The Harbinger

A Triquetra Chronicle

by Sarah Heximer

ISBN: 979-8-9990482-0-2

Any references to historical events, real people, or real places are used factiously. Names, characters, and places are products of the author's imagination.

Front cover and book design by Sarah Heximer
Edited by: Eleanor Smith
Proofread by: Ashley S.

sarahheximer@gmail.com

www.sarahheximer.com

Prologue

They were running.

Bare feet running through the forest. It was pitch black and becoming ever darker. Only the light of the full moon on this vernal equinox could be seen through the trees, and only then because the branches were still bare and the moon so bright tonight.

And her. Gaining on them with full force on her ebony thoroughbred, her jet-black hair falling around her shoulders in long tendrils, coupled with the velvety dark violet cloak flowing behind her, created an aura that she was flying through the dense night air right at them.

Suddenly, she tripped. The root had come out of nowhere on the soft emerald floor of the forest so familiar to them. They knew these woods like the backs of their hands. *Where did that come from?* she thought. But she couldn't focus on that right now. "Get up!" she heard the voice she'd come to know as her intuition and guide yell. It was as if that voice had reached her friend running just ahead, who then stopped in her tracks and reeled around. *No!* she thought as she tried to yell, but her throat was raw from breathing in the cold night air. She wanted her beautiful soul sister to keep running, but instead she circled back to try and help her up. It was but a moment, but it allowed their pursuer to get within reach. They huddled together, each trying to shield the other.

How had it come to this?

har·bin·ger /ˈhärbənjər/
noun

1. a person or thing that announces or signals the approach of another; 2. anything that foreshadows a future event; omen; sign.

Chapter 1 – March, Present Day – Sophia

I woke up in a cold sweat. The dream was as strong as a memory, and one that had plagued me for years. For as long as I could remember, the dark woman on the even darker horse would visit around the same time every spring like clockwork. While it was only a dream, and I often consoled myself with that, it felt…deeper.

I brushed it off as I always did and moved on with my day. Recurring dream or not, there was no room for it amid my schedule of meetings and lectures today. I had stumbled into teaching at a local university later in my career, but it was incredibly satisfying, and it appeared it was my calling. Sharing my experience from the working world made all those years of highs and lows worth it. It was an opportunity to share a gift, my gift, with others. Whatever that was.

There would be no time for a hot shower this morning. In all the panic, I had slept through my alarm and was running against the clock. Our team was preparing for an industry competition, and I needed to be on time to commence run-throughs of their presentation. These students were the best of the best, and while they didn't need me, I needed them. I loved watching them puzzle out their responses to the case questions and come to their own conclusions. It had become my favorite "recurring memory" in my time there, watching them grow into the critical thinkers I knew they always were and apply what they had learned in class to a real-life scenario.

They had been working for months on this latest case and were coming down to the wire. This year's presenters were particularly impressive, though they had also learned from the best in their predecessors. I always thought fondly back to that first group of students, as they allowed me to haphazardly navigate my way around my first semester of teaching and advising on such a competition. They were patient and let me figure things out as I went along and were seemingly happy to be my guinea pigs – who had all gone on to lead incredibly successful lives in their chosen field of study and were well on their way to becoming "red bottom" owners.

The inside joke about a particular brand of shoes I owned never ceased to make me smile. Since then, we had developed a historical knowledge system of handing the team lead responsibilities to whichever upcoming upperclassman had been on the previous year's team. It was a newer strategy but one that was already paying off.

After letting Violet, my eight-year-old Heinz 57 pup, outside to romp in the fresh air and feeding her breakfast, I quickly washed my face, threw my brown, mostly wavy, sometimes curly, hair up and drew black liner across my top lash line to help open up my oh-so-tired eyes.

Taking a moment while brushing my teeth to stare into my own face, it always amazed me what one could see. I remembered a long time ago as a child staring into the mirror and into my own dark-hazel eyes and almost scaring myself. If you stared long enough, you could see into your own soul. It had almost gone dark once while I was doing that, like the light of my soul had suddenly been extinguished through no fault of my own, and I swore I would never look that closely at myself again.

Thankfully, the coffee maker had done its job and brewed a deliciously piping-hot pot of snickerdoodle coffee, my flavor of the week, so that I could fill my thermos and run out the door. I grabbed my overly stuffed backpack, water bottle and puffer vest before kissing Vi on the head and headed to the car. My carefully curated Spotify station decided to grace me with a favorite, "Ants Go Marching," to which I enthusiastically cranked up the sound system and rolled down the windows, despite the early spring chill. Today was going to be a good day, regardless of my recurring dream. It became a distant memory as the roads changed and the Spotify station kept playing my favorites one after the other, almost as if it knew I needed a bit of a pick-me-up on this frantic morning.

Driving onto campus at this time of year always conjured up old memories from my time at my alma mater. The smells, the optimism, the vitamin D. It seemed every campus had the same air about it at this point in the semester – a listlessness, an excitement. For freshmen, it was moving on and away from being the new man on campus. For the sophomores and juniors, they were finally moving up the food chain, and the seniors, well, senioritis had kicked in back in January, if not in the fall semester, so we were lucky they were even gracing us with their presence. It was an electric time to be involved in a campus setting, and I loved every second of it.

I pulled into the closest spot I could find to our meeting building and put the parking pass in the window. I was still running late, so this would be a huge help in not making me run like a crazy bag lady all the way to the meeting about to start in three minutes. Thankfully, I had gotten there just in time to avoid an insanely long walk in the brisk spring breeze. Sun or no sun, this campus had a biting wind that could cut through any ski jacket.

My students were anxiously awaiting my arrival so they could get going. We had finally agreed that enough research had been gathered, and they were ready to move through the same process we always had...the brutal construction, deconstruction and ultimate reconstruction of their presentation before it was go-time. We had two weeks, which meant adrenalin was running high.

Ready to dive into my time-tested methods of poking holes and putting them under pressure, they were feeling giddy and decided to poke holes at me instead. "Hey, Prof, what's with the frazzled look this morning? Stay up late grading our papers again?"

I loved the nickname they had come to call me, the warm familiarity. While it was simple, the tone in which it was used was endearing and made me feel like I was making an impact. The mutual respect was unlike anything I had experienced in the corporate world, and I appreciated it more than they would ever know.

"No, Josh. Just your paper. It was truly horrendous! It took me hours to figure out what your actual thesis was and what you were trying to say about the upcoming industry trends..." I joked. Sounds of "ooo" and laughter filled the air, and Josh took it in stride.

Amanda then cut through the noise. "But seriously, you good? We can't have a weak link in our chain this year!"

Impressed by her quick wit and yet uncomfortable accusation, I swiftly moved us into presentation mode. These kids had the impression I was a laid-back professional. They didn't need to know I was completely neurotic around this time of year thanks to an odd dream I had had since my childhood, or was it senior year of high school?

"Moving along." I winced and took a long sip of my scrumptious coffee while putting my clog-adorned feet up on the long lecture-style desk in front of me. "Let's set up for the beginning of the presentation. Who's standing where, and most importantly, who's holding the clicker?" I winked.

It was always a source of debate, especially since each team had taken to naming "her" like she was a boat. It was somewhat of a physical baton that was passed on every year and of the utmost importance. It seemed we had settled on "Gwen" this time but had yet to decide who was her keeper.

We nestled into our regular cadence of the presenters practicing, the support team asking brutal questions and myself interjecting with more theatre-like directions on their stance or speech than the actual content of their presentation. It was theirs after all, and they were proud of their work.

I just relied on that little voice in my head that I had come to trust. It was a comforting voice and one that never led me astray, once I realized I wasn't completely nuts and it was natural to have an internal guide...You just had to learn to listen. I had discovered the hard way that if I didn't listen to it, I would regret it. After all, isn't that what ultimately had led me away from the corporate life into teaching? It would always help me visualize how things could go, and it was beyond helpful in these situations when the group was about to be up against some of the strongest schools in the nation.

Now came my favorite exercise...forcing the speakers to sit in a circle and present their parts to each other without looking at the slides on the screen. It was an exercise we started a couple years ago, one that had been suggested by that internal guide and had proven effective in building team comradery and chemistry on stage – which always made us stand out against the competitors.

"Alright, guys...you know what's next." The four of them groaned. Stacey, Andi, Melissa and Stephen had seen this happen the last couple of years, but only Melissa knew of its effect, being the team lead and designated upperclassmen who had been to the competition the year prior.

"Do we have to?" Stephen whined.

I raised my eyebrow and slowly turned my gaze to Melissa for full professor effect. She warmly rolled her eyes and shot Stephen the Queen Bee look she had been honing, and he quickly backed off.

"Sorry, Prof."

I chuckled under my breath and let them begin again. There was silence in the room as they went through the dreaded exercise of sitting in a circle facing one another and were forced to look each other in the eye to practice. What always amazed me, and the rest of the team that was watching, was how their posture became elevated throughout their discussion, their voices grew stronger and more confident, they no longer stared at the screen behind them, and the energy in the room went from stagnant to buzzing. I swear if it had colors, it would go from a comforting blue to an electric green or even purple. Their purpose and determination brought to life by connecting with each other instead of the slides, or their shoes.

By the time the team finished, they looked at each other, as if to indicate, *OK, now what?* Clearly not seeing the impact of what just happened.

Once more they assembled themselves around the screen and delivered the presentation as they would in two weeks. Then they felt it. It clicked. Things were humming. They weren't stumbling over themselves or each other. There was chemistry. The exercise had worked yet again, and the voice in my head seemed to smile. My intuition had paid off. When they concluded this time, applause broke out across the room from the support team, and Stacey, Andi and Stephen all looked at each other with amazement. Melissa smirked at me.

"And that's how it's done," I said triumphantly as they took it all in.

Soon it was time to go and get on with our days. I had four more classes to teach, and they all had to get back to reality. I loved the bubble we created each Tuesday and Thursday morning leading up to the competition and was always a little sad when we had to burst it.

"Alright, guys, great work today. Be sure you take notes on what you liked or didn't like, and what worked for you and didn't. Let's meet same time next Tuesday. I know I have most of you in class today at some point, but have a great weekend!"

Resounding hoots and hollers ensued as most packed up their bags to depart. Julie and Rachelle from the support team were in my first class and thus simply moved their belongings to their normal seats in the front left of the classroom, while I fired up my laptop and nursed my last few sips of sweet snickerdoodle nectar. It had been a godsend this morning, but I might need to do another coffee run in between classes if I was to make it through the day.

The room had a quiet hum to it as students came in and took their seats. I was busy syncing the technology, crossing my fingers that it would actually work. Technology and I were not always known to get along, and it was a gamble whether I would have to pivot to plan B for my lectures. I always felt as if it signified I was truly from another time. I hoped it made me a more lovable professor versus what I felt, which was pathetic. I wasn't that old, but the seamlessness of technology that was supposed to be supportive never ceased to escape me and made me feel like a grandmother who doesn't know how to use a cell phone.

Which reminded me, in all the merriment of the morning, I had missed the few notifications on my actual cell phone. As I was reviewing the daily morning meme from my bestie and checking my emails, something caught the corner of my eye out in the hallway. That voice in my head almost yelled at me to look up. I did so immediately with my heart racing, and yet it was gone. Something about it was disquieting, as if it was a warning.

I tried to shake it off, but something about it hit a little too close to home, especially after how my day had started...

Chapter 2 – March 1563 – Ann

The three girls had been raised in the same small village in Northern England for nearly two decades. They had grown up with the tale of two sisters who nearly killed each other over the English crown and vowed they would never do that to each other, in a manner of speaking. How could they? They were not born as blood sisters, but chosen, as friends.

It was the early part of Queen Elizabeth's reign. Their days were filled with helping their families with their younger siblings, a little farming, running around the fields and forests collecting all kinds of herbs, and dreaming of love. While other girls their age had already been married off or had fathers that forced them to play a more active role on the farms and in their family businesses, they had fallen under the divine protection of Sophia, or so they said out of range of their families. Divine Sophia, the goddess of wisdom and the divine feminine side of God they had been taught about through local folklore.

Thankfully, it was no longer the stifling Catholic England they were born into; however, it had shifted to a Protestant-focused country that would still have them hanged for anything that denigrated talk of the "Lord." For what their families did not know was that their love of collecting flowers from the field had turned into experimenting with the "magic" of herbs and remedies made therein. They were bewildered how a simple flower brewed in boiling water could provide calm and assistance in falling asleep, or a plant that could aid in comforting symptoms of "wamblecropt" or their courses was also believed to assist in longevity, or work as a simple perfume, for those willing to pay.

They knew that people were willing to pay since one of their mothers was the village healer. However, they had yet to share their newfound appreciation with her, fearing how she would react. Each had trained with her at one point or another but had feigned disinterest since theirs was of a more fanciful, girlish take on the subject rather than functional.

Lately, they had turned their attention to how best to use the herbs at their disposal to bring about love for themselves. They had discovered a large grouping of rocks in the wood that provided shelter for a makeshift altar. It was there they hid their latest concoctions and attempts at using the amply provided ingredients from the forest for their imaginings. It was silly, they knew, because magic was not real, but they still felt alive while they were pretending all the same and the space became sacred to them.

While they were grateful for not having been married off or unwittingly betrothed to any of the local boys, their families grew anxious to be rid of them and the increasingly bigger mouth to feed as they sped through the transition from child to woman. In their minds, they were approaching cronehood and would soon be too old to marry, let alone have children.

They playfully relished the thought of becoming the Three Fates, constructing a house in the woods from which they could work with their flowers, tell stories to each other and grow old with one another, though each of them also longed for someone to love outside of their created sisterhood. Of course, one of them had been close to capturing the otherwise elusive opportunity, but it went unexpectedly awry.

They were blissfully unaware that just a few days' horse-ride away, London was experiencing the worst episode of plague they were to have in the 16th century. Scores of people were to die that year during the outbreak, causing mass panic and hysteria, which, as they would come to find out, would bleed into their lives.

Still, as London grew to the epicenter of the European world under Queen Elizabeth's rule, it never held an interest for the trio. They loved being surrounded by, and living in, the wonder of nature too much and continuously reveled in all it had to offer, if you knew where to look.

It was just turning to spring. There was still a chill in the air and frost on the ground in the morning, but you could tell the sun would be radiant by midday. March was a glorious time of year; Shrovetide had just concluded, and they were swiftly moving toward Lady Day. Shrovetide was not the favorite among most since it was the last day before Lent began and the fasting commenced, but it was worth it to move closer to the Annunciation of Mary and true year's start in the English calendar. The girls were also planning on honoring Divine Sophia and quietly recognizing Ostara and the equinox and "the old ways," as they could.

The snow was beginning to melt, and the earth was waking back up – which only meant more fun was to be had! They took to their morning walks to welcome the new day as early as they could before commencing with their chores. They would each steal a chunk of freshly baked bread with butter and some cheese from their family kitchen to keep their rumbling bellies at bay, or feed the local wildlife along the way, whichever they fancied. Then, while communing with the forest, they would share any dreams from the night past, "visions" – as they had come to call them – they had seen during the waking hours, or anything else that came into their head.

They had discovered that they each had an affinity for one thing or another and would try to develop that gift with individual exploration, which they would then share with the others at this time. If nothing else, it was the calm among the storm in the sea of their chaotic households of siblings, parents and endless conversations among the permutations available under one roof.

It truly was their favorite part of day, and they cherished this sacred opportunity to commune with Sophia.

On this morning, Ann, the eldest of the group – though they were only months apart – was being particularly quiet. Margaret – or Madge, as she liked to be called – and Lizbeth – because she did not want to be confused with the Queen – were chattering among themselves, not paying any mind.

Ann was tall for a woman of the time, but not so much as to be considered unattractive or intimidating; in fact, her stature was partially why people liked her because she had a significant calming presence. Her dark-brown hair was curly on good days, loose waves on the not-so-good ones, and thanks to ancestors to the north, she had amazing deep-hazel eyes that seemed to change with the season, almost like the deep greens and grays of trees depending on the amount of sunlight or moonlight they received.

Her energy seemed to some like the constant, calm flow of a creek. Her intuition had always been rock-solid, and she would often use it to read people, places and situations to help her family and friends as the occasion called. Her friends loved her presence and often craved it. She herself was not sure where the sense of balance emanated from but found she relied on it heavily, especially during times of trouble.

Madge was the youngest of the group. She was of average build, though she was carrying a little extra baby fat that hadn't loosened yet. She had long wispy strawberry blonde hair and slate-gray eyes with flecks of brown. She wasn't a traditional beauty, but what she lacked in looks, she more than made up for with her character. She was quiet, reserved and one of the kindest humans you would ever meet. As the eldest of eight, she knew how to balance patience...or perhaps tolerance, with love. She was curious by nature, given she came from a long line of healers, and loved learning the old ways from her mother.

Lizbeth, caught in the middle of the matron and child, was contrary to both. She was also of average height but with dark-raven hair and eyes to match. She seemed to hypnotize everyone she met and was certainly the village beauty. Her wild, rebellious ways seemed to counteract any marriage proposals she should have gotten given her gorgeous face, plentiful hips and the position her family held among the village elders.

The three of them made an odd grouping, but they did not care. Their "trinity" was perfect to them, and they relished each other's company whenever they could!

I was lost in thought about what I had experienced the night before. It was a dream, and I had been glad of that, for if what it had shown was a prophecy, it could only truly be labeled as a nightmare. I had been running through the forest. It was the blackest of black nights. I did not know why I was running, but I could feel panic ripping through my veins and knew my bare feet were carrying me along the emerald carpet of the woods for a reason.

But what was that reason? Why would I be running in such terror? What could possibly have happened that would cause me to flee in the moonlight? And barefoot? It was silly to think since Lizbeth's father provided all their families ready access to whatever they wanted, given his profession, that I would go without anything without a true purpose.

Suddenly, I became aware of Madge and Lizbeth's enthusiastic conversation, and I snapped out of my reverie. I would think on it more later, when I could concentrate.

"Ann, what is on your mind this morning? You have not touched your piece of bread, and I specifically made that fresh butter just for you!" said Lizbeth, playfully getting my attention.

"Yes, Ann, you are positively morose and completely missed Lizbeth's story about Robert from last night!" piled on Madge.

"My apologies, my dear ones, I was lost in thought and unable to raise myself. I am here now. What, pray tell, has the inscrutable Robert done now?"

Robert Evans was an anomaly in our village. Quiet and pensive, with a far-off look, as if he was always experiencing life somewhere else, most of the town felt he was impossible to interpret, which made him all the more attractive for Liz. She had a fondness for anything that repelled convention and thus aways pushed the boundaries of her already flexible family.

The only female in her house, she lived with her two brothers, Matthew, eighteen, and George, twelve, and her well-respected father, Henry, who was the village cobbler-sometimes-cordwainer for the local gentry. Her mother, Jane, had died during childbirth with her youngest sibling, George, and she had been without a female influence since. Her dark complexion had come from her raven-haired beauty of a mother, who had come with her own set of rules and suspicions.

Having come to England as a little girl with her Romani family, she was a rarity in the countryside, which always made people talk. Fortunately, the musings about her died down as time went on and thankfully Lizbeth was never mentioned in the same breath as those original suspicions. However, having lost a mother so young, it explained her need for our chosen sisterhood, as well as her complete disregard for appropriate "ladylike" behavior, something that confounded her family of men.

"We'll never be rid of her, Father," Matthew would complain, "for what sane man will want to wed THAT?"

To which her father would retort, "And what lady will want to marry you for your lack of concern of how to empathize with the fairer sex?" Her father always won these conversations since Matthew would lose patience, loudly sigh and stomp away as if he was as old as his younger brother.

"Welllll…" started Lizbeth, dragging the word out for dramatic effect – a common if not somewhat lovably annoying trait of hers. "We went for a walk in the moonlight!" she crooned.

"Lizbeth! With your father's permission of course?!" I cried in mock shock. This only caused her to giggle more.

"Why of course, my sweet Ann," she replied with equal sarcasm. "But fear not, while I had less than admirable intensions for our evening rendezvous, he was yet again in another world."

"Go on," I said, blushing from her admission.

"It started off as all fun and games. As soon as we passed through the opening to the wood, I brushed my hand against his, and he thankfully took it. I was relieved, of course, as it was the boldest action I yet have taken, but one never knows how any boy will act, let alone one as mysterious as he."

Madge and I looked at each other with smirks on our faces. Lizbeth sure did love sharing a story.

"Anyhow, we glided along the path, hand in glorious hand. It was truly delicious. The goddess Diana shone down in all her full moon brilliance, and I felt warm all over. Suddenly, Robert stopped. I was not sure if he had seen an animal cross the path or heard something, so I stopped with him for fear of stepping on a furry rodent or crunchy bug."

She was in full storytelling mode now, acting out her words with enthusiasm. As much as Madge and I never liked to admit it, we were rapt with attention. She continued.

"Only, he just stood there. Saying nothing. I looked into his eyes and it was as if he was seeing nothing as well. Truly, had I not been holding onto his hand anchoring him to this world, I am sure he would have floated away! Just as suddenly as he had stopped, he flicked his head toward me and settled his silver-blue eyes on me, as if he was looking right through me. It was most disconcerting. And then he was back." Lizbeth continued to walk along the path among the trees and bent over to pick some wildflowers, as if she had not a care in the world despite what she had just shared.

Madge and I stayed rooted to our original spot and looked at each other once again. We were not quite sure how to respond. Madge, of course, had heard the telling already, and yet she seemed equally perplexed as I, and no better for having witnessed it a second time. We had each heard about Robert's "fits," as the villagers were wont to call them.

Poor Robert. He had come from the Northlands, though not quite all the way to Scotland. There were rumors that he came from a long line of "seers." While no one was certain of what this meant, they inferred it was not always accepted as a positive quality. Most of the highly religious town folk would spit over their left shoulder if the term was mentioned, and yet it was Madge's mother, Eliza, the village healer, who usually showed the most compassion. Surely seers could not be all bad if she held a soft spot for them.

"So, what do you deduce from that?" I prodded.

"I am unsure," Lizbeth admitted as she began braiding the stems of the wildflowers together for a crown. "I know Robert has been known to have 'fits,' as others call them, but I had not believed it until now. As I said, if I had not been holding onto his hand, I fear he would have disappeared for those few moments. And the look in his eyes when he looked at me, and then became aware again that I was even there..." She hesitated. "I could have sworn I saw a look of fear and disappointment, but for what reason, I know not."

She seemed distant herself as she relived the tale in her head and began to contemplate what it meant. I was about to ask if it was something they should approach Mrs. Williams with to gain clarity, but Lizbeth finished her flower crown, placed it on the elder tree close by as an obvious offering to Divine Sophia and started toward their sacred space where they left their latest herbal concoction out to be infused with moonlight.

Our families were not deeply religious in any one denomination; in fact, I had heard them talk of their ancestors being tied to the word "gnostic" more than once. We all believed in a higher presence and had attended lessons when we were young. We had borne witness to too many things in our short lives to think there was not a higher power. However, the current interpretation of a purely masculine and seemingly vindictive and judgmental version did not completely resonate with us girls and the beauty we saw in the world, nor the relatively matriarchal families we lived in.

When we were little, our mothers would all share stories they had been taught of the different versions of a higher power, carried down from their ancestors. Lizbeth's mother, though none of us could quite remember her, would confirm similar versions of the stories from her heritage as well. Admittedly, it had been little since she seemed reticent to remind others of her background, given the air of mystery her looks already provided, an air she did everything in her power to suffuse so her family could live in peace. It was enough to provide some confirmation in our minds that perhaps there was more to religion than was currently being taught on England's stage.

Thus, we girls found our way to Sophia and the thought that there were two halves, masculine and feminine, to one whole God. We also thought it appropriate that she had three daughters, Faith, Hope and Charity, so why not three friends who acted as sisters to keep her name alive?

Lizbeth's story was finished. But something about how it had started, how she had described the walk in the woods, brought me back to my original preoccupation, one I was not prepared to return to just yet. I withheld my thoughts of an entreaty to Madge's mother and let the girls walk ahead to continue their discussion. Though I did not have a clue how to interpret Lizbeth's latest experience, it did not keep Madge from asking a thousand and one questions to try and get to the bottom of it. I knew Lizbeth was in good hands until I could focus on it again.

Chapter 3 – March, Present Day – Sophia

Classes finished for the day, I packed up my things and headed back to the car. It had become a beautiful spring day while I was inside talking through the fourth level of category management and progressing through the food ecosystem in my capstone classes. The warm breeze was refreshing, so I threw my bag in the passenger side, jumped in my trusty used Mercedes GLE, Etta, and promptly rolled down the windows so I could feel the air rushing by me on my way back home.

I had taken to naming my cars from the start; after all, I spent enough time in them that they practically became friends. Etta had been the latest in a short but honorable line of sojourn partners and named as such because I had "At Last" gotten an SUV, and it was a Mercedes. Oddly enough, Etta's namesake song was playing as I signed the paperwork, which, for all intents and purposes, sealed the deal for me.

Pivotal moments of my life had always been marked by music – usually personal favorites that meant something to me – and in such a way that if I didn't know any better, I would think they were a way for the ethereal "someone" to communicate with me.

Being it was the weekend – at least as a teacher whose last class was on a Thursday, it was effectively my weekend – I thought a stop off at the outlet malls on the way home to get a fresh batch of Lindt truffles was in order. They were a little treat to myself after the back-to-back days of nurturing young minds, and I found as I reached into my glovebox, I was completely out.

I parked at a spot near the door on the end closest to the shop, made sure my computer bag was hidden and strolled in. As I walked through the doors, my phone started buzzing, as did my watch, and I saw that Kit was calling me. She was probably checking on me since I hadn't reacted to any of the memes she had sent that morning, my mind otherwise occupied. Feeling slightly guilty about the fact I had yet to call her back and I was going to buy myself a sizeable bag of chocolate instead, I told myself I'd call her as soon as I got back in the car.

There were always so many decisions to be made on which truffles made the bag. This time, inspired by the spring air, I thought I'd try some of the "fresher" flavors, as opposed to the heavier ones, and popped a couple orange and white chocolate crème and stracciatella in for good measure. I paid for the embarrassingly large bag of goodies as the clerk smiled to herself, and I went back out to the car.

As I passed through the exit, again I felt a quiet nudge to look up, as if someone was calling my attention, but there was nothing to see.

I got back in the car with haste, connected my phone to the media player and immediately called Kit. She would be the perfect antidote to the weird goings-on. Sure enough, I was greeted with a "Hello, my love!" and I sank comfortably into my driver seat and took off toward home.

Katherine, otherwise known as Kit to her dear ones, was a soul sister I had found later in life. While we had grown up in the same hometown, attended the same school and had some mutual friends, we were in very different social circles in the time of our youth. If only I had known how much we actually had in common. Who knows what trouble we could have gotten into!

As it was, she was a vivacious redhead in her late thirties, married with children, twins in fact, and a noted abnormal psychologist. She was incredibly kind and thoughtful, an amazingly patient mother and an all-round good human being; she just did not tolerate anything disingenuous, which also kept social vultures at bay. Coming from a family with two brothers and one sister, she was a natural born leader and knew how to stand out in a crowd.

Her husband, Erik, was a modern-day Viking. Former military, strong and muscular build, tattoos and long golden hair he mostly wore pulled back in a ponytail or man-bun, he was everything you would want in defense of our country. Kit had really won the lottery, as he was a good man too.

They met at the VA Hospital where Kit was giving a seminar on abnormal psychology and PTSD. The tall, light and handsome man was there visiting some friends. Trifecta not to be foresworn, he had brains to boot, being a self-taught astrophysicist, having taken to the subject while overseas and experiencing some unexplainable phenomena in what some considered spiritual lands.

He still wouldn't talk about it much, but you knew it was enough to prompt him to explore parts of the unknown.

Together, they were a power couple that many looked up to and aspired to be. You couldn't help but feel their love when in their presence, and it was a beautiful thing.

Kit and I had originally connected over the shared psychology background, as we both had our undergrad degrees in the subject, only she chose to go down the path I had dreamed of, while I decided to use it in "a more practical sense" and fell into the business world, leveraging the expertise in a marketing capacity.

"You'll never believe it!" she exclaimed on the other end of the line.

"What?!" I responded in equal measure.

"Well, you would know if you answered any one of my texts this morning. Where were you? I thought you had fallen off the face of the earth!" she said jokingly. I knew I wasn't going to get away with the silence from earlier today easily.

"I know, I'm sorry. It's just...a dream I had, and I overslept, and just, ALL the things." This was becoming our usual response – with arms flailing if we were in person – to describe when it was one of those days.

"Oh yeah, was it that dream you've mentioned before? I think you've said you've had it a few times?"

Blast her recall. While we had become fast friends, and knew we were soul sisters, I had yet to delve into the neuroses that was my recurring dream every spring. I knew how it looked and sounded to me as an undergrad psych major. I was a little afraid of how a respected abnormal psychologist would interpret it, and I wasn't prepared to be committed to the nuthouse just yet.

"Wow, good memory! Yes, something like that. Anyway, it happened again, and I lost all track of time. I had to scoot to campus this morning—"

"Oh right! You're in full competition mode." Once again finishing my sentence.

"Yes. They are so ready. Today was my favorite stage of the prep though because…" I was happy to veer her away from the dream conversation and go into the magical exercise, and then I heard a loud crash come from the other end of the line.

"Hold on a sec." She clearly held the phone away from her mouth, but I could hear the reprimand all the same and was glad not to be on the receiving end. Her twins must have just gotten home from school, and they had made holy terror on their way into the house. It would not end well for them. I chuckled to myself.

"Soph, I have to call you back. T-squared is going to bring the house down if I don't take matters into my own hands…"

"No worries," I replied, thankful once again for the distraction from the path our conversation had started to take. "I have no plans, just going home to chill with Vi and maybe start on a new crocheting project." I could almost hear the smirk at this on her end.

"You do realize you are not a granny yet, right?! It's Thursday, you have no teaching responsibilities until Tuesday, so why don't you go out and live a little?" It was a classic argument we had started to have once she realized I was unattached. I knew she meant well, but we had yet to dive into all the whys and why nots, and right now was clearly not the time. I smiled at her concern.

"I know. But after today's start and—"

"I know, ALL the things." We left it at that.

After she hung up, my previous Spotify station from this morning piped back up. I forgot how exuberantly I was listening to it in the wee hours of the morning because "#41" suddenly blared at me from all Bose speakers in my car, and even with all the windows open, I nearly jumped out of my seat.

I started thinking about what Kit had said, that I should go out and act my age. But the comfort of sitting in, throwing on a movie, pouring a rich glass of cab and snuggling up on the couch with Vi while I determined my next crocheting project was just too enticing. I got lost in thought about stitches and hook sizes for the remainder of the ride. As I pulled into my driveway, I could see a little reddish-tan head peering out the curtains and a black nose pressed up against the glass.

I loved my sanctuary. It was a cute little cottage-like house I had found for myself a few years ago when I was still working in the corporate world. I was tired of paying rent and not building up my own equity, so I started the house search. I had loved all of my apartments, the coziness and central location, but I found as Vi and I both got older, we appreciated a little more breathing room. So, I found this great piece of property in the northern suburbs of the city and fell in love.

It was a cute white house with an old stone path that led up from the street line. There were some spectacular trees on the property that the previous owner had planted herself decades ago, along with a resplendent garden all the way around the little ranch with its loft. While I had never been particularly good at keeping plants alive, she had done an amazing job with capturing seasonal beauty with relatively low-maintenance flowers and bushes, so all I had to learn was the difference between a weed and a young flower stem – something that required an app on my phone, as I had more than once pulled out something that would have otherwise been a gorgeous flower of some sort.

I loved my little slice of heaven, and the fact it had such lush history, being built in the late 1800s, was the cherry on top. It reminded me of the time I had studied abroad in London. We had lived in an apartment building built in the early 1900s, young in comparison to most of the buildings surrounding us. That was when my love affair with living in old places began. Difference being that now, I had an appreciation for the "village" atmosphere instead of the compact city life.

I pulled into the little unattached garage, parked and heaved my backpack onto my shoulder, knowing full well that if it wasn't safely secured on my back, Vi would ultimately knock it off in her excitement at my return. Man, I loved that little rescue and often wondered who had rescued whom.

She had come to me at a time in my life when I was getting overwhelmed by my work life and needed something to keep me out of a funk. My dad had helped. He always had a sixth sense when it came to adopting dogs, and this time was no different. I had steeled myself against looking at rescues online to try and find the perfect companion but could not physically set foot in a shelter, knowing full well I would want to adopt all of the wayward creatures.

It took months of me sending links to him for him to approve or reject, mostly reject, until we found her: "Sandy." Sandy was a recent acquisition by the local SPCA from Virginia. Unfortunately, I had had unbreakable plans the weekend we discovered her and was unable to go see her for myself. My dad was certain she would be scooped up in no time, so he ventured over after work on that fateful Friday in July. He went up to the desk and asked for her.

The story goes that she had been taken to the back for some shots, and they were just bringing her up front again. As soon as she saw my dad, she went between his legs, jumped up, wrapped both front paws around his leg and looked up at him as if to say, "Are you here for me?" The call I got after that was either I was to take her, or he would. The rest, as they say, was history. I renamed her Violet since my favorite color had always been purple, and I liked the ease of her nickname "Vi" for training purposes.

My perfect pup did her happy dance as I came in the door and set my things down. It hadn't been an abnormally long day for her, but I could tell she was ready for her Thursday routine to commence – a walk around the block so she could properly relieve herself, a snack upon returning, and cuddling the rest of the night. If I was honest, it was my favorite routine too.

"Alright, baby girl, let's get your leash on. I don't think you'll need your coat today!" She bounded over to her hook where the leash and poop bags were hanging and waited as patiently as her little wiggle butt could. We were off.

As I was walking and taking in the fresh air, my mind drifted back to my conversation with Kit. Why was I so reticent to tell her the details of my recurring dream? I already knew we had a deeper connection than most, even if we had met later in life. She wouldn't honestly commit me, and in all actuality, it might be helpful to have a "professional" opinion on the subject. At least then I might be able to make some sense of it and even put it to rest. Yes! That was it. Perhaps she could help.

I resolved to message her after we got back from our walk. If nothing else, we were way overdue for a coffee and venting session, and with the weather finally starting to turn, we might even be able to go walk in one of the local parks for added atmosphere. Vi and I continued our jaunt around the little neighborhood in the sunlight while I milled over the possible reactions of my friend.

Chapter 4 – March 1563 – Ann

Back from the morning amble and ready to begin the daily chores, I walked into the village and parted ways with my friends. We deemed our latest experiment successful and spread the flower trimmings along the wooded path as we walked back so as to encourage our loves to find their way to us – at least Madge and Lizbeth's loves; my need was different these days. The morning conversation and activities proved to be an ample distraction from my experience the night before, and I had high hopes that the litany of things my mother needed help with would do the same.

"Good morning, family!" I cried as I entered the four-room house. While not particularly spacious, it was cozy and warm, and all the things a little cottage-like home should be when filled with as much love as our family had for each other. The outside was a combination of wood beams and gray stone, with some earth to help hold everything together. The thatched roof provided enough cover in the winter to retain warmth while also not sealing it so much that we choked from heat in the summer. The tall multi-paneled windows were always my favorite feature because of the way the sunlight danced along the waves of the glass on the inside and created gorgeous patterns along the floor.

There was a room, a loft really, where I slept with my siblings. It was whitewashed to help release any unnecessary heat rising to the top, whereas the lower floors had darker walls to try and retain it. My parents' bedchamber was the smallest of the rooms on the first floor, containing their simple oak bed with a matching cupboard. There was also a receiving room where we had a few oak and maple chairs with thatched padding for comfort, and of course the kitchen.

The traditional heart of the home was always bustling with active children, a warm stove and herbs drying overhead. The stone floor provided the necessary though incredibly unforgiving foundation on which it all lay, and in the winter, we would attempt to lay down a large piece of cloth my mother had woven to help keep out the cold.

Izzy, the youngest of my siblings, bounded in from the receiving room with a joyous "GOOD MORNING, SISSY!" as only an eight-year-old could muster. She may have been the youngest, but she certainly contained the most energy of all my sisters.

My father belly laughed and said, "Well, you must be ready to go back out to the fields with me and accomplish a good day's work with that entrance!" Izzy immediately tempered herself and looked around for help. My mother simply smiled, shook her head and kept on stirring the laundry over the fire.

My father, John Hughes, was one of the main grain farmers for our village. Well-liked and a hard worker, he was respected by many, which was why he was on the town council and had a voice in the community. My mother, Sarah Hughes, not for wont of being any less because she was born a woman, had become a well-known seamstress in the area. Not that the village had much need for an accomplished seamstress, but she had a few odd clients from the nearby lords, who commissioned much of her work. When that was slow, she managed some laundry for those who needed the help. Our village was built on trade of goods and services, and as such, we never wanted for anything.

My mother finally looked up from her stirring, took one look at me and came right over. "Not sleeping again, are you, love?" She must have seen the dark circles and bags under my eyes, though she mistook their meaning completely. She kept going in a knowing voice. "I know. It must be hard, but you must have hope that he could still turn up."

He was almost a long-distant memory now. I had not looked upon his face in nearly...I calculated in my head and realized it had been three-and-a-half years. He was meant to have returned to me three years ago this month in fact, but no one had heard from him since he had sent word of his intentions.

I shook my head, as if to shake away the memory. "No, it was not he that kept me awake last night, but..." I stopped myself short. If I mentioned anything of the nightmare I had seen, I would have to go into great detail, and that was not something I wanted to do for myself, let alone my well-meaning mother, who would be horrified, resulting in her crossing herself several times, calling on the goddess and then creating a perimeter of salt around the loft. For while she was a somewhat religious person, she still took to one or two "mystical" habits to keep out the bad luck.

She looked at me expectantly. "Just thoughts of the harvest and what this new season will bring," I lied.

She sighed. "Yes, I know. With the drier winter weather, your father has been concerned with the harvest, but no matter – we will make do," she said cheerily and walked back to her laundry pot. As she prepared the sheets and other undergarments for bucking by soaking in the hot water and lye, I thought I should at least pitch in and get the bucking tub prepped so she could easily transfer the goods.

Usually reserved for finer households and dedicated services to lords and ladies, the villagers recognized my mother's talent in being able to "buck" just so. Hers was always the whitest of whites and cleanest of cleans among them, so those who had the spare coin at odd times of the year outside of the traditional trading would seek her out to help them with their own laundry, so that when Easter came round or any other major holiday or celebration, they could make a good show in their own homes of all their fine linens. For as we learned, there was a certain pattern to the folding of the linens to be placed in the buck tub and subsequent sticks lain in between layers so that the dirty water would run off "just so" and not leave behind any marks on the freshly washed garments.

Going into my mindless self-imposed task, I set to humming. Just then Thomas came bounding into the room asking if he could go run around town with his friend George. His appearance went unnoticed by me until he started mocking my humming and dancing around with one of the previously laundered petticoats drying on a line in the receiving room, as it was too cold yet to take the line drying outside. My mother turned in haste and set to chasing him with the washing bat in her hand until he placed the petticoat back on the line.

Given his outburst, I did not think it likely that he would be allowed out, but my mother must have decided she did not want him around as she finished her work, so off he went with a spring in his step to play with George, Lizbeth's little brother, but not before he turned to me to share a bit of gossip.

"George said that Lizbeth went walking in the woods night last..." He trailed off, trying to create a sense of intrigue. When I did not bite, he continued. "With a boy."

I kept my face devoid of expression, as it would not do to feed into the conversation.

I heard my mother gasp in the background, and she fired off, "What boy?!"

Glad for the attention, Thomas continued. "Robert," he responded as proudly as he could on hearing something before our mother had.

"Robert, that odd fellow who came from the Northlands? Well, why on earth would Lizbeth want to do that?"

Thomas was about to continue with his own less than appropriate supposition when I interjected. "Honestly, Mother. You are to believe a twelve-year-old boy on this story? He is probably just trying to sensationalize his sister. You know how brothers can be," I said and shot my own brother a look of reproach.

With his manhood and honor at stake, Thomas exclaimed, "Na-uh! George saw her leave with his own two eyes!"

My mother heard the little boy tantrum coming to the surface and decided not to believe what was being said. Instead, she turned to him with washing bat in hand and retorted, "I am sure he did, son, but perhaps it is unwise to go telling tales that are not your own."

At this, he pouted and turned on his heel to go out into the daylight.

We were alone again in silence with our tasks. Thankful for the break, but sensing my mother was about to poke around more about what had kept me up last night, I quickly finished the buck tub setup and asked if I could be excused to the fields to see if Father needed help. Not seeming to notice my true intention, she gladly agreed, and I too went out into the bright spring day.

I was walking down the main street on the well-trodden path to my father's field when I had this cold sensation drift over me from head to toe on my left side. With a furtive glance to my left then my right, I sighed in relief as I saw Lizbeth sitting in the window of her father's workshop, eyes to the sky.

Chapter 5 – March, Present Day – Sophia/Maddy

The weekend flew by without another thought of recurring dreams, case competitions or anything else work-related. Monday morning, I woke to a rebound in the winter weather and thought twice of taking Violet for her morning constitution without her doggy coat, given the bone-chilling dampness.

Deep in thought about my schedule for the day, my phone buzzed. While I grabbed it out of my pocket, I amused myself with the thought of how at one point in my life I would have paid good money for just the right ringtone or notification sound and now, unless on rare occasions, I would pay good money for it never to make a sound again!

It was Maddy. She was texting because she was coming into town this week and wanted to know my plans and if she could crash on my couch.

Maddy was a whirlwind. She always had been! We had been friends from a young age, even if we fell into different circles, but she had been there for me in times of need. A self-identified party girl who loved life, she worked in the fashion industry and rarely came into town. Her wanderlust was too strong to keep her in one place for too long, but she would use her hometown as a launch pad whenever it was convenient. I always had a sense that she was running away from something but could never quite put my finger on what. This week's unplanned visit felt like another one of those "launch pad" moments.

I quickly shot back a *Friends* meme of Rachel and Phoebe doing a happy dance and left it at that. Less was always more when it came to Madeline Baker.

Violet wasn't digging the bipolar weather either and took to her morning duties quickly and efficiently, keeping us from having to walk the entire block and facilitating a faster return to the warm coziness of our home. She adored when I would use the well-worn fireplace, something I had a bit of anxiety over if I was honest – due to a young adulthood experience of not opening the flue at my parents' house – but I couldn't help but take a picture each and every time she curled up in a little ball by the hearth and sighed, as only a contended little furry freeloader could.

My phone buzzed again. Maddy had sent me a picture of her as a hint to her latest location, or at least the one she was flying in from, and asked if I would be a dear and pick her up from the airport. I saw her slight build fashionably clothed in the latest designer she was repping, light-brown hair – though no one truly knew her natural color since she dyed it all the time – and her unique blue eyes shone from her fair complexion.

The blue wasn't the unique part; oddly enough there were flecks of black I had discovered at a sleepover back in the day. She was telling a ghost story – she had always been an avid storyteller – flashlight pointed upward for dramatic effect. The light seemed to bounce off little spots on her eyes, which made me curious. It had been a hot topic at the time because everyone was saying it was impossible to have black in your iris, but one couldn't argue with the evidence, or Maddy.

To the wrong person, they had a chilling effect, but they intrigued those trying to get to know the real her. Some of the kids who didn't get it dubbed her "black hole" after the void that she seemed to create between people, places and things when she wanted to through her words, actions and vibes. It wasn't the worst thing she had been called, but I was certain it stung her nonetheless, even though she'd never admit it.

There looked to be the shoulder of someone next to her on what I quickly recognized as the Ponte Vecchio, but it also looked like the person had been cropped out of the shot. Must have been the latest in her thrall of suitors. I wasn't worried. I would hear all about it once she was here.

Sure, I responded with a quick auto-type. *Let me know the ETA of Your Highness and your carriage will be waiting.* I knew she'd kick me for that one, but it was worth it. For all her bravado and attitude, she really was a sweet person on the inside, some might even say vulnerable, even if she didn't show that side to everyone. She sent me a screenshot of her itinerary, which made me realize it was not only this week but 11PM tonight that she was due in! My to-do list for the day just grew exponentially and I got right to work.

Maddy woke with a start. She had fallen asleep on the flight from Newark. It was a quick flight, so she impressed even herself but blamed her previous flight over the pond from Rome to Newark and the first-class ticket she had negotiated with the ticket agent right before departure. Being her had its perks – including access to the flowing champagne and delightful steak dinner in seat 1B.

What had jolted her awake? There wasn't any turbulence. The layover had been grueling but not enough for her to have fallen into such a deep sleep so quickly. Then she remembered the dream. It was a dream she had had for as long as she could remember, and one she couldn't decipher. It always started the same...she's riding horseback with a cloak flowing behind her as she's chasing someone. She looks down at her hands holding the horse's mane. They aren't her hands, but somehow, they seem familiar. She's in a dark forest at night, but the moon can be seen through the trees...

It wasn't an enjoyable dream; in fact, it was downright ominous, and always seemed to plague her when she was coming back home.

The plane swiftly descended into the Regional International Airport, and she readied herself to disembark. Checking her watch, she saw they were going to land slightly past the hour at 11:11. *Make a wish*, she heard her inner voice cry out with joyful childlike glee.

Shaking her head, as if to shake off the memory, she rummaged in her purse for her mirror and made sure she was presentable. While she knew that Soph wouldn't care about her appearance, and her hometown airport might as well be her parents' living room, there was always someone who knew someone around the next corner, and she had a reputation to uphold.

She was one of the first to stand to leave the plane so she could get down the escalator and retrieve her luggage. The anticipation of this process was almost too much to bear. This airport wasn't too bad when it came to luggage, but "Sew-ark," as it was called by her friends in aviation, was less than reliable. Who knew if her latest splurge purchase of an Italian leather travel set would have made it in good condition, let alone at all.

She texted Sophia that she was off the plane while heading to the baggage carousel and asked where she would like to meet her. As she hit send and walked out of arrivals, she saw a familiar face in the sea of loved ones milling about for their own travelers. She should have known her friend would never let anyone arrive from a long trip, even at this hour, without a personal welcome.

They did the mock slow run toward each other laughing and then fell into each other for a warm embrace. It had been a while since she'd seen her…she tried to recall the last time, but then Sophia was constant and reliable as Niagara Falls, and time never changed anything. The huge bear hug from her tall friend revived her in a way she didn't know she needed, and then they turned to get her luggage.

The brown curly hair and hazel eyes turned on her while they descended the escalator. "Italy, huh? Fashion week or something?" Sophia prodded.

"Or something." Maddy donned her wicked smile and fell silent.

"So, you're going to make me work for it, huh?" Soph quipped.

"That depends…What are we doing after this?" Maddy questioned.

By now, Sophia knew the pattern. Stop at the local pizza joint to grab a large double cheese and regular pepperoni pizza, head back to her quaint little house in the Northtowns, and enter to an already prepared set of dirty martinis on the table, to be washed down with a bottle of juicy cab afterward. All while having changed into their PJs and gorged on pizza, Maddy sharing her latest tales.

"I thought we'd change it up and stop by Domino's or Taco Bell on our way to your parents' old house and egg it," Sophia mused.

"Sacrilegio!" Maddy exclaimed in mock horror, as these two chain restaurants alone brought locals to their knees out of spite for their more lauded non-chain options. And Sophia knew she hadn't gone near her old house from her childhood in years, though she didn't know why.

"The usual – you know me better than that," Sophia remarked upon seeing Maddy's fake indignation.

"Excellent, then you can wait until we have properly comforted ourselves to hear the tales of my latest adventures. Sally forth so we may get to what needs getting to!" she cried in an English accent that would leave a true Brit plugging their ears.

11:11. The plane landed a little late, but not as bad as it could have been given the weather.

I knew, and expected, Maddy would be on rare form, but this seemed above and beyond, even for her. Wanderlust or no, she looked wary. Jetlag could be a pain, and arriving near midnight was no picnic, but I couldn't help but feel like there was something else beckoning behind her normally protected eyes.

She was generally so composed and put together, yet tonight she was bordering on frazzled. Maybe she had a bumpy ride? I would have to ask her once we settled in back at the house and she had a few sips of her preferred apéritif in her, though I was certain, knowing her, that champagne had been involved on her long haul back to the States.

Ah well, at least her sense of humor was intact, and I had already preemptively called in my traditional pizza order. A must on the "Maddy is Back" list, I just had to hope that Vi hadn't gotten curious about the perfectly made dirty martinis sitting on the island, likely starting to beautifully condense, since I had the fireplace lit earlier in the day.

Some traditions were never meant to be broken, and I was happy this was one of them. Sitting in our PJs on the floor and cramming our face with hometown pizza was the perfect amount of nostalgia, now with an adult "twist" of martinis and wine.

I helped her grab her bags, five luxurious matching leather pieces in all, and we started off to row G in the covered parking area. Once again I was happy to have Etta, as I'm not sure my original car she knew back in high school, Subie, would have been able to take the challenge of her wares! We drove off in the direction of our food and comfort, with an amiable silence between us as she shifted into "Maddy without the Mask" mode, and

I gave her the space to do so. Her energy seemed to finally calm once the rich smell of cheese, pepperoni and par-baked crust was sitting in the backseat, calling our names to get home faster.

We pulled into the driveway and my Wi-Fi security light clicked on to light the way. Once again, I saw a reddish-tan head peeking through the window, which made Maddy start at first, then laugh once she realized what it was. She practically bounded ahead of me to be greeted by the pup so she could have some fur-apy before we did anything else.

"OK, don't worry about me. I'll just grab ALL your bags. Go on in, you'll find what you're looking for on the island," I called out. She raised her hand above her head and waved me off as she continued through the door without a care in the world.

She really did seem to be preoccupied by something. Perhaps this latest heartthrob had really gotten to her? No, impossible. She was never serious about anyone, just as she was never satiated by being in one place too long. Her taste in men shifted as her location did: constantly and quickly. I was definitely going to get to the bottom of it, but not tonight. Tonight was about pizza.

I managed to get all five pieces of luggage inside the side door, impressing myself and thanking my apartment days for training me to carry as much as possible all at once so I didn't need to make multiple trips. That and, this set really did stack together nicely! I didn't want to know what she spent on them, but they were pretty awesome.

"I will put Your Highness's luggage in the loft, should that please you so," I called into the front room with mock irritation. I could hear Vi playing up while Maddy tried to give her squeezes. It was not apparent who was winning in the struggle, but both were having a bang-up time since neither noticed me.

The loft wasn't much, but I had made it into a makeshift studio space with a section for a guest room and storage. The murphy bed functioned as a desk as well as a couch and suited my limited square footage any time I had a random guest.

I ran back out to the car to grab the pizza and lock up. Normally I didn't think twice about being outside at night, but something spooked me as I was walking back. It was a cold feeling that went up and down my left side. I looked around to see if the wind had picked up, but it was still for such a cold and damp day. I saw the silhouette of my friend in the front window through the curtain and bucked up. Maddy was the last person that needed to see me weirded out. I would never hear the end of it!

Heading back inside, I triple-checked the side door locks, placed the pizza on the counter next to the remaining martini glass, as the other had clearly already been pilfered, grabbed paper plates and napkins, and went into the front room to settle in for what was sure to be a great story.

Chapter 6 – June 1563 – Ann

Spring came and went, and soon it was summer. Both April and June saw changes happening in how England and Scotland viewed and dealt with witches, a hot topic of the current climate, especially among Londoners. While their village was outside the immediate impact, it was still something the girls had to keep in mind as they explored their respective talents in the safety of their woods. They did not consider anything they did to be in the realm of witchcraft but also knew others had been tried for less. They were lucky that everyone in their village kept their religious misgivings to themselves, but with one such as Robert already getting odd looks, no one wanted to draw unnecessary attention.

Spring saw Lizbeth falling even more in love with Robert. While he was still prone to his "visions," Lizbeth found it ever more interesting and enjoyed the sideways glances cast at them as they walked the village streets.

Her father was none the wiser, though her brothers teased her mercilessly. George because he was the younger of the two and that was what young boys did when they were anywhere remotely near what they sensed as "love." Matthew, her middle sibling, because he was jealous. Jealous that because she was their father's crown jewel and only female in the family, she was allowed to be rebellious and roam free from the traditional tethers of their life, while he had to begin his apprenticeship under their father to become a cobbler in the family business, even though all he hoped for was the freedom to ride in the fields and become a soldier for his queen's army. He longed for adventure, and his sister, though only a female, had the freedom and was wasting it on an infatuation.

For me, watching my friend fall head over heels for the strange boy was endearing, but it also hurt. The spring and all of its associations with new beginnings and new life only reminded me that I may never love again. It marked another year that James had not returned to me, and he likely never would. If he had, we would have already been married and started our brood of children by now. Oh, how I missed those days of lying listlessly in my father's fields with him, dreaming about our future and all that lay ahead.

James Clarke was a farmer alongside my father. Because of that, he was instantly welcomed and encouraged to pursue me. I played hard to get at first, but it was clear from the start we were destined to be together. I had heard whisperings of it in the wood and even tried the old wives' tale of where you skin an apple, drop the peel into the water and the letter it formed was the first letter of your true love. All those years ago when I saw it float and shift into a J, I just knew.

Walking along the main street in the village in early June, I felt my mind carry me away to the last time I saw James. I asked him not to. I even begged for him to stay.

It was silly at the time, I knew, but I had yet to fully believe in the internal voice that spoke to me, and I felt its tug on my heart all the same. It conveyed a sense of dread. I had a dream a fortnight before he was to leave of a big dark owl. It shadowed over him as he was returning home and suddenly eclipsed him, and he vanished. I knew that owls were considered portents of death, so I worried.

"Dinnae worry, my love," James said as he cupped my cheek in his rough hand. "Yer dream is merely superstition based on old tales. I will be fine. Besides, I journey with my trusty bow on my back. Should I see a shadowy figure loom overhead, I will merely shoot it!" he jested, trying to assuage my concern.

"But pray tell why you must make this journey? I do not understand. They are not your immediate family, and we are to marry this year!" I pouted, hoping that this extreme change in manner would be proof enough of my displeasure at him leaving. I was not traditionally a "whiner" or one who was easily concerned.

"Because my uncle ails, and my auntie needs help tending their lands. My cousins are yet too young to know what to do and their training has not started. I am the only one in my family who can help. It is my blood-sworn duty as the eldest in the line. We Clarkes take our family pride very seriously, and while my parents are not here to bear witness, I must do right by them. Besides, I have nae seen the Scottish Highlands in a fair moon and would like to see them with my adult eyes again before we settle into our life of contentment."

I swooned. I always did when he mentioned our future. I knew he was doing the right thing; he was a noble man, and it was one of many qualities I loved about him – besides his curly auburn hair, broad shoulders and strong calves. Which I knew was wicked to say, but given his Scottish heritage, I had seen him in his family's blue, black and white patterned tartan kilt a fair number of times at recent celebrations, and I could not help but admire them.

"If you must. But perhaps I shall not wait for you until your return. Perhaps another may take me as their bride while you manage your family so very far away," I had teased, starting to walk away from him.

I had done it. He turned on me in the field and we toppled to the ground, his hands and arms making sure I had a soft landing. My jest had had the intended effect, bringing our bodies close one last time. I loved being in his arms and could not bear the thought of not having him by my side for the next few months.

Our bodies seemed to always vibrate with energy when we were near each other. The sensation through every fiber of my being was exquisite, and I had come to rely on it to keep me satiated while he worked in the fields. There was no way to bottle it for this long of a journey, so I tried to absorb all I could as he lay on top of me, softly pinning me to the ground.

He stroked his fingers through my curly, dark-brown hair. He loved that we both shared the natural look in our locks, compared to those who attempted to bring the wave to their hair through other means. We looked deep into each other's eyes and were lost for a moment. Our heartbeats slowed to match each other's rhythm, and we just lay there. Letting the world pass us by.

"I love you, my bonnie lass." A not-so-secret pet name that had further endeared me to him, especially when his

Scottish accent came through. "I will return for ye, and we will start our life together as man and wife. This is my solemn vow, for ye are my one true love, and I ken it from the first time I lay my eyes on ye in your father's fields."

A tear started to fall to my cheek at these words. They were in such contrast to the dread I felt, and yet I knew how true they were, for I felt the same.

"We will be married." I wiggled under him at this comment, my excitement escaping me for a moment. "We will have bairns, three strapping young lads and two bouncing lasses, all with our curly hair," he said as he continued to caress my own hair, slowly moving his strong hand down to my face. His fingers moved to my lips, and I was about to kiss the tip of his forefinger when the number of children he had mentioned struck me.

"Five children?! What, you think me a workhorse for birthing babes?! Well then, the boys best have your midnight-blue eyes and strength to work the fields, and the girls have my deep-hazel eyes with which to work their soft magic and win you over, so they have you wrapped around their little fingers forever!" I giggled. I could not be mad at him. Not now.

His strong hand took to the side of my waist, my breath caught, and his mouth came down for a kiss. I loved his kisses, as hidden as they had to be since we were not yet wed. I pressed my left hand to his strong chest to feel his heartbeat. I drank in his wild open-air scent, somehow mixed with a distant smell of the sea, the strength of his jaw, and how much we both loved and desired each other.

My mind would always wander to the anticipation of our wedding night, though I knew I should not be thinking such thoughts. The way our bodies seemed to fit together like a puzzle, the way our hands met, or the sublime feeling of his lips on mine. We were two pieces to one whole, and we knew it.

The kiss had brought me to tears once again, surging from the depths of my soul, as if I was already feeling the loss of him, and then the moment was over. We had to get back to the village. He to depart to the north, and I to make sure my siblings were preparing for supper. As we walked back through the woods and away from the fields, my dread crept back, even with my soft hand tightly held in his rough work-worn one.

It was dusk, and I suddenly heard a soft whir overhead. I did not see anything, so we kept walking, making our way to my house where he would drop me off for the last time. As we left the wood, I felt something pricking my back. Confused, I turned my head around. I did not see anything at first, and then there it was. At the edge of the wood, sitting on one of the tallest branches, a large dark owl.

I came back to myself at the sharp memory, not realizing I had walked clear across town and through the woods to the very field in which we had lain that last moment together. Tears no longer fell. It had been three-and-a-half years since the moment we had received word of his disappearance, and even longer since that last moment.

I still struggled to understand how my world could come crashing down so violently. Like a tower crumbling. He was only supposed to be gone those few months, six at most, then it was extended. Even still, he should have returned the following March.

We had heard there was a great uprising between French troops and the current Scottish Reformation. It took place near Glasgow, a city I knew he had to pass on his way back to Northern England and home. Home to me. But he never made it. It was supposed that, as he was traveling, he got caught in the middle of the conflict.

As it was his way to travel in his full family colors and kilt, he could have been mistaken for one of the Scots in arms and, since he was not from there, went unrecognized and unclaimed once bodies were identified after the fight. At least, that was the theory I heard my father tell the village elders. There were others floating around out there, but I did not care to hear them.

I did not like to think of it. While I had come to terms with not seeing him these past years, a part of me still held out hope. Hope that he was alive somewhere and would yet make his way back to me. I had even taken to visiting our sacred space in the middle of the night to pray to Sophia for his safe return. I tried different combinations of wildflowers, sticks and other items from nature I found on the mossy wood floor to offer to her in exchange. I had begged for her to return him to me in any way possible, but nothing ever worked.

I had stopped with the rituals by now since we as a group had taken to other foci with our practices, but every once in a while, I would still venture out at night to see if I could commune with Sophia, or if not her, perhaps him, to finally get some closure through a ghostly encounter. While I was disappointed she had not yet answered my prayers, I did not blame her. I knew she would provide a response in time, even if it was not on my preferred timeline.

It was also at that time I learned the importance of listening to the voice in my head, and heart, and the ability to connect dreams and omens. The owl had made it so. I did not talk about that part much, but it was what further drove me to my sisterhood with Madge and Lizbeth, and what had propelled us into learning even more about the "craft" with herbs, flowers and such. It was a beautiful distraction from the pain of loss, and many times as I worked, I would hear that little voice inside affirming my actions.

I looked around me once again in the field. These flashbacks had become few and far between over the years, but this one had been the strongest yet. It was as if I could feel every ounce of that day in my bones and imagine him right by my side once more, like I was living two timelines. It was painful and magnificent all at once.

I shook my head to eliminate the sense of foreboding that had come with it. I decided once and for all I needed to bury these thoughts and emotions so that I could move on with my life, even if it would not include getting married. How could I ever give myself to another man when I had lost my one true love?

I moved slowly through the trees back to the village, resigned to my new destiny and trying to determine what it would hold when I heard a soft whir overhead. I looked up, half expecting to see a shadow as I had before, but nothing. Lost in my thoughts, I carried on.

Upon exiting the oh-so-familiar path, I felt a strange pricking sensation on my back. I turned, this time with my whole body, to face whatever it was head-on. At first, I saw nothing, and I was about to turn around and chalk it up to my flashback coming alive again, but then I saw it. On the top branch of the elm tree, on the edge of the field, was the same large owl, blinking its liquid gold eyes back at me yet again, a harbinger of things to come.

Chapter 7 – May, Present Day – Sophia

Maddy's stay was entertaining as always but didn't go deeper than sharing the latest hijinks in her choice of career and man. I was wrong in assuming this latest one had made any such impact on her, and her thirst to move onto the next thing was as strong as ever.

She had seemed on the verge of sharing something after two martinis and a bottle of wine…but the flash was gone as quick as it came.

The week of her "crashing on the couch" quickly turned into a month, and then two. It worked out nicely in the sense that when I had to escort my competition team to Las Vegas for the week of their festivities, I didn't have to put Violet in the kennel, and she could stay with Auntie Maddy.

The competition went incredibly well. My students were the most prepared they had ever been. The "non-presenting" team that built up the research had played their supporting role beautifully and even called in before each time slot to tell them to "break a leg." I loved the comradery and relationships they had built.

I, as usual, had found a small talisman worthy of the presenting teams' efforts to take with them on stage as a good luck charm. I had started the tradition with my first team as a way to be with them while they presented, and it had worked. They had unseated one of the reigning top teams. Each year, it was something different, so that if I had recurring students, as I had intended, they didn't have a collection of the same item from year to year, but it always contained the power color of purple, incorporating an essence of strength and resolve to fuel their fires.

This year's competition was rough. Ever since our team had unseated the majors, more and more teams were breaking the mold and becoming authentic in the way they presented and approached the challenge statement. But I wasn't worried. I knew we were ready, and that trusty internal voice told me this was the year – and it wasn't wrong.

First round turned into second round, and second round led into finals. Though the wait in between presenting and finding out who made the cut was excruciating, it was worth every "whoop" and sigh of relief that escaped Stacey, Andi, Melissa and Stephen. They deserved every moment.

When, finally, they held the unveiling ceremony of who won and the check was presented, I burst with sheer momma pride as they were called up to the stage. I quickly got the rest of the team on a group chat so they could witness the excitement for themselves...though I had to mute them, otherwise they would have deafened the entire room.

It felt good. And I thought I had further solidified my position within the school and program for the future. However, on the flight home, I had had an overwhelming sense of foreboding that I couldn't shake.

Now, the semester had ended, and we were quickly moving into summer – my escape time. I had big plans to refine my curriculum for the upcoming fall semester and determine what my research topic would be. While it wasn't my favorite idea, I had been encouraged by my department head to pursue my PhD so that I could become full tenure. In order to do that, however, I had to develop a research project and get published. It wasn't something I relished, but I knew that if I wanted to firmly plant roots in academia, it was something I had to do.

Having Maddy around was not helping. She was constantly coming and going as she determined her next steps, and this wasn't happening as swiftly as one would have liked. I loved my friend, but that didn't mean a long-term living situation was the healthiest thing for either of us. Sensing my walls going up, she found more and more reasons to be out of the house, yet her stuff remained. Even Violet seemed to have lost her puppy eyes for the new human in the house, as she could sense my mood shift.

"I invited Kit over for a girls' night!" Maddy came bursting in the door as I sat pretending to tap keys on the keyboard and muster up an idea for a thesis. "Soph?"

"In here," I yelled back, letting her know I was in the office.

She came bounding in. "I ran into Kit while I was out. I guess I forgot to tell her I was in town, as she was surprised to see me."

I mentally added an apology to my list of to-dos. Kit and I had had a few quips over text in the past months, but as I had been busy with the competition and end of the semester, and her with her latest speaking circuit, we hadn't spoken properly in a while. Nor had I had the chance to get her thoughts on my dream as I had promised myself I would.

Maddy continued, not waiting for a reaction. "I invited her over tonight so we could have a girls' night!" I was busy processing the information while also mentally constructing the apology, so when I didn't respond with an equal measure of enthusiasm, she added, "I hope that was OK?"

Her tone brought me out of my reverie. "Of course! It will be great to have her here," I assured her. "I haven't had a good Kit conversation in months!"

"Great," she said, "so what shall we have? I can buy the wine!"

I should have known that the preparation of this last-minute soiree would fall to me. The only thing Maddy knew how to cook was reservations, or an open bottle. Her traveling had not given her the time to learn the basics, and as she was constantly chasing after figureheads in the modeling world, food was most likely forgotten.

I smirked to myself. "Let me think. I will check the pantry for what I have, but it's probably not much."

Maddy didn't eat a lot, but what she did eat had already eaten me out of house and home the past few months. With how busy I had been wrapping up the semester, I had neglected to do my bulk food shop.

"Tell you what, why don't I finish up what I'm working on here and then we can run to the corner store up the street?" I said.

While I clearly wasn't making any progress on developing a core thesis, she didn't need to know that, and at least one of us had to appear to be responsible. I also knew this girls' night would devolve from healthy eating to wanting all the old favorites, so why even put up a pretense? We may as well just go straight for the goodies. The corner store would have the old standbys, and we wouldn't have to go too far.

"Sounds great!" Maddy whooped and then at least had the wherewithal to pick up some of her stuff lying around. She wasn't a complete disaster of a house guest.

Soon it was the "bewitching" hour, as the three of us used to call it, and Kit's headlights pulled into my driveway. As much as it was impromptu and slightly annoying that Maddy had made such a grand assumption, I was excited to see Kit. It had been months, and with twins, a husband and her private practice along with public speaking gigs, she was hard to nail down for anything in person, let alone a last-minute girls' night of old. It must have been serendipity at play.

Kit came crashing through the doors with paper bags in hand, overflowing with all the healthy snacks. God, I loved her. She knew that with this being a Maddy-led event, heaven knows what would be served.

Maddy rushed at her and immediately enveloped her in a huge hug around the neck, inadvertently knocking some of the fresh goods out of the bags. Violet watched the produce roll until it stopped and then inspected it to see if it was something she should help with. "Oh, sorry!" Maddy cried.

"No worries, doll, it all goes to one place anyway," Kit said. I let her make her way over to the island to relieve herself of the bags before I stepped in for my bear hug too.

Now it sounds weird, but I consider myself a connoisseur of hugs, having grown up with a dad who gives the best. Kit's were right up there. A hug from Kit could revive you for months, and we were way overdue! Not one to be left out, Maddy piled on top, and it was high school all over again.

While we had each grown up in different circles, they had all crossed paths at one time or another. As we grew into adulthood and recognized the similarities in each other, and a unique ability to finish each other's sentences while also peacefully co-existing without any drama, we became our own little trifecta.

Without prompting, I held out the pitcher of dirty martinis and three upturned glasses. "I hope you wore your comfies." I nodded at Kit, and then looked at both of them. "Who's first?"

They both smiled a cheshire grin. I poured, Kit took over the kitchen, organizing all the food, and Maddy just started talking. She had yet to regale Kit with the tales I had already heard a million times, and once again her storytelling abilities kicked in.

Kit didn't mind. She patiently listened to every excruciating detail while she made her famed tomato onion salad, which stood out like a sore thumb against all the junk we had bought that afternoon.

Once Maddy finished, we could each get a word in edgewise. We had moved from the kitchen to the front room and were lounging around on the floor in front of the food-filled coffee table, listening to our favorite 90s station on Spotify. Conversation quickly turned to Kit's twins, her hunk of a husband and then her work.

"...he's just a little man already and only eight!" Kit said as she spoke about Tate. "I know they're twins, and birth order shouldn't ultimately matter all that much given they are minutes apart, but damn if he doesn't act like a firstborn. He's practically an old man already."

Maddy was swirling her martini in her glass. We were already on our second pitcher of the evening. I was glad that Erik was happy to watch the kids and let Kit spend the night so we could all let loose.

"Are you really surprised? He's just an old soul," Maddy said, almost to herself, and then realized what she said and silently crossed herself.

For all her vim and vigor, Maddy was supremely religious. Something that Kit and I had spent hours discussing and trying to reconcile with the party girl who worked in fashion. She went through men like one would go through paper towels, and yet when it came to anything spiritual, she would start reciting Hail Marys or crossing herself while turning around in a counterclockwise circle. We both found this counter-intuitive and amusing, but it just added to Maddy's charm, so we didn't feel the need to point out the dichotomy of her actions.

"No, you're absolutely right," Kit reassured her.

"What about Thora? Is she just as old-timey as Tate?" Maddy asked, trying to change the subject. Kit and I both laughed out loud.

"Ha!" I responded.

"No, not quite. As much as she is still a reserved child, she's a bit more feral," Kit said.

"Oooo, I like her already!" Maddy smiled.

"Yeah, she's unconventional and would prefer to be homeschooled and 'be one with nature,' as she calls it," Kit shared.

"Well, that still sounds fairly adult-like to me. Who wouldn't want to be in school with a ton of friends and having fun at recess?!" Maddy questioned.

"Oh, she still loves having fun, but because her idea of fun is slightly different than the rest of the kids her age, she prefers to make her own fun...which can lead to some interesting experiments and Erik and I finding animals around the house. I don't know where she gets it!" Kit exclaimed.

Maddy wrinkled her nose in response. We could see she was curious and wanted to ask for details, but that was warring with her desire to start reciting a prayer multiple times over. The religious side won out, as she didn't poke any further, and Kit and I just shook our heads in silence, once again not being able to reconcile the two versions of Maddy.

"So," Kit started, turning the conversation back to Maddy, "what's your next move?"

I sent her an appreciative look while Maddy gathered her thoughts. She was doing her typical reverse-reverse psychology thing to help move her along and out of my house, without my even asking. It really was like we shared one brain sometimes. It was comforting to say the least.

Maddy's face lit up. "Well, I have a new offer to head back to London! It is an up-and-coming designer out of the West End and her latest sketches are simply to die for. She heard about my recent work in Italy and her people reached out to my people, and voila!" she said with flare. Kit and I giggled.

"London, huh? Tell me, how many times have you lived there again?" Kit asked sarcastically, knowing full well we had both lost count. Maddy threw the pillow at her from behind her back. It smacked Kit in the face, nearly toppling her martini glass in the process. "That was almost alcohol abuse!" Kit cried.

"Serves you right." Maddy pouted. "And, Miss Smarty Pants, while the designer is going to be based out of London, she has a family estate in Northern England that she plans to use for her brainstorming headquarters. She wants me to meet her up there and we will plot out her plan to take over the fashion empire!" Maddy laughed her evil villain laugh.

"Sounds great!" Kit said. "When does that new adventure start?"

"Oh, um, well, I hadn't had a chance to share with Soph yet, but tomorrow." Maddy looked up at me sheepishly.

I, in turn, spat out my latest sip. "Tomorrow?!" I half squealed, half choked.

"Yeah, sorry, Soph. I just found out all the details and negotiated the deal yesterday. I guess in all of the excitement and then running into Kit, I forgot to mention it. I hope it's OK. That's partially why I was excited for tonight, serendipitous timing and all for a final sendoff," she said in a gush of words.

"Why on earth are you apologizing?! This is incredible for you. I don't need notice of when you're leaving; I'm not your landlady!" I said while reaching across to give her a quick hug. "This is fantastic news, and I couldn't be more thrilled for you." I said and quickly ran into the other room.

They must have heard the clinking as I rummaged around for what I was looking for, because they were both looking at me expectantly when I came back into the room with three small cordial glasses in hand, a cold, dark, cherry-colored syrup in each. We had started a tradition at the beginning of our friendship where whenever anyone had something exciting going on, we would mark the occasion with our favorite – ice wine. It was more of a local thing and hard to come by outside of the area, making it even more special.

We clinked, we sipped, and then we slept. It was 2AM by the time we all passed out from pure exhaustion. Maddy may have been used to this lifestyle, but Kit and I were out cold. We were drunk on our shared bond and randomly being together in one spot on an early summer's eve, and surprisingly not the alcohol we had just consumed.

None of us had taken time to notice that it was a full moon that evening, the first of the summer months. She shone down us with her brilliant light through my front window, while we all drifted off to dreamland, comforted in each other's presence, as one can only be with their true friends.

Chapter 8 – July 1563 – Ann/Lizbeth

June turned into July. I felt every one of those days pass after seeing my harbinger again. I was not sure what to take the dark owl as a sign of, but I assumed it was not good, or at least not all good. As I understood it, true harbingers could represent both dark and light.

That morning, as I prepared to help my father in the fields, there was a soft rumbling of commotion out in the streets. While it was not an alarm, there was certainly something happening that fell outside the village's daily routine. I grabbed my hat and ran to the door.

There was a carriage coming, with a gentleman on his horse riding ahead of it and several of his men flanking his sides. He was not royalty but certainly of nobility judging by the way he carried himself at first glance. I knew enough to curtsy as he passed by.

He was most certainly of a higher station than anyone in our village, but perhaps not to the level of the local barons who liked to trade with us when the occasion called. I had a ripple of cold travel up and down my spine as he rode past. I could already tell I did not like this man and what he represented and hoped that he was simply passing through as he journeyed elsewhere.

The whole town came out of their houses and workshops as he made his way along the main street. He was clearly traveling to the village center to ascertain who the highest-ranking male was. He would be shocked when he determined there was no knight or "reeve" to be found here. For this was a place unto itself, most uncommon at the time. We supported the local lord and his family as needed, but they left us to our own devices otherwise.

Lizbeth's father's workshop was toward the center, and since he was one of the elders, in both years and craftmanship, I supposed he would be the one to take the call to arms and speak with the newcomer. I ambled down to his shop as others followed the carriage.

As I suspected, Mr. White came out of his shop after one of the village boys ran in to tell him of the stranger's arrival. He approached the rider, who dismounted and bowed with a condescending air of incredulity. I grimaced. This man clearly held an air of self-import that none of us were used to, and I did not care for it. I quietly made my way toward Mr. White, both to know what was going on and offer my support should I need to speak on behalf of my family.

"Good day, sir. What brings you to our humble village?" I heard Mr. White ask in his most respectful tone. I tried not to giggle.

"I seek shelter for the week as my men and I are searching for new accommodations outside the city," he said.

A gasp escaped most of the crowd and you could hear mumblings of: "The city?" "London?" "Here?" "He is already days away, why so far?"

His answer, said at a higher volume than necessary for a conversation with Mr. White, had the intended effect, and he beamed. Mr. White's puzzled look urged him to continue. "Yes, I bring my small household with me from London. You may or may not have heard of the latest plague that has overtaken the city. I seek to make my home elsewhere after having lost my sister and brother."

I heard James in that moment. *He doth protest too much. He has other motives for coming here.* I shook my head, first in agreement, though no one else heard the comment, then in surprise at my internal voice taking on James's tone. Was it a memory?

"May I know your name, sir?" Mr. White asked.

"Richard Acton" was his response.

Just then, I saw my friend Lizbeth exit her father's shop. She must have been in the backroom reading and had not heard the commotion, otherwise she would have been the first on the street. At the sight of her, Mr. Acton immediately bowed in mock chivalry intended to catch her eye.

Instead, Lizbeth looked around the village congregated and was bewildered. I could see her trying to work out what was going on, and as her eyes searched the crowd, they landed on me. I silently shook my head and tilted it to indicate we should meet in the wood. She understood and turned back to the stranger, who was still attempting to gain her favor with that horrifically awful bow.

I saw Mr. White give her a look and suppress a cough. She did her best to curtsy and I heard her say in her most demure voice, "Sir." He rose, as did she, and he put his hand out for hers.

"It is a pleasure to make your acquaintance, fair maiden. Are you the lady of this house?" Mr. Acton inquired. I cupped my hand over my mouth and had to turn away to stifle a laugh. What was he playing at? Why the façade? He clearly took pleasure in the attention he was garnering from all of us, but it was most impetuous.

Lizbeth smiled and said, "As it happens, sir, but only because my father is a widower, and I am the only daughter." I breathed a sigh of relief. At least Lizbeth had the good sense to play along.

"Ah, I see," Mr. Acton responded, and I saw him turn to his men with a devilish look in his eye.

Mr. White spoke then to break the odd tension building in the air. "You may disperse and go back to your routines, my friends! We are not besieged." I was not so sure and thought it best to remain and be inconspicuous. He turned back to the traveler. "Sir, we have no inns in our village, but I have room enough. You may stay with us until you find more adequate dwellings for your household."

Mr. Acton lowered his head in thanks. "I would not usually entertain such an offer, but..." he began and then looked Lizbeth up and down, "how can I refuse?"

Mr. White turned to his daughter. "Lizbeth, would you please escort Mr. Acton and his men to our house? I will tell Matthew to follow. You may well find George there still. Have them clear out their rooms so Mr. Acton and his men can rest after what must have been a long journey."

I could tell this was the last thing that Lizbeth wanted to do. Clearly conversations needed to be had in our space of respite, but they would have to wait. Her eyes found mine again as the crowd thinned and I simply shook my head. I took off toward Madge's, and she knew that the two of us would be waiting for her once her task had concluded. I could only imagine how the boys would react at being forcibly removed from their rooms to sleep in the receiving room on the long benches with some straw padding or on the hard floor.

Lizbeth did as her father bid her and led the strange group toward home. Her older brother, thankfully, was on her heels in a moment, as he had only been in the shop, his day's work ahead of him. He had just begun the apprenticeship with their father and was already most capable. This early in the morning, he would have been evaluating the materials to be used for the day to be sure they were suited to the tasks, arranging the leathers, preparing the necessary dyes and making sure the threads for stitching were not knotted.

They led the motley group slowly down the street to their home. Matthew looked at his sister with an inquisitive glare while Lizbeth simply shrugged her shoulders and kept walking. She could feel an icy breath of air moving up her back and she turned to see what had caused it. When she did, she saw the traveler, Mr. Acton, staring at her.

This stare was wholly different than when her Robert stared off into space with one of his "fits," though she liked to call them "journeys" once she understood what was going on. No, Mr. Acton's had a completely different feeling and purpose. It was cold, it was calculated, and she suddenly felt very aware of the way her hips moved under her skirt while she walked, how her hair blew in the breeze, how straight she held her back. She quickly turned ahead and tried to suppress a shudder.

I walked with a brisk pace to get to Madge's just up the road. I had not seen her in the village, and she was going to want all the details. I knew it would be a while before Lizbeth could break herself away from their new visitors and join us, but we needed to get to our wood.

I approached Madge's door and knocked thrice. I heard the pitter patter of footsteps running around inside. It was Joan, Madge's second oldest sister, but fourth sibling in the line of eight, who answered the door. "Hi, Joan, is your sister at home?" I asked.

Joan, only ten but wanting to act older, answered with a sarcastic attitude, "Which one? For I have four sisters." She clearly knew I did not mean the youngest ones, Amelia and Rebecca, as I saw them chasing the baby of the family, John, around near the fireplace, nor Mary, the thirteen-year-old who usually kept to herself in the corner, sketching whatever she could.

Not in the mood for her despondence this morning, I was about to retort with a haughty answer of my own when I heard Mrs. Williams call out from her still room, "For heaven's sake, Joan, let her in and run and get Margaret!" Clearly Mrs. Williams had already been on the receiving end of Joan's mood today and was having none of it.

I walked back to the heart of the house. Mrs. Eliza Williams was the village healer and known in the neighboring villages for her talents. The care with which she worked and the joy she had for her craft was evident in all her tinctures, salves and ointments.

I loved going into the still room. It felt like it held secrets and magic within, with the upturned drying herbs and flowers creating a unique potpourri of scents in the room. It also held various glass jars and containers on the wooden shelves, and other such equipment with which Mrs. Williams made her concoctions. Her "book of knowledge," as she referred to it, sat at the center of the room on the wood block island she had created for herself, resting open on the iron holder.

"Good morning, Mrs. Williams. What magic do you brew today?" I asked with a smile.

"Ha, magic. You girls and your notions. No magic here, just good old-fashioned herbal knowledge to set what ails you right as rain!" she responded.

I liked Mrs. Williams. Slightly taller than most women, with a medium build and warm chocolate-brown eyes, she always had an air of the mystical about her, though she never let us dive too deep on the subject. She was one of the few women I could look in the eye rather than at the tops of their heads. She liked to focus on the ancient heritage behind what she did and knew it well. Her mother's mother's mother and beyond in her line had all been healers, each adding pages to the age-worn tome in the middle of the room.

I heard Madge come bounding downstairs, though I could have easily mistaken it for one of her younger brothers, William or Robert, with the speed at which she came. She was not used to me making house calls so early in the morning and was clearly eager to find out why I was there.

I turned to her mother. "Mrs. Williams, do you need any provisions from the wood this morning? As it happens, I am on my way there now and would be most happy to help collect anything for which your inventory is low."

She gave me a knowing smile. "Were you now? Well, I suppose my Margaret could go with you to help if only to save you dropping off what you collect on the way back. Here, let me make you a list."

She turned to write down the few flowers and herbs she needed that were known to grow wild in the wood – primrose, cowslips, nettles and elm bark. Madge furrowed her brow in confusion at me while her mother's back was turned. I put my finger to my lips and shook my head to indicate we would talk later. She nodded her head in response and gathered her things and the basket.

Mrs. Williams turned, handed me the list and we both took off out the front door, eager to go about our task. "Good day, girls, be sure you do not forget anything!" she called after us with a smile.

As soon as we were out of ear shot, Madge turned to me and was about to ask what this was all about when I realized I had yet to inform my father of the goings-on or where I would be. He thought I was coming to the fields to work with him today. I cursed my luck and was about to divert us on our path when my little brother Thomas went running by. I called after him, "Thomas!"

He stopped abruptly and turned. "What?!" He was clearly agitated that he had to stop.

"Where are you going?" I yelled.

"Father asked me to run home to see where you were. He was worried since you had not shown up," he said as he approached us. My luck was still intact, it seemed; I would not have to go to the fields after all.

"Could you please tell Father that I am now tasked with helping Madge gather important herbs and flowers from the woods for Mrs. Williams, and I will see you when you all return from the fields for supper?" I asked.

Thomas was none too pleased. He did not like it that I had as much free rein as I liked and had been shirking my duties in the field lately while he had to help, and Susan and Izzy, my younger sisters, got to stay home with our mother while she worked.

He groaned. "Alright, but he will think it a thin excuse!" And he was off.

Madge and I looked at each other in delight and swiftly moved arm in arm toward our path.

"Now pray tell, what is all of this about?!" she queried.

"I know not the details, but a strange traveler showed up in the village this morning. Mr. White spoke with him and took it upon himself to give him and his men lodging for the immediate future!" I said. Madge stared at me as I continued. "He had Lizbeth and Matthew walk them back to their house to let them settle in after their long journey."

At this, Madge was confused. "Long journey?" she questioned.

"Yes!" I exclaimed. "Supposedly from London! He says he escaped the plague that has gripped the city once again, and to which he lost both of his siblings."

She turned to me. "But you do not believe him?" she asked. Madge knew me too well. It was as if she could read my thoughts and complete my sentences, sometimes before I had even finished the thought myself.

"Correct. There is something about this man that seems off. I do not trust him, or his intentions. He has too proud an air for his station and thinks much too highly of himself," I responded, while still clearly thinking things through.

"And you think it suspicious he should want to leave London during a plague?" she continued.

Now that, I could understand. We had heard of the great plagues before. Thankfully, in the north, we had yet to be touched by one. I always credited Mrs. Williams and her exquisite healing practices with that escape, though she would take no such credit.

The plague going on this year, however, was especially caustic. We had heard tales of scores of people perishing from fever, headache, chills and swelling of their body. It would come on fast and leave one dead in days! It seemed to be taking a large population what with the clear sanitation problems happening in and around such an overpopulated city such as London.

No, it was not necessarily the plague that "plagued" me, but his claiming to be an orphan with no family ties left.

That was not something someone usually shared in introductory or civilized conversation. It was a private fact one usually kept to themselves until one knew their audience better. Just then, the little voice that had popped in my head this morning spoke up again with the "I think he doth protest too much" and I found myself nodding my head in agreement.

"What?" Madge inquired, clearly seeing me nod my head to an unspoken thought. I repeated what the voice had now told me twice. She looked at me and then we forged ahead in silence as she absorbed the saying.

We started to pick some of the herbs and flowers on her mother's list as we entered the woods but realized if we picked them too early, they would lose their necessary fragrance and liveliness, so we had to wait until our business here was concluded.

We sat on the stumps in our circle among the trees and our stone altar and waited. It was so peaceful here, with an unspoken sense of security. I knew we had all felt it on some level, which was what made it so special for all of us. The remnants of the latest love spell Lizbeth had worked up with Madge fluttered in the breeze on top of the stone.

I hoped that whenever Lizbeth came to regale us with her story from the morning, she had sense enough to bring some food. In all the morning's events, I had walked out of the house without having eaten a bite of cheese and my stomach was loudly reminding me now.

Madge and I sat silently, each lost in our own thoughts, when we heard someone approaching. Assuming it was Lizbeth, we both continued sitting, waiting for her to break through with a spectacular entrance. Instead, it was Robert, looking as bewildered as ever.

"Robert?" I called to him. He turned and saw us and walked over. "Whatever are you doing here?" I asked.

He looked at me, then to Madge, then back to me, as if he was assessing the situation, why we were here, and what he should say. He clearly had not expected to find us here, or had he?

"I came looking for Lizbeth. I needed to tell her something, something I have just seen in one of my vis—" He cut himself off and looked down at his feet. He suspected that Lizbeth had told us about him but could not be sure, and it would be un-gentlemanly to ask.

I softened my voice to reassure him. "Go on." He looked up and then stared straight into my eyes. I felt the earth shift under me and energy vibrate around me. I had not felt that vibration or surge of energy in...I started and looked away. His gaze fell and suddenly he ran off, as quickly as he had come.

Madge came over, sensing something had disrupted me.

"Are you alright?! What was that all about?" she asked as she looked off in the direction he left. I slowly started to shake my head, trying to figure it out myself. I was just about to tell her what I had experienced when we heard someone else approaching.

This time, it was Lizbeth. She was completely out of breath and heaved herself down on her tree stump with a sigh of relief. Madge was the first to react. "Lizbeth, what on earth..." but Lizbeth held up one of her fingers as a sign to give her a moment and Madge stopped.

I gingerly sat down on the stump nearest me. My legs were still shaking from the moment before with Robert. What had that been? It was as if James had been standing right next to me and our bodies had touched in some way. It was the only time I had ever felt the fission of energy in the air in that way, but James was not there. Lost in thought, I had not heard Lizbeth start until she abruptly said my name.

"Sorry, what?" I said, coming out of my stupor.

"I am trying to tell you both what just happened. Are you with us?" she asked.

I glanced at Madge, who looked at me with sympathy and moved her head slightly to indicate we should keep the moment with Robert quiet for now, lest we interrupt Lizbeth's train of thought and lose the story completely. It always amazed me how we could communicate in that way.

"Well, Matthew and I took Mr. Acton and his men back to our house. They will be most interesting house guests indeed!" she squealed, though not in her happy way. "They immediately removed their boots and ordered us around as if we were in their service. Matthew is too good and obeyed. I, however..."

Madge and I looked at each other and half groaned, half laughed. We knew where this was going.

Lizbeth carried on, not noticing our reaction. "I stood there with my arms crossed and refused. Matthew shot me a glare, but I cared not. Who are these men?! He is not even a lord or baron. He does not own anything in our village, so why on earth should I be subservient to him!" She sat down again on the stump next to her, having taken a standing position to tell the tale after she caught her breath. She was clearly flustered by the experience.

"So where do they stand now?" Madge pushed on.

"I do not know." Lizbeth huffed. We both looked at her.

"What do you mean you do not know? Did your father not ask you to get them settled in so they could rest?!" Madge asked.

"Of course he did, but when has him asking me to do anything ever forced me to comply? I left. I could not stand it. And that *man*..." she said with a little too much emphasis. "That man frightens me. Not like my Robert."

"Whatever do you mean?" I said, finally finding my voice.

"The way he looks at me, he is no gentleman at all. I doubt there is even a plague ongoing in London. He was probably run out of the city for being a scoundrel, and now he is in my house!" she exclaimed.

At this, we all broke out into a belly laugh. We could not help it, given the novelty of the situation and the drama with which Lizbeth told her story. Madge was the first to recover herself and speak. "Was there anything else you noticed about him other than his wandering eye and disrespectful manner?"

"Yes!" Lizbeth cried. To make matters worse, Lizbeth had noted the thick silver chain that hung around his neck with a large ornate cross on it. Also, among his belongings, a Bible had fallen out of his bag along with a few other religious markers. We fell silent.

While no one in the village was a "nonbeliever," there were plenty that were not orthodox either. In fact, they had all kept their beliefs to themselves and worshipped how they chose to in their own homes. We had heard of the English Reformation that had started with our queen's father, but those strong divisions had not reached us where we were in the north.

"Do you think him an orthodox or dissenter?" Madge asked, barely aware of what those terms meant, but the mood ostensibly changed.

"I know not," replied Lizbeth, "nor do I wish to find out. I hope my father does not let him and his men linger and they find where they are meant to go with haste!" she finished.

Madge and Lizbeth carried on with their line of inquiry, trying to parse out as many details as they could about this new arrival.

Religion? Plague? Civil upheaval? Had all of those just wound up on our doorstep in one fell swoop? I did not want to believe it, but between the voice in my head, the owl at the edge of the wood the other day, and the encounter with Robert, I could not help but feel they were all warnings of things to come.

Chapter 9 – August, Present Day – Sophia

The summer was flying by. Unfortunately, my latest thesis was not. If I was honest with myself, I had shifted so many times on my theme and intention I had lost all originality and just kept starting over every time I sat down at the keyboard.

Perhaps I should have gone into psychology, I mused. More times than not over the years, I had said I already knew what my dissertation topic would be – "The Male Ego and Its Inability to Let Women Pass Them While Driving." I had been conducting my own focus-group-of-one for years. Anytime I approached a car on the left and saw it was a man that I was about to pass, I counted down until they realized, sped up, and either wouldn't let me pass them or changed lanes and blocked me in mine. Nine times out of ten was what I had concluded at this point.

My phone started to vibrate on the desk, bringing me out of my reverie. I groaned. I couldn't afford any distractions. I needed to buckle down and get this dang thing written, if not outlined, before the day's end, so I could remain on schedule with my "voluntold" PhD.

I ignored my phone and set my eyes back on the blinking cursor on my laptop screen. I needed inspiration. I needed a muse. I needed a miracle.

Then, my phone started vibrating across the desk again. Clearly, whoever it was, they were persistent. I knew it couldn't be my parents; they were off on one of their European adventures again, thoroughly enjoying their well-earned retirement. They would be sleeping at this hour in Italy.

Suddenly, a sense of panic kicked in as Kit came to mind. I immediately picked it up and saw that my intuition had been correct. I answered. I was about to say some quippy hello when she just launched into her speech.

"Hi, I'm so glad you answered. I know you're working and need to be focused, but I could really use someone to talk to about something and I honestly don't know who else I can turn to. I think I'm losing it," she said, all in one breath.

"OK, I'm here! What on earth has you so frazzled?!" I said.

Kit was the calm one. The rational one. Whatever this was, it had to be off the charts.

"First of all, take a deep breath. You sound like you're about to hyperventilate!" I instructed. I heard silence, and then the soft intake and outflow of air on the other end. "Good, now do it again," I said in a soft tone. Once again, I heard a soft intake of air. "Now, what's up?" I queried.

Still frazzled, but the calming breaths clearly starting to center her, Kit responded. "Thanks. Holy cow, I haven't had to do that in a while," she said, more to herself than me. "Listen, I know we only became true 'friends' in the last few years, but I do feel a kindred spirit with you that I haven't with others. But this, this might push the boundaries of our soul sister-dom," she said.

I didn't know how to respond to that. It wasn't like her to be dramatic.

She went on. "I think it might be better if we speak in person."

"OK, where do you want me to meet you? I'm not getting any writing done right now anyway and could use a break," I said.

"Could I come to your house? I would feel too self-conscious sharing this in a public place and I can't risk Erik hearing me. He would commit me for sure!" I was surprised but agreed. "Thanks, I'll be over in twenty."

I quickly went into the front room and kitchen to straighten up for company. Violet looked at me lazily from her bed, wondering why the sudden movement at midday when I had so clearly been dormant just moments ago.

"I'm sorry to disturb your sunshine, Your Highness, but Lady Akelsen is coming over for a quick chat, so you may want to make yourself presentable!" I quipped in my best British accent. She almost looked like she shook her head before she laid it back down and tucked it under her tail.

Twenty minutes later, I had changed from my comfy sweats to more appropriate jean shorts and a short-sleeved shirt, throwing my hair up into a ponytail and slapping on more deodorant for good measure. I knew Kit wouldn't care what I looked like, but as she was always so put together, I had to try.

I heard the car tires crunch on the driveway and come to a halt. The car door slammed, and within seconds, Kit came rushing in the side door, kicked off her shoes and sat a bottle of bourbon down on the counter.

I whistled. "Wowza. This is going to be a doozy of a Tuesday afternoon...Where are the kids?" I mused. It may be the end of summer, but I knew they were still yet to go back to school, even if my own countdown for going back was dwindling down to single digits.

"They're at their grandparents for the week, thankfully. Just dropped them off yesterday." She walked around the kitchen, grabbing rocks glasses and ice, clearly making herself at home, which, even given the circumstances, made me smile inwardly at the familiarity we had developed over the last couple of years.

She popped the bottle and started to pour. I immediately took the bottle out of her hands, grabbed the already ice-filled glasses and corralled her into the front room. I had thought about pulling a saloon reference out and asking her to "saddle up to the bar and tell me your worries," but the look in her eye told me this wasn't the time.

We walked into the room, and she patted Vi's extended head absentmindedly and took her usual seat in the large chair in the corner facing the window, while I plopped across from her on the sectional couch on the chaise lounge end. I sat in anticipation, not wanting to break the obvious concentration on her face. She was clearly trying to figure out how best to start.

"How about some liquid courage? Cheers!" I said, finished pouring our glasses, handed her one and raised my glass in her direction. She half smiled and took a slug.

"OK," she said, finding her words. "I may be making a bigger deal out of this than I should, as I'm sure it is nothing but a child's musings, but something about it felt so...real."

I gave her the space to continue and noted whatever this was included one of the kids. She felt my eyes on her and looked up.

"It was when I was dropping the kids off yesterday. We were singing in the car, having a great time listening to 'Stand Back' by The Arrows, when Tate stops and says, 'I had a dream about an arrow!' He seemed pleased and, expecting it to be a cowboys-and-Indians-themed discussion, I turned the music down so Thora and I could hear him." She took a breath and was about to continue when she thought better of it and took a swig of the bourbon instead. "He said he had seen me, only it wasn't me, running through a forest at night. I was barefoot, in what looked like very old-fashioned clothing. He saw someone chasing after me and someone else behind me, and we looked scared. Then, there was an arrow flying through the air and both of us fell to the ground."

My mouth was agape. I didn't say anything. I couldn't say anything. She continued.

"At first, as he was talking, I figured it had just been a scary dream, but he kept saying it was me and someone else. He was insistent. He also seemed to be talking from the first person, as if he was seeing me, but from my vantage point. The detail he was sharing was so incredibly vivid, and yet he couldn't tell me who I was with. He was getting mad at me for asking so many questions, but I honestly thought perhaps he was having a psychological break! He just kept going into more and more detail about the surroundings and a time period he could know nothing about and, in his eight-year-old way, telling me that he saw me – or maybe it was him in some way, given his perspective – get shot by an arrow. Well, I tried to remain calm, but after I dropped them off, I ran home to look up a few things. Of course, nothing in my books was going to help..." She couldn't stop the words flowing now.

"...and then I thought of Erik. Whenever there is something he doesn't understand, he meditates. I've been trying to do that for a while now, but I never found it to be helpful. I had started the practice when I realized that sometimes it can help soldiers with PTSD. I thought it would make a good study if I tried to experience it for myself before I started talking about it with patients." She took a breath, everything seemingly running into one sentence while she tried to work it all out. I just sat in awe, never having seen her like this.

"...I do find it oddly soothing, though I haven't really gotten beyond that. Anyway, I figured at this point it can't hurt, so I sit down, turn on the music, and try to put my mind into a state of 'flow,' as Erik calls it. I sat there for a good thirty minutes, not knowing what I was waiting for. I kept telling myself this was nuts and if anyone in my professional world saw me now, they would think I had gone to the other side of the abnormal psychology train...and then I saw it. The whole scene just as Tate had described it. I not only saw it, but I *felt* it..." She took another swig of bourbon and continued again.

I sat stunned as she described my recurring dream to a T. The carpeted forest floor. The bright full moon. The running. The terror. Only, in her version, she was the one ahead of me, and she could see what happened before my version went dark.

"Soph. I know it sounds absolutely insane, but I am at a loss as to what this is," she concluded.

If I hadn't been gripping my whisky glass in sheer panic, it would have surely fallen to the floor. She mistook my silence as not being sure how to respond to her, when in fact I had no idea how to tell her that if she was crazy, then I was too.

She stared at me, beckoning me to reply, to say something, show some sort of reaction. Not thinking, I slowly got up, placed my now sweaty half-empty glass on the coffee table and quietly left the room. Kit watched me with eagle eyes. I heard her sigh and sit back in the chair, unsure of what to do next. I heard the clink of the ice cube hitting the side of the glass as she finished off the bourbon.

I went to my bedroom and into the nightstand where I kept it. A log of all the times I had experienced the dream. The first couple never made it into the journal, but once I realized it was something that happened a lot, I started keeping a record to see if there were any patterns, my latest dream in the spring being the last one of many.

As I kept the record, I started to notice that the dreams were strongest in the spring, March to be exact, and always around a full moon. I would have them throughout the year too, but they were more glimmers of the full story, not like they were in the spring.

I grappled with the decision, but finally resolute, I walked back into the front room. I silently handed the leatherbound journal to Kit, poured another large dram of bourbon for both of us and took my spot on the couch. Kit continued to watch every move, not sure of what I was doing or how I was handling the situation. I took my glass with a shaking hand and motioned for her to open the journal.

It was our unique way of communicating, where we didn't need to say a word. I knew she wouldn't question me further. She took a swig and set her glass down on the side table to open the journal.

March 19, 1999

It happened again. I had the same dream I've been having, only as I get older, I see more and more each time. I am going to try to capture it here so I can start keeping a log of when it happens. I feel like there is some important reason behind it, but who knows. I might be completely deranged.

We were running.

Bare feet running through the forest. It was pitch black and becoming even darker. Only the light of the full moon could be seen through the trees, and only then because the branches were still bare and the moon so bright tonight.

And her. Gaining on us with full force on her ebony thoroughbred, her jet-black hair falling around her shoulders in long tendrils coupled with the velvety, dark-violet cloak flowing behind her, created an aura that she was flying through the dense night air right at us.

Suddenly, I tripped. The root had come out of nowhere on the soft emerald floor of the forest so familiar to us. We knew these woods like the backs of our hands. *Where did that come from?* I thought. But I couldn't focus on that right now.

"Get up!" I heard the voice from inside me yell. It was as if that voice had reached my friend running just ahead of me, who then stopped in her tracks and reeled around.

No! I thought as I tried to yell, but my throat was raw from breathing in the cold night air. I wanted whoever was in front of me to keep running, but instead, she circled back to try and help me up. It was but a moment but allowed our pursuer to get within reach. We huddled together, each trying to shield the other.

And then it ends there, as it always does. I don't know who the girls are, what they are running from or why I am seeing it from the first person, but it's creepy. I tried bringing it up to my dad before and he just laughed it off, saying, "Well, our ancestors were witches and warlocks!" and made a joke out of it. My mom thinks I'm crazy and says it must be part of my female cycle, and I should just drink more water and rest more when it starts. They don't understand that this has been happening for years, ever since I turned ten.

I've looked up "recurring dreams." The search engine spews out the obvious that a recurring dream "can be a sign of underlying issues and may be a way to process trauma or unmet needs" and then goes on to give examples of interpretations. For "being chased or attacked" specifically it says, "this dream may symbolize a fear of evasion and avoidance of confronting unresolved emotions or conflicts."

DUH! Anyone who has ever taken an interest in psychology could see that. What it doesn't tell me is why I have the same one, and why it happens every year around this time. I've decided I can't talk to anyone else about this for fear of being committed, not a good look for someone who wants to go into psychology when they get to college. I will just have to keep this to myself and see if any of my future studies will help me understand this.

It could also be leftover childhood whimsy, though super sketch, and perhaps I will eventually grow out of it.

TTFN!

Kit finished and looked up. I just nodded my head and took another sip. I held it in my mouth, both to warm it before it went down and to get every ounce of flavor out of the thick brown liquid. I blinked at her. Kit looked back down at the diary and read the passage again. Then she turned a few more pages and saw the log of dates.

January 1, 2000 – New Year's

March 19, 2000 – Spring Equinox

March 15, 2001 – Ides of March

December 8, 2001 – ?

March 18, 2002 – near equinox

The list went on until this past March. Kit looked up at me again. We both remained silent for a long time. What could this possibly mean? I thought I was crazy enough having this recurring dream. Now, there was another person who had seen and experienced it too...and an eight-year-old boy? How was it even possible? Apart from trying to tell my parents when I was younger, I hadn't spoken about this to anyone.

Kit slowly closed the book and set it down on the table while simultaneously picking up her glass. It had become wet on the outside from the condensation of the ice melting and the sun shining through the window. She opened her mouth to say something, raising her finger to point at me, and then seemed to change her mind.

"I know," I said, breaking the silence and pouring into our glasses. My words barely cut through the tension and wonderment in the room.

"But how..." she started but decided to leave it at that.

"It started when I was ten, at least that's when I think it started. First, little bits and pieces. They seemed like a fairytale the way they were presented, and I assumed I was pulling from all the fables I had read and movies I had watched. Then, as I got older and they kept coming, I didn't know what to think. But I thought I was alone in my crazy," I said, then continued. "This spring, this last one, I almost said something to you. It had been an especially long day on campus, and I think you called me on my ride home. I didn't answer right away and then when I called back, we were trying to catch up on all the things."

She smiled and nodded, letting me know she remembered the day.

"I thought to myself after we hung up that I should say something to you, but we were...are still so young in our friendship, even though it feels as if I've known you forever. I didn't want to sound completely off my rocker. But the more I thought about it on that drive home, the more I thought with your psych background, maybe you'd have a theory."

Kit sipped. I breathed.

"Then one thing led to another. Maddy was visiting, and I just forgot to ask. I certainly wasn't about to bring it up in front of Maddy. Poor girl would have shot out of this house so fast screaming 'devil' that she would have left a burn mark on my floor!"

We both laughed at that, breaking the heaviness in the room.

"So. What do we do now?" she asked.

I stared at her blankly. "I'm not sure," I responded. Whatever we did though, the answer was not going to be found in a book.

I was glad to hear that Kit had at least started meditating. While I wasn't an overtly spiritual person, I had my own misgivings and thoughts on religion as a whole. I could tell we were going to have to go in a completely different direction than either of us had dared try before.

"This may sound odd," I started.

Kit cut in with "And this doesn't?!"

"But I think we may need to find some guidance of 'alternative means,'" I said with air quotes. She cocked her head to look at me like a dog who had misheard a sound. "I think we may need to find someone who can help us interpret this dream, like a psychic or something," I clarified.

She made a face but ultimately agreed.

We both jumped on our phones to see what we could find and both came to the same conclusion. We needed a Shaman. Kit reached out to one and booked an appointment for the two of us for a week from Friday. I made sure my day was blocked. It wasn't like I was actually going to be successful in writing a business-minded research paper now. We both sat back in silence to sip our bourbon.

That next Friday took forever to come.

Chapter 10 – September 1563 – Lizbeth/Madge

Unfortunately, the week that the traveler had stated to Mr. White had quickly become two, followed by two months. Lizbeth knew if her mother, Jane, had been there, this would not have happened. Her poor brothers continued to be put out by Mr. Acton and his supposed household, not having slept in their own beds since they arrived.

Richard Acton was not a nobleman in any sense of the word. They had thought by the grandeur of his arrival that perhaps he was a viscount or at the very least a baron. The local earl and his family that sometimes came into the village to use their services had never heard of him. So, while he carried himself with import, it was soon determined he was not of nobility.

It seemed he had come by his money in unknown ways, and no one could quite pin down the true story. Whether it was shrewd business deals, or perhaps more likely, he had come upon his ill-gotten gains through games of primero and main – popular card and dice games – no one was certain. Whatever it was, there was a dark energy around Mr. Acton, and not many of the villagers enjoyed his company after the novelty of a "Londoner" wore off.

His dark, beady eyes were constantly shifting around a room, wary of anyone in it, his long dark hair always unwashed and hanging in oily strands. His face could have been handsome once, but as he only partook in ale, mead and the occasional solid food, it had become sallow with dark circles which only punctuated his sharp nose.

Over the course of their stay, Mr. Acton made it known that one of the other reasons for his journey was to find a wife. He no longer wished to find one in the city, and the girl to which he had been betrothed perished on the tenth day of being sick with fever. He had shared the story with anyone who would listen, even if it was said without emotion or remorse.

Mr. Acton had taken a strong liking to Lizbeth. She knew he had since that first walk home when she felt his cold eyes appraising her like a prize cattle. She tried to keep out of his way, but he had somehow befuddled her father, who was only too pleased at the interest.

At first, it caused her to stay away as long as possible from the house she loved so dear. She found ways to spend extra time with Robert or steal away with her friends. After a while, however, her father found tasks that kept her at home in the company of Mr. Acton. She despised those days. The look and manner of this man revolted her, and she could not possibly think what had so captivated her father.

It was now fall. The leaves were showing their true colors and demonstrating to the world how beautiful change could be. Lizbeth feared that if Mr. Acton did not take his leave soon, he might stay through the winter. She could not have that. He was already driving a wedge between her and her beloved Robert.

She had had enough. She decided that night, she needed to see Robert and devise a plan so they could be together. Robert always took a walk in the afternoon in the village.

She would make an excuse to go visit her father and brother at the shop and run into him. No one would be the wiser!

She made haste as noon was quickly approaching. She let what felt like her captors know she had to run a few tools to her father at the shop and she would be back to prepare their supper in time. The men of Mr. Acton's household paid no mind, but the man himself certainly did. He stood at once from the corner which he had been occupying in the kitchen to offer his assistance. "Mistress Lizbeth, allow me to run the errand for you, as you are but a fair maiden and should not have to do such labors."

It took everything in Lizbeth not to roll her eyes.

"I thank you, sir, but it is a task I do all the time for my father. It also allows me to get fresh ingredients with which to prepare your meal," she replied with reserved indignation.

"Mistress, I have told you, please call me Richard," he purred like a large cat on the prowl.

"Thank you, Mr. Acton, but as we are neither friend nor kin, I could not imagine to be so bold," she responded.

He frowned. He had been trying for weeks to get on a more familiar basis with her, but she had not allowed it. For her, it was the last vestige of boundary she had control of before her father seemingly gave her away to him.

With that, she quickly turned to depart. Mr. Acton called after her and she tried to hustle away, but he caught her by the arm. She turned, startled at his touch. "I think you forgot the tools with which you were dispatched,

Mistress," he said and handed her the few things she had gathered to take with her on her mission. She blushed a little at her blunder and took the tools readily.

"Thank you, sir." And she turned and walked swiftly away.

As she made her way to the village center and her father's shop, she saw Madge. She was walking along the streets with a boy of her own. He had recently come into her awareness, though his family was a staple in their village. Simon Oliver was a quiet and simple dairy farmer. Known to be wonderful with animals, but less so with people, Lizbeth was confounded at what Madge saw in him.

Did his stutter not give her cause to run away? How could they carry on a conversation without her going mad waiting for him to stammer out his meaning? Sure, he was comely looking with his fair sandy hair, rich brown eyes and tall lean stature, but those freckles on his face made him look but a boy ten years younger than Madge!

She made a mental note to ask Madge what they were doing later – and why he was not at the farm! She had to find her Robert and deliver the tools to her father. As she got closer to the shopfront, she saw him. He seemed to be walking by in a daze while other villagers stared. She immediately ran up to him and startled him out of his latest "journey."

"Robert!" she cried, and she practically flung her arms around him but caught herself. He backed up in horror, not wanting any additional attention. He walked her over to the side of the building so they could have some privacy.

"Lizbeth, what are you doing here? Are you not supposed to be keeping company with that Mr. Acton?" he questioned.

"Yes, but I stole away so I could see you. I miss our times together and had to break free," she said.

He chuckled and said, "You make it sound as if you are in a prison."

She frowned. "I feel as though I am," she said under her breath. He stared at her and was about to speak when she said, more loudly this time, "I must see you. Meet me in the woods at our usual spot tonight. It is a new moon, so even Diana offers us cover!"

Robert thought about this. "I suppose I can. But will you not get in trouble leaving the house at such a late hour?" he questioned.

"I care not" was Lizbeth's emphatic reply. "I think..." she started to share her concern for her father's plans for her and Mr. Acton when they both saw her brother come out of the shop.

Robert stared at her for a moment, kissed her on the top of her head with those thin but strong lips of his and moved back in with the crowd along the streets. She lingered in that moment for a second before she walked forward to give her father the tools he had forgotten at home.

Her heart ached to simply run after Robert and suggest they go away together. All she wanted was for his towering frame to wrap her in those long arms and hold her close, tell her all would be well, and she would not have to deal with Mr. Acton anymore.

Lost in her daydream with a small smile on her face as she walked into the shop, her heart stopped. There was Mr. Acton. He must have followed her.

"Oh, there you are, Lizbeth! We thought you had gotten lost," her father exclaimed. "Mr. Acton said he had business in town today and stopped by to say hello and escort you back to the house from your errands. I assured him you had yet to arrive, but he insisted."

She blushed. "Yes, sorry…" She had to think quickly. "Only, I saw Madge in the streets and wanted to speak with her since I have been staying at the house so much." It was a lie, but at least it was a reasonable one, and she knew if Madge was questioned, she would cover for her friend.

"Mr. Acton, I still have errands yet to run. No need to wait for me," Lizbeth started, but her father interrupted.

"Nonsense, girl, I'm sure Mr. Acton would be more than happy to accompany you and help you home. Why not run along now? Matthew and I have been working nonstop today, and a big meal will be just the ticket when we get home," Mr. White said.

Richard smiled. "Have no fear, Mr. White, I will be sure to get Mistress home in one piece. It would be my pleasure."

Lizbeth felt like he said it with a sneer but tried to ignore it. At least she would be able to see Robert tonight and devise a plan to get away from Mr. Acton.

Her father seemed far too pleased as they walked out the door. No sooner had they left the warmth and safety of the workshop than Mr. Acton took her arm and led her along the street. "Now, where was it you needed to go to get provisions for the evening?"

She did not like his tone, or his handling of her arm, but she knew she could not make a scene.

"I have devised a different recipe for the evening, so I will not be needing to stop anywhere, sir," she responded as she subtly tried to remove herself from his grasp. He was not giving up.

"Ah, but are you sure, Mistress? You seemed so adamant in coming down here today."

Could he have known? Did he follow her when she saw Robert? If he had, then she had to be extra cautious. However, she sensed, even through his bravado, that he could not be that clever and it was likely something else that caused his suspicious smile.

They made their way back to the house, he holding onto her arm as if she was a horse on a rein, and she moving as quickly as she could so as not to be seen in the company of this man. She was certain there had already been speculation and rumors.

Once they were back in the house, she noticed his men had dispersed and her little brother George was nowhere to be found. The thought of going inside with only Mr. Acton gave her a wave of anxiety unlike any she had ever experienced. She tried to remain calm as she walked to the kitchen to prepare the meal.

Richard had stopped at the doorway to remove his boots and doublet, revealing his starched linen shirts underneath. They seemed to be stained with unsightly sweat and grime, and she wondered when they were last laundered. She really was quite uncomfortable with how casual he had become in their home.

Before she knew it, he was behind her, grabbing her by the waist and spinning her around. She gasped as his face came right in front of hers. She could smell an acrid, bitter scent coming off his breath, and his large sharp nose came in direct contact with her button one. He was seething under his breath, "You know, if you were mine and you pulled a stunt like that today, you would be taking a beating, from one end or the other, until you learned some respect."

She could not believe what she was hearing. If she was his? Beating? And how could he stay so incredibly calm while forging such violent thoughts?

She wheeled around and clambered out of his grasp. "First of all, sir, I am not nor will I ever be yours." This seemed to amuse him. "Secondly, I know not what you speak of with a 'beating on either end, but if you do not clean up your vulgar language in my father's household, you will surely be thrown out on your rump!" she continued, with fire behind her eyes now, surging from a place of which she was unsure. "And lastly...there were no stunts pulled today other than my needing to take tools to my father and running into a dear friend."

He opened his mouth, as if to say something in response when she continued. "Nor do I owe ANY explanation to one so vile as YOU!" She turned on her heel and stormed out of the kitchen to her room at the back of the small house. She needed to put distance between the two of them.

When she got to her room, she took her mother's rocking chair, secured it in front of her door and went to sit on the bed. Her whole body was shaking. What had just happened?! She knew this man to be one of ill repute, but not to this degree.

If she was his? Wait until her father came home. There would be no dinner ready, as she was not going back out there alone with him, and now she had cause to remove this man from their lives forever, she hoped. What had been the look behind his smirk? It seemed to hold knowledge she did not possess.

She must have fallen asleep after her ordeal, because when she woke up, night had already fallen and everyone in the house was asleep. She had missed the opportunity to speak with her father, and now she had no idea if Robert would still be in their agreed-upon location.

She had to get away, more than ever. She quickly changed out of her gown from the day that made far too much noise for sneaking out of the house and draped her cloak over her face. She quietly moved the chair from in front of her door, thanking her mother for her protection in her time of need, and shuffled out the front door past her snoring brothers. She knew explanations would be needed in the morning, but for now her only thought was getting to Robert.

Madge had had a lovely day. Simon was not usually off in the middle of the week but had been able to take a break to wander the streets with her. She thoroughly enjoyed his company, even if others did not. She could not understand why. The tall boy with sandy blonde hair was an incredibly kind soul, even if he could not speak well. It mattered not. He spoke through those liquid brown eyes of his and she could understand every word.

Dairy farming was not the grandest of occupations, but it was a respectable one. Her friends had laughed and teased her about being a milkmaid when they first heard the story of their meeting, but it was all in good fun. They were happy for her, and she was thrilled there was someone who was interested in her. Her, Madge, after all this time.

Of course, he preferred to call her by her given name of Margaret, and she loved it. He was so incredibly shy and formal with her. She appreciated him not wanting to get too familiar too quickly, and he was one of the few that she did not insist call her by her nickname. The sound of her given name coming off his lips was magical, as though only he understood its true meaning.

They had been walking through the village when she saw Lizbeth, making a beeline for her father's shop. It was odd to see her out and about after the past few months. The longer Mr. Acton stayed in town, the less she and Ann had seen of their friend. She had stopped attending their morning ambles altogether and had not been able to work on their creations in the sacred space in weeks.

It seemed as if she was slowly becoming a prisoner in her own house, and Madge could not understand why Mr. White would allow it to be so after years of giving his daughter complete freedom. Madge had not told anyone, but her talent at rune casting had grown, and she had foreseen major changes coming. Until now, she did not know what they would be, though she suspected they stemmed back to the day Mr. Acton arrived.

She made a move to go speak with her friend, but in an instant, she was gone. She thought she had seen Robert walking nearby, so perhaps they had gone to steal a few rare moments together. Good! Poor Robert had been wandering aimlessly for weeks since Lizbeth was not around to fill his days.

She gladly turned her attention back to Simon, his freckles dancing in the sunlight. She absolutely adored him! He was carrying on about the latest challenges with the herd and how some of the farmhands had unexpectedly taken off without a word. It was not incredibly riveting conversation, but it was part of Simon, so she loved it.

Love. She could not believe she had just admitted the word to herself, but perhaps that was what this goofy feeling was. It did not feel soul-stirring, as Ann had described her feelings for James, but she was incredibly fond of Simon and his kind heart. She hoped there was a future to be had here.

They continued through the center toward the fields. Even if Simon was not on the farm for the day, he loved being near the country. She took in the scents and sounds on this early fall afternoon. The way the grains blew in the breeze, the clouds casting shadows across the tops of the fields, and the smell of the fresh air mixed with fertilizer from a field beyond. Yes, she could see herself growing old with this kind, soft-spoken dairy farmer and resigned herself to making it happen.

Lizbeth practically ran all the way to the wood, to Robert and her favorite clearing under the dark new moon, but he was not there. This was exactly what she had been afraid of since waking to realize she had missed nightfall.

At least, she did not think he was here. She sensed someone might be and decided to proceed with caution until she was sure. She called forth a small whistle meant to sound like a bluebird, just as Robert had taught her. Nothing. She tried again. Still nothing but the silent breeze blowing through the trees and rustling the fall leaves.

Just as she decided it was safe to move forward into the field, she saw something flash from behind and envelop her in darkness...

Chapter 11 – August, Present Day – Sophia

Kit and I had wound up draining the bottle of bourbon she brought with her that day. Not because we were talking and mindlessly pouring, but because we sat in silence contemplating everything that had just been shared. We needed it to fortify us as we embarked on something so foreign that the only way to "digest" it was with swallows of brown liquid.

The Friday was finally upon us, and I didn't know what to expect. Kit and I drove separately to the Shaman's location, not realizing that she had only just recently moved from an actual business location to her personal apartment. We parked side by side and looked at each other as we locked our doors.

Kit nervously laughed and I said, "I hope we didn't sign up to be axe-murdered…" We approached the door to her split-level apartment building, #234. I laughed internally at the numbers. I had always loved seeing recurring numbers and wondered if they held meaning.

We rang the doorbell and were greeted by a pleasant smile and warm rush of air. Our Shaman, only known to us as Terease, opened the door wider to allow us in. Directly in front of us was a steep set of stairs. We took off our shoes and climbed up cautiously.

As we got upstairs, we saw a clean white apartment overtaken by boxes. Terease had clearly just moved to these lodgings and was in the midst of setting things up in her new space. We found out she had to relinquish the previous business rental based on some changes in how she wanted to practice, and she left it at that.

I eyed the beautiful new Keurig on the counter with dual-purpose k-cup and espresso, secretly hoping she would offer us a cup. I was out of my element and a sip of coffee would surely put me at ease. As if reading my mind, Terease said, "No coffee today, I'm afraid! I am completely out."

Kit and I looked at each other and back at her and smiled.

She led us to a back room, which was really the front of the condo. As we walked closer, we could smell smoke, and she clarified that she had just smudged the room to cleanse the energy. Noting the look of confusion on our faces, Terease asked, "Are you new to the practice?"

Not knowing how to respond, Kit and I simply nodded our heads. "Oh! That's surprising, your people give off an air that you have been intuitive for a while. No matter."

Kit and I both started looking around in mass confusion, but decided it was best not to ask too many questions. Kit looked at me and mouthed "your people" with a huge question mark on her face before Terease turned her attention back to us.

"Now. What is it you all wanted to accomplish today?" Terease asked as we entered her room.

It was painted with white walls, as most apartments were, but she had done her best to turn it into a sanctuary. Sheer pink curtains hung by the windows and a wooden and glass bookshelf stood on one wall, housing many different crystals, feathers, and other charms and talismans. One could only imagine what they were used for. The other wall had what appeared to be the top of a drum leaning against it, painted with Native American markings. There were a few pictures on the wall of fierce, strong-looking animals. It was easy to tell that Terease came from one of the local tribes and took great pride in it.

Kit spoke up first. "Well, it all began with my son telling me about this dream..." she started.

Terease shook her head and interrupted. "Yes, I remember, but what is it you want to accomplish today?" she asked again.

Kit was lost for words. She was still trying to reconcile this entire experience in her logical brain. I stepped in.

"I think we are just looking for some clarity on the whole thing. How is it that Kit's son had almost the exact same dream that I've been having my whole entire life, only from a different perspective? Why is it that we feel like we've known each other forever and yet we've only been friends for the past few years? Why can't I ever see the ending to the dream and what does it mean?" I couldn't stop the questions flowing now. The years of having to bottle this up and pass it off as nonsense were now exploding out of me like word vomit.

She held her hand up to make me pause.

"Breathe," Terease said. "I understand it is a lot. I am surprised to know you two haven't been practicing your strengths because you positively radiate them from your core, but all in due time." Kit and I once again looked at each other in confusion but thought it best to let it go. "Your people have been showing up all morning and they are anxious to provide the answers you seek. Let's begin."

She set us down in the two chairs she had placed in the middle of the room, side by side. We did as we were told after placing our bags down in the corner of the room by the door. She then lit what she referred to as her smudging stick and passed smoke over us with a large brown and white feather and walked around us in a clockwise circle until we had been completely enveloped in a thick plume.

I was beginning to enjoy the smell and felt like it was helping to calm me down. *I might need to find my own smudging stick*, I mused to myself.

"Are you open to holding some crystals? I like to use them to help filter energy and intention," she said, interrupting my thoughts.

Kit and I, somewhat mesmerized, just silently nodded our heads.

In my hand, she placed an amethyst, rose quartz and lapis lazuli. While I may not have been "practicing," as she called it, I had always had a fascination with rocks and minerals growing up and remembered seeing these in the blue suitcase collection I used to study when I was a child.

In Kit's hands she placed a green aventurine, rose quartz and some purple bespeckled thing I had never seen. It was pretty, whatever it was. At our feet, she placed long milky-white wands. They looked like large shards, and I seemed to recall them being named sele-something, but I couldn't place it.

"Do you have a specific frequency of music you would like to hear?" Terease asked. The scientist in Kit laughed and I cocked my head, wondering what she meant. "I take that as a no," she said and went to turn on her sound system.

The room filled with low notes that sounded vaguely similar to a didgeridoo, then female voices singing vowels in different pitches. It was beautiful and hypnotic, and unlike anything I had heard before. Kit must have been transfixed too because her laughing stopped.

"Now, I will work with spirit as I guide you along in your visions. This is a silent exercise. Spirit will help me show you what it is you seek. All you must do is keep your eyes closed, listen to the music and let the visions unfold. It is like meditating. Let thoughts come and go in flow. There is no right or wrong way to meditate, and you certainly are not keeping your mind quiet!"

We quietly agreed and closed our eyes. I whispered, "See you on the flip," and our session began.

While I was not a regular practitioner of meditation, I had done enough sessions to know that it took a while for my mind to focus. I knew the biggest key was letting thoughts come in and helping them flow out, so nothing remained too long in your brain and disrupted the experience. If you didn't, before too long you would be ruminating on the grocery list for twenty minutes instead of allowing a different state of consciousness. This one was different.

As I listened to the music and heard the low vibrations of instruments mixed with the ever-changing harmonies of the female voices, I could feel something breaking loose in my chest. The sounds took me to a completely different place and the rest of the room fell away.

I was mildly aware of Terease moving around Kit and me in a circle, using different implements from around the room. Every once in a while, she would tap the top of my head, or I would feel the brush of her hand along my shoulder, as if she was swiping away a spider.

It was electric. I could feel every hair on my arm stand up. I felt like I was in one of those vampire movies when a new vampire awakens and experiences all the sensations they had been missing out on all those years. It was almost as if the electrons in the air were on fire, and I could sense each one.

As I experienced the physical, so too did I experience the mental, or perhaps more accurate, spiritual. At first, it was just flashes of color. Dark purple. Emerald green. Chocolate brown. Bright white. Then the colors started converging into actual images and I was in my dream.

Running on a dark path through the woods. The path was clearly known to me, otherwise I wouldn't have been able to run with such speed. I looked above me as I ran and saw the bright white full moon. I also saw something flutter overhead – that was new. The unexpected disturbance made me trip and I fell to the ground. I looked behind me in terror as I realized my pursuer would gain on me. I could hear the hoofs now, faster and faster they came...

At that moment, I felt Terease place the crystals I held into my left hand and shift my right hand away from my body to hold onto something. I realized she had Kit's hand in mine. Neither of us moved and suddenly an electric current ran through our palms and up my arm into my body. As it did so, I looked up in my vision and saw ahead of me another person, also running.

When I fell, they must have heard the thump and turned back. As they approached, I saw it was a woman, with strawberry blonde hair, average build and slate-gray eyes with flecks of brown that twinkled in the moonlight. I had never seen this woman before, and I gasped. There was something oddly familiar about her, but I couldn't place it.

I saw her come back toward me and heard my voice cry out to her to keep running. She didn't listen and was back to me in a few paces. She placed a hand around my arm and tried helping me up.

We hadn't been quick enough. We both heard the pounding of the horse hooves coming and turned to see another woman. She had raven hair with matching eyes. There was a flash in them that didn't seem natural. The cloak she was wearing only added to the sinister aura as she rode atop a massive black stallion. It was something I would have expected out of Sleepy Hollow.

We tried to run, but it was too late. As we realized that we weren't going to escape her, we turned to each other and came together in a strong embrace of sisterly love and hid our faces in each other's hair. I, or my first-person perspective, tried to move to shield this woman as much as I could from what was about to come, and she tried to do the same.

Then it happened. I felt the searing pain of something going through me like a hot blade through butter. It went through me to the other woman, and we collapsed on the mossy floor of the forest. The blood started to pool from both of us and just as my eyes were beginning to close, the one who shot us came into view from above, with her lips curling into a half smile at what had just occurred.

The vision was gone. My mind was blank. The music was softly coming to a close and Terease had stopped moving around the room. She was smudging again, and I was starting to fully appreciate the smell. My body felt like it was still hovering, as if I was having an out-of-body experience. Mine and Kit's hands were still clasped and there were still fissions of electricity running through them, or mine at least.

I heard Terease say in an incredibly soft voice, "I'm going to count to ten. I want you to slowly walk up a set of stairs. When I get to ten, you can open your eyes, but do so very slowly," she cautioned. I nodded to show my understanding.

"One...two...three...four...five...six...seven...eight...nine...ten."

I opened my eyes. I slowly glanced around the room, as if I was seeing it for the first time and needed to get my bearings. I looked to Kit, who was seemingly doing the same. We were still holding hands and clearly neither of us wanted to let go. Becoming self-conscious, we each squeezed each other's hand and then let them drop. Kit was crying. I was silent.

What. Was. That.

Terease spoke, again with a soft voice. "How are you?" We both remained speechless. "That was a lot. I don't normally do a past life clearing with two people because you never know where it will go or if the lives are truly linked, but your souls..."

Kit found her voice first. "Past life clearing?" she inquired, clearing her throat and wiping her eyes.

"Yes. I had a feeling that's what this was all about. Then when your people started arriving in droves this morning, I knew it was going to be an interesting day!" she responded.

My turn. "I'm sorry, I'm afraid I don't know what you mean."

"Oh! Forgive me. I keep forgetting. You two really do have practiced old souls emanating from you. Anyway, your dream, Sophia, and your son's dream, Kit, are from a past life. As I assume you experienced just now, it didn't end well."

How the hell could she have known that?!

Terease saw the surprise in my eyes and carried on. "Your souls are inextricably linked because of the shared traumatic experience. It's why I had you hold hands, something I also don't normally do, but your people wanted it to happen to help things along. Now I can't tell you all the details of the whys and hows and whats, but whatever led up to your demise in that life was horrific. Since you died trying to protect one another, it stayed with you and clearly left a mark."

Neither Kit nor I moved. Had she seen the same thing I did? What was going on?

Kit found her voice again. "OK, putting aside the 'past life' concept for a moment, why is it that my son saw this and not me?"

Terease responded almost as if it were a reflex. "Well, because he's a fractal of that soul!"

Kit and I blanched at the same time. "What?" was all she could manage.

Terease saw we were out of our depths again. "This would be so much easier if you had already been practicing. OK, fractals are pieces of one soul that can be found in others. Literally a soul fractured into many pieces that can live many different lives, resulting in an unseen connection and synchronicities. Have you ever felt like you understood someone else's point of view without ever trying? Or someone on the other side of the world or in a different generation leads an eerily similar life to yours? Oftentimes, though not always, mind you, they are fractals."

"But why…?" Kit started to question, but Terease cut her off.

"I don't know the whys. What I do know is that you both have some soul searching to do, and on a deeper level than either of you have ever tried before. There is a lot more to learn here, and it will only be mastered if both of you sit with it and extend your minds."

We looked at each other and then back at her. I was still trying to make sure my mind was tethered to my body. I couldn't begin to comprehend everything she was saying.

"Your session is done for today," Terease started. "It was a doozy! You opened your own Pandora's box with this one and now you have a lot of work to do. That said, because of all your ancestors and guides showed up today, I was able to clear away this past life for you so that your soul still clinging to it could be healed. You may need to find some answers, but it shouldn't besmudge you to the depths it did before."

Again, we shook our heads as we took all of this new language in. "You take your time getting up and drink a ton of water today. It will take a beat for everything to settle back in, but it will," she finished and walked out the door, giving us the room to collect ourselves. Kit was still sniffling and calming herself while I just continued to stare in front of me.

We stood up in silence, still holding the crystals. Not knowing what to do with them, we each set them on the chairs we had been sitting on, grabbed our purses and went out into the hallway. It was odd that I found it difficult to walk straight, but then again, if I had just time traveled or some such craziness, it would only make sense. Kit asked if she could use the restroom before we left, leaving me standing with Terease in her kitchen.

Clearly reading the emotion on my face, she said, "You can ask."

I looked at her and blinked, wide-eyed. "How..." I started but quickly changed tack. "What is it we were supposed to have 'studied' before having come to you that would help interpret..." I waved my hands around in all directions. "All of this?"

She laughed. "You will find your path. Some call it spiritualism. Others call it paganism. Others don't know what to call it."

"What do you call it?" I asked.

"I don't call it anything, because it means something different to everyone. Ultimately, your practice is a collection of your own beliefs, culminating in whatever your soul's gifts are. You're not there yet, and there are different ways to discover these things, but now that the two of you have found each other, you will be unstoppable." She winked.

Kit came up from behind me and asked if I was ready to go. I nodded and we said our farewells. Once we were out by the cars, she asked if we should grab some coffee or food, to which I said yes. We ran across the street to the closest diner we could find.

I wasn't hungry but knew I needed more time in her presence to try and understand what just happened and learn what she had experienced. We grabbed the first booth we could find, hidden in the corner away from the late morning regulars. We didn't need anyone overhearing the conversation that was about to ensue.

"So," I said, after the first thick white porcelain cup of coffee was placed in front of me.

"So..." Kit responded, even quieter and more reserved than normal.

"You go first," I offered.

"OK," she said, then looked down at the white paper tablecloth to gather her thoughts. "It was odd. At first, I was just taken with the music. I hadn't heard anything like that before and it was hauntingly beautiful…" I was nodding my head in agreement. "Then, it was like in *The Mummy Returns* when the kid says that he's blasted to different monuments in the blink of an eye in the visions the bracelet gives him. That's what it felt like. I was inside of the exact dream that Tate had shared with me that started this whole thing."

She took a breath and a large gulp of the steaming-hot tea she had requested rather than the diner coffee. "Only this time, I could feel the blood coursing through my veins, I could sense the woods we were in, I could smell the mossy mustiness of the ground…I was experiencing it all in first person."

I kept nodding in encouragement so she would know she wasn't alone, but also because I didn't know what else to do.

"Then I heard a branch snap and a thud. I looked behind me to see a girl on the ground. Well, young woman. She was tall from what I could tell, even if she was splayed out, and had brown curly hair with deep-hazel eyes. She looked at me with such fear and I could tell she was willing me to keep running, but I felt this compulsion to go back and help her. Like I couldn't leave her."

I breathed a sigh of relief. If we had to be experiencing this together, at least she wasn't the one doing the chasing!

"I know, me too," she responded, as if I had spoken my thought out loud. We both took swigs of our warm drinks. It wasn't the fortifying whisky from ten days ago, but it was something.

"Did you..." I started.

"Yeah. What the heck was that?" We were both referring to the electric pulse that went through our hands.

"I don't know," I said, "but it was at that point in my dream that you, or who I am assuming is you, snapped back to help me," I finished.

"It does seem like we are experiencing the same moment from two different points of view."

It became clear we had a lot of synthesizing to do. Since we were both still absorbing, we decided eating something and changing the subject might be the best course of action. We had time to figure these things out, and as Terease had indicated, this was only the beginning.

Chapter 12 – September 1563 – Ann

It had been a couple months since I had spent time with Lizbeth. After hearing Madge tell me she saw her yesterday, albeit from afar, I was a bit jealous and annoyed. So, she could run tools to her father and steal away in alleys with Robert, but she did not have time for her friends? Her sisterhood?

I resolved to go visit her at her house today so I could get some answers. I was surprised to hear she had even seen Robert, since when I ran into him last week, he said it had been at least a fortnight, if not more, since he saw her. I could tell he was distraught and looking for answers as well. He may be a quiet man, and Lizbeth may have come on strong, but he had taken to her and gotten used to having her around.

As I was leaving the empty house – my siblings were all out for the day, either tending the fields with my father or running errands with my mother – I grabbed my hat and turned left toward the Whites, but a shiver ran down my spine and I had an odd feeling that I should turn right and head to the woods. The voice seemed to concur, so I set my sights on the path ahead.

As I approached the entrance, I saw a figure exiting the same path. They had their cloak pulled tight around them. I could not make out who it was until they were right in front of me, and I realized it was the one person I was seeking.

"Lizbeth!" I exclaimed. She jumped nearly out of her skin. I had plainly startled her, as she had been lost in thought and trying to hide her eyes, clouded and unseeing. "Where on earth have you been? Fine morning to be wandering about the wood. Something we used to do if I am not mistaken..." I trailed off as I noticed her hair falling in her face and her tear-stained cheeks. "Lizbeth, whatever is the matter?!" I stammered.

She hesitated, and when it was clear she was frozen to the spot, I approached her to envelop her in a hug. She winced and darted back. It was an odd response, as if she was afraid of physical touch. "Lizbeth..." I started to say when we heard footsteps coming our way and both turned our heads.

Madge appeared, as if called to the wood the same way I had been.

"Ann? Lizbeth? Whatever are you doing here? I had this odd notion that I should come this way this morn. I was practicing with my runes and saw there was an accidental meeting in the future, but who knew it would be so quick! Whatever are the chan—" She dropped off as she took in the sight of Lizbeth wrapped tightly in a cloak, me halfway to her, and a staleness hanging in the air.

"I think we better reconvene by the stones," I suggested, knowing we would be safe there from whatever had drawn us here. Lizbeth seemed as if she was going to protest but instead quietly turned and led the way.

Madge nudged me in my side and gave me a quizzical look. I responded with my own uncertainty, and we walked in silence behind Lizbeth to our tree stumps and rock center. I noticed that it looked like there was something smudged on the back of Lizbeth's cloak, and there was certainly grass stuck to it.

I pointed at it for Madge to see and she broke out into a large smile. We both looked at each other with girlish understanding. Lizbeth must have finally wooed Robert into the circular field last night, though why she was acting so forlorn was beyond us. She would have a tale to tell soon!

We each took a seat on our individual tree stumps. Something about being in our space and in front of our stone "altar" set Lizbeth at ease, but only for a moment. Before she could get a word out, she popped up from her stump and started pacing. Clearly whatever troubled her was going to take a moment to divulge.

I saw Madge's wheels turning and she had a smirk on her face that told me whatever she was about to say would be inappropriate to the tenor of the times and swiftly caught her eye and shook my head. She had clearly not yet seen Lizbeth's full face that showed whatever it was, it was not exciting.

"Liz..." I started but then hushed because Lizbeth started speaking as if I had not said a word.

"I know not what to do," she whispered, almost to herself. Madge and I exchanged glances. "I cannot go home. If my father finds out, he will never let me stay under the same roof. And yet, I definitely will not go while *he* is there..."

The wild contempt in her eyes was indication enough of whom she spoke, so I dared not clarify. I saw her body start to shudder uncontrollably. I got up to put my arm around her and bring her to a seated position, hoping that might take some of her stress away, but my attempt to touch her caused her to withdraw.

"I only mean to comfort you, Lizbeth! You are shaking and need to sit down. Allow me to help you," I said, trying to keep my voice calm so as not to startle her any more.

"DO NOT TOUCH ME!" she cried and then burst into tears, the likes of which neither of us had ever witnessed, and dropped to the forest floor.

Some dark sense in the recesses of my brain started to creep forward. Madge must have been coming to the same realization too as we each put the puzzle pieces together.

"Liz. Darling girl, did he hurt you?" I asked as I crouched down next to her on the leaf-strewn ground. It was a small gesture, but not one easily missed, as she shook her head.

"What happened?" Madge asked, also coming over and crouching down beside her distraught friend.

I was afraid that was going to send her over the edge again, but it somehow mollified Lizbeth into a sort of precarious calm where she could speak. "He must have followed me," she forced out. "He must have followed me and heard me talking to Robert by my father's shop."

"Oh yes, I thought I saw you there..." Madge started in a jubilant tone, to which I quickly hushed her, and she stopped.

"He who?" I pushed further. Silence. "Lizbeth, if it was Mr. Acton who did this to you, you must tell your father at once. Hitting a young woman..."

Lizbeth laughed at this. It was not her usual lilt that one found so infectious, but something cold, dark and unnatural, coming from a different part of her now torn soul. It was at that moment that I realized that whatever had happened had changed my dear sweet Lizbeth forever. She looked up at me then and I noticed what appeared to be flames coming from her dark eyes.

"Hit me! I only wish that was the case. I know not what it actually was that he did. One moment I was looking for my Robert to try and plan how I could get away from my house and the situation as it was so obviously unfolding, and the next...a darkness overtook me in the field." Her story was coming fast and furious now.

"I fell to the ground and felt someone on top of me. It was so dark out I could not see anything, but I could smell him. It was the same acrid, sour smell I had come into contact with earlier in the day when he cornered me in my father's house," she continued. I was about to question this new information but set it aside for later.

"He was pinning me down on the ground and making such horrible grunting sounds. He tried forcing his lips onto mine and all I could do was feel his rough skin scraping my chin. I cried out and tried to move, but it just forced him down on me harder. I tried biting his lip to see if it would make him stop, but it only made him angrier and almost happy to have me struggle against him. That is when I felt him starting to lift my skirts and heard him unbuckling his large leather belt, and I blacked out. As sure as if he had struck me across my face, I blacked out. When I woke just a while ago, my skirts were torn, my cloak a mess, and I...I...had blood on my undergarments," she said sheepishly, barely audible.

Madge and I were silent. Our mouths were agape.

"I remember crying out to Sophia to help just before I blacked out. This made him laugh. A deep, guttural, soulless laugh that sounded like the devil himself rose up from hell. But no one came. I was forsaken by her."

"Oh no, love…" I tried to assure her, but she held her hand up.

"Please. Do not try," she said.

"Lizbeth, he cannot get away with this. We have to go tell your father. There is no way he will let Acton go without repercussions!" Madge encouraged. I nodded my head in agreement, trying to get her to move, to breathe, to do anything that would bring her back to some sense of normalcy.

"No. He will not. He intends to have me marry him. I know it," she whispered.

"Are you sure?!" I gasped while Madge covered her mouth in shock.

"He has not shared as much, but I can tell how he carries himself around Mr. Acton. He is always trying to push the two of us together. And I have foreseen it."

At this, we both gaped in awe. We had each been practicing our own gifts when we could, but we had not talked about them since Mr. Acton came to town. Madge with her runes, me with my intuition, and Lizbeth with her herbal knowledge, using them in different ways to get answers from nature.

"Do not look so surprised, my doves," she disingenuously cooed. There was something haunting in her voice, that darkness I was starting to recognize as a different side of her coming to the surface. "With so much time on my hands at home, practicing in my room or sneaking to our sacred space has been my only joy. Have you not noticed that I have missed all of our usual jaunts and gatherings? I have been locked away in the house, having to spend as much time with *that man* as my father wishes. Practicing with whatever herbs and flowers I can find in whatever mediums are available has been the only thing to bring me peace, thus my abilities have grown."

"Of course we noticed you were gone!" I yelled, not meaning to have spoken with such fervor. "For months now we have not known what happened to you. We would get glimmers of you skulking around, but when you would ignore us and turn away, we knew not what to think. For it to now be headed in this direction..." I let my words hang in the air, not wanting to bring them to fruition. Lizbeth smarted at my tone but understood.

"After this, I know not what Mr. Acton will do or what he is capable of. I fear he will further manipulate my father into a marriage contract, and I will lose everything. My sisterhood, my Robert, myself." She looked down at her hands then, wringing them out as she tried to keep herself together. Something in the way she had ended on "herself" sent the same cold shiver up and down my spine I had only just experienced that morning, the one that had brought me to our place.

As if it heard the call and understood the impact, I looked up to see none other than the large dark owl peering down at us. We must have been interrupting its sleep since it was mid-morning by now, but how and when had it started to make its home above our altar? I realized that I needed to consult with my intuition when I got home to see if I could glean any additional information, something I should have done the last time I saw the same harbinger. I did not know what the knowledge would do for us, but perhaps my internal voice would know.

"We will figure this out. We have to. Perhaps you can come stay with me and my family for a few days while we make the case to your father," Madge started.

Just then, we heard footsteps. They were heavy, brooding and unlike any we were used to. We all crept to the other side of our stones to hide ourselves away from whoever approached. We held our breath as the footsteps came ever closer. It seemed as though they breeched our circle and then stopped. None of us wanted to peek for fear of being caught. They stayed there for a long time, surveying the scene in front of them.

To an untrained eye, all they would see was a stack of stones in the middle of a few moss-covered tree stumps. However, to anyone looking for more, they may notice the bits of singed twine or flower stems strewn over the top stone, along with charcoal markings on the perimeter and sides of the structure. They also may realize that the stumps were arranged in perfect symmetry as the points of a triquetra, representing the three phases of female, as well as the Holy Trinity, and family, with each positioned in the east, west and south as guardians, something we had picked up from the old tales for protection.

After what felt like ages, the footsteps retreated, but none of us took comfort in that. The air was left with a heaviness so uncommon in this sacred space.

When we felt we were in the clear, we all stood and started to make our way out of the woods and toward home. We did not know what we were going to do next, but we had to do it together.

Chapter 13 — August, Present Day — Maddy/Sophia

Maddy was loving life. This new job couldn't have come at a better time, or a better place, as it turned out. Not only could she sense she had overstayed her welcome with Sophia, and to be honest, she was over the accommodations too, but she was tired of the same dark dream of chasing people on horseback. As soon as she made the decision to leave her hometown, it stopped, as it usually did.

Now, she was spending her time helping the latest British designer Mary Carmichael bring her collection to life while living in the English countryside. So far, the adventure had been everything she hoped. She was able to reconnect with her friends from Italy, Estelle and Rosemary. Both had been pivotal in her landing this latest role and she couldn't be more grateful. Sadly, neither could stay for long and were already off to the next networking call, but she had enjoyed seeing them at least for the first week or so.

Maddy's room was on the top floor of the old English manor Mary had rented out for the remainder of the year, not a family estate, as she had thought, but elegant and wonderful nonetheless. Once having belonged to English gentry, it had been kept up by the local historical society. With the latest trend in movies being made in buildings like these, they were only too flattered when *the* Mary

Carmichael had inquired about using the space as her latest headquarters.

It was no Downton Abbey but resplendent in its quiet glamour. The property itself encompassed a small plot of land, in comparison to most, with only fifty-six acres. The outside walls were made of light brick, and most had years' worth of dark-green ivy growing up the side. Whatever modesty it shared on the outside was only to beckon you into its beautifully kept rooms on the inside.

Her favorite, apart from the room she claimed as her own, was the main sitting room, with its vast stone fireplace and original exposed brick. The whitewashed walls and wooden parquet floors transported its visitors to a long-forgotten period. At times, she could almost see men, women and children living within these walls, walking around in their skirts, corsets, doublets and boots. It had to have been the reason Mary chose this place, aside from being incredibly English herself, as inspiration for her new line of clothing, which harkened back to the clear distinction between masculine and feminine, natural fibers and minuscule details.

Mary Carmichael was attempting to bring back something lost in fashion from the earlier centuries. There was a romance with which people dressed back then, and by recapturing the essence and influence of staying in one such manor as those would have lived had only helped to fuel her creativity. Maddy was overjoyed. There had always been something that had drawn her to the clothing, and she often longed to dress in multiple layers and support herself with corsets, voluminous skirts, feminine fabrics, etc. – not that she would have admitted that to anyone out loud.

This morning, she was sitting for breakfast in the main dining area, another room with an open fireplace and exposed stone. However, above this one was an ornately carved piece of chestnut wood that showcased the crest of the original owners. The walls were also lined with the same chestnut in the box-like wainscoting popular of the time. The most unique feature of the room was the curved ceiling, with Celtic knots and sconces sculpted into the plaster. The modern area rug was a bit of an eyesore if she was honest, but she understood the need for it to help protect the deep mahogany floors.

Mary came in off her latest midnight brainstorming binge. Clearly on a tear for fresh coffee, Maddy quietly got up from the table and went over to the maple sideboard where the silver coffee service was laid out.

While there was no technical "staff" assigned to the property, the historical society had provided a chef and porter to make sure they were well taken care of. The porter, Bill Graham, had just brought in a freshly brewed pot and Maddy made sure Mary got the first piping-hot cup.

Maddy liked Bill; they understood each other, unlike the others staying in the house. Each had a specific purpose to help people and accommodate their requests. They had become thick as thieves with the ability to commiserate on what a life of "service" was like, though Bill's tales were far more interesting and salacious than Maddy had expected from the English.

Mary Carmichael was a typical English rose, brimming with female energy and gentile in nature. While this was not her family estate, her family did come from the upper crust of society, so she was used to a certain level of comfort. Of average height for a female, she had porcelain-white skin that came into harsh contrast with her jet-black hair, kept in a short bob with a severe fringe across her forehead. Her look was simple with black mascara and red lips, so as to make sure her face never took too much attention off what she was wearing, though in all honesty, you could most often find her wearing black, like a lot of artists.

"Up all night, I see?" Maddy queried.

"Brilliance never sleeps!" Mary exclaimed without a hint of ego and took in a deep breath of the pungent aroma of black coffee. She heaved a great sigh of relief and drank the first blissful sip.

Maddy walked back to the sideboard and gathered some fresh fruit and a croissant onto the small white china plate with gold-painted rim and brought it back to the table for herself. She knew Mary wouldn't be ready for anything solid until at least the second cup of caffeine coursed through her veins.

"How are the secondary set of sketches going? Do you have any other errands you need running?" asked Maddy as she tore off a piece of croissant, dipped it in some Greek honey that had been procured and shoved it in her mouth. She hadn't always been a honey fan, but once she had her first taste in Greece five years ago, she couldn't get enough of the stuff. Being the assistant to a major designer had its perks. Bill gave her a sideways glance as he exited the room to tend to the chef's plans for lunch later that day.

Mary seemed lost in thought and hadn't heard her, so Maddy pushed again. "Oh, right. Sketches are coming along nicely, though there is a detail on the hem of one of the skirts I can't get right. I'm wondering if there needs to be a cloak overlay instead of the detail on the skirt itself. I'm trying to create some depth and dimension that is getting lost in the shuffle if I leave it to just the one layer…"

"Right, so do you need me to go into town and grab anything for you as inspo?" Maddy asked.

"No, not quite yet," Mary replied, suddenly pushing back her chair and bolting for the stairs. She must have had divine inspiration hit with the way she took the old creaking stairs two at a time up to her "drafting room," as she referred to it.

From the look of it, it was the old master's study. Smaller than the library on the first floor, and adjacent to a bedroom on the second, it shared the same chestnut walls as the dining room, only floor to ceiling. The fireplace in this room – this manor was not lacking in them – was a combination of carved stone and wood. The leaded windows had the original wooden shutters and a bench that sat over the radiator, which must have been added once the technology was available.

While she was sure a grand desk would have once stood in the middle of the room, now it was filled to the brim with tables and easels holding sketches, mood boards and Pantone color squares, strewn about in no particular order. Mary had declared the room hers after her first sight of the jacquard drapes, knowing they would be the perfect inspiration for her sketches. She was paying homage to the house itself in a way.

Well, since Mary clearly wasn't going to need her at the moment – sometimes these brainstorms of hers would last well into the afternoon – she thought she should finally explore the grounds. She had been there for a month and a half already, but with the whirlwind of getting the house set up and running to town to get bits and bobs from the antique shops and historical society for Mary to adorn her drafting room walls with, she hadn't much time. She picked up her plaid coat from the butler's entry hall in the back of the house by the kitchen, grabbed a large shawl, threw on her black lace-up boots and walked out into the sunshine.

The front of the house was deceiving. It was nestled among trees and bushes and looked rather tiny. But when you went outside, there were several outbuildings along the east of the main house, which was where many of the staff were setting up the "manufacturing" for when they needed to start spinning out samples, organize all the materials and, thankfully, keep all the dress forms to be fitted.

Mary had always found the headless forms to be rather creepy, especially after having experienced a dark room behind the stage at Paris Fashion Week a few years ago. They looked like an army that had all lost their heads at the same time. Maddy had a tendency to agree with her employer and was just as grateful the forms would be kept in an outbuilding.

The "backyard," if you could even refer to it as such, was a vast expanse of green leading into a few small woods.

With rolling hills and countryside as far as the eye could see, Maddy wasn't sure if she was supposed to be running through it à la the *Sound of Music* mountaintops, rolling down the hill like a five-year-old, or taking high tea in the gardens with a parasol and hat.

It was beautiful, and peaceful, and everything she didn't know she needed right now. She took a deep breath, filled her lungs with fresh country air and decided to take a walk to the first set of "woods" she saw. She always loved exploring the local wildlife while she was on one of these adventures, and who knew? She might run into some flowers or herbs that would look nice in the sitting room, or even her room, and bring some natural fragrance into the house.

As she walked, she turned her face up to the sun and let it warm her from head to toe. She could almost imagine walking along a long-forgotten property, petticoats and skirts swishing, bodice cramping her middle from being tied a little too tight and hearing the soft footfalls of feminine boots crunching on the ground beneath her.

She was disturbed from her reverie as she heard another set of footsteps approaching, only these were not part of her daydream. They were much louder, heavier footsteps coming up from behind her, which made her gasp and whirl around – to find nothing there. Instead, in her trance, she had collided with an unsuspecting person now directly behind her and knocked them over. In her daze, she hadn't seen the man with the tripod set up at the foot of the hill, and he had been so concentrated on his landscape he had not heard her approach.

Thankfully, they had not fallen into the camera and knocked the equipment over, but both were startled to say the least. The man managed to get to his feet first and offered a hand down to Maddy, as she seemed to be a bit tangled. She gratefully took it and allowed him to help her up. She started to ask "Who the hell…" but stopped short when she finally looked into the face of the stranger. Here was a classic example of a "TDH" – tall, dark, and handsome.

He chuckled and said, "So you're the American, are you? I guess by your stunned silence you've figured out I'm Mary's younger and significantly better-looking brother," he mused.

She hadn't thought about that. Her mind was still going over the details of his face: stubbled cheeks, amazing dimples, eyes that transformed to different colors in the sunlight and dark-brown hair that seemed to shimmer from the inside out. She found herself absentmindedly nodding her head.

"Oy, did you hit your head too?" he asked, facial expression shifting from playful to concerned. Maddy realized how daft she must look and quickly shook her head to release whatever was keeping her transfixed.

"No, I'm good, thanks," she muttered. He didn't look convinced. "So, Mary has a brother, huh?" she tried, hoping he'd take the bait.

"What, she never mentioned me?! I'm hurt," he said playfully in a cockney accent. Man, this guy was all over the board. Now that she looked at him without the halo shining around him, she could see the family resemblance.

"No, she has, I just didn't think you were here!" she said, not wanting him to get too upset or tell tales to her employer.

"Just arrived on the train this morning. When I got to the property, I couldn't help but run out back to capture this view. This vantage point should be spectacular at sunrise! I wanted to be sure I set myself up for tomorrow morning to capture it," he sputtered as his passion shone through. Clearly, their family was into the arts, with his sister being the well-known designer and he a world-famous photographer.

"I hope I didn't mess up your equipment too much with my bump and tumble," Maddy said.

"No, all good here. It's kind of why I went down with you. Thought it might be safer if I fell over and away from the equipment to change your trajectory. There was no chivalry in it at all, just a selfish attempt to keep my new baby out of harm's way!" he exclaimed with a smirk.

The conversation went quiet. He clearly wanted to get back to his camera settings, and she was ready to remove herself from this embarrassing situation. "Well, I'm off for my walk then. You enjoy getting your 'new baby' comfortable in her crib," she said.

He smiled at her. Oh, that smile was trouble. Not only was he the younger version of Mary, but she could see he was the flirtatious and wild second child of the family, and that was a deadly combination for her. His eyes suggested he could read her thoughts, and she started to blush.

"I'm actually all done for now. Nothing I can do until tomorrow morning when I get up at the...what do you yanks say, 'the ass crack'?" He winked. She was transfixed again and simply nodded her head. "I was just going to pack up and head back to the house for a spot of breakfast, if there was anything left by Mary's lot. But, if you'd like, I could accompany you on your walk. I assume you have the morning free since Mary hasn't dispatched you on some mission," he mused.

She started to simply nod her head again but caught herself. What was this guy doing to her?! "Oh, I wouldn't want to trouble you. I'm just out for a morning stroll to explore the grounds and look for further inspiration for your sister. She has a whole 'natural vibe' going with the cloth she's trying to emulate for the designs, and with all these gorgeous woods around here, I hoped I could bring something back for her to use," she blathered. Now she was rambling. What the actual hell?

He smirked, again as if reading her mind. "I would feel awful if you did in fact have a concussion after that tumble and I left you out here to fend for yourself. Tell you what, why don't I pack up here, leave my bags and we can wander over there together? I can pick them up on our way back."

She rolled her eyes at his mock concern and waved her arm. "Oh alright, come on then, Sir Lancelot, and walk with me thus," she joked.

"A sense of humor too! I like that. You're feisty. We're going to get along just fine," he said and picked up his stride as she started to walk away but quickly realized he needed to pack up.

She watched him put away the equipment and admired how well he fit into his dark jeans and black leather coat. He seemed to be aware that he had an audience and was relishing the attention. After he had put everything away, he sauntered over to Maddy and offered his arm.

"I figure it is safer for the both of us if I steady your steps as we go into the woods," he said with a grin.

Maddy saw this as a challenge, and not one to back down, she graciously hooked her arm through his and they walked forward.

The day really was breathtaking. The greens weren't quite as brilliant as those in Ireland, but they were close. As they walked into the woods, Maddy took a deep breath. She always loved the smell of the moss-covered trees and sounds of the forest. That seemed to make him smile, though he kept his thoughts to himself. Wanting to break the awkward silence, Maddy thought she'd start small.

"Sooo, may I know the name of the man whose arm I am holding?" She was trying to sound as nonchalant as possible, even though her mind was already going to places she shouldn't, feeling the muscles of his forearm flex under her hand. She would wager he had those strong, sinuous forearms that only people who worked with their hands had, a divine quality she was always drawn to. *He is trouble*, she thought to herself again.

"You mean to tell me that my sister has not told you my name, seeing as you've talked about me so much?" He laughed.

Maddy shook her head. "No, I'm sure she has mentioned you, but as you were not here and none of my concern at the time, I filtered it out as unnecessary information."

He grabbed his chest in mock pain. "I'm hurt to the core!" he exclaimed.

Maddy slapped him on the chest with her free hand. "As if you know my name, the lowly assistant to the great Mary Carmichael!" she said reproachfully.

"Maddy," he responded. Well, now she felt like a proper ass. "HA!" he said with triumph, as if again reading her thoughts.

"Fine. Well played, but can you still remind me of yours so I know what to call you other than TDH." Rats, she hadn't meant for that to slip out. Why on earth had she said that?! He stopped walking and turned, letting go of her arm slightly.

"TDH?" he queried.

Maddy sighed. "It's nothing."

He dropped her arm completely and crossed his arms over his solid chest to wait.

"Ugh, OK, fine. Tall, dark and handsome," she clarified. Grinning, he looked at her as she continued. "It's something my girlfriends from home and I use in reference to someone when we don't know their name and they happen to have those features. It's common, so don't flatter yourself," she quickly added, pointing her index finger at him for added measure.

He seemed to consider this, then said, "Ryan," dropping his arms into a mock bow then quickly taking her arm and hooking it over his as they began to walk again.

She stayed silent. Ryan Carmichael. Yes, how could she have forgotten! Just last month when she had first gotten to England, she remembered hearing Mary carry on about how he had just won some journalistic photography award for his work in Africa. There were articles left all over the house that she had to pick up as Mary had wanted to collect anything out there about her baby brother.

It was endearing to Maddy at the time to think how much an older sister could care for a younger sibling and not feel jealous. She had never had that kind of connection with her siblings or family, or anyone really. It was easier that way, given her lifestyle, or was her lifestyle born out of never feeling, or wanting to feel, a connection to anyone?

Ryan and Maddy continued to walk in companionable silence until they came upon a patch of wildflowers. Maddy instinctively walked over and began picking some of her favorites for the current season: corncockle and bluebells, and even some late-season cornflowers abounded here!

Ryan watched her in quiet reverie. When she turned to catch him staring, he smiled, completely unconcerned with having been caught in the act. Maddy walked back to him to say they could go, and he surprised her by cupping his muscular hands around her face and drawing her in for a kiss. It was a deep kiss that went to the depths of the soul she didn't know she had. She lost sense of time and space and wanted to float there for eternity.

She realized after a few moments that he had pulled away. They both seemed to be shook by what they just experienced, only their responses were very different. Ryan smiled a knowing grin that she had already come to interpret as his own concoction of playboy mixed with childlike innocence.

Maddy was simply dumbfounded. She had been kissed by a lot of guys before, and maybe even within minutes of meeting them, but nothing like that had ever happened. She became aware that she had dropped the bouquet of flowers she had just picked and bent to retrieve them.

As she stood, she heard Ryan say, "Sorry. I've been wondering what it would be like to kiss you since you tumbled into me. While I was trying to be a gentleman and wait, I figured here in the woods while you were picking wildflowers was as good a time as any!"

Having regained her cool composure, Maddy simply responded with, "Oh."

Ryan laughed and took her arm over his again and they headed back out of the woods and onto the grounds. "Well, you're a cool customer," he quipped, aware that she did not seem impressed. "Perhaps I should try again…not enough power for you, that?" He playfully turned to her.

Excited at the prospect of being lost in the pool of nothingness again so soon, she challenged him. "Do your worst, Mr. Carmichael."

Apparently, that took him by surprise, but he didn't let it last long. Before she knew it, his mouth was on hers again, his strong arms tucking around her waist and pulling her close to his warm chest. She couldn't help but reach her arms up, tangling her hands around his neck, and she just stayed there, bouquet be damned. In her mind all that was missing was the *Princess Diaries* "leg pop" and the scene would be complete. Maddy didn't know how long they were standing there in that amazing embrace, but she hoped he would never let go.

Chapter 14 – September 1563 – Ann

The return had not gone as planned. We thought if the three of us went to Mr. White's shop at this hour in the morning, we could be there to support Lizbeth as she told her father what happened. He would have noticed she was not there last night, surely, and would likely be frantic. Then, once the tale was told, Lizbeth would stay with me and my family, since there were less of us under one roof than what Madge had to contend with and this would allow for relative peace and quiet.

We had made our way quietly to the center of the village, with much coaxing of Lizbeth, as she stopped thrice on the way there. We each stayed silent, Madge and I not wanting to spook her any more than she was, and Liz gathering her thoughts, or so I assumed.

We were just approaching the shop when we saw a now familiar dark-brown cloak with gold trim come out of the exact door we were wanting to enter. The profile showed the pointed nose and long, dark, greasy hair of Mr. Acton. I never noticed how his nose, so pointed, seemed to hook as well, like a bird of prey. It was remarkable really, and I mused to myself how I was now seeing his true colors. His mask was off, and it was an ugly sight to behold.

He turned abruptly and began looking up and down the street, as if he did not want to be caught, which was lucky because neither did we. I yanked Lizbeth into the closest doorway and Madge did an about face to walk away as if she had been alone. Madge was the least likely to have been recognized by Mr. Acton, so he would not think twice.

I held my breath while Lizbeth sank down against the doorframe, trying to make herself as small as possible, holding her stomach, as if she was trying to keep herself together. As soon as I saw him walk away from the shop and on a clear path to the Whites' house, I moved out of the doorway.

Lizbeth looked like a small, scared cat huddled up in the corner. I reached down to help her up and she looked up at me, eyes glistening with unspilt tears, such fear and hopelessness as I had ever seen. "Liz, he's gone, darling girl. We can go."

"No. No, we cannot," she said with more vigor than I expected. I gave her a quizzical look. "Do you not see? He has already been to my father. He has woven some tale he is sure to believe over me. No, I cannot speak with him now," she determined. Madge had heard us moving and returned to our side.

"But surely your father will believe his own daughter over a stranger."

Lizbeth laughed at this. "Do you not understand? He is not a stranger anymore, not to my father. To my father, he is the ticket for me to be married into a 'successful' household. A man above my station and likened to a 'gentleman' from London. To him, Mr. Acton is the answer to his now obvious prayers of being rid of me at last," she said with despair.

"Elizabeth," I started, with her full given name, knowing full well she was going into hysterics, but she stopped me.

"No, I will not go speak with my father just now. Can we return to your house so I can get some rest? You can send word to him in his shop that I am well and over at your house to see my friend after so long a time away," she reasoned.

"As you wish," I replied.

Madge decided it would be suspicious if all three of us showed up on my doorstep, so she went to find Simon. It was late morning by now and he should be taking his midday break soon. She beamed at the prospect of seeing him but, not wanting to cause any more anguish for Lizbeth, settled her face into a slight grin and moved along.

Lizbeth and I walked arm in arm back to my house. She seemed to need the support, and I needed to keep her close. I could feel her slipping away from us with each step and was trying to hold on for dear life. Whatever had happened in that wood had certainly changed her forever, and I started to wonder if that was the reason my dark portent of danger was lurking about again. I really needed to take some time to think when we got back to the house, but I would not dare do so in front of my friend until I knew better the meaning of all of this.

When we walked in the door, the house was warm thanks to the fire in the hearth. Mother must have lit it to bake bread for dinner, otherwise it would not have been going with such fury on a fall day. It was cool enough for need of a cloak, but the true chill of the season had yet to settle in.

"Who is there?" I heard her call from the kitchen, clearly surprised that anyone was coming in at this hour.

"It is just me and Lizbeth, Mother," I returned.

"Oh goodness, Lizbeth! How are you, love? I have not heard mention of you in weeks!" she said cheerily, obviously in the midst of preparing dinner for later.

My father and brother should be working their way back from the fields to have their dried beef, bread with butter, and a chunk of cheese. Mother did not approve of father having ale and then going back out in the fields, especially with Thomas in tow, but it looked like she had set aside a small amount of mead and watered it down so he could at least take the chill off what was undoubtedly a cooler morning.

Lizbeth was silent. My mother came around the corner as she sensed something was different. I quickly devised an excuse. "Lizbeth is tired. You know those men from London still stay at the Whites. Apparently, they were up quite late last night, and Lizbeth did not get much sleep. I told her she could come rest here for the day."

Knowing all too well the carousing that men could get up to when they wanted, my mother shook her head and said, "Of course. Good plan, Ann. She is welcome to have some bread and cheese as well. I must save the meat for Mr. Hughes and Thomas, as they will have to go back out to the fields to finish up later, but you are looking a tad peaky, love," she said as she took in the sight of Lizbeth.

I did not want her seamstress eye to fall on her cloak, so I removed it from my friend with haste and folded it in my arms. "Thank you, Mrs. Hughes," she said, coming out of her stupor enough to acknowledge what was being said to her. "I am not hungry at the moment. I just need a bit of a lie down."

My mother observed the dark circles under her eyes and drawn pale face. "If I were to guess, love, it has been more than just one evening you have not been getting proper rest. Let Ann take you to the children's room and you can stay as long as you like."

I walked Lizbeth over to the loft and up the stairs. She obeyed my every move as though she were a well-trained dog. I had her lie down on my bed, still rumpled from my quick rising this morning. She climbed in and removed her shoes. I tucked her in under the thick quilted comforter my mother had made me for my sixteenth birthday. I think it was meant to be part of my dowry when I was wed to James, but after his disappearance, my mother took pity on me and let me curl up with it every night. Lizbeth seemed to sink into the bedding and almost disappear.

"I will send word to your father with Thomas as he goes back to the fields with my father," I whispered. Lizbeth only nodded slightly and turned over, escaping from the world. I set my hand lightly on her shoulder, trying to transfer some calming energy. I knew she did not want to be touched but needed to feel like I was doing something to heal the darkness overtaking her. Thankfully, she either had not noticed or perhaps did not care and allowed the energy to flow.

I walked quietly down the stairs back to the kitchen, steeling myself for whatever inquisition was to come.

There was no way my mother was going to let this go without more information.

As I entered the room, she was warming some chunks of bread so the butter would melt and be ready for consumption. As it turned out, my father and brother walked in just then and she turned from the bread to them without another word in my direction.

"Where is Susan?" my father asked as they came to the kitchen and sat down.

"She is over at the Williams' today. Poor Eliza has her hands full with her brood and asked for some help with the young ones since William is apprenticing with Nicholas, and Mary does not have the stamina to wrangle the rest of the lot on her own," my mother replied.

"Ah," my father said as he sat down on the closest chair. I was not sure if it was a sound of relief at finally sitting or one of understanding how it must be with that many children under one roof.

"Yes," my mother continued, "ever since Margaret has started taking up with Simon, she has been otherwise engaged during parts of the day," and turned to me with a wink.

I sat down next to Thomas to take my dinner, still anxious to steal away and have some time to think. "I cannot believe she likes Simon!" he cried rather boisterously.

"Shhhh," I admonished, and he gave me a questioning look. "Lizbeth is resting upstairs. Her own household is besieged by supposed gentlemen who know not the meaning of a restful night's sleep."

Thomas laughed, rather too loudly for my taste, so I elbowed him in his side, to which he responded with an emphatic "omphf."

"Now, you two," started my father, "no more of that. If rest is what she has come for, rest is what she will receive. If Henry has his wish, she will not have much time for rest in the near future," he finished and shot a knowing glance at my mother.

At this, I winced. Perhaps my father knew not what he said, but I had a feeling there was something more to the glance. I thought it may be an opportune time to play naïve and do some information gathering. After all, how could we create a campaign against Mr. Acton if we did not have all the facts?

"Whatever do you mean, Father?" I asked innocently. He looked at my mother again and a silent question passed between them, along with an answer. Ultimately, she nodded, and he continued.

"Well, just that Mr. Acton has been courting Lizbeth for several weeks, if not months now, and has been making his intentions known to Henry, that is, Mr. White, that he wishes to take Lizbeth as his wife!" he said with jubilation.

I sat there in shock. Lizbeth had been correct, as had her vision, or whatever she had received through her flowers and herbs. I must have been mulling it over too long without expression because I realized my whole family was expectantly staring at me.

"Oh!" was all I could manage. My father was surprised at my reaction; my mother cocked her head, as if she knew why and I could see her wheels turning, trying to back up the news with why I should be happy for her and not dwell on my own situation.

"OH!" I started again. "'Tis just that I would not think that would be such common knowledge without Lizbeth knowing. And are you sure, Father? I mean, we do not even know this man and I get the sense that he is…" Words were flooding out of me, and my father held up his hand after he finished tearing a chunk of bread.

"It is not common knowledge, only to those of us on the elder's council. Henry has been positively beaming as of late, the likes of which we have not seen since his poor Jane passed," he said. I started to interrupt, but he continued. "And whether he is a good man is not for us to decide. Henry seems to think he is a perfect match for his Lizbeth as none other in this village has been. He may not be titled, but he does have money, being that he is from London, and he will be an advantageous marriage for Lizbeth so that she may rise in society and give her children an elevated life," my father said, convinced in his own words.

I chewed on my lip, weighing my options. Was this my opportunity to tell my father about what happened and gain him as an advocate for our cause? Would Lizbeth want this information shared in front of my family while she slept? How much of what was just said could she have heard above in the loft?

"But Father," I started, and he held up his hand again.

He finished chewing the piece of dried beef and said, "Not another word. It is not our decision, and she sleeps right above us! It is not for us to spoil the happy tidings before they come to fruition. Really, Ann, I thought you would have been happy for your friend to have found such a match."

"I am, Father, or rather I would be if it was an actu—"

"No more of this. The accord, as I understand it, will be confirmed within the week. Not a word of this to Lizbeth. I mean it, Ann." He bit a piece of cheese, as if to signal the conversation had ended.

I hung my head and pushed my plate away. It clearly was not the time or place to make the case for Lizbeth not marrying Mr. Acton, but with the finality of my father's words, I was concerned that there was never going to be an opportunity. I had to strategize, and the food was only going to distract me.

We finished our dinner in silence. Thomas was worn out from such an early start, my mother was perhaps anxious to say anything lest it upset me as someone else was getting married and not me, not aware that was the furthest thing from my mind, and my father clearly did not want to reopen the discussion.

As the dinner concluded and the men readied themselves for the afternoon, I wrote a quick note to Mr. White and asked Thomas deliver it along the way. My father looked at me with a raised eyebrow, and I told him it was merely a note to let him know that Lizbeth was resting here for the day, and she would likely stay for supper as well. He seemed satisfied and allowed the transaction, reassuring me that he would not let Thomas forget.

As soon as they left, I whirled around to my mother. "Mother, she cannot possibly marry Mr. Acton!" I cried.

"I know, darling girl, it will be hard to lose your dear friend to marriage, but it really is time. Past time if you think of it. You girls have been very lucky not to have already been married off and started families of your own yet." I tried to break into her obviously rehearsed soliloquy but was rebuffed. "I know you were closest and poor James – God rest his soul wherever he may be – is not an option anymore, but I am surprised you would be so selfish as to block your friend from such a grand opportunity!" she finished.

"But Mother, that is just it. It is not a grand opportunity. Mr. Acton is not the man he says he is!" I cried.

At this, she turned. "Ann Marie Hughes, you must not make accusations for which you have no proof. I did not raise you to spread unkind words."

I rolled my eyes, supremely frustrated that no one was listening or caring, but how could they? They were not in possession of the information I was, of what had happened to Lizbeth just the day before, and her true reasons for resting in our loft instead of her own room. "I am not—"

"No more of this. I agree with your father. He shared too much just now, and I will not have you ruining this for your friend, regardless of your intentions."

I was infuriated. I now saw what Lizbeth was so worried about. If my own parents, who I considered to be levelheaded people with good hearts, were so clearly taken with the façade Mr. Acton and his men had created, then how could we convince Mr. White? A man so focused on his beloved daughter's future since she grew up without a mother, a fact for which he was always outwardly guilty of, though there was nothing he could have done to save her.

I needed air. Without a word, I grabbed my cloak and walked outside so I could pace in private and think about our next move. Leaving Lizbeth's cloak still surreptitiously folded in the corner so as not to attract unnecessary attention to the stains, rips and filth, I went outside to clear my head.

I do not know how long I was out there, but my pacing left me with no better conclusion, so I went to check on Lizbeth. As I walked back in and set my cloak down, I realized hers was missing. Perhaps my mother's keen seamstress eye had sensed the garment's mishandling, and she had taken it upon herself to rectify it.

While not ideal, maybe it would be a conversation starter into the truth. I slowly walked into the kitchen to see what she was up to, only I found her busy with supper preparations, no bucking bath to be seen. She looked up at me from kneading the bread dough on the center island with soft eyes, her way of apologizing after being so harsh earlier.

A sinking feeling crawled into my belly. I quickly pivoted and ran up the stairs, taking them two at a time to check on Lizbeth in the loft. When I got up there, I saw a lump in my bed and started to relax. I quietly but swiftly walked over and sat on the edge of my bed to soothe my friend awake, only the lump was my sheets balled up and her shoes were gone. My breath caught. What had she heard at dinner below?

I ran downstairs and into the kitchen. My mother looked at me with shock on hearing me tear around the house as such. She was just about to question me when I asked, "Where is Lizbeth?!"

She looked confused. "She is sleeping upstairs, love. Are you alright?"

I ignored her question and said, "No, she is not. And her shoes are gone, as is her cloak I left by the front door!"

My mother thought about this and said, "Well, perhaps she overheard us at dinner and was too excited to contain herself at the news. I suspect she ran home so she could wait for her father's return for the evening and talk," she said, smiling to herself.."

I knew that was not the case. I ran to the door and looked up and down the street. No sign of the raven hair anywhere. There was only one way in or out of our house. How had she gotten past both my mother and me? Was I that caught up in my own thoughts that I had not noticed her departure?

I did not know how or when she had left, but Lizbeth was gone.

Chapter 15 – September, Present Day – Sophia

The next few weeks after our Shaman experience were a blur. While we communicated a fair amount before, Kit and I had become inseparable now. Every waking moment was spent diving deeper and deeper into the history of what we experienced to get answers. When we weren't working our day jobs and Kit wasn't tending to her young family, we were meeting at coffee shops, talking through video chat, or texting back and forth.

We had decided that Kit would focus more on the psychology-related topics, as that was the area she was most comfortable with, and I would investigate the more esoteric elements, like fractals.

Me: *Check this out, I found more on fractals.*
Kit: *OK, hit me.*
Me: *"Spiritual fractals: The part of a human that detaches from the body after death, which is separate from influence, body, genes and evolution – the soul – is fractal. Fractals are spiritual because they explain human's innate understanding of the world." – The Oxbow School.*
Kit: *...*
Me: *Also, "What is fractal consciousness? Fractals are highly entropic, and this is one of the reasons several researchers have suggested that our consciousness is fractal." – Fractal Institute*
Kit: *This is just too...I don't know.*

Me: *Wait, it goes on to say, "...secondly, our central nervous system, which governs the most functions of our body and mind, has a lot of links to fractals."*

Kit: *That's true. If you remember, the CNS has the brain and spinal cord, which takes and responds to all the sensory information in the body and allows all bodily functions...*

Me: *Yes, Professor, I do recall the definition of the CNS.*

Kit: *LOL, sorry. I forget that you studied this too. OK, so if the CNS is technically built of up fractals, I can see where it would be further split into other cognitive, and not so cognitive, parts.*

Me: *Yup.*

Kit: *So, we're saying that whenever what happened, happened, our souls were so traumatized that the experience not only imprinted on our DNA but caused a splitting of our soul? That's a little too Voldemort for my taste...*

Me: *Splitting yes, but as I understand it, not in the way of the Voldemort horcruxes, because those were intentional and created for an evil purpose. Hold up, what do you mean "imprinted on our DNA"?*

Kit: *Oh, didn't I tell you? There's a whole study around "epigenetics" whereby people have studied "how experiences leave chemical signatures on genes, which can alter how genes are expressed."*

Me: *Now who's looking into the esoteric?!*

Kit: *Not really. It's been scientifically proven through studies. They found chemical tags, methyl groups "that can be passed onto offspring through genetic material."*

Me: *Huh. But that's not the same as what we are experiencing, is it? Imprinted on us, yes, but are we saying what we saw was ancestors of ours, or our own past lives?*

Kit: *Agreed, not exactly the same, but could be why there is imprinting happening with Tate and possibly Thora.*

Me: *Say more.*

Kit: *Well, I'm still trying to wrap my head around why Tate had the dream and not me. With Thora being more "old school," it would make sense that she could have picked up on that part of my life, but still, why did they get those attributes and not me directly? I have a theory but am reticent to say it out loud yet.*

Me: *Interesting. I respect that. But if not now, when?*

Kit: *...*

Me: *I won't force it, but it might be important.*

Kit: *Well...what if she...*

Me: *Yes...*

Kit: *...what if she, or I guess in this case me, was pregnant at the time of the "event" and the trauma imprinted on the pregnancy? Thus, the fractal of me that is Tate and/or Thora is the epigenetics of that experience now manifesting itself in Tate's dream for him to relay to me because my soul in that past life could not bear to carry it.*

Me: *Woah.*

Kit: *Yeah, like I said, it's just a theory.*

Me: *I will have to ruminate on this...*

Kit: *I know, right?! I'm probably overthinking it.*

Me: *Um, no. My entire left side is lit up with goosebumps...Alright, love, I have to focus on prepping for tomorrow's class. As much as I would much prefer to spend ALL my time on this topic, I do need a paycheck. Not everyone can be a world-class psychologist with a massive following in their chosen field!*

Kit: *Ha! Massive following, I think not. No worries, love. Erik took the kids out tonight so I could have some peace and quiet. I'm going to finish up here and then try to*

meditate before bed. It seems to be the best time for me to tap into whatever is going on.
Me: *Excellent. Enjoy! Nighty night.*

I put my phone down and turned my attention to the latest lecture. Marketing 101: Segmenting and Target Markets. It was usually a favorite of mine since I loved to tell stories about the importance of "Knowing Your Audience" and "Demographics vs. Psychographics." I loved the look of understanding that passed like a wave over the students. For them, it was either a hook into becoming marketing majors or the confirmation that they couldn't care less, and this would be fulfilling a Gen Ed requirement for their other major. But the word "psychographic" got me thinking about other things and I had to look away from my computer.

A snack. That was what I needed, brain food. And apparently what Violet needed too. I had completely forgotten to get her dinner, a fact she was none too happy about. She reminded me by jumping on my foot.

"Ow! Sorry, girl. I got lost in the research," I said, looking down at her. I patted her head, and we walked into the kitchen. She ran over to her bowl and practically willed it onto the countertop for me to fill. I realized she was out of water too, for which I quietly admonished myself. I promptly filled it, throwing a few "water cookies" in for good measure. Vi loved her ice cubes and surely that would help her forgive me.

I filled her bowl with her favorite kibble, set it down on her stand and turned my attention to the fridge. I hadn't been grocery shopping in a few days, as I had squirreled away this weekend and wasn't sure what I was going to find. I settled on the jar of bread and butter pickles and started the tea kettle.

When in doubt, pickles were my go-to comfort food, having acquired a taste for eating them by the jar in college. Now, they were just super convenient, if not the most nutritious option I had at my fingertips.

If I was honest, I wasn't too hungry. There had been some weird goings-on at the university of late and I didn't know how I felt about the energy shift. I still loved teaching, more than any corporate job, but the vibe was off this semester. I couldn't tell if it was because of all the wild stuff Kit and I were going through, or if it was something else.

My phone dinged, breaking through my thoughts, and I went to retrieve it, thinking it was Kit having stumbled on some other scientific fact. Instead, I saw it was Maddy. Maddy! I had completely forgotten about her. Oh, thank goodness she wasn't here as we were uncovering all this madness. She would be running away from us for sure! Or bringing the mob to drag us in the streets and burn us at the stake.

I smirked. I opened the text to find a picture of her against a green backdrop with an English country manor in the background and next to an amazingly good-looking guy. The picture was tagged, *Pure bliss! <3*. I opened the picture into a bigger window so I could get a better look at this guy that was giving Maddy the goofiest grin I had ever seen.

Tall, dark locks, a few freckles on his face between gorgeous eyes, of which I couldn't quite determine the color. He was fully clothed, but you could tell from the way the sweater stretched across his chest that he was well-muscled. I wondered who this new Adonis was.

I realized it had been a while since I had last checked in on her and made a mental note to do so tomorrow. While I just received the text from her now, Lord only knew when it was sent given my cell signal of late. The picture had clearly been taken in the daytime, and it would now be well into the wee hours of the morning over in England.

My kettle went off and I brewed a cup of decaffeinated cinnamon tea, a fall favorite as the weather turned, and contemplated how long it would be until I burned my first fire in the fireplace. I cupped the tea mug in my hands as I walked back to my place in the front room. The mug was an oldie but goodie, black with dancing skeletons. I kept it out all year because of my love of Halloween and the childlike glee it brought me.

Not wanting to spill the hot liquid all over my papers and computer, I set it off to the side. Oh, who was I kidding? I wasn't going to be able to focus on the lecture. Besides, I could give that thing in my sleep at this point. I needed a distraction.

Instead, I jumped on the couch, curled up in the corner with my well-worn knitted blanket and turned on the TV. Vi came over and stared at me with her biggest puppy eyes, willing me to let her up on the couch, to which I relented, still trying to make amends.

Oh, my pickles! I left them on the counter. Oh well, Vi was snuggled in now and I didn't want to disturb her.

I opened the guide to try and find something distracting.
I scrolled through, finding lots of options, but nothing
was catching my eye. *The Mummy Returns* was on, which
made me smile thinking back to Kit's comment after the
Shaman experience and how she was "whooshed" to the
different time and place. It wasn't quite time for
Halloween movies to be out, though that was exactly what
I was in the mood for. Instead, I settled on a lesser-
known channel that was showing a series about "Ancient
Civilizations." It looked a little Indiana Jones-esque,
which seemed perfect.

I came into the episode halfway and tried focusing on
what they were saying. I took a few sips of my cinnamon
tea and set it down on the end table again, snuggling
deeper into the couch. Before I knew it, I was out,
succumbing to the coziness of the couch, the warmth of
the blanket and the sweet fur baby sleeping at my side,
nestled in the nook of my legs.

It was a tumultuous, furtive sleep. Nothing concrete, just
images flashing. A stone altar, woods, a village that
looked like what I knew as Salem, a man in a cloak, then
mountains, rolling green hills, tartans and castles.

None of it was making sense, but I also couldn't seem to
wake. Then in the midst of it all, I heard my phone ring.
When I opened my eyes, the sun was creeping into the
room, my tea had long gone cold and Violet was sprawled
on the other side of the couch, probably having gotten
tired of my apparent thrashing since the blanket was all
which ways around me.

I looked at the time, 8:15AM. Wow! I had slept on the
couch all night?! I must have been cooked. I realized I

had been woken by the phone ringing and turned back to it to see "Mom" on the caller ID. I cleared my throat, not wanting her to know she was waking me up.

"Hi, Mom!" I said, trying to sound bright and chipper.

"Hello, darling, how are you? I didn't wake you, did I?" How did she always know? Mother's intuition, I guess. I could no longer knock her for this with all I had discovered.

"Not really, just first human I'm talking to today," I covered.

"Oh good, well, I just wanted to check in. Dad and I are coming back from our latest adventure on Wednesday and wanted to be sure you could still pick us up at the airport?" she asked.

"Yes, of course, I have it on my calendar. How's Italy?" I replied.

"Bellissimo!" she exclaimed, clearly proud of herself for picking up a few of the local words, something we had always tried to do as a family anytime we traveled to show respect for the local area and its people.

I smiled. "Excellent to hear. Yes, I will see you and Dad on Wednesday. I assume the regular pizza order will be required?" I asked.

"No, I think we have seen enough pizza and carbs to last us for a while on this venture, sweetie. Perhaps a juice cleanse is in order." She laughed to herself.

"No worries. I will follow your flight on the app and let you know where I'm parked once you get to the luggage area." I hurried along, not wanting to keep her on the phone for too long, given the distance.

"Sounds good, love, can't wait to see you then!" She ended with, "Love you!"

"Love you too, Mom. Say hi to Dad for me and have a safe trip home." We hung up.

I knew I should capture my dream and send it to Kit, as we had promised to do if anything relevant came up, but it was all becoming fuzzy and I wasn't sure what to tell her I had seen...mountains?

Instead, I got up, went to the bathroom and got ready for the day. Thankfully, I wasn't too far behind, so I didn't need to rush out of the house. I packed up my laptop, got Vi fed and out, and filled my thermos once again.

Classes didn't start until 10AM, so I had plenty of time to get to campus, park and walk to my classroom. I checked my email and saw something waiting from the dean of the college. That was weird. Why on earth would he be emailing me?

I quickly opened it and scanned the message, and my heart dropped into my stomach. He wanted to see me in between classes today. While I knew full well I had done nothing to support the sinking feeling in my gut, that voice in my head woke up and started to jabber away about how I had known something was coming and this was likely it.

I decided to ignore it and enjoy my drive instead. I said goodbye to Vi, locked up and jumped into Etta. This time, the first song that came on my Spotify was "Witchy

Woman." I laughed to myself, turned it up and drove off to campus to face the day, and whatever it was to bring.

Chapter 16 – September 1563 – Ann

The only thing I could think to do was run to Madge's and see if she had turned up there. Maybe she had fled from one haven to another, seeking comfort in what was sure to be chaos in the walls of the Williams' home.

As I passed by the cobbler shop, I took a quick glance inside to see if she happened to be there, but she was not. I did not want to worry her father when I had only just sent word that she was resting at our house. I pulled my hood over my head so he would not see me should he happen to look outside.

When I got to Madge's home, I could clearly hear the kids running around. Susan must not be managing the young ones as well as Mrs. Williams had hoped. I was about to knock when I saw Madge coming around the corner with an odd smile on her face. She did not notice me until she almost walked into me, hands on hips.

"And where have YOU been?" I asked.

Startled, she looked shy and said, "With Simon."

"'Tis way past dinnertime and well onto supper. Should he not be focused on his work?" I wondered aloud, sounding more annoyed than I intended. She started to respond, but I had grown tired of the conversation if only because of my worry for Lizbeth. "Never mind, we can speak of that later. I have to find Lizbeth," I choked out.

With a look of incredulousness, Madge said, "I thought she was with you?"

I shook my head and told her what had happened. No sooner had I finished than the front door to the house was thrown open and the littlest Williams, John, came tearing out, followed by the second youngest, Rebecca, and my own sister Susan in tow, clearly trying to keep up with them and stop whatever game was ensuing. Susan turned around as she ran after them with her arms held open wide and a shrug of her shoulders. Madge and I took the opportunity to look inside the house, and while we saw a lot going on, Lizbeth was not amid the disorder.

I looked at Madge. "I better go in and help with all the children while your sister wrangles those two. You go find our girl," she said.

I nodded my head, turned and left. I was not looking forward to what I was about to do next, but it had to be done. Even the voice in my head, while reticent, was urging me on.

I walked up the lane to the Whites' house. As I approached, I could not help but feel a chill run down my spine as I looked at a house that once held such warmth but now seemed devoid of anything remotely resembling that. I pulled my cloak around me to strengthen my resolve. I was not going to give away that Lizbeth was missing if she had not come home, but I was also not going to miss confirming she was safe after what had happened only a few hours before.

I suddenly remembered one of the sigils from Madge's rune set passed down to her from her father's side, which was meant to be a protection sign – a long center line with two short lines at an angle on the top third of the main line. I quickly drew it in front of my chest. It could not hurt to have a little extra help!

I stepped up to the door and knocked thrice. Thankfully, it was one of Mr. Acton's men that answered the door. He looked at me silently, though with his roaming eyes I could tell his thoughts were racing. I straightened my stance.

"Who is it?" I heard a voice call from within. Not immediately recognizing it as George's or Matthew's, after the visceral response that followed, I knew it was Mr. Acton.

His man turned to respond, but I did so instead. "It is Miss Hughes, a friend of Miss White's, come to inquire as to her health." I thought it best to pretend I had not seen Lizbeth at all today.

I heard the scraping of a chair across the floor. He must have been sitting with his feet up on the table, chair tilted back, from the thud and then scrape before he could get to his feet. I watched as he lumbered forward, clearly having imbibed more of Mr. White's mead, and approached like a goblin out of the dark.

"Her health?" he slurred. "Why, her health is just fine," he sneered. "If you are her friend, why have we not been properly introduced?" he asked as he looked me up and down and then jokingly elbowed his comrade in conspiracy.

"Proper? I daresay you know the meaning of the word...sir." That last word I added with an unnecessary emphasis.

His jesting manor quickly took on a tone of disdain. "Watch it, Mistress, you should learn to respect your betters," he said.

"Did you mean elders, sir? For I see no betters here," I responded as I looked both he and his man up and down, though not with the same intention as they had with me.

Seeing that I was not backing down, Mr. Acton paused for a moment and thought about how best to proceed. He obviously knew who I was and who my family were to the village, as well as my importance to Lizbeth. Better to win me over than to have me for an enemy.

I could see the wheels turning behind his bloodshot eyes – how much did this man drink? The smell he effused left something to be desired, and I could see why Lizbeth referred to him as acrid. I did not know if I could have ever removed that odor from my nostrils if he had gotten as close to me as he had my friend.

"Well, Mistress." He emphasized the word with an odd timbre I did not care for. "Our dear Lizbeth is out and about at the moment. I am surprised you have not seen her, as I could have sworn she said she would be with her friends today. Perhaps not as close as you thought?" He tried one more time to get a rise out of me, but I refused to let him win.

"Or perhaps closer than you care to understand...sir," I responded, with a knowing glint in my eye.

He must have intuited something from that casual exchange because he became immediately suspicious and edgy. "Whatever it is you know, or think you know, Miss Hughes, is clearly not for me to decide. But you should be aware that your friend is even more of a hussy than I suspected, and anything you say will fall on deaf ears, as I have already spoken with her father. The announcement is to be made in a fortnight and the ceremony a few weeks after that. We shall see how friendly Miss White remains with you and *your kind* after that!" he finished, almost in celebration.

My kind? Hussy? Who did this man think he was talking to?

Just then, George came running around the corner to break the standoff happening between us. Completely oblivious to what he was walking in on, he burst past Mr. Acton and into the house to fetch something. Just as quickly as he was there, he was gone, yelling "Hello, Ann. Goodbye, Ann." as he went. He and Thomas must have been in the middle of some game.

I was about to respond to the gauntlet just thrown down, but Mr. Acton beat me to it. "Miss White is not here at present, Miss Hughes. As to her health, I have her well taken care of and looked after, I can assure you. You need not worry your little female head about such matters." He and his man grinned at each other, and I could almost read their thoughts. As it seemed we might gain a further audience, and not wanting to make a scene, I bowed my head to him, turned and left.

I had no other choice. Now that I had heard it directly from the man himself, I had to find Lizbeth and take her to her father to make her case. She needed me more than ever and I would not fail her. Whatever had begun to unravel in her this morning would only continue if she spent one more second around that vile, repugnant louse. Clearly her father had to see that.

I went to the only other place I could think of, our sacred spot in the woods. Knowing that Lizbeth had shared it was her only place of respite over these past few months, she had to be there. I quickened my pace, but not so much as to draw attention to myself. As I entered the path, I heard the familiar fluttering above, but this time I did not look up. I rushed to approach the stones and immediately stopped.

Lizbeth was there, but she was in the middle of a ritual the likes I had never seen. She had shed her cloak and was moving around the altar in a counter circle, meaning to "undo" or take away something, while waving her arms about above her head and chanting something incoherent.

As she moved past the center, I saw it. There on our sacred altar were not the traditional herbs and flowers we had practiced with to build her skills, but something lay in a heap and was leaking a dark liquid. I froze. What had she done to our space? Held so sacred for purity and joy, now engulfed in a feeling of darkness and fear.

My breath caught in my throat and made the smallest sound. Lizbeth, even in all her fervor, heard and sensed me there, but did not stop. She kept moving around the circle backward, chanting and calling out, but when she got to a point where she could see me, she stared into my eyes, imploring me to understand. She had to do this. She had to go over to the dark side to save herself from her unraveling future. If this did not work, nothing would. She had tears streaming down her face. I knew it was not something she wanted but felt compelled to do. She was desperate.

My tears started falling as well as I watched in shocked silence. I did not want to bear witness to this, but I also could not look away. I could not leave her in this time of need. I closed my eyes, which only half helped, as I could still hear her, chanting and wailing, her steps quickening, the sound of her voice transforming from its usually sweet and light notes to something dark and guttural. I worried someone from the village would come. It was only midday, after all, but as time was of the essence in her mind, she clearly did not care.

Lizbeth. My gorgeous, wildly rebellious, raven-haired storytelling Lizbeth was doing something we promised we would never do, nor did we know how. Had she been practicing these dark crafts alone? Or was this coming from somewhere else? It seemed to be emerging from that dark place that had started to overtake her this morning, a place of fierce protection against what was to come and an unknown chaos driving her forward. We were losing her. There was an unnatural anger that was eclipsing her otherwise effervescent self.

Soon, it was over. The chanting stopped. The movement halted. And I opened my eyes. Lizbeth stood in the center of our sacred space, the triquetra, arms raised to the heavens, sobbing, imploring Sophia to help her.

Surveying the scene, I knew that Sophia was not likely to come. If she had not shown up for me all those years ago, how could she now? We had always talked about her as love and light, and this...what I had borne witness to was anything but.

Lizbeth brought her arms down in front of her chest and then they fell to her sides. Whatever mayhem she had just concocted had concluded and she was clearly spent. I stood in awe, partly in wonder of how far she had progressed and partly in shock at how awful the space now felt.

Lizbeth crumpled to the ground. I ran over to her and took her head in my lap, cradling it gingerly so as not to hurt her neck. Whatever had been pouring out of her while she had been moving around had clearly left her spirit worn. She fluttered her eyes open and looked up at me. For the briefest moment, I could have sworn I saw a flash of dark lightning. It scared me and I had to remind myself that this was Lizbeth. She seemed to return to her senses then and sat upright.

"Ann, whatever are you doing here?" she asked, as if she had not seen me just moments before.

Confused, I said, "I came looking for you. Whatever are YOU doing here when you are supposed to be resting in my loft?"

She looked down at the ground. "I..." she started, but then heaved a huge sigh and could not continue. I knew what she was going to say but let the silence hang there between us anyway, for once not wanting to finish her thought.

"We need to go talk with your father. We can make him understand the gravity of the situation, that he must not allow this union," I said instead. Lizbeth just sat there on the forest floor. I was not sure if she could even hear me, so I tried again. "Lizbeth, we must," I started, but she cut me off.

"It will matter not. If what your father said is true, then it is done, and so it must be," she finished.

"Shhh, Lizbeth, you must not utter those words, for you will bring it upon yourself so!" I exclaimed. "Your father—"

"My father is doing what he thinks best for me. I have been a burden to him far too long and this is his chance to be rid of me and give me my own family."

The fact she was so resolved to this, especially after what I had just witnessed, did not ring true, but I could not continue to argue with her. I would have to plead her case myself and see if it got her out of harm's way. I looked at my friend again, so frail yet resolute. I watched as she set her shoulders and began to stand, like a soldier preparing himself for battle, even if he was not convinced it was the best course of action.

"Would you like me to walk you home?" I asked.

"No, I do not want you near there. I will be fine. I think I may go find my brother first," she said.

"I saw George come and go..." I stopped myself, as I did not want her to know I had confronted Mr. Acton already. Best she come into that knowledge when she regained her true spirit. "I saw George just recently, running about. I think he may be playing a game with Thomas."

"Oh" was all Lizbeth could manage.

I had one last attempt. My ace in the hole. "Should you not try and speak with Robert about all of this? What will he say?" I queried. I watched as her face dropped again.

She sank her long, slender fingers farther into the earth around her, as if she was trying to soak up its energy.

Then she looked up at me with her dark eyes. "I will have to let him go. I do not want to hold him back any further." The quietness and ease with which she said this stunned me. How could she give him up so easily? I thought for sure the mention of him would bring her back to her senses. I was aghast.

"It is going on suppertime. We should really be heading back if you do not want to cause trouble for your father," I managed, hoping to at least get her up and walking so I could remove some of the dirt and leaves that had collected on the back of her skirts and cloak.

"You are correct. I should. Will you help me up? I know I must move, but I do not trust myself just yet," she admitted. So, whatever she had been up to had taken her energy. I wanted to ask her what that was but at the same time was hoping to intercept her father on his way home from work and have a word alone with him. I had to try.

"Yes, dear one," I cooed, trying to sound as normal as possible. She placed her hand in mine, and I steadied her as she stood. Her hand was so cold, perhaps because she kept sinking it deeper into the earth.

We turned away from the altar, me not wishing to see what still lay in the middle and Lizbeth not wanting to disturb whatever she had conjured, and walked on along the path in silence. Just as we began, the winds picked up through the trees and I heard a moan shudder through the wood. I looked at Lizbeth to see if she had heard the same thing, but she kept walking as if she had not.

We left the woods without a word. As soon as we got to the edge of the village, we went to part ways, but Lizbeth grabbed my hand and turned me toward her. "Please, Ann, please do not do anything. I know your way and you will want to help me, but it will only make trouble. What I did in the wood…" She trailed off, almost as if she did not want to speak of it but then mustered up her courage and continued. "What I did in the wood should take care of all that. If Sophia is what we think she is, she will help," she said. I had not told anyone of my reaching out to Sophia in despair, so she could not know this was for naught.

"But, Liz, what I saw, that was not the way of Sophia, or us for that matter."

Lizbeth put her hand up. "We will not speak of it again. I will have my answer from her either way."

I looked into her eyes, hoping to find my friend there, but she was fading, and fast. I knew what she was asking of me, but I was not sure I could stay out of it. I had to try speaking with her father. I could not just let this happen to her, with this man who was the antithesis of the reputation he had created. Lizbeth must have sensed what I was thinking and half smiled at me through desolate eyes.

"I have always admired your tenacity and nobility, Ann, but this is the one time you must let it go. For my sake…please," she emphasized.

I let out a sigh, not realizing I had been holding my breath. "Alright. If you think it best. But know that if you change your mind, I will be there in an instant to speak on your behalf. This cannot stand," I replied. I was not sure I was comfortable with this decision, but she had pleaded so heartily I could not help but pause my plan.

"Thank you," she said softly, squeezed my hands and turned to walk away.

I did not know it then, but things were about to radically change for us and our planned future.

Chapter 17 – October, Present Day – Sophia/Maddy

The day had been a blur. Classes went well and I managed my segmenting lecture with ease. I was still processing the meeting with the dean, however. I wasn't sure if it was good or bad and would need time to mentally review the conversation and dissect it, but also didn't have the brain capacity to do so now.

Instead, I looked at my phone with anticipation of all the texts I had missed. While I had hoped there was an update from Kit – I had become quite reliant on those for a pick-me-up during the day – no such message waited. Instead, it was screenshots of flight information from my parents, and another picture from Maddy with her oh-so-juicy hunk.

I decided now was as good a time as any to reach out and see what was going on. It would be verging on late evening with the time difference, but knowing Maddy, she was likely just getting started. Video chat would be best, give her a real surprise.

I opened her contact info and pressed the video camera button. It rang, and the longer it did, the more I regretted the decision. I would hate to interrupt her and the boy toy "in situ" and was just about to hang up when I heard the unmistakable sound of a call connecting.

"Soph!" she exclaimed. "Oh, how brilliant. I'm so glad you rang," she said with continued enthusiasm. She had only been overseas a few months, but clearly her English accent was coming back in full swing.

"How goes it, doll? That's a juicy fella you have by your side," I dove in.

She smiled. The goofiest smile I think I had ever seen on her round face. She practically turned to goo on the screen.

"Yeah…" was all she could say.

"So…are you going to tell me about him, or do I have to go all MI6 on you?"

She giggled and looked beyond the phone. So, he was there, I thought sheepishly.

"He's just gone down the hall. We are having a small soiree here tonight in honor of next year's fall line concluding. Mary hasn't told anyone a thing about it, but we all have to get dressed up," she said, clearly ready to embark on one of her stories. It was then I noticed her scarlet satin dress and dangling chandelier earrings, and were those opera gloves in the background? Oh, the life of my dear sweet Maddy, dressed up in such elegance on a Tuesday evening.

"And…?" I led her on.

"Oh, Soph, I don't even know where to begin. It's been such a whirlwind!" She paused. I thought it best to let her collect her thoughts instead of interrupting. "He's just so great. I've never felt like this before, and it's gotten so serious so fast! Not heavy, just, I want to spend every waking moment with him," she gushed.

"So, who is he?" I asked.

"Ryan. Ryan Carmichael," she said with a dreamy look on her face. Carmichael. Why was that so familiar? Then it dawned on me.

"Your boss's husband?! Maddy, how could you…"

"Soph, honestly. Do you think that little of me?! No, silly, it's her brother."

I took an audible sigh of relief but fixed my face to play it off as mock shock instead of fear. While I didn't think Maddy was the kind, she also wasn't the type to go ga-ga head over heels.

"Brother. Got it. But what the heck is he doing there? Do they always travel as a set?"

"No!" she cried. "Soph, are you going to let me tell you the story or what? I only have a few moments until he gets back!"

I made the gesture to zip my lips and throw away the key and let her continue. She was pacing around her room now. I only caught glimpses, but it didn't appear to be your typical English household. I made a mental note to follow up on that later.

"…and then he just kissed me!" she exclaimed.

I must have been focusing on the room longer than I thought because I had missed the entirety of their meeting. Ah well, I could blame the connection and I'm sure she would tell me again.

"I only got parts of that, doll, you will have to tell me again, but I know you're crunched. But with that ending and the pictures I'm getting, I assume it's going well?" I said.

"More than well. I'm so happy I could cry, but I'm also waiting for the other shoe to drop," she admitted.

That was Maddy. When everything was going "too well" for her, she always worried the sky was about to fall. I had no idea where it came from. She led a wonderful life! I wasn't saying it didn't have its imperfections as everyone's did, but this sense of foreboding she carried with her at all times, well, it confounded me. I swear it became a self-fulfilling prophecy half the time and she willed the "shoe- dropping" to happen by purely bringing it into existence with her insistence and expectation. From what I was learning through research with Kit, it was quite possible.

"Now, Maddy. Don't do that! You know you create your own shoe-dropping! If he's that great, and you really are that happy, try not to think like that. You will only self-sabotage and then you'll be miserable," I rallied.

"Well, look at you going all psychology degree on me. Hanging out with Kit much?" she mused.

I laughed to myself. She didn't know the half of it.

"Anyways," she continued. "He's a pretty famous photographer, like I said, and has a lull in his shoots at the moment. He has always been a sucker for the English countryside since he and his sister grew up in the city, and when he heard she was setting up shop out here, he thought he'd come surprise her!"

"Lucky for you, huh." I smiled.

She grinned again. Then she stood to attention. "Soph, he's coming back. I hate to run but—"

"But you have a fancy glitzy party to go to with your TDH Englishman and I need to scoot," I finished.

"Something like that," she started to whisper, blew me a kiss on the screen and managed to squeak out a "cheers" before the phone went dark.

Well, that was interesting, I thought to myself. I would have to give Kit the latest when we spoke next. Given it was only Tuesday night, she would be in the throes of all the kids' activities and working on her day job. I had already taken too much of her time over the weekend so thought better of reaching out.

I was thrilled for Maddy and had so many more questions. Not just about the guy, who I now knew was named Ryan, but the house she was staying in and the work she was doing. Maddy never really spoke about what it was she did; she always kept everything pretty close to the vest, but I was wondering with this latest change in her, likely because of Ryan, if she might be more forthcoming. At least outside of her usual stories that had to wait until she was back home with a few martinis in her.

Ryan Carmichael, huh. I turned my attention to my laptop. *Let's just see if this guy is all he's cracked up to be*, I thought. I entered his name into the search engine and several things popped up at once.

Thankfully, he had created quite the reputation for himself. His portfolio was breathtaking! While his bailiwick seemed to be landscapes, he did quite a bit with architecture too. He definitely had a keen eye for design and how to frame a shot, as well as capture the true essence of color. I could see why Maddy would capture his attention as well. Our Maddy was a stunner on all levels, and with his obvious appreciation for the depth of textures and colors, her beauty would be high on his list, like one of the landscapes he had traveled around the world for.

It didn't seem like he was a player, which made me happy. Someone at his level usually wound up in the tabloids for their exploits, and yet there was very little to find on him personally, which I liked. Maddy needed someone who was stable and didn't give in to drama.

After not finding much else other than where he went to school – University of the Arts London, for which it seemed his family were benefactors (go Maddy!), with a short stint at University of Edinburgh – and a list of favorite shooting locations along with a couple interviews, I thought it best to put Mr. Carmichael aside.

I needed food. The fridge had not restocked itself from yesterday's search, so I would need to go out if I wanted anything healthy. Or…I could order some Chinese to be delivered so I didn't have to leave the house. It was only fall, but the air had turned colder earlier than normal. After the long day I had on campus, I did not relish the thought of having to fight the crowds at the grocery store. Violet seemed to agree with me and did not want me to leave her again either.

"Chinese it is!" I said to her as I picked up my phone and rang the Crystal Palace. I placed my usual order of sesame chicken, fried rice and an egg roll: seventeen minutes. Well, that would be faster than anything I could cook, even if I did have ingredients, I thought, and put the phone down. I grabbed Vi's bowl and fed her her kibble, as I knew she couldn't wait any longer, and then went to the fridge to get a glass of water.

I stood there at the fridge sipping my water, trying to make sense of the meeting with the dean from earlier, the memory having come back into my awareness. That voice was silent, for once, and was allowing me to ruminate uninhibited. I must have stood there longer than I realized because before I knew it, the doorbell was ringing, and my food was being delivered! My stomach bellowed in anticipation as I walked to the door to retrieve the piping-hot meal. I thanked the driver, handed him a tip and quickly closed the front door. It wasn't one I used often and let in a frightful cold breeze.

As I walked back to the kitchen to plate my dinner, I contemplated which movie I would throw on in the background for this evening's research and wound up back in my reverie of discerning this afternoon's meeting.

Maddy switched off the call from Sophia as Ryan entered the room. That was close! While she didn't care that Sophia had called – she was thrilled in fact – she didn't want Ryan catching her gushing about him. It wouldn't suit, especially since she was already far "gushier" than she knew herself to be in front of any man, and did not want to lose all semblance of cool.

Ryan strode back into her room with a confidence that made her weak in the knees. She loved how different he was from other men she had been with over the years. None of the same bravado, though he certainly had earned it with his career path. No, he was much more secure in himself than "the others," as she was increasingly referring to her past beaus and sighed with contentment.

"Mary is almost ready!" he said and walked over to sit beside her at the chaise in front of her bed, being careful not to wrinkle his freshly ironed pants. It wasn't quite a full tuxedo, but it was a formal suit of sorts. Clearly designed by his sister, it fit him in all the right places, and he wore it very well. She also appreciated that he wasn't going super formal and chose to leave the first few buttons of the white shirt open to reveal his strong neck and the top of his collarbone.

"What is this party theme she is being so secretive about?!" Maddy asked with anticipation, slipping on a black satin opera glove.

"I have no idea." Ryan smirked.

"Yes, you do. And I vow to get it out of you!" she replied while securing the second glove on her left arm.

"Oh yeah? Do your worst," he prodded, in homage to their first meeting. Maddy turned to him to topple him to the ground in a playful swoop, but just then a knock came from the already ajar door.

"Oooo, saved by the knock," Maddy said as she stood up and walked over to the door.

"Yes?" she answered.

"Ms. Carmichael is ready to receive you now," said Bill, the porter, dressed in a costume that Maddy didn't recognize.

She swallowed a laugh as she looked him up and down and noted his obvious displeasure at the role he had been asked to play in tonight's events. Bill raised an eyebrow at her, as if to challenge her further, and she simply put her hands up to her sides in a gesture of surrender. Bill nodded his head in acknowledgment and moved on down the hall.

She turned to Ryan and said, "Ready?" to which he rose from the velvet chaise, grabbed his evening coat from the nearest chair, slinging it over his shoulder, and strode over to her, offering up his arm. They walked out into the hallway arm in arm, and both had a saunter in their respective steps to once again be in each other's company.

Maddy thought back to the first day they had met. After the surprising and life-changing kiss on the grounds, they had gathered Ryan's things from the hill and walked back to the house. Upon entering the side service door near the kitchen, they were greeted by an all-knowing smirk from Bill.

Maddy flushed; he must have witnessed everything! She gave him a pleading look, as if to say, "Please don't tell her yet," and he had just nodded in his way and walked on.

Ryan had thankfully not seen the exchange, as his back was to them while he removed his black leather jacket and placed his equipment in the corner. He looked up and all around the hallway in which they found themselves. It was then that Maddy recalled he was not only a landscape photographer but also specialized in architecture. She assumed he had already been inside to drop off his things, but perhaps Bill had taken everything for him.

Maddy led him out of the hall and into the front of the manor so he could see everything in the bright sunlight. They had yet to say a word and just kept looking at each other and smiling. It was then she recalled he had wanted food. She took him by the hand, as if she had always done so, and led him to the dining room.

As they entered, still in their bubble of silence and looking into each other's eyes, they were greeted with a shrill, "There you are, brother!" and before Maddy knew it, they had dropped hands and a blur that looked like Mary went rushing past her to tackle him. Mary, for all her fashion designing brilliance, was not the most observant of humans, so Maddy hoped she had not noticed the hand-holding or general air about them as Bill had.

She wasn't that lucky. In an unusual burst of awareness, Mary turned to Maddy and looked between them with a knowing look. "So, Maddy, you've met my brother, have you?" Maddy flushed again and nodded sheepishly.

"Oh, lay off, sis, we only just met out on the grounds!" Ryan admonished quickly. He truly was a knight and Maddy gave him a side look of thanks.

Mary smiled, responded with, "I approve" and turned to walk away. Maddy had looked on in surprise and Ryan just laughed. His laugh sounded like a golden sunrise.

She had never heard something so magnetic in her life and wanted to listen to it all day.

Maddy smiled to herself at the memory. It had been several weeks since that first meeting, and they had only grown closer. Ryan would join her on her escapades into the village, and she would wander the grounds with him on her breaks. It was almost like they had become a symbiotic organism that existed for its other half. The fact that Mary had so knowingly "called it" from the start and given her approval had both stunned and excited Maddy. She wouldn't normally go in for any spiritual talk, but there was something different about this.

Just then, Maddy became aware that they were entering the main hall. It was draped in all sorts of fabrics, rich in color and texture, and the whole place was lit by firelight. Candles and candelabras were everywhere, all the fireplaces were going, and you could hear the roaring and whooshing coming from each room.

In the center of the hall, there was a table. At the table sat an older woman. She was dressed like a traditional Romani, long salt and pepper hair falling around her shoulders under a jewel-tone satin headscarf. She had cards spread out on the table in front of her.

It was then Maddy realized, to her utter dismay, the theme of the party. Mary had been incredibly focused on the 16th century for her designs and gone deep in her research of the era. In it, she had also come across all the superstitions of the time and found them fascinating. She had even tried to gain Maddy's thoughts on the subject, but Maddy had politely declined so as not to give away her staunch religious beliefs and complete disregard for anything that went against them. It would have made working for Mary impossible, and yet now there was Ryan.

The party's theme was set around "superstitions," not just those related to the Elizabethan age but throughout time. Mary had found some inspiration in the details that surrounded the topic and woven them into all of her designs for the fall line of the following year.

Every fiber in her being told her she was going to hell for attending this party and she should turn around and go back to her room. She could make a quick and quiet exit, and no one would be the wiser...except for Ryan. She couldn't leave Ryan; she didn't want to leave Ryan. He wouldn't even know why, and she wasn't ready to share that part of herself with him just yet. It was usually the final step in losing someone close to her, as they never understood her fervor.

To be honest, she never understood it either. Her family was not super-religious; her scruples were born completely out of her own mind and not any "nurture" effect from super conservative parents...She would have to find a way to reconcile attending the party with Ryan and any personal misgivings she had. She supposed she could just keep herself on the periphery.

Ryan had noticed the tensing of her arm as they had approached the hall and gave her an inquiring look. He saw the wheels turning behind her eyes and concerned look on her face, but then it quickly faded. She smiled at him, tilted her head, as if to say, "Let's go," and they forged ahead into the night.

Chapter 18 – September 1563 – Ann/Madge

Madge felt guilty. For all the goings-on with her friends, she knew she should be more invested in the outcome, but she could not focus.

The last few months with Simon had been pure bliss. Yes, he was a dairy farmer and that came with its own set of malodorous challenges, but she had ceased to notice the smell in the time they had spent together. Yes, he was also the boy that used to tease her mercilessly when they were children. He, who used to be one of the most unkempt children, running around the village like a feral cat. It was all in good fun, she realized now, as she watched her younger brothers do the same and realized it was simply a boy thing.

Simon as a grown man, however, captured her attention in a different way. His wild sandy hair had grown into rich locks, still unkempt but in a "devil may care" kind of way. His eyes, that seemed to burrow into her soul, were a luminous brown, verging on gold. They were kind and looked at her now with such intensity she felt like she could get lost in the safety of them forever.

She could not believe her luck. Madge was not one to stand out among the other girls in the village. She knew she was not nearly as beautiful as her friend Lizbeth, and being the youngest of her group, she still possessed some naivety, but Simon did not seem to mind. Her shy demeanor was endearing, and she appreciated that she did not have to change herself for him.

His father was older than hers and had already handed over the farm to his care. He had been working there since he was thirteen and had a way with the animals. She thought he seemed to be more comfortable around the cows over which he tended than humans, a fact she secretly loved. It was that awkwardness that drew her to him at first. Gone was the wild child who would run around and pull on her braids, and here was a soft, gentle man who adored her.

It was three months almost to the day that he had approached her. She had been on her way home from her morning walk with her friends in the woods, one of the last she could recall in fact, when he bumped into her on the main street. She had been in her own world, musing about the latest love blessing they had tried at the altar that morning. They did not like to use what traditionally was called for with frog bones and such – it felt wrong and not what Sophia would want – so kept to their herbs and flowers.

They had tried all sorts of combinations in the past, but none of them had seemed to work. That morning, Madge was the only one truly into the task, Ann having stopped doing it after James never returned, which Madge could understand, but she at least had a co-conspirator in Lizbeth. That was until that Mr. Acton had come to town. That morning Lizbeth was not her usual self, and Madge could tell her heart had not been in it. However, she was determined to figure something out.

She was also missing an article of the desired one's clothing, but as they had taken to trying this ritual, they had always said that it mattered not who it was as long as they were kind and loving and chosen by Sophia – they put their trust in her, even though they still knew very little. They loved the notion of a female "higher one" versus the contemporary male version that only seemed to judge. They had gotten the notion from her mother's family tome where she derived all her healing tonics. When looking back through the pages, there was often blessings invoking a "Sophia" and so they took to calling on her.

On this particular morning, she was remembering, she had taken some extra basil from her mother's stockpile. They had tried it in combination with rose petals and lavender before, which was supposed to be the right mix of herbs, but it had yet to do the trick! This time, she loathed the bitter edge it added to what would have been a gorgeous floral bouquet, so she wanted to add something else. She had read vanilla was another great ingredient, but as that was nowhere to be found in her village, she decided to add a pinch of cinnamon, a spice of good luck and abundance.

They would normally mix these things together in a hollowed-out piece of rock they found nearby, go through an entire ritual of placing this on top of the altar and then circle the structure three times sunwise to bring in the abundance they so hoped for. However, on this morning, as Madge was the only one in the spirit of the endeavor, she let the other two sit off to the side. Ann was at least assisting with the process, but Lizbeth seemed to be in another world.

Madge did not let it stop her. She mixed the herbs, placed them in five heaps along the top of the altar and drew the Nordic rune she had memorized from her set that represented love, which to her looked like an upside-down key, in the middle of the stone. She started around the altar with a new saying she had written the night before. It had just come to her, like a dream, and she thought it worth a try, though she knew full well that she was trying so many different things this morning that, if it worked, she would not know which to thank!

North, South, East, West
Come to me at my behest
On wings of a dove, bring love to me
Hear my request
So mote it be times three

She proceeded to say it three times as she circled the altar. Ann had complimented her on the new word play for the blessing and thought it very fine. She asked where she had gotten it, and Madge had told her it just popped in her head the evening before. Ann smiled and sat down. Her friend had often guided them in this same way.

The ritual done, they did not like to burn the offering as one might do and instead always left it atop the stone and let the winds do with it what it will and give it back to nature. Madge had thought to bring an extra rose for good measure and left that in the middle of the stone, hoping it would so honor Sophia that maybe this time they would be heard. She had not realized she had spoken the words with such fervor until she felt her raspy throat, in need of a drink.

The girls had all walked out of the wood together and went their separate ways. Ann to likely check on her father and brother in the field, Lizbeth to go back to her house, though she seemed reluctant. Madge wondered why. Mr. Acton had come to the village, and surely as he was a gentleman, Lizbeth would be more interested in being around him and learning news of London and such, especially since it was quite uncommon for someone of any stature to visit this part of England. She was so lost in those thoughts as she headed home that she bumped into Simon.

She was about to protest when she looked up to see the face of her "assailant" shining down on her with bemused awkwardness. He was clearly flustered at having unwittingly knocked her to the ground and yet anxious to help her up to her feet. "I-I-I-I…" he started to sputter.

Madge stepped in. "It is fine. I was not looking where I was going, lost in my own head."

He breathed a sigh of relief and yet seemed to want to say something else.

Madge looked at him expectantly, which only turned his face redder. "I am fine, really," she said and turned to move on when she heard him, half under his breath.

"I am glad, Miss Williams. For I would not want to have c-c-caused damage to your person…or your he-he-he-head," he forced out.

She blushed. Well, that was kind, she thought to herself. For the first time, she looked up into his eyes, which was troublesome, since he kept them downcast. "Thank you, Mr. Oliver. You are very kind."

She turned and started walking away. She ventured a look back at him to see if he had left the spot and found, much to her surprise – and delight – he was still in the spot where they had collided, watching her walk away.

If she had not believed in magic before that day, she surely would have converted right then. She felt her heart skip a beat and suddenly knew, if she had to conduct the ritual in the woods again, whose clothing she would be hoping to add to the center. But something told her that was the last time that particular combination of offerings would ever be used. Sophia had heard her and granted her heart's wish.

She had been right. The next few weeks and months passed as a blur, and she recollected each stolen moment with relish. Simon had begun to call on her in the evenings after his work was done for the day. The first time he alighted on the doorstep, her mother gave a knowing glance while her father seemed to be completely oblivious. When Simon asked if they could go for an evening stroll, he looked concerned, but thankfully her mother stepped in and cajoled him into allowing it.

It would not be a long walk, as the days were getting darker quicker and quicker as the fall wore on, but she drank up every moment. Madge had to carry most of the conversation until Simon got comfortable enough with her to loosen his tongue and then the stutter would almost disappear. They talked of many things during these times: likes and dislikes, hopes and fears, future plans. At first, their answers had been separate, but the more time they spent together, the more they began to intertwine.

Three months had gone by in a flash. Now, their walks became more frequent during the day, such that they were no longer relegated to just taking evening strolls, as it was getting far too dark to enjoy them anyway. Simon would find any time he could to spend in her company, even if only for five minutes when he had to fetch water, a task usually reserved for the farmhand – he had taken to doing it himself for the excuse to see Madge.

Only yesterday he had stolen a kiss on her cheek when no one was looking. She immediately flushed and whipped her head to give him a questioning look, but he was gone, back to the farm to conclude his chores.

When she had come home, her mother could tell something was different and merely smiled to herself and remarked that she had been spending an increasing amount of time with Mr. Oliver and perhaps it was time they had him over for dinner to sit with the family. Madge was so happy she threw her arms around her mother's neck and cried, "Oh, Mother, yes, please!"

"Good, I will talk with your father," she replied and went back to making her latest tincture. The winter months were coming at a rapid pace, and she was busy preparing the salves, ointments and elixirs, ready for the villagers' needs.

Madge was practically beside herself waiting for her father to come home so they could set the plan in motion. She was most anxious to know whether he would allow it, and how soon it could be planned, and the look on Simon's face when she told him. She stopped her flow of thoughts just long enough to begin doubting his intentions and whether he would truly be happy at the invitation, then quickly realized that was a silly notion and let it pass through her mind.

That evening, Madge made sure she attended to her father's every need, in such a way that amused him. She knew her mother would not make the request until after the children had gone to bed and her parents were sitting by the fire going through their individual days with the last of the season's cider warming in their mugs. She vowed she would try to sleep instead of listening in on the conversation, as she was afraid she might let out a sound at whatever response was given, but found when the time came, she was too restless. She crept out of her room and toward the front of the house, staying in the shadows and being as quiet as she could, or so she thought. She came upon the conversation already underway…

"Yes, dear. Simon Oliver," Eliza said.

"But whatever for?" Nicholas replied.

"Honestly, Nick, you can be quite thick-headed at times. Madge and Simon have been going on walks together practically every day for the past several months. Have you not noticed?" she asked.

"I guess I had but had gotten so used to the idea of Madge always being around that I turned a blind eye, not thinking about our baby girl leaving the household."

Madge felt a pang of guilt for making her father feel that way, but also a touch of reproachment. Was she not to have her own life? She turned her attention back to the conversation, not wanting to miss anything.

"I know, my husband, but she is of age, past it some would say, and Simon is a good man from what I understand. He has been running the farm on his own these past two years since old Mr. Oliver became too frail to do so himself. He takes such care with the animals and is known to be incredibly kind," her mother continued.

"If not known to be very well spoken, my dear. How will Madge manage with someone who can barely speak to people?" her father asked.

"I do not think conversation is a problem between the two of them. I think our Madge brings out the best in the young man and it is a solid match," Eliza said with as much confidence and support as she could. At this, Madge heard silence and could picture her father taking a sip of his warm cider and leaning back in his heirloom rocking chair to contemplate the situation.

"Oh, alright," she heard him huff. "I suppose it is about time, and if they have been spending as much time together as you say, then it is the proper thing to do. You can tell Madge in the morning, but send William to make the request. I will not have her bounding over to the poor man while he is working with his cows and interrupting his very important job!" he concluded.

"No need to tell her in the morning," her mother said, and before she knew it, Madge was being summoned. "Madge, come here, we've something to tell you, though I am certain you already heard."

Madge could not deny it, so she sheepishly came out into the light of the front room. Her father looked confused and then realized what she had been doing with an amused smile. She padded across the stone floor of the house, watching the light from the fireplace dance across the whitewashed walls and wooden beams in the ceiling.

"Yes, Mother?" Madge tried being coy, but that only annoyed her mother.

"You know very well what, my child. Your father has consented to having Simon over for dinner. What shall we say, in a fortnight?" Eliza thought out loud.

Nicholas saw Madge's face fall at having to wait for so long and quickly stepped in to help his daughter. "Let us say one week from now, Eliza. I think the poor girl will faint if we wait too long."

"Thank you, Father." Madge beamed. "I will tell him tomorrow!" and she turned on her heel to get back to bed before they could say otherwise.

"You will do no such thing, young lady!" her father called after her. "We will send William with the invitation so as not to invite unnecessary speculation," he finished.

Madge turned to face them again. Blast, she was not fast enough.

"Oh, come now, Nicholas. William may delay in getting the message to him, and you have that big job for Mr. Acton. Surely you cannot spare his apprenticeship, and Robert is too young to send the invite. Best let Madge ask him when she sees him in the morning to be sure it is delivered," her mother said with a wry smile.

Madge looked expectantly from one parent to the other, secretly crossing her fingers behind her back.

As if to test her patience, her father waited an extra measure before responding with, "Oh, alright."

At that, Madge practically ran back to her room, on tiptoes so as not to disturb her sisters while they slept, and jumped into bed. The morning could not come fast enough.

Chapter 19 – November, Present Day – Kit

Where was it? Kit was rummaging around on her desk for the latest article she had been reading on sound baths and their calming effects for those with PTSD. It was a lesser form of treatment that had not caught on in the community at large yet, but she found the topic fascinating and was trying to bridge the gap between the medical community and the spiritual one.

It had become her raison d'être of late. Anyone who knew her growing up would have known her to be a slightly sensational girl, though still logic-based. That was why the thought of psychology had been so titillating to her, a true marriage of science and conscience. The human brain was a marvel, and she loved diving in to learn about the way neurons formed and fired, affecting people's ability to make decisions and the motivations behind them. The further she delved into the world of the energetic healing modalities, and the known effects, the more she wanted to lean on it for solutions over traditional medicine.

There was a whole world opening up to her, one of herbal medicine and holistic practices. She was certain that if she could only absorb everything that was out there, she might find a better way to approach the abnormal psychology field, while also helping to devise non-pharmaceutical strategies for those with PTSD.

Thora had come in just then, as she had gotten home from school a few moments ago. When Thora saw the piece of paper on the floor with pictures of herbs on it, she picked it up and excitedly handed it to her. "Mommy! Are you into plants too?! They are so good for you," she said.

Kit, always wanting to support her children's interests, replied, "Yes, baby girl. I'm looking into how plants and herbs might be a better approach to help my patients than traditional medicine."

"Well, that's cool! There are so many good ones out there," Thora continued.

Still searching for the paper she just had in her hand but not wanting to lose the conversation thread, Kit replied, "Oh, yeah? Like what?" Ah, there it was, buried under a different article on the efficacy of sound baths and opening of chakra points.

"Well, there's ginger for upset tummies, chamomile for making you calmer, and mint for helping your belly too..." she started. Kit was impressed. "Then the one I can't quite say...something about an echo..."

"Echinacea?" Kit asked.

"Yeah! That's for staying healthy, and lavender can help when you are feeling anxious," she continued. Again, somewhat basic if one had ever looked into herbal medicine, but how did her eight-year-old know these things?

"Where did you hear all this, baby? Are you studying something different in school?" Kit inquired.

"No, I just like to learn about all the different plants and what they do. Did you know that back in the day, instead of doctors, a lot of villages had people that were called 'healers,' and their job was to help people feel better?!" This was amazing knowledge for someone her age. Kit wasn't completely shocked since Thora did have an old-school way about her. She was smarter than the average bear.

"I did know that, pumpkin. How did you?" Kit asked.

"I saw it in my dream." She tipped her head and walked away.

"Oh, that's ni...what?!" Kit said. She processed what her daughter had just said. Based on Tate's revelation that started this whole spiral into the unknown, she wasn't sure what to expect with his twin also having a somewhat alarming dream that revealed secrets of the past. She thought she better investigate while the house was still calm and followed Thora out into the kitchen.

"What do you mean you saw it in a dream, pumpkin?" she said.

"What?" Thora responded, already moving onto another topic in her head. Kit just looked at her. "Oh, yeah, I kept seeing plants and flowers in my dreams a couple weeks ago. You always said that I should look up what those things mean if I remember them in the morning, so I did. I found out that there are a lot of plants out there that have very cool ways of helping people. A lot used to be based on the belief that the shape and look of the plant would tell you what it was used for. I don't quite get that part yet, but I felt like in my dream I knew what I was doing with the plants, picking them, hanging them to dry, so I thought maybe I needed to know in my waking life too!" And with that, Thora turned and walked away, as if they had just been describing the weather.

Kit stood there, not quite sure how to respond. With Thora's obvious nonchalance on the topic, she thought it best to take the cue from her daughter and not delve further, although that was all she wanted to do. Mental note made to speak with Sophia about it later, she moved farther into the kitchen to get a snack prepared. It was a Thursday, so Tate would be coming home from the Ninja Warrior gym in a little bit. She and Erik liked the twins to have separate activities too so they could have their own friend groups. It was important that they developed their own identities.

Tate had taken to ninja as easily as if he were a cat. She said it had to have been Erik's genetics, as hers were more likely to have made him fall flat on his face. He loved it! He would glide across the agility courses with ease and had already won a few local championships for his age level. Erik couldn't have been prouder and saw a real future for him, if he was to maintain the speed and agility with which he performed now. For what, she didn't know, and with his military background, she was afraid to ask, but she was glad they got some father/son bonding time during the week.

Thora was a bit more of a challenge. She wasn't a super girly girl, but neither was she a complete tomboy. She loved when her dance season was in full swing, but also when she had golf and softball going too. In fact, there wasn't much she couldn't do when it came to sports and activities, which was awesome for growth, but difficult when it came time to choose what she was going to dedicate herself to. There were too many choices and things she enjoyed, so sometimes she did nothing. She was in between seasons of everything at the moment so was relegated to two dance classes on Monday nights.

"Mommy…" Thora started.

"Hmmm" was Kit's response as she opened the fridge to contemplate the options for dinner. Thora paused as she wrestled with what her next statement would be.

The secondary choice must have won because the energy shifted and she responded with, "How was your day? What are you working on?"

She may be a handful at times, but Thora really was the most thoughtful child she'd ever met. She wasn't sure if all children asked their parents these questions, but she truly appreciated when hers did. Even if they didn't understand what she did at times, it was the thought that counted, and she was always touched when they would think to ask.

"Well…I'm working on that paper I was telling you about before. The research on how sound can potentially help those who have PTSD," she said.

"Right," Thora acknowledged and then turned pensive again.

"What is it you want to ask, pumpkin?" Kit inquired, realizing that perhaps it was her being distracted that was keeping her daughter from asking what was on her mind.

"Um, nothing really," she said coyly.

"It's OK, doll, you can ask me anything. Shoot!" Kit turned her full attention to her daughter.

"Um, OK. So, all the plant research I've been doing…I was wondering. Could I get a special book to start keeping notes in and find different recipes to try?" she asked sheepishly.

Kit wasn't sure why this was so hard for her to ask but responded with, "Of course, dove. Why on earth would you be so nervous to ask that?" and turned to look in the fridge again. Maybe her own episode of *Chopped* would do the trick for the mish-mash of ingredients.

"Well, because I've read that when you do that, the books are called a grim-something-or-other and I might be a witch then," Thora said, mumbling the last part under her breath.

Kit whirled around. Where on earth would she have gotten that notion? And how had they gotten back on that topic? Thora seemed to have been disinterested at the time.

"Where did you hear that?" Kit asked in as calm a voice as possible.

"When I was looking up information about what effects plants can have. I saw something about how healers back in the day had special books and that their ability to heal people was compared to powers and that a lot of them were accused of witchcraft," she said and looked like she was about to cry. "I've always loved plants and got excited when I thought I could do more with them than just look at them or use them in my art projects, but I didn't want to be called a witch!"

Kit tried not to laugh. For all the ways her children were incredibly old souls, there were times when their innocence shone through.

"And I heard you and Auntie Sophia talking on the phone the other day about how you had to be careful exploring all the new spirit stuff you were looking into because you didn't want to set off another witch hunt in the 21st century, and then I got nervous that what I wanted to do was bad, if what you guys are doing is bad too," she poured out, almost as if her sentence was made up of one long word.

Kit sat down at the tall chair near the breakfast island and patted her lap. Thora may be growing like a weed, but she could still fit on her mother's lap, and she wasn't ready to give that up yet. Her daughter walked over with her head bent down and hopped up into her rightful place.

"First of all, what Auntie Sophia and I were talking about…we were joking. Second, what we are researching is not bad, or witchcraft or anything like that. Third, what were you doing listening in on my private phone call, little one?" She looked at Thora with an eyebrow raised and tickled her. Thora giggled but didn't answer. "And lastly, what you are talking about is quite advanced for your age, but then again you always have been ahead of everyone else. It may not be common practice to keep a book of plants and herbs and study their effects, but there is no harm in it!" Kit assured her.

"OK," she said in a meek voice. "But…" Kit waited again to let her finish her thought. "Why are you and Auntie Sophia being so secretive? If it isn't bad, I mean. You are whispering all the time, or texting her, or going to the bookstore and looking up topics that you seem to be afraid of other people knowing about," she continued.

That smarted. Man, was her child observant. Thora was right. If it wasn't bad, why was she behaving that way? There was nothing wrong with wanting to educate oneself on a different modality for health, or a different way of understanding the world, or finding out more about what had happened in the past. Why was she acting like she was guilty?

"Well, those are all very valid points, little one, ones that I will have to take under advisement. Nothing we are doing is wrong. I think Auntie Sophia and I are being so secretive because it is something new we are both learning, a new perspective, and until we each become much more fluent in the knowledge, we want to keep everything to ourselves. Does that make sense?" she finished.

Thora seemed to consider this while also eyeing the fridge. "Yes," she answered.

"Good. If you'd like, once we get through this week, we can hop online and look at grimoire options for you and choose one. Christmas is coming and will be here before we know it!" Kit said while patting Thora's back.

"GrimOIRE!" she repeated. "That's the word! Thanks, Mom."

Kit couldn't help but smile to herself after Thora hopped off her lap and bounded back to the play area just outside the kitchen. She was so observant and had clearly been watching every move Kit made. She would have to be more careful in the future, especially if she didn't want her daughter to catch wind of anything before she was ready.

Just then, her cell phone buzzed. It couldn't have been the boys, but she had a sense she should look anyway. It was Sophia, as if the mere thought of her conjured her into existence. She answered, "Soph! How the heck…" but she was cut off.

She sat and listened as her eyes grew wider, trying to take in the incoherency from the opposite end. "Say no more. Erik should be home with Tate any minute. As soon as they're home, I'm grabbing my keys and heading to you. We can walk through everything then. We will get this sorted, I promise!" Kit said emphatically.

The change in the tone of her mother's voice drew Thora back into the room with an inquiring look. Before Thora could ask, Kit held her hand up to silence her while she finished on the phone. As soon as she hung up, she called Erik to see what their ETA was.

"Great, thanks, love. As soon as you get home, I have to run over to Sophia's," she shared with her husband. "Yeah, she was a mess. It will take more than a phone call for this one. I want to make sure she's OK, with everything going on…Thanks! Love you. See you soon."

"Mommy…" Thora started.

"It's OK, everything is fine. Auntie Sophia just had a rough day at work and needs to talk with me. As soon as your brother and Daddy get home, I'm going to pop over there. Do you mind helping Daddy fix dinner?" Kit said, almost in one breath.

"Sure!" Thora said excitedly. This kid was from another century. This seemed even more evident now with the latest revelation of her wanting to learn "plant magic" on top of already loving to cook and play housekeep. No sooner had Thora walked over to the fridge to cast the same inspection Kit just had than they heard the garage door open. With that, Kit grabbed her keys and her long puffer vest and raced out the door.

Whatever had happened had been enough to practically unhinge her friend, and that wasn't something that could be left to a phone call. On her quick fifteen-minute drive to Sophia's house, she mused to herself about the interaction she had with Thora that afternoon. Plant medicine, grimoires, past lives and Goddess knows what else; there really were more mysteries than answers in this world. And it was an exciting thought. There was so much left to discover...

Chapter 20 – November 1563 – Ann

It was a cold morning. Made even colder after what had happened the day before.

I could not believe it. The fortnight had come and gone, as did the weeks leading up to the supposed "blessed" occasion. The traditional "Crying of the Banns" had been used, though not in a truly traditional sense since our church had no bell. Still the announcement had been made thrice and no one objected to the marriage. I had to fight every urge to speak with Lizbeth's father. I had made her a promise in our sacred space. I could not break that vow, but after yesterday, how I wished I would have.

The village gathered for the wedding of my dearest friend and soul sister, Miss Elizbeth White, to Mr. Richard Acton. Everyone was there, save one. I had not expected him to show up, as I imagined it too painful for such a sensitive soul, but I had hoped. Perhaps if Robert had made an appearance, Lizbeth would have been snapped out of her trance and remembered not only who she was, but that this match was not what she wanted. However, Robert, I was informed, had not come within a hundred yards of the place and spent the day and best part of the evening wandering in the woods, as was his way.

Mr. White was all smiles. Not only was his daughter marrying someone of a more elevated station but to one who had offered a reverse dowry – an unheard-of accord – thus ensuring her future happiness, or so he thought.

For how could she not be happy to have won such a prize? Had he known what I knew, he would have reconsidered what he was essentially forcing Lizbeth to do. I knew he was not disappointed at having taken her away from Robert, a man with low prospects. However, if Lizbeth's father had known the full measure of the man to which he was giving his only daughter, he may have thought more of poor Robert and his simple ways.

Of course, Lizbeth looked gorgeous. She had taken her mother's wedding gown to my own mother for modifications. Made of a blue taffeta, the color had faded slightly with age. Its bell sleeves had a beautiful gold trim of a higher fashion unavailable to the villagers at the time, but since our mothers had been girlhood friends, and my mother was an expert seamstress, she was always able to get her hands on some extra "bits and bobs" to make things special. The lace that lined the decolletage area was sorely in need of repair after some moth-eaten holes were discovered. My mother was able to fashion a fill-in scrim with a thin linen such that it created a similar effect but was a bit warmer, a thoughtful consideration given the time of year.

The effect was magnificent. I had gone over in the morning to help Lizbeth with her hair and make sure she had everything gathered for her evening. She was to stay on the outskirts of the village on the land Mr. Acton had procured after the engagement announcement. That had been what Madge's father was working on for him. As a carpenter, he was able to set a base structure for which the happy couple would be able to start the first building on the property. Richard said it was his wedding present to her, and they would build their house there.

I thought it interesting that he had not referred to it as a "home" but chalked it up to him being a man. He could not possibly be so without feeling that he could have purposely meant it, could he? After all, at least he was not taking Lizbeth back to London or somewhere else in the kingdom, and we could still be nearby. While the house was not nearly ready – they had only broken ground a couple weeks ago – there was a rudimentary outbuilding erected on the property that Mr. Acton meant to use for their wedding night.

I admired my sad friend as we worked her dark locks into a Guineverean look. Lizbeth had opted not to place her gorgeous raven hair in a high motif to frame her face, as ladies were wont to do in formal social situations, but rather wanted it to be simple, unfussy and, I thought to myself, something she might be able to hide her face with throughout the day. She may be sad and have succumbed to her fate, but nothing could take away the natural beauty. I thought I would try one last-ditch effort.

Madge and I had been attempting to talk sense into her for weeks now. To come clean with her father about what Mr. Acton had done, what we were told he had then accused her of to her father and forcing herself on him, and how she could not possibly marry someone of his character. She would not hear it. She was defeated and did not want to speak on it any more.

I think she still secretly hoped that her ritual in the woods would manifest a way out, something that would block whatever it was fate had in store, but clearly that was not the case. I had not mentioned it to her, but I had seen that fateful harbinger nearby, my dark owl, as she finished that day. As I suspected, Sophia had not shown her guiding hand through any of this, making our sacred spot feel more abandoned than ever. What Lizbeth had done, wherever it came from, had significantly affected and altered the energy of our space and none of us had been back since.

I opened my mouth to speak, but before I could get a word out, Lizbeth's hand was up in a calm repose, and she simply said, "No. What is done is done. If Sophia sees it fit I should marry this man, I must believe there is a greater purpose. For that is what we have always learned, is it not? That the universe has a grander design, and we are at its mercy?"

I closed my mouth. I could tell anything I said today would be in vain. Plus, had I not said it all already?

Poor Madge had run herself ragged trying to find the right combination of words and herbs to help, but to no avail. Her mother was baffled by the sudden increase in remedies and advice needed, and asked who was ill, but Madge had kept it to herself. If she revealed one, she would have to reveal all, and that would not be staying true to Lizbeth's wishes. Even her runes had not changed their sad message, that there would not be a change for the better. We ignored the warning that constantly crept alongside them, one of darkness and death.

As I watched Lizbeth approach the church doors, I saw her steely resolve. I also saw flames of pain behind her eyes, those dark, expressive eyes, once lit by stardust and magic, now full of something else. Madge and I stood together with Simon next to her. We decided to stand apart from our families, as we struggled with what was taking place and could not hold a steady face. The vows were said, rings exchanged, and nuptial mass conducted. Everyone filed out of the chapel to go to the barn of old Mr. Tracy for the celebration. He was the only one with space enough to host us all under one roof.

The night had worn on. Madge and I did our duty by pretending to smile and accepted platitudes on Lizbeth's behalf. "Oh, is it not wonderful!" and "Quite the catch he is!" and my personal favorite, "She is so lucky, that one!" After a while, my head felt as if it would fall off from all the nodding.

Simon had sensed something was amiss but had the good graces not to ask while in public and instead chose to whisk Madge away onto the dance floor, any excuse to have her in his arms. I was happy for them. Madge deserved to feel special, especially as one of many in her household. I sat there thinking it probably would not be long before we went through the same ritual all over again for those two. Simon had taken to dining with the Williams almost every night for the past month. He was sure to ask her father the question soon.

Staying in the corner on my little wooden chair, I began having an internal conversation with a familiar voice. "He will not treat her well," I heard a man say in a soothing but warning tone.

"I know, that is my fear," I found myself saying aloud. To whom I had not a clue, yet a response came.

"Why did you not talk with Henry?" it said.

"I made a promise to her that I would not," I replied.

"Ann." I smiled at the way my name sounded, the deep, masculine voice smooth like honey. "Ann!" it said more powerfully and urgently. And I woke up.

Was the voice part of my dream, or had I been remembering what had actually transpired last night? I did recall sitting in the chair in the corner of the barn, watching the party pass by. And who was the voice? I did not say the possibility out loud, to prevent both raising my hopes and sounding positively mad.

My intuition had sometimes taken on a voice of its own, but this was markedly different. Like I was having a true conversation. Under normal circumstances I would go to the wood to commune in our space to understand what was happening, but as we had not yet purged it of the dark energies Lizbeth brought forth, I did not think it wise.

I lay in bed deliberating. Of course, with the temperature outside my covers, I did not want to move. Adding in everything I had just remembered from the day before, I was even less inclined to get up and start the daily tasks. Given the place the sun occupied in the sky, I was well past my normal early morning chores and should be going along to check on Father in the field. I would have to pass by the new outbuilding on Mr. Acton's property…

That was motivation enough. Perhaps I could convince Madge to come for a walk with me. She too did not appreciate the cold, but I was positive that for this endeavor, she would make an exception. I may even be able to share my dream with her, tell her about the voice without her thinking me infirm. We both knew I had a stellar intuition, which manifested itself as a voice at times, but this was different. It had taken on an effect of...I dared not say it.

I jumped out of bed and hurried to at least get my stockings and shoes on before bearing the cold wooden floor beneath my feet. My chemise was like ice as I replaced my nightgown and layered my woolen tunic followed by my daily dress. The wool chafed as an additional layer, but the extra warmth would be needed for my walk. I pinned my hair up so I could more easily put my winter bonnet on and create a barrier with the collar of my cloak, then walked down from my loft into the kitchen.

It was warmer here, as any heart of the home should be, and my mother had kindly left some toast, beans and sausage out by the fireplace. She knew I was not happy about what had transpired yesterday but thought it merely a girl's misgivings at losing her friend to marriage. She could never imagine all I had witnessed and heard, that Lizbeth was gone to me in more ways than one.

There was a note on the counter. My mother had gone to pick up her parcel of seamstress supplies she had ordered from Mr. White and to place another request. The alterations she had made to Lizbeth's dress had cleaned her out of her "fancy" trimmings, and since cobbling often required similar resources, she and Mr. White had started pooling their orders to his vendors years ago for cost-efficiency. That, and it was much easier for Mr. White to make and receive requests as a man than it was for my mother. She had tried for years and receipt of the items for which she had pre-paid was half at best.

I shoveled the slightly warm food into my mouth, washed it down with some ale my father had left out and walked to the door, with a new resolve to check on my friend under the guise of delivering well wishes for the happy couple. But I would need something to bring if that was the case!

I looked about to see what we had lying around that would suffice. Instead, I grabbed the basket by the door, walked out into the daylight and set off to Madge's. Her mother would likely have some extra herbs and tinctures that we could collect and deliver to the happy couple as remedies for the winter weather. It was perfect!

I hurried along to the Williams' and knocked on the door. Joan, the middle daughter, answered with Amelia and Rebecca at her heels. She rolled her eyes when she turned to look behind her to see what I was smirking at. "Uggghh, why are you two always following me?!" she said with exasperation.

I stunted my smile and looked at her with as much seriousness as I could muster. "Joan, it is likely because they look up to you and want to be just like you," I exclaimed.

She paused to consider. I saw a smile creep onto her young face and soften her previously reproachful glare.

Just then, Robert, the middle son, came into view and shouted, "No, they do not. They find you annoying and were hoping you were leaving out the front door!"

Joan's smile dropped and she turned to yell back at him but decided against it. She turned to me with the grace of the woman of the house and said, "How can I help you, Miss Hughes?"

I stifled a laugh at the formality. "I am here to see your sister," I replied.

"She is not in at present. Is there something I can help you with?" she answered.

Just then, I heard Mrs. Williams call from the back of the house, "Who is it, Joan? Close the door before you let out ALL the warm air!" Joan ushered me in from the doorway but stood in my path so as not to enter any farther than necessary.

"It is just I, Mrs. Williams!" I called.

"Oh, Ann, dear girl. How are you this morning? You looked a bit peaky last night if I may be so bold."

My cheeks flushed. Had she seen me talking to myself? "Too much excitement in one day, I imagine," I quickly said.

"I can imagine, love. First one friend and soon..." She trailed off, realizing she had started to say too much.

I arched my eyebrow in response and wanted to question her further, but with so many little ears around us, I did not think it wise. I nodded my head slightly, as if to indicate I understood and continued. "I was looking for Madge. Joan said she is not in?"

Mrs. Williams kept working on her latest batch of horseradish. Once I realized what it was, and why she had a piece of linen tied over her nose, my eyes started to water. "Sorry, love, the Gilman girls up the road have a touch of the congestion and Mrs. Gilman is stopping by soon to pick up this chest compress." I nodded in understanding and waited for her to continue. "Madge went out early this morning. Earlier than I expected after all of her exertions last night, but I have a fair mind she was taking some of my fresh honey and wine mixture to Simon to keep him from getting sick while he works outside. Would you like some, dear?"

I shook my head. "No, thank you," I said, slightly deflated.

"Was there something else you needed?" she asked, sensing that I was there with a purpose.

"I had only thought..." I started, "that perhaps we could go visit Lizbeth this morning and bring the happy couple some of your winter remedies, should you have extra that you can spare. They are only living in the outbuilding at this time, not that it is not a fine building – being built by Mr. Williams and all – but I would not want either of them to be caught without some of your wonderful elixirs!" A few extra compliments could always go a long way, I thought. Or had I just heard the voice tell me that? I shook my head to silence it.

Mrs. Williams smiled. "I know what you are doing, Ann Hughes, and it will absolutely work! Yes, of course. I have an extra jug of the honey and wine mixture I just spoke of. They will want to take that in the morning and evening if they feel a cold coming on. I also have..." She trailed off as she wiped her hands on her skirts and looked in her stocked cabinet. "Here. It is a bottle of ache and anise with violet seeds. Sounds awful, I know, but if they cook it with wine until it's thick, it will help with any dry coughs. Oooo, I also have this..." she said as she reached toward the back of the cabinet and took out a small glass container. She held it out for me.

We may not have done so in a while, but all three of us at one time or another had trained with Mrs. Williams to learn about the different remedies and herbs. "Can you guess this one?" she queried.

I took a strong whiff; it smelled sage-like, but not quite sage, mixed with mint and something subtle. "Hmmm," I thought out loud, "is it your wormwood, mint and balm salve?"

She beamed. "Very good! You always were a quick study. Now, what is it used for?" she asked.

I stared at her, completely blanking, and then that masculine voice piped up. "Well, they may need it after all the mead and ale consumed last night," it chortled. I smiled. I had not heard that laugh in far too long. I looked at Mrs. Williams, who had now dropped her playful gaze and was evaluating me.

"To treat stomach pains and sickness. Likely something they will need after last night's festivities," I added, more for the benefit of the voice than myself.

"Yes," she replied, more warily this time. I looked back at her, trying to fix my face so there were no telltale signs of what was actually occurring.

"Do you think that is enough? I am afraid that is all I can spare at the moment," she finished.

"Absolutely! I appreciate this more than you know. Thank you, Mrs. Williams," I said, feeling her gaze on me.

"My pleasure, love," she said, turning back to her horseradish.

I packed the goodies carefully into my basket and walked toward the door to leave. My eyes were beginning to water from being so close to the ground horseradish and I needed some fresh air, even if it was cold. The children who were home scrambled around, either chasing each other or performing their chores. It was a warm and welcoming home. I hoped it was something Lizbeth could create for herself, but I had strong doubts.

"Thank you again!" I called and swiftly went out the door.

I had hoped to have strength in numbers as I went on my self-assigned errand. However, with Madge's attention elsewhere, I would have to take care of it myself. I kept walking farther away from the center of the village to the outskirts. The land was rather stark, a perfect place for a person such as Mr. Acton, but I had trouble seeing my lively Lizbeth there, though it had been months since she had been lively if I was honest with myself. What was there to do to keep her entertained?

I supposed once the house was built, she would have her own garden to tend to, but right now, it looked as though they were serfs squatting on the nobleman's land without permission, in a faraway corner where they could not be found.

I approached the scruffy door and knocked, as lightly as I could so as not to push the door off its rickety hinges but loud enough to be heard. No one came. While I had not yet had my own wedding bed, I assumed by this time they would be up and about. I knocked again. Finally, I heard stirrings from within and stepped back from the door so I would not be in the face of whoever opened it. There were boots scuffing the floor and low grumblings could be heard coming closer and closer. I was not sure if I was about to be met by a human or animal.

The door opened and a bloodshot-eyed Mr. Acton peered out to see who was disturbing his obviously fretful slumber. He practically recoiled into the darkness at the bright light streaming in, making me think of the vampire stories I had heard. I tried not to laugh.

"What. Do. You. Want," he forced out. There was that acrid smell again; he must have over-imbibed at the celebration last night.

"I am here to see Miss Whi...Mrs....the lady of the house," I corrected, keeping my voice as even and calm as possible but not able to call her by her new last name. This man truly set my skin aflame.

"She is indisposed," he curtly replied.

"My apologies, sir. I only came to bring..." I started and saw a door crack open in the background. "I only came to bring some of Mrs. Williams' treatments, most helpful to have on hand during the winter months. There is one for—"

"There will be NONE of that sorcery in this household," he seethed, the large silver cross glinting on his chest.

I was taken aback. I had known others to be wary of herbal practices, but Mrs. Williams' salves and elixirs? "But sir..."

"But nothing!" he bellowed. I saw the figure behind the cracked door recede into the anteroom and the door silently close after them.

"Where is Lizbeth?" I questioned, more firmly this time. He just stared back at me, not aware that I had seen her face appear behind him.

I was clearly not going to get anywhere with this man, nor was I going to be able to put my eyes on Lizbeth to be sure she was well. I would have to find another way to get the basket of Mrs. Williams' goodies to her. Without a word, I nodded my head to him to bid him good day and turned to walk away. I had only taken a few steps when I heard his unmistakable sneer, "Thou shalt not suffer a witch to live."

It almost stopped me in my tracks, but the voice inside my head urged me on to safety. I felt a pair of eyes boring into my back until I heard the door close, and I started safely back on the road home.

A witch? Was that truly what he thought of us? Herbalists at the most, silly girls playing with flowers and herbs at the least. Was it he who had ventured to the woods that day and broken the boundary of our sacred space? It would not surprise me. Perhaps, under the right light, one could see us as such, but having kept up with the laws from London and Edinburgh, none of us thought we qualified as witches. For this repugnant louse of a man to make such an accusation against us, and in light of basic herbal remedies, my concern flew to Mrs. Williams before the rest of our trio.

Whatever the case, his fervor spelled trouble for Lizbeth and possibly the rest of the town if our original musings about his chain and Bible turned out to be true.

Chapter 21 – November, Present Day – Sophia

Where was I going to start? I had just hung up a call with Kit, who was now on her way over.

The day had begun like any other. Wake up, get ready, grab coffee and bag, kiss Vi, head to campus. Even classes seemed a bit mundane, probably because it was the end of semester and everyone was starting to zone out. Winter break had been well earned by this latest crew, and I was happy I could do for them what I had done for others in the past.

Thankfully, their midterms had been so exemplary I had canceled the final. All that was left for my older classes was the capstone project, which they were to present at the next class, then I was going to give them the entire week of Thanksgiving off. I knew all too well that having a class the week of Thanksgiving would be in vain, so I rolled with the punches.

It was another email from the dean that had set me off. I had an odd sense come over me anytime I saw his name in my inbox. Chalk it up to old habits dying hard from the corporate world, and possibly some latent PTSD from being "attacked from behind" in a past life, I just sensed something was off. He wanted to see me once classes concluded for the day. Since there wasn't much going on, and I had given them class time to finalize projects with their groups, I dismissed my last section a little early, packed up my things, shut down the tech hub and moseyed on over to the dean's office.

I waited outside his office for about fifteen minutes before LaShonda let me in. She had tried to make small talk with me, but with my anxiety through the roof, I wasn't much of a conversationalist. Finally, I was allowed to enter. I walked tentatively into the room, and LaShonda closed the door behind me. I knew it was a gesture of politeness; however, I couldn't help but feel like she had shut the lid on my coffin.

Dean Smith was a nice enough guy. He had been Dean of the College in which I taught for going on fifteen years now. He was well respected in his field but wary of outsiders; this he had made clear to me on day one. He prided himself on hiring classically trained academic staff and had not fully embraced bringing professionals from the corporate world into teaching, thus taking away important jobs from those who should have received them, in his less than humble opinion. Instead, he was required to maintain a certain quotient of academic to professional staff in his college, a fact he was none too happy about.

I thought I had made headway with him on that front since I had started working toward my PhD, something I still felt "voluntold" to do, but if it would help me secure my place in this world, I was willing to do it. That last meeting I had with him toward the beginning of the semester, however, had been odd, jarring and made it evident that my efforts would not bear fruit.

"Hi, Dean Smith," I said, with as much reverence as I could muster under the circumstances, since I was being ambushed.

He swiveled in his chair to face me. He was an odd-looking fellow. Older, slightly balding, though not enough that it had become a full-fledged problem, but enough for a man of his stature to be overly sensitive about it. He stood just about eye level with me, maybe a little under, and took pride in his suits. He used his gold-rimmed glasses more as a prop than for a functional purpose from what I could tell, and his tobacco-stained teeth evidenced his pipe use.

I once had an image of him sitting at home in a smoking jacket next to a well-drawn fire, pipe in one hand and brandy in another. The thought returned now, and I had to keep myself from laughing. He clearly was not in a joking mood, but my nerves were killing me!

"Huh? Oh, hello, Miss Aitken. Please take a seat," he said without emotion and more than a little distraction in his gaze as his hand directed me to the chair opposite him at his large U-shaped desk.

I sat down while I observed the odd surroundings. His office was tidy enough, but his desk? Pure disaster zone. I wondered how he could find anything, let alone get any work done. He had a few desk awards scattered on the backside of the U, but in perfect sightline of those who sat down across from him. They had all been academic in nature and, to me, not all that impressive, but I always made sure to show them as much deference as possible if they made it into the conversation.

Why was he so distracted? He was the one who called the meeting, not me. He was acting as if it was a bother that I was even there. I sat quietly, taking my department chair's original advice and saying as little as possible, allowing him to lead the conversation.

"Miss Aitken...uh, it is Miss, correct?" He eyed me suspiciously, as if an unmarried woman of my age was to be dealt with delicately.

"Yes," I replied, "though if it makes you feel better, you are welcome to refer to me as Sophia. We've certainly known each other long enough at this point, wouldn't you say?" I asked, trying to make light of the obvious tension in the room.

He clearly did not agree. "Miss Aitken, there's been some complaints," he delivered. I just looked at him, waiting for him to continue, but he did not.

"Complaints, sir?" I queried, hoping he would elaborate. Meanwhile my brain was going a mile a minute. Complaints? Complaints about what? My students loved me, I had built great relationships, I'd gotten a lot of repeats in each semester because they wanted to take my classes...I couldn't begin to imagine what he was talking about.

"Yes," he said, without continuing.

Again, I tried following my department chair's advice but couldn't stand the suspense. "About...?" I began.

He took a breath. I had never seen him so flustered, which was saying something. He sighed. "About you, I'm afraid," he finally pushed out.

I stared at him, needing more information. When he saw that I wasn't going to respond, he kept going.

"Miss Aitken...Sophia," he relented. This sudden softening of his resolve shocked me. I watched as he got up from behind his desk and came over to the other side to sit next to me, instead of leering down at me from his pedestal.

I started to stammer, "I don't understand. My students love me. I..."

"Yes, exactly."

I cocked my head with a confused look. "I'm sorry?" I managed.

He reached across and took my hand. In the corporate world, this would have been the oddest thing one could do, but in this environment, he had instantly gone from stern dean to endearing grandfather.

"It's the staff. Not your department, mind you. You have rave reviews there as well, at least from your department chair..." He looked down, almost trying to hide his eyes, as if he was going to give someone away.

I just sat there silently, letting him tell me whatever it was he was trying to choke out.

I watched him nod to himself as if he was agreeing with some unspoken statement. "Sophia, the rest of the faculty has complained because of your high marks from students. They, not all of them, mind you, just a vocal few, a very vocal few," he said, almost to himself, "are concerned that your unorthodox teaching methods are undermining their ability to teach in their classroom. The enrollment numbers came in for the past three semesters, and your class enrollment is the strongest in the college."

He stopped for a breath. "Naturally, because of the high marks from your students, you are drawing attention to yourself. While some of the other faculty are wanting to learn from you and adapt their methods to see if they too can engage with students better, there are others who see it as an afront to their profession and are lobbying to the provost to change the number of professionals we allow into the faculty versus 'true academics,'" he finished.

I scowled.

"Their words, not mine," he clarified. This came as another surprise. He was not known to support the initiative himself, but here he was, almost defensive of the anti-corporate rhetoric.

"I...I don't know what to say," I admitted.

He looked at me, patted my hand and stood to walk back to the other side of his desk. Apparently, the human side of this conversation was done, and he needed to get back to his usual persona for the next part.

"Miss Aitken. I'm honestly not sure what to say either, other than we need to fix this. It is why I asked for your syllabi earlier in the semester to see if I could help guide us to a solution. I've come to the conclusion that either you need to amend your teaching methods to adhere to the traditional pedagogical practices that our esteemed faculty follow, or we need to determine your true place here at this college and in this university."

I was aghast. He actually looked disappointed at having to deliver this ultimatum. I sat in stunned silence, trying to think through my options. At least that last interaction now made sense. Surely this couldn't be happening. I was being challenged because I was too...good? I had a sudden flashback to a time in high school where I was ousted by a friend group for being "too noble," as they had put it at the time. And here I was again, being accused of something which made absolutely no sense.

I stood. Rather abruptly judging by Dean Smith's reaction. "I...need to think about this," I said.

"Certainly, Miss Aitken," he responded.

When it was clear he was not going to offer anything else, I asked, "May I go now?"

Dean Smith simply shook his head and turned back to his laptop. He clearly wanted to be done with this conversation too.

I walked to his door, opened it, tried to compose myself and walked out.

LaShonda obviously knew something was up, as she was standing there waiting for me with a chocolate in hand. "Here, sweetheart, take this." It was a small gesture, and one that did not align with the situation, but I appreciated it all the same.

"Thank you," I croaked out. Oh no, my body was starting to react to the conversation, and I could feel my eyes pooling. I didn't want to cry, but as all women know, sometimes your body just reacts without consulting with you first.

I hurried out of the office and the building, raced to Etta and jumped in. I threw my bags in the passenger seat and sat there for a good five minutes before I started the car. I became aware of other cars circling the lot like vultures and people eyeing me in my spot, wondering if I was coming or going. I started the engine, flipped off my music and backed out of my spot.

As I pulled away, I saw two of those vehicle vultures go after the vacancy and narrowly miss each other. How appropriate. That was exactly how I felt right now, being assaulted out of nowhere. It was a vaguely familiar feeling and one I did not appreciate.

I drove, not knowing in which direction to go, until I found myself pulling into the parking lot of the closest grocery store to my house. In times of need and confusion, snacks and binge-watching something with vampires was the only way to clear my head. I found their cool nature and grand perspective – having lived so long – reassuring somehow. The food was purely for a serotonin rush.

I parked the car and glided into the store as if I was floating, but not a good float, more of a trancelike state of one who was just going through the motions. Everything was a blur. I walked over to produce to get my favorite fresh salsa, the deli to get pepperoni, the chip aisle to get tortilla chips and cool ranch Doritos, the cracker aisle for wheat thins, and finally the bakery in the back for some half-moon cookies. This one clearly called for ALL the vices. Thankfully, I already had some wine stocked at home, so I didn't need to stop again. I cashed out through the self-checkout – not my favorite, but avoiding humans was essential for keeping it together until I got home.

I walked back out to Etta, threw the newly acquired chemical-laden junk food in the trunk and jumped in. The rest of the ride home was as much of a blur as the shopping experience, and before I knew it, I was pulling into my driveway, loading the bags onto one arm and walking to my door. I unlocked the door with the keypad, praising myself for setting up the finger touch technology for the millionth time, and went inside.

Violet was there to greet me as always with her wiggle butt wag and her favorite toy in her mouth, but she immediately sensed my tension and ceased. Instead, she waited for me to drop everything on the counter and then slowly walked up to me, nuzzling my leg. I dropped down to pet her head and wound up sitting on the floor against the island with her in my lap for a very long time. She let me hold her and use her as a child would a stuffie, squeezing and trying to transmute the upsetting energy and release it from my mind, body and soul.

I suddenly became aware of it getting much darker in the house. How long had I been sitting there? I needed to do something. This whole thing just felt off. I needed Kit. I kissed Violet on the head, and she took it as the signal that it was time to get off my lap. As I slowly uncrossed my legs and grunted to rise, I grabbed my phone and dialed.

Kit answered on the third ring, and I didn't even let her finish her greeting before I dove in. I became a blubbering mess. She only got every other word, I'm sure, but once I finished, she said she had to wait for Erik to get home with Tate and she would be right over. That made me breathe a sigh of relief. Kit was coming. We would figure this out.

In the meantime, I prepared my smorgasbord of snacks and grabbed the first bottle of red I saw, Phantom – matching my mood exactly. No sooner was I done pouring the two glasses than I heard a car door slam and feet crunching up the stairs. We were past politeness at this juncture and Kit burst right in.

"Tell me everything," she said. I just looked at her. I picked up the two wine glasses and thrust one in her face. She lifted her left arm and put a bottle of Jefferson's Reserve in mine, my favorite bourbon of late. I nodded and set it on the counter, knowing we would be breaking into that next.

We carried the glasses and bags of goodies into the front room, curled up in our respective spots on the chair and a half and the crook of the couch, and settled in for my tale.

Chapter 22 – December 1563 – Ann

It was Advent, and the village was in full fasting mode. Of course, for most, it gave them the excuse to simply drink ale and eat fresh bread with butter by the fistful. I always loved our house at this time of year. To be honest, I loved it every time of the year, but Christmas held a special spot in my heart for all the greenery, candles and berries with which my mother decorated.

Being a seamstress, she had an eye for detail, so no corner went without holly, ivy, mistletoe or yew. The mistletoe was hung in strategic places around the house, more so for my parents' benefit than anything, but they knew full well it had to be out of reach from the young ones or they would tear it down. The tallow candles from Mrs. Williams always added to the smells of the season and, unfortunately, made me even hungrier than usual.

It was an evening of preparation. The twelve days of Christmas would soon be upon us, and as was our tradition, we would be rotating to different friends' homes on each evening. My youngest siblings, Thomas and Izzy, were busy teasing each other about what Saint Nicholas would bring each of them while Susan was on her best behavior, helping my mother in the hopes of going to a party with one of her friends the next night before everything started. She was just of age, fifteen, so parties were now of great interest to her, and the fact she had been invited to one outside of her home had excited her to no end. I was not sure Mother would allow it, but she was certainly taking advantage of the extra set of hands to make sure the house was in tip-top shape.

"Ann, how goes the preparations at the Williams'?" my father asked from his seat by the fire.

"They are well, Papa. They are happy they do not have to host first, given the litany of children they have to pick up!" I responded with a sly smile.

My parents knew only too well the chaos that ensued at their house with such a large brood and, while they never said as much, were quite happy they had only the four of us versus the Williams' eight.

"I am quite sure Mr. Williams is still helping them rather than sitting with his feet up by the fire with a drink!" my mother quipped from the kitchen, not miffed, merely joking in a good-natured way.

My father smiled. "Yes, Sarah, I am sure of it, for either he is a better man than I, or I am the luckier to have married one such as yourself who recognizes when a man needs his rest after a long day's work." My father knew exactly what to say for my mother to demonstrate her enigmatic guffaw.

"Well, perhaps it is so. However, perhaps it is also because I recognize how OLD you are and would not want to overwork one such as yourself into an early grave," she responded.

My father looked up in mock shock, blew a kiss to my mother and took a sip of his drink. My parents were usually in good spirits, but it was always a thing of beauty to witness around the holidays.

Just then, there was a knock at the door. Not knowing who it would be at this hour, I offered to answer it, but my father jumped up from his position instead. He placed his drink down on the side table and strode to the door, straightening himself as he went. We all paused our work to see who it could be. I had a pit in my stomach, though I could not place why.

The door opened and my father started to ask who was there when we were all greeted by carolers with the wassail bowl! I let out a nervous laugh while the rest of my family joined in. "Here we come a-wassailing, among the leaves so green!"

As the household sang, my father went to his coin purse to withdraw a couple of shillings for the donation. When the verse finished, the hot spiced ale was offered, but my father placed his hand up in refusal. "No, thanks, ladies and gents, we have enough in our home, but take our donation with hearty thanks all the same."

The group bowed their heads in gratitude, while one in the group shouted, "Well, do not mind if I do" and plunged a cup – that seemed to appear from an unknown place – into the large wooden bowl to take a sip. All laughed, and they moved on to the next house down the lane.

My mother took up her work in the kitchen again while humming, and my father repositioned himself at the fire. Realizing what time it was, Susan offered to get the little ones to bed. My mother, never refusing any help when she could get it, nodded her head and kept up with her tune, now switching to "The Coventry Carol," a personal favorite of mine.

I re-focused on folding the table linens, as they had finished drying, and the pit in my stomach came back. What on earth was causing it? Perhaps it was because Madge's family had been asked after, but there had been no mention of the Whites? Or of Lizbeth?

It had been a couple of weeks since the wedding and an odd silence had fallen over the couple. It was as if an invisible barrier had been placed around the outbuilding in which they were living and everyone from the village felt it an unwelcome space. Even Mr. Williams, who had helped build the structure, was no longer allowed to work there. Madge and I had made a couple of attempts to visit our friend and determine her condition, but we had not gotten past the rickety old door with either Mr. Acton or one of his men standing sentinel.

I was quite confused as to this behavior and set to writing to Lizbeth, hoping a different approach would work, but not one letter had been responded to. I even questioned if they had been received at all. I was careful not to put anything incriminating in them, knowing full well Mr. Acton was the type of man to open all correspondence but hoping he would think it innocuous enough to allow Lizbeth to write.

Madge had suggested we leave it for the time being and take up our campaign after the holidays. Perhaps once they had gotten through the first month together as newlyweds, and we gave Mr. Acton some space, he might come around. That was Madge, ever hopeful and optimistic. I was less so. I had a sinking feeling that something was truly amiss, the owl never quite leaving my mind. The vivacious energy of our friend had been diminished when I saw her last, the morning after her wedding. She was clearly frightened of him, as under any other circumstances, she would have fled into my arms, man be damned.

That night, as I lay in bed and started to drift to sleep, I heard that voice again. The same dulcet tenor tones I had been hearing since the wedding. They were warm, and rich, and I welcomed hearing them, knowing full well I might be becoming "tetched," as they said.

"Ye have right to worry, love," he said. I did not respond, hoping he would continue and expound his meaning. "He is not to be trusted, and I fear, no longer is she." At this, I frowned. "Aye, I know this troubles you. It is why the pit in your stomach has grown. Listen to your intuition. It has not failed ye."

At this, I quietly giggled and asked, "Am I not listening to my intuition now? Has it not taken on this voice of yours?"

There was a pause before it responded, "Nae."

At this I started. What did that mean? I swallowed hard and considered if I should ask my question.

"Go ahead, ask," I heard it say.

I hesitated, then decided I had nothing to lose.

"If you are not the intuition in my head, then what are you?" I whispered.

"Ye already know the answer," he responded. My pulse quickened.

"Do you mean to say, that after all this time, it is you?" I choked out.

"Me who?" he said, and I swore if there was a face with the voice, it would be smiling. I could envision those bright teeth of his, dimples on either side of a lopsided smile, scruffy face from a long day's work, auburn curls falling at random intervals all over his head.

"James?" I squeaked out. There was another silence. I thought I had lost him or perhaps I was falling asleep. Disappointed, I lay down in bed and rolled over to curl up in despair until I heard him say ever so softly…

"Aye, my bonnie lass."

I woke the next morning as if nothing happened but wondered, as I started to come to, why my cheek felt like a tear had frozen there overnight. I stood to make my bed when the realization hit me. "Aye, my bonnie lass" was what the voice had said. His voice. It was him. James.

I fell back onto my bed. Was it possible? Our group had read that some with magic in their blood could hear and commune with spirits from the beyond, but surely I could not be one of those people. We had just been playing around with our herbs and rituals; they were an interesting pastime and made us feel special, different from the rest of the village, but it had never got to the point where we thought any of us had true gifts.

I wanted to test my theory. Thankfully, my siblings were already gone, having been called out to the fields with my father for the day to tend to the wheat and rye, the last few tasks before the Christmas celebrations commenced. I steadied myself on my bed and listened. Only my mother should be left in the house, but once again I seemed to be alone. She must have had an errand or two to run. Feeling fairly confident I was the only one, I whispered, "James?"

Nothing. I shook my head at myself, knowing how silly I must have looked. However, I was not deterred. It was now or never. "James?" I said, a little bit louder and with more confidence. Still nothing. One more shot. "James Clarke, if that is you and I am able to communicate with you, give me a sign!" I said more emphatically than I meant to.

Just then, I heard a jar fall from a shelf downstairs. I guessed my experiment was over. I stood, finished making my bed, got dressed and went downstairs to clean up whatever mess had just been made. My mother would not be happy to come home and find things amiss.

As I walked into the kitchen, I looked around for whatever had caused the racket. Then I spotted it. A jar of calendula tea. A specific tea my mother used only for special occasions, as it represented protection and prosperity. The last time we had it had been over three years ago on the evening of my betrothal to James.

Thankfully, the jar had not broken, only fallen to the floor and the top had gone askew, spilling some of the fragrant flower. I fell to my knees and gently began to sweep what I could into my hands and back into the jar. I cautiously stood and placed the jar back on its shelf and turned away.

Without thinking I said out loud, "I assume that was for me." I waited to see if there would be any response. When there was not, I carried on. "Is there something you need to tell me?" I waited again.

Nothing. I was about to turn and move out of the kitchen when the jar that I had secured on its shelf started to move again. This time, I caught it.

I must be losing it, I thought to myself. *This is not real.* No one would believe me, and yet I needed to talk to someone.

Instead, I felt the urge to go to the woods. I had not been back in so long and was still wary of the place, but it seemed like I was being called there once again. Perhaps it would be easier to think and determine what was happening in the space where all this had started. I sighed as I realized what I was now doing.

"James, I am going to go to the woods. Not our space, but the altar. I am assuming you know about it, and I have no idea why I am saying this out loud to you, but I wanted you to know." I waited to see if anything would happen, but when it did not, I left the kitchen, grabbed my cloak and hat, and walked out the door.

As I made my way to the woods, I did not pay attention to the bustling village. Everyone's spirits were high because of the approaching holidays. It was usually a time I relished, drinking in the positive energy, admiring the smiles on everyone's faces...but not this time. This time I was preoccupied by a different kind of spirit. I did not notice when someone called out and waved. I also did not notice that I had made it all the way into the woods until I bumped into someone, completely unexpected at this time of day and in this location. I looked up to see who it was, half anticipating I had imagined it, but was relieved to see it was a real person.

Robert looked down and quietly pardoned himself. "I am sorry, Miss Ann."

"Not a bother, Robert. I am actually happy to see it was you and not my imagination!" I exclaimed, not thinking of what I was admitting.

He looked at me then and cocked his head to the side, as if trying to understand. "Miss? What...whatever do you mean?"

I reeled myself in. "Oh, nothing. I forget myself," I quickly responded.

We both stood in an uncomfortable silence. This was the most attention Robert had ever paid me, and I him. He had not budged though. He seemed to be regarding me in a different manner than he had previously, reading me almost. I pulled my cloak around me tighter, feeling a little self-conscious.

That seemed to break him out of his stupor. "I am sorry, Miss, it is I who forget myself now." He bowed his head again.

"Not to worry, Mr. Evans...Robert. I do not mind. In fact, I think you may be the perfect person to whom I can ask this question," I said, once again not thinking before the words escaped my mouth. Had I meant them? It would stand to reason that outside of Lizbeth and Madge, Robert may be the only one to believe me, or even begin to understand what I was experiencing. Some part of me must have known that...

He looked at me questioningly, and then it happened. The "fits" I had always been warned about, and that Lizbeth had described in detail. He was staring at me, and then it seemed he was staring through me. His eyes became hazy, like the sky on a covered night. It did not last long, and I was not sure what to do while it happened, and then it was done, and he had recovered. He looked at me with a new awe and what almost felt like appreciation.

"Perhaps we should find a place to sit, Miss Ann. I feel this may be a…different conversation," he said.

"I think you may be right. I know just the place," I said and started to lead him to the altar. He suddenly reached for my arm, as if to keep me from tripping. I gasped at his touch; it was the first time in a long time that a man had held me in his grasp. He apologized but did not let go, nervous of some unseen danger.

We came upon the stones and stumps, and I halted. It took me a minute to drink it all in. Though it had only been a few months, the whole place looked different, felt different. Moss had already begun to grow over the top stone. Thankfully, no remnants of whatever Lizbeth had placed there remained, blown away by wind and washed away by rain, no doubt. I was grateful, for I would not have wanted Robert to experience it. He maneuvered around the space with a familiarity that struck me. Perhaps he had taken over this place in our absence?

We each took a stump across from each other and sat. Not knowing who should go first, I was mustering up the courage to admit what I had been experiencing when he said, "You have got the sight."

It was my turn to look up at him. "I'm sorry?" I said.

"You have got the sight, have you not? The ability to communicate with the spirit world," he clarified.

"How would you..." I started, not sure which to respond to first, his abrupt declaration or the fact that he somehow knew without me saying anything.

"I recognize one such as myself," he softly replied and then looked down.

I took a deep breath and let it out. "I am not sure I would call it 'the sight,' as such. It is more 'the sound'..." I trailed off, not sure how to explain.

He once again cocked his head to the side, as if I was speaking a different language and he was struggling to keep up.

"I do not see things but rather hear them. And not just anything..." I paused. He was engaged now and was not going to interrupt my train of thought. I sighed. "I do not know. Perhaps I am going mad. I will be the lonely spinster woman of the village that everyone thinks is tetched and live out my days in the woods or a small hut." I laughed at myself.

Robert clearly was not amused by this. "Miss Ann..." he started and then took on a different tone entirely. "Ann. You are not tetched. You are part of what others may call the 'cunning folk,' but you are not going mad. I promise you. I know what others think and say of me, but there is a purpose."

I laughed at that. I too knew what people thought and said about him. I always held a soft spot for Robert. He was a kind man, clearly dealing with a "gift" that he had not asked for and yet had no one to talk with about it, especially now that Lizbeth was gone. The fact he was opening up to me at all was impressive, so I thought I should repay the gesture.

"'Tis James," I said.

Robert looked up again, unsurprised. "I know," he said.

My jaw dropped. He laughed. I had never heard Robert laugh before. It was light and airy, much like his demeanor when he walked around lost in thought.

"How do you—"

"I have seen him. By your side. For quite some time now, in fact. He has not left you since he made his way here," he admitted. I did not know what to do with this new information. "You have no doubt seen me stare off to your right side in the past, no?" he continued. I nodded my head in quiet confirmation. "It is because that is where he stands. He has been trying to get your attention for a while now. He knew you had the gift," he finished.

I let that sink in. "I just thought I was dreaming at first. A longing manifesting itself. I have always had a strong intuition and internal voice, but when it started to speak back, and began sounding like his voice, his laugh, I thought something had gone wrong in my head." I looked up with an apologetic look, but Robert seemed to take this in stride.

"Some can see. Others can hear. Still others can smell, feel, taste or know. My ancestors have many stories about each of these abilities. They all come out at different times. Some people have one while others may have multiple," he said.

I listened and tried to digest all of this. "I guess that would make sense," I said, working it out in my head. "So, when you have stopped and stared beyond us in the past, that is when you saw them?" I asked.

"No. That is actually something else entirely," he said with a smirk. I did not know he could be this playful. I was quickly seeing what had so appealed to Lizbeth.

"So then what is it? Do not tell me you have another sense?" I queried.

"I do. I can see what will happen," he said matter-of-factly.

"Like a fortune teller?!" I cried.

"Something like that," he said, "but not on demand. It is more like visions that happen when I am near the person they will happen to."

Then I remembered a time in the wood several months ago, when we had come upon Robert while we were leaving the sacred space. He had in fact stared off to my right and I wondered what he was looking at, but he had also had one of his fits and looked positively forlorn. Or maybe that was the story Lizbeth had relayed to Madge and me on that morning so long ago when I had been preoccupied by my dream. He started speaking again and I turned my attention back to him.

"For instance, as we were walking, when I grabbed your arm. You did not see it, but my eyes had clouded over, as they do, and I had seen you tripping in the woods. It was darker out in the vision, as if it was a different time of day, but I thought it best to take precautions anyway."

Something niggled at the back of my brain at that, but it was not dislodging itself easily. Something about tripping in the woods and the darkness…"It must make it hard to have normal conversations with people. Does this happen all the time?" I asked.

He looked at me. "There is a reason I am considered anti-social and not invited anywhere."

I felt for him then. How much life had he missed out on simply because he could do something that others did not understand, or did not take time to understand?

"Great, well, if this keeps up for me, you might gain some company!" I laughed, trying to lighten the mood.

He smiled. "Yours seems to be quite specific. You have a guide in James. I would highly recommend you hone your skill to hear him better. If what he is indicating to me is true, you are not quite there yet," he said, nodding to my right shoulder.

I snapped my head to the right, as if to yell at a live person. "What?! You mean you can see him right now?! James, I am trying my best, but this is all new to me!" I admonished.

Robert was amused by that and chuckled. "He knows, Ann. Are you still in the stage of being able to hear him right before you go to sleep or right after you wake up?" Again, my jaw dropped. "That is because those are the times when you are most vulnerable, when your brain can process what is occurring without logic interfering. Eventually, if your connection is strong enough, you will be able to talk with him whenever you please, and he with you, I would wager," he said enthusiastically. I must have looked dubious because he quickly followed that with, "You will. I have seen it."

Chapter 23 – November, Present Day – Sophia

We were a bottle of red and half a bottle of Jefferson's into my dilemma and neither of us had made heads nor tails of the situation. Kit was astounded when I walked her through my conversation with Dean Smith, clearly as confused as I was. We were very much still at the "S" of the S-A-R-A-H model of grief, shock, and had both gone quiet contemplating what was next.

The bottle of Phantom had gone down easily for both of us. Dark and smooth, it had tempered my nerves just enough to allow me to get my story out in one fell swoop before I started my next breakdown, this time under the watchful eye of my dear friend. The bourbon…we were slowly sipping, taking our time, as we each attempted to process the day.

"I just can't believe that it would be the faculty coming at you like this," Kit finally said.

I was wondering what she had been thinking as she sat in what I now considered "her chair," swirling the amber liquid around the large cube of ice in the rocks glass. I stared at her with a blank expression.

"I mean, it just doesn't make sense. There HAS to be something else at play. I mean, if they are true professionals, wouldn't they be welcoming ways to teach this new generation of students?" she asked.

I could see she needed to outwardly pontificate, so I just shrugged my shoulders, knowing there was more coming.

"And how can they call themselves true academics if they don't want to learn new methods? Isn't that what they literally preach to their students?!"

"I know. But to be fair, I don't think it is 'the faculty' so much as one or two of them," I said.

"Right, what did he say again?" she asked.

"A vocal few. 'Very vocal few' was then said under his breath," I repeated.

She shook her head. "So, who? Surely no one in your department," Kit said and then took a sip from her glass.

I had to swallow fast after holding the bourbon in my mouth to warm it up and bring out the full bouquet of flavor. "Well..."

Kit shot a glance over at me with one eyebrow raised. "Say more," she encouraged.

I didn't want to sound paranoid, but I wouldn't be surprised if one of the "very vocal few" had been someone in my department and his fellow like-minded cronies. He had been at the university for decades and at one time held a similar position to Dean Smith's. He and I had not seen eye to eye since day one and I could absolutely see him taking offense at me achieving the strongest enrollment numbers. That said, I didn't understand why, when there were plenty of students who loved him as well and I had heard as such directly from their own mouths.

"So, you think it could be Professor Mathers?" she asked, draining what was left in her glass and setting it aside on the little marble end table next to her chair.

I shrugged. "I mean, it could be. But it could be a lot of people," I responded, finishing my glass, not wanting to be left out from the next round. I got up to retrieve Kit's glass and moved to the kitchen.

"I think we need to break into your haul before we have any more, otherwise I won't be able to make it home later," Kit called out.

"I'm on it. I was thinking the same thing," I yelled from the kitchen. "Just give me a sec while I feed Vi. Do you need to check in with your brood?"

I heard her pick up her phone to check for any missed notifications. "Nah, Erik's got this. That's the thing when you marry a military man; he takes his duties seriously!" she quipped.

I laughed from the other room. "Yeah, and a Norse god. Seriously, you won the lottery with that one. You better hold on tight!" I said as I walked back into the room, snack bowls balancing precariously on my left arm and two drinks in my right.

"Oh geez!" Kit said and jumped to help me safely land the bowls.

"My offerings, my lady," I mocked. She shot me a glare as she lowered herself to the ground in front of the coffee table, opened the bags of chips we had brought in earlier, poured them into the proffered bowls, and started mowing down on the chips and salsa.

"So, what are you going to do? Find out who said it so you can confront them?" she asked between bites.

"I honestly don't know." I sighed, sitting down beside her and sidling up to the grub. "I guess I could, but what difference would that make? I don't think the dean would have brought it to my attention if it was as easy as confronting someone. It should have been his job to put a stop to the nonsense if it was that easy. He has the authority," I mused. "Short of my..."

My phone started buzzing. I didn't really want to answer it, but there was something aggressive about it, and after the day I had, I thought it best not to ignore it. I reached for it and saw it was a video call from Maddy. I turned the screen to show Kit, and she grabbed it out of my hands and answered the call.

"'Allo, love!" Kit said in a heavily Americanized British accent.

"Hey, what? I...I thought I called Soph," she said, confused as she looked at her screen again to check who she had dialed.

I popped my head next to Kit's. "You did, Govna!" I quipped in an equally as awful British accent.

"Oh boo, no fair. I'm missing a fun girls' night?!" Maddy pouted.

"Not quite," I said with a sideways glance at Kit.

"Trouble in paradise?" Maddy crooned.

"Kinda, but that's not why you called, silly, unless you've developed a sixth sense," I said, eyeing her suspiciously and trying to lighten the mood. She shook her head and withdrew a bit. Ugh, why did I always forget not to joke around with her about the spiritual world?

"No, no, it isn't," Maddy said sheepishly.

Not wanting to lose her, Kit piped in. "So, what's up, chica?" she said, almost too brightly. "It's gotta be the dead of night or early morning there," she continued, checking her watch and visibly doing the math.

"It is, I'm afraid, yes," Maddy said, fully in her acquired British accent now, and she paused. We both grew concerned.

"Mads, what's going on?" I asked. She hesitated, almost unsure if she was going to speak. Given Maddy was usually ready to jump into storytelling mode at any given moment, we were getting worried.

"Maddy?" Kit cajoled. "Honey, talk to us. Did something happen?" she continued.

"Did Ryan do something?" I jumped in.

Kit shot me a questioning look, as if she didn't know who Ryan was. I just gazed back at her to indicate I would fill her in later.

The moment seemed to pass. "Oh, I'm fine, guys, really. I guess maybe I'm a little homesick or something, which is why I called, wanting to see a friendly face," she said, a bit misty.

Homesick? Our wild child? Something was definitely up, but she wasn't going to be berated into sharing it, and we both knew that, so we sat silently waiting.

"It's just..." We saw her get up and move around her room. It really was magnificent, even in the dark. I could clearly see the mahogany four-poster bed behind her and the velvet chaise at the foot of it. Kit was obviously watching the background too, riveted by the glimpses we were getting in the moonlight. It seemed she had the window drapes slightly pulled open and there was a sliver of silver light across the wood floor and crossing onto the Persian rug.

"I think I may be going crazy," she finally said.

Kit and I looked at each other and then back at the phone. We didn't know how to answer that, so Kit did her famous "say more" line.

"OK. So, Soph, remember a couple of weeks ago when you caught me as we were getting ready to go to the party Mary was throwing for the new line?" she asked.

I nodded my head and kept my mouth shut, not wanting to break her train of thought. Kit took a breath, as if she was going to question something, but I swiped my hand under the coffee table to smack her leg.

"When we got down to the lobby, I found out that Mary was taking the theme of the party quite seriously. She had based it on all the superstitions of the periods she had taken inspiration from."

Kit and I silently groaned as soon as we heard the word "superstition." No wonder she was in a tizzy. We both relaxed and shoved back from the coffee table to lean up against the chair. Both of our backs were not thanking us for hovering on the floor, but it was the only place we could stay close enough together for the video call.

Maddy must have heard our groan, to which she added, "Exactly. I got down to the foyer with Ryan and there was a gypsy-looking woman sitting in the center with a table and she was doing tarot card readings. It took everything in me not to bolt immediately, and I'm fairly certain if Ryan hadn't been holding my hand, I probably would have." Kit and I nodded dutifully, and she continued. "I resigned myself to ignoring her, desperately wanting to enjoy the party. Ryan was in such a good mood and things were going so well I didn't want my personal misgivings with the 'eclectic' to ruin the evening."

She was wandering around her room now, not paying much attention to the screen, so Kit and I took a moment to look at each other, impressed that our overly religious rebel could do such a thing, and for a guy!

"The problem was to enter the party, one had to be proven 'worthy' as part of the fun Mary had cooked up, so I had to do the reading if I wanted to go in. Ryan sensed my hesitation and went first, showing me that 'it didn't hurt,' not realizing why I was so reluctant. He passed with flying colors and was admitted through what looked like an old-fashioned speakeasy door that had been built for the occasion. He said, 'See you on the flip, toots' in a 1920s accent and went through. I, thankfully, was left alone in the foyer, as we were still a bit early for the party and most of the guests were going to arrive fashionably late. I said a few prayers in my head to keep me from harm and sat down. The lady seemed harmless enough and I just told myself it was an innocent game; nothing would come of it."

"Maddy," I stopped her. "Honey, you should probably sit down now. You are going to wear a hole in that side of the carpet if you keep pacing like that," I said with a laugh, trying to ease her tension. I knew she was upset, but she was making me more anxious than I already was with my own situation. She made a nervous sound and found a chair where she could sit and continued, leg bouncing this time. Oh well, at least she was staying in one place.

"OK, so Gypsy Zabina – that was her name – went through her whole show. She closed her eyes, shuffled her deck and seemed to speak words at it. She had some wooden block next to her that was smoking and emitting an odd smell, I presumed for ambiance. Anyway, she only pulled a couple of cards for Ryan, so I figured this would go fast. She pulled the first few, nodding her head, and then she pulled a few more. Before I knew it, she had pulled ten cards! She started shaking her head and said I must not be a believer, and all this other stuff about karmic cycles being entrenched and needing to be broken. I wasn't sure, but when I saw a card labeled 'Devil,' I nearly jumped out of my seat. Her mood had gone quickly from fun to very serious, almost trancelike. I didn't listen too much because the next group was coming, and I just wanted to get out of there. She finally sensed my discomfort and noticed me eyeing the door, so she picked up all the cards, shuffled them again and said I could go. As she was shuffling, another card fell out and she handed it to me, saying it was a message for me. I took a brief look at it, but at this point I just wanted to get away from her and back to Ryan," she said.

Kit and I were holding our breath. This was the most Maddy had ever spoken about a subject like this, and we were riveted. Kit let out the breath she had been holding. "What was it?" she quietly asked.

"What was what?" Maddy said. "Oh, the card? The Knight of Wands."

I made a mental note to look up the meaning later. "OK, so was that it?" I cautiously asked.

She seemed unnaturally riled up for that to be it, but perhaps it was, and she was only now processing it weeks later. Maddy bit her lip, a habit she only had when trying to figure out what to do or say next. "No," she finally said. "No, it wasn't. The rest of the party was OK. Uncomfortable because there were moon phases, herbs and other costumed people around all evening with crystals and other evil implements," she said, looking away from the camera.

Kit and I had to stifle a laugh when she referenced crystals as being evil, and I glanced around my room to make sure none of my growing collection was in view.

"Ryan could sense I was uncomfortable and thought he had done something wrong. He spent the first part of the night trying to make it up to me. When I finally told him it was because of the party itself and I didn't believe in any of it, he laughed and escorted me out. We went outside to the grounds where I could get some fresh air. We spent the evening talking about beliefs, something I have never done with anyone, and then he walked me back to my room."

At that, Kit and I looked at each other and thought we understood. They must have broken it off, either because she was too resolute, or he was too whimsical.

Maddy read our thoughts and said, "No, we're still together. Better than ever actually," and she half smiled.

"Seriously, Mads?! That's great!" Kit exclaimed.

"Yeah, normally you avoid that topic like the plague, but you're telling me he was cool with where you're at?" I added. "That's awesome."

"He respected it, but as I listened to him talk through his own set of beliefs, or even nonbeliefs, something clicked, and I could see where perhaps I have been too uptight about my own."

Our mouths dropped at this admission.

She laughed again softly. "I know, I know. Shocking."

Kit and I did not know what to say.

"But that's not even why I called. I'm proud of the progress I've made, and while I think most of it is still bollocks..."

After a minute, Kit said, "Earth to Maddy..."

"Right, sorry," she said, shaking away whatever had made her drift off.

"There's more?" I asked.

"Uh...yeah," she said. She hesitated, twisting her fingers and ringing her hands.

"Maddy, it's us," Kit cooed, just as I had heard her do with her own children when she needed them to come clean about something.

Maddy's hands stopped moving. "There's something I haven't told you guys before. Something...that I've always tried to ignore in my awareness, but ever since that night and the tarot lady, it's...intensified," she admitted.

Kit and I exchanged glances again. We couldn't imagine what this would be.

"Ever since I can remember, I've had this recurring dream. It usually only happens when I'm back home, which is why I'm away so much. When I'm not there, it doesn't happen, and I can get some peace," she said.

I stiffened. Recurring dream? Kit was obviously on edge too after what Tate had revealed to her over the summer, what had started the two of us going down this rabbit hole. It had been Alice in Wonderland ever since with what we had uncovered, and now this? Maybe it wasn't as bad as she was making it out to be.

"Go on," I encouraged.

"I always come into it at the same point. I'm riding horseback with a cloak flowing behind me as I'm chasing someone. I look down at my hands holding the horse's mane. They aren't my hands, but somehow, they seem familiar. I'm in a dark forest at night, but the moon can be seen through the trees," she said.

Kit slowly grabbed my hand on the floor, out of sight from the phone. We couldn't look at each other, and she could feel me starting to shake.

"Only now, since *that* night, I've been having it here, and it's been more intense. I'm seeing additional parts to it, and it's dark, guys. Like, really dark. And I'm not only experiencing it visually from the first person, but it's almost like I can feel the emotions of this person, and they are angry. It's hatred and darkness, and almost religious zealotry that I can empathize with, and unlike anything I've ever experienced. I honestly think it's that part that scares me most, that I can identify with that fervor on some level...Anyways, I keep riding on this huge black horse, and then..."

"You pick up a bow and arrow and shoot?" I interrupted.

Kit squeezed my hand. Maddy was stunned, and I instantly regretted saying something, only I couldn't help myself. It just came out. What she had been describing I had seen so many times in my own dreams, only from the opposite perspective. I was staring at her now through the phone, and she was staring right back.

"Soph...how did you...how could...how could you possibly have known that?" she stammered.

I turned my face to Kit's. There was a silent approval that I should tell her my story, but perhaps we should keep the other part out of it for now. She had admitted she was opening up to other perspectives, but only moments ago, and this was already going to rock her world.

"Well...I've never told you something either. I too have had a recurring dream for as long as I can remember, and it is about someone chasing me through the woods on horseback. Only recently was I made aware of the ending...and...it involved a bow and arrow."

Each of us was silent.

Kit spoke first. "Maddy, you OK, hon?"

Kit knew how I was. She was holding my shaking hand, trying to pass calming energy through it, a new trick she had been practicing. She had gotten good at it, but this moment was too much even for her to manipulate. Knowing she couldn't do the same for Maddy, she tried to use her voice. Maddy started by nodding her head up and down slowly. "You sure? What you've just shared is a lot to process on a good night, let alone layering in this latest revelation," she said, going into full professional mode.

"Yeah…" Maddy started to say. I continued to sit there, processing. "Yeah…I'm good," Maddy said, looking off into the distance.

"Maddy, I—"

"Listen, it's late here. I have to be up in a few hours to get out to the shop and make sure Mary's team has the next round of pieces done. She is trying to have a show in this house over the holidays and we are way behind." The pretense had returned, all solidarity gone.

"OK, doll. Whatever you…"

The screen went black. I looked at Kit. "Well, that was received as I expected it to be," I said, shrugging.

We both started to get up from the floor, groaning with the effort.

"This is almost forty." Kit laughed, trying to break my mood.

"Yeah," I responded.

"Soph, what we just witnessed tonight was a breakthrough in and of itself. If you told me a few hours ago that we would have heard Maddy Baker talking about tarot cards, let alone getting a reading, I would have said you were off your rocker," she said jovially.

"Yes, I agree, but that's not even the problem right now. The problem is—"

"The problem is, it is a Tuesday night and we both had a long day and tomorrow promises to be even longer if we stay up one more moment," she said as she made her way to the kitchen to grab her vest and keys.

"But—"

"No. Not right now. You were already processing too much before that call, and it will all still be there tomorrow," she admonished. I went to argue, but she put her pointer finger up and did the mom shake. "No. Right now, we are both going to get a good night's rest and start again tomorrow. All of this will still be there in the morning, and we will be the better for having cleared away the cobwebs."

She was right. Today had turned into an absolute disaster on all fronts, and now we had an added mystery to solve.

How the hell was it possible that Maddy could be having the same dream I had – and Tate! – but from the other perspective, and for all these years? What did that mean? And why had it taken an interaction with a fortune teller for her to come clean about it? Knowing how she felt about religion, I was shocked she even approached the old Romani woman.

I cleaned up our snacks, which had basically gone untouched thanks to the unexpected video chat from over the pond, placed the spent rocks glasses in the dishwasher, let Vi out for one last constitution and went to my bedroom.

What was going on?

Chapter 24 – December 1563 – Ann

After my conversation with Robert, I doubled my efforts. I did not know what I was doing or how I would strengthen my now identified gift, but he had said, "If the connection is strong enough, you will be able to converse with him and he with you." That was all the motivation I needed. I was certain our connection would be strong enough. I just needed to find out how best to develop the ability, which was where I was lost.

We were past Advent at this point and well into the twelve days of Christmas leading into the new month. The rotation of celebrations around the village was jovial as always but wearing thin. No one else seemed to be bothered by it, and I was surprised myself, but this year was different in so many ways. Not only was I missing having my friends by my side – Lizbeth had not been seen at any of the social gatherings, and Madge was always with Simon – but being around so many different energies was affecting me as well. It took longer and longer for me to recoup after each party. I felt heavy after all the interactions and needed a release. It was entirely new and foreign to me. Was this how Robert felt being around others?

At least today there was a break from all the merriment, and I could find a way to discharge everything. I was also going to see Madge, which I was positive would help. We had decided it was time we try to go back to our space in the woods and make it our own again, though she no longer needed to practice her own gift since she had Simon. It was something we could do together. Maybe we could even try calling our friend back to us somehow.

We met at the village center to begin our trek. Madge's cheeks were rosy, and I did not know if it was from the cold air whipping around this morning, or if she had just left her early visit with Simon. Either was possible, but based on the smile plastered on her face, I was leaning toward the latter.

"I see you have had a brisk walk this morning, given your cheek color, my dearest," I joked.

Madge looked at me with smiling eyes. "I do not know what you speak of," she said and smirked.

"I see," I said, looped my arm through hers and we turned to walk the path into the wood side by side.

There was a slight murmur behind us, but we assumed it was simply the normal hustle of the morning and continued. I thought I felt a pinprick at the center of my back, but as it had been some time since Madge and I could truly be unto ourselves, I chose to ignore it.

We walked together in silence for a bit, enjoying each other's company in a way we had not been able to do for a while. The air was crisp and smelled of more snow to come. The wind had a bite to it, a warning of a storm not far off in the distance. The trees rustled their bare branches in response. As we entered the woods, it was as if we all took a collective sigh of relief: the trees, the wind, Madge and I.

"So how is Mr. Oliver this morning?" I said, breaking the silence.

Madge smiled to herself and asked, "Why do you think it is I saw him already?"

"Madge, I know it has been a fair bit since we sisters could truly catch up, but do not think it so long that I cannot recognize the dubious grin on your face or flush in your cheek!" I said with mock indignation.

She laughed. "Oh, fine, you are right. Mr. Oliver, Simon, is doing well this morning, I suppose."

"You suppose?! Do you not know?" I queried.

"Well…" Madge started, but something was holding her back.

"Madge, dear, what on earth is it that you feel you cannot share with me?" I asked.

"'Tis silly, really. I just…" she said, then stopped herself.

I stopped walking and turned to look at her. Now was as good a time as any to practice my new awareness. I looked into her face as she turned over whatever thoughts were consuming her.

Before she could respond, I said, "You are wondering why it is taking so long for him to ask the one question you are dying to hear after all of this supposed courting."

She looked at me with eyes wide and jaw open.

"How on earth…" she stammered.

"…did I know that and finish your thought?" I said impishly, raising one eyebrow. She continued to stare at me. "We have much to catch up on, dear one," I replied, and we resumed our steady gait into the woods.

I looked around as we approached our old spot to be sure Robert was not milling about. Not that it would be a problem for me, but I wanted to respect the space he had taken over since our unceremonious departure. I felt Madge's arm tense as we walked into the circle of stumps with the rock tower at the center. Thankfully, she did not have the same last vision of this place as I did, but it had been a while since we had been there together all the same, and the fact our sisterhood was down to two still stung.

"Why do we not sit for a spell and enjoy the morning?" I suggested. I knew the stumps would likely still be wet from the latest snow, so had brought some extra cloth with which to wipe them down and add another layer between the cold seat and our bottoms. As I set to the task, I noticed Madge looking the place over, as if she sensed what had happened last but did not quite understand it.

"I know," I said, in solidarity with the expression on her face.

"It is just...has it really been so short a time since we were all here last?" she asked with pain in her eyes. "It feels like ages and yet only yesterday that we were here, all three of us, working on our latest combination, and now..."

"In truth, I have only been back a couple of times since. The latest was an entirely different experience and set me to thinking we should reclaim the space, with or without our full triquetra," I said.

Madge eyed me suspiciously.

I was not sure if I should divulge what I saw Lizbeth doing here last, as it may startle her into leaving, so I put that aside and dove into my latest encounter with Robert. "It was only a week ago, right before Christmas. I woke that morning with a sensation that I should come here, so I did."

Madge slowly sat down on "her" stump, keeping her eyes on me as she did so.

"I had not been back here for some time before that for similar reasons as you and it was...is too painful to remember what we have now lost," I continued.

Madge kept silent, taking it all in but nodding in agreement.

"As I approached the space, I ran into Robert."

At this, Madge's expression changed to one of surprise.

"I know, I had not expected that either, especially since I had felt called here. I had half expected to find you and Lizbeth here, as had happened with the three of us before, all feeling the pull to our space at once. Anyway, it was not, and I was surprised to find Robert. I was mulling something over in my mind at the time that I desperately needed to tell someone, and with Lizbeth gone and you with Simon..."

Madge dropped her gaze into her lap. "I am sorry," she started.

"Oh no, love, I did not mean it in that way at all! I am beyond thrilled for you and Simon and glad that we do not have need of this place in the same manner as before.

You have found your match, and he is wonderful!" I clarified. This made her smile, at which I continued.

"It is just, since the unhappy occasion…" I glanced at her to be sure she got my meaning, to which she smirked and covered her mouth. "I have…progressed in ways I am not sure I myself understand," I stammered out, not knowing how to approach this news but needing to tell her all the same.

Things had changed between us. Was it wise to even share this with her now? What if she had begun to change in the way Lizbeth had now that she had a love, and she would see me as a danger or a threat? I shook my head to dislodge the memory of Mr. Acton's harsh warning the last time I saw him.

"You can tell her, lass," I heard to my right.

"Are you sure?" I asked out loud, forgetting for a moment I was not sitting there alone.

Madge cocked her head to the side at this. "Ann? Am I sure of what? Are you alright?" she asked with a look of concern growing across her face.

I took a deep breath and exhaled, the intake of cold air down my center and into my core helping to steady me. I continued. "Since the unhappy occasion, I started to hear a voice at night. It continued to get stronger and yet always came back to me as a memory or dream the next morning."

Madge looked relieved. "Well, you have always said you have a strong intuition, which we have all experienced at one time or another. It must be that!"

I took another deep breath; it was now or never. "So I thought too, love, except that it was more than that. I do not know how to explain it other than…the voice started to talk back. Not just coming forth to tell me things I already knew, but also things I did not. And…" I continued, her eyes widening with each word, "the voice was not my own."

At this, she gasped. I forged ahead, not wanting to lose my nerve now. "The voice was male and known to me. However, because it only ever happened as I was going to sleep at night or as I awoke in the morning, I thought I was dreaming. Then, one day last week, as I was drifting off to sleep, I asked it if it was my intuition, to which it replied, 'No.'"

Madge was not running away yet, and it seemed she was leaning ever closer to me, so I assumed she did not think me completely delirious. "Then who or what is it?" she asked in a hushed whisper, as if she was afraid to even admit the connotation out loud.

I looked into her eyes to be sure I was talking with my Madge. Our eyes locked. She was there.

"James," I said, not breaking our gaze.

She sat back. "James? Oh, Ann, are you sure? I mean, I can understand you wanting it to be…" she said but trailed off as she saw my head shaking back and forth.

"I thought the same thing too, but it was confirmed by his response to my question, as well as Robert," I said with some emphasis and finality.

Madge looked stunned but not scared. "How did he…?" she started.

"When I ran into him in the woods. He knew something had me unnerved and suggested we talk. At the time, it was the most I had ever heard him speak! We walked here, sat down and before I could say anything, he said that I had the gift of sight. I clarified that it was more sound than sight, but then immediately questioned how he knew." I stopped short then. His story was not mine to tell, but I was not sure how I could keep going without including it.

"'Tis fine, lass. Robert will not mind, given it is Madge, and Madge will more than understand, having witnessed Robert's fits for herself. Keep going," I heard my guide gently say.

Madge had not budged and was looking at me in anticipation of my next words. "How did he know?" she asked with enthusiasm.

"Because he said he recognized one such as himself."

Madge's jaw dropped again, not in surprise as one would expect but in finally having confirmation of a long-held wisp of an idea.

"He can commune with the spirit world through sight and said that I could do so through sound," I continued.

"So that is what happens when he has one of his 'fits'!" she half asked, half exclaimed.

"No," I responded, "that is something else entirely."

Madge looked confused again. "So how did he..." She was clearly trying to work this out for herself.

"When I told him of what I was hearing and that it had said it was not my intuition, he merely replied, 'I know.

James has been with you for some time now, waiting for you to develop your gift further,' so matter-of-factly, as if he had been telling me of the weather!" It was my turn to exclaim. It felt good to be saying this out loud, and to someone who knew me well enough to know I was not spinning tales.

Madge stood and I was afraid for a moment that she intended to run away, but she clearly needed to walk some nervous energy out. I gave her space as she paced. Suddenly, she dashed at me, and I almost toppled off my stump, fearing she was about to ring my neck, but instead, she grasped onto me with a fierce hug. "

Oh, Ann, I am so sorry!" I was not quite sure for what she was apologizing, so I started to say it was fine when she interjected. "No, I am not sorry about what you have said, only that, if James is with you by your side in the spirit world, then he is truly dead and there is no hope of him returning as we once thought."

I was amazed. As much as I had been shocked to find he was with me, I was also not surprised, and yet the thought of grieving him had not occurred to me. Madge was right; he was truly gone from this world, and I would never hold him in my arms again. I had known that on some level already, which was why it never crossed my mind to be sad that he was here. I was too preoccupied with being able to hear his voice again, and yet perhaps as I developed my ability to speak with him, I would now get answers as to what happened. I put the thought aside.

"Oh, Madge, you really are the best!" I squeezed her back. Bless my friend, who was not upset at me or afraid of me, but worried and sad for me at what this latest revelation brought. Only she could have looked at this whole situation and seen it from that point of view. She let go of me then and went back to her stump, wiping her eyes with her knuckles.

"You are too kind, friend. I am alright. While I had not thought of it in those terms, I think I had always known that he had passed. At least this way, I know he is with me, and I am learning to talk with him."

Madge smiled at that. "I guess that is the next best thing, but oh, Ann, how are you managing? This is truly remarkable, and you must feel as if…" She stopped and caught herself before saying the next words.

I laughed. "It is fine, love, I am managing. Robert is helping. I am not so proficient at it yet that it is bothersome during the day, but it does bring me comfort at night when I can finally make contact."

"Why at night, I wonder?" she pondered.

"Oh, Robert clarified that for me too. Well, guessed, more like. It happens at night before I go to bed and just as I wake up in the morning because that is when your head can process what is going on without logic getting in the way. You are more vulnerable at those wee hours and willing to understand what is happening," I replied.

She nodded her head slowly in understanding. "How is it that Robert knows all of this?" she asked.

"As we suspected, he comes from a whole line of people with varying gifts. He understands, which is helpful for me!" I finished.

"Varying gifts?" Madge asked. "You mean there is more than seeing or hearing?"

 "Yes! Consider all your senses...there is a gift for each."

She thought on this for a moment. "It is all so much to take in. How are you managing?" she asked again as she weighed up everything I was throwing at her.

I simply shook my head. "Honestly, I am not sure. This last holiday week has been particularly hard, and it is as if now that I am aware of it, I am picking up on other's energies as well and they are being displaced onto me. I have been exhausted each night after we get home from one gathering or another, feeling like I need to find a way to release everything that is storing up inside me," I admitted.

Madge slapped her legs and stood then. "Well, then we need to get to work!" she said. It was my turn to look at her with my head tilted. "My mother says, whenever someone feels stagnant like that, they need to go to a place of security and ground themselves to let all the bad flow out of them and into the earth so it can be transmuted back to what it should be," she said.

I must have missed that lesson but was glad Madge knew what to do. "So, what do you suggest, dear friend?" I mused.

She looked around. "We may be down to two, but this area of the woods once helped us perform a different type of emotional release. With a little bit of work, I think we could get it back."

I surveyed the stone altar and stumps in front of us. She was right; it was not so far gone that it could not be saved. I stood and we both got to work, clearing the ground of all the debris that had fallen into the circle, brushing the stones of twigs and forest droppings. It was mindless, and it felt good to be back in a rhythm together, working in our space with purpose.

At one point, I thought I heard some rustling among the trees and fallen branches breaking under someone's feet. We both stopped with anticipation, and I was fully expecting to see Robert appear out of nowhere. After a few moments the sounds passed, however, and the woods grew quiet again, save for the wind that was making itself known.

We worked until just past suppertime and midday. We knew we should be making our way back, but having toiled to give the space new life, neither of us wanted to move. We looked around to see all we had accomplished. Madge reached into the pocket of her cloak and pulled something out. "It just so happens I have this with me!" and she waved the tied bundle in front of my face. It was a dried stick of sage leaves wrapped together in twine.

I smiled. "What do you know?"

Madge smiled back. "Mother gave it to me a while ago...but here it sits, and now I know why," she said triumphantly. "Would you like to do the honors?" she asked.

"No, I think it best if the Mistress of the Procured Herb does it herself," I said in a mocking tone.

"Fine," she said and dropped to her knees with the bundle in hand. She needed a flame with which to light the sage so we could create the smoke and banish any negative energy that still hung in the air, even after all our purging. Thankfully, Madge was brilliant at striking two rocks together to get a spark and she had the sage bundle lit in no time.

We let the flame go out of its own accord to ensure there would be enough smoke. Madge led the way against the sun around the stone center and we said in unison what we had devised so long ago:

Let evil be banished from this place
Take it away from us with grace
From West to East, South to North
Let it harbor here no more-th

We laughed as we said the last word, knowing full well we had made it up at the time because we could not think of anything else that rhymed. Once we walked counter-sun three times, we switched directions to sunwise and said:

We welcome in good in abundance
Let this space transform repugnance
North, South, East and West
Please keep us safe at our behest

We once again circled three times and concluded with, "So mote it be."

The smudging stick smoke held out just long enough to conclude the ritual. We both knew this had only been something crafted in childhood, and yet after having performed it again, it felt so reassuring, like a favorite cloak wrapped around one's shoulders.

Neither of us knew what the future held, especially with all of the changes lately and more that were yet to come. However, at this moment, in this time, the familiar provided a sense of comfort and release that had not been felt in so long.

As we walked back to the village much the way we came, in silence and locked arm in arm, we sensed the same buzzing as we had when we left. We got to the village center and Madge's eleven-year-old brother Robert ran by but stopped short when he saw us.

"She has been seen!" he shouted to us with a wild look in his eye. We looked at each other, not quite sure what he could mean. By his exuberance, you would think he saw the Queen.

"Who has?" I asked him with a smile on my face, thinking he was playing a prank at our expense.

"Lizbeth!" he called and then kept running in the direction he had been going.

Madge's arm tensed in mine, and we looked at each other. We immediately looked over at Mr. White's shop to see if she was in there, as she used to be at this time of day, keeping her father company and annoying her brother as he apprenticed. However, she was not. Perhaps young Robert had gotten it wrong, but then Catrina, the daughter of the baker, came over to us. Clearly sensing our confusion, she lowered her voice as she approached.

"It is true, Miss Hughes and Miss Williams. I saw her with my own eyes, though I almost did not recognize her 'tis been so long and she looked…different. The whole village has been abuzz, seeing as no one has seen her since their wedding! How is she?!" she asked us, clearly expecting us to have an update. When she saw we had nothing to offer, she scooted back to the bakery before her mother bellowed after her.

Lizbeth had been seen. It had caused such a scene in the village, and we were devastated we had not been here to see it. If she had come, where had she gone? Surely, it had to have been only recently, and we could not have missed her by much.

We started walking again, arm in arm, silently marching forward as we were each lost in our own thoughts. Then there it was. That pricking sensation in the middle of my back again. The pit in my stomach was back too, and I had a sinking feeling that something else had happened while we had been out in the woods, reclaiming our sanctuary.

Chapter 25 – December, Present Day – Sophia/Maddy

The student presentations quickly concluded, as did the Thanksgiving holiday. My preconceived week off for the students turned out to be serendipitous for me as well since I needed time to myself. Kit was right; there was a lot to process and the only thing that was going to help was not having any distractions so I could dive into my own head and figure things out.

Violet must have sensed the change in energy because ever since that "Night of Revelations," as I referred to it, she had not left my side. She was usually one to lounge in her favorite bed and watch me go from room to room, or sleep in her bed in my room to stay warm, but now she was watching my every move, something which I would normally not let happen, but under the circumstances the little warm furry body next to me was the only thing that would let me sleep, fitful though it was.

Thanksgiving had been late this year, so we were already into December by the time classes resumed. Not wanting to focus on my dilemma the entire break, I decided to focus on Maddy's. I got my hands on a deck of traditional tarot cards to better understand the one card she recalled, the Knight of Wands.

The cards were easy enough to find, and there were sites aplenty online to help one learn the art of interpretation, but I was old school when it came to learning new tricks and wanted a physical reference. I found one at the local Five Below of all places.

In the days since I had discovered the book, I was amazed to find the similarities between the tarot deck and a deck of traditional playing cards, and how, historically, people used to read playing cards like tarot. Once I learned the Major from the Minor Arcana, I started to understand the different suits and how to interpret the pictures. It all came to me pretty easily and I impressed myself, though I was wary as to the why and suspected it had something to do with my strong intuition.

When I finally had what I felt was a strong base knowledge, I pulled out the Knight of Wands to see what information it held and why Gypsy Zabina would have said it was a message for Maddy. I was pretty sure Maddy would not be looking into this herself, and as her friend who held a natural interest in the modality anyway, I thought maybe I could help.

The depiction itself wasn't overly remarkable. There was a knight clearly dressed for battle and charging ahead on his noble steed. The way the horse's head was cocked certainly looked like they were in the thick of it, and yet the knight himself appeared calm. I imagined it was because of his nature and meant to indicate the energy of the card. I had learned that each of the suits represented a basic category: Cups = Emotions, Swords = Conflict, Pentacles = Money, and Wands = Ambitions.

If I was to interpret the card's meaning based off this alone, I would say that Maddy was being given a message to pursue her ambition with passion and charge ahead, calmly. The book I acquired said that the card represented "a surge of energy and confidence to take action; a challenge to be faced with a determined attitude; a need to put ideas into action and finish what they started." Still other interpretations I found pointed to discovering a new interest or – more interestingly – spiritual path and that one should take it slow and steady.

I laughed to myself, given the conversation we had and Maddy's admission that perhaps she had fought too hard against other ideologies. It always surprised me how dogmatic she was when she had traveled and seen so much of the world and its cultures and beliefs. It was almost an unnatural security blanket with which she held onto for no apparent reason, while also seemingly running away from herself.

I told Kit about my findings, and she too was impressed with the speed at which I had picked all of this up. "You seem to have a natural affinity for this subject, Soph," she said and let the thought sink in.

It did feel weird. The more I looked at the cards, the less I had to reference the book, and I could give a pretty good indication of how the reading was going.

Distraction time over, however, I was headed back to campus for the last full week of classes before finals. I didn't broadcast beyond the classroom that I didn't set a final, but the students were buzzing with the knowledge. Today was the day we would wrap everything up and tie it with a nice bow. Thursday would be the end-of-semester party I liked to throw, with bagels for the morning classes and pizza in the afternoon, while everyone watched the same movie on repeat.

It was my way of paying homage to my Latin teacher from high school. He would do the same thing just before winter break to celebrate Saturnalia, giving each of his students a chance for respite during the day and somewhere to escape. Only then, it was *Monty Python and the Holy Grail.* Now, so as to keep with the spirit of my servitude, it was *The Founder*, a movie based on the man who made McDonald's what it was today, particularly appropriate for students studying food marketing.

I was looking forward to Thursday. By then, I would have made a decision on how to proceed within the university and what my future held, at least in the short term. Today, however, offered no such relief as I had a follow-up meeting scheduled with the dean to talk through my options and determine where we went from here. We were both in new territory and I could tell he was uncomfortable, wanting to put an end to this as quickly as possible.

Kit had checked in with me throughout the break, even inviting me over to her house for Thanksgiving dinner if I wanted. My parents had an opportunity to head down to their Florida property for the long weekend for a friend's daughter's wedding, and while my mom was remiss at not hosting this year, I was grateful for the space. Even with no distractions, I hadn't yet figured out what my next steps should be. I was truly at a loss and hoped Dean Smith would have more luck.

Should I try to find out who was behind the complaints and defend myself? I knew I couldn't change my methodologies based on this; that was tantamount to accepting bullying behavior. I had never succumbed to that in my life and certainly wasn't about to start now. Would I stop teaching altogether after I had found my calling, a career I truly enjoyed? I was at a standstill.

The day of classes flew by, everyone discussing their holidays and asking their last questions before the presentation feedback. They knew they wouldn't get their final grades until a couple weeks from now. They were excited for the most part, considering how well they had done in front of the live clients the week before. It was similar to the aftermath of the spring competition when everyone finally got to put into practice what they had been learning and test their skills in "real world" situations.

I smiled, but it was also painful. I had impacted so many students and in such a short time frame, and their exuberance and thoughtful commentary was truly motivating and inspiring. Was I ready to give this up?

Josh, from the competition team, picked up on my general mood. He came up to me after class and said, "Hey, Prof, you good?" It had become a bit of a joke between us since the last competition when he was a ball of nerves. I had simply walked up to him, put my hand on his shoulder and asked him the same question. We both knew he was nervous as hell, but I felt him physically relax in that moment. Since then, it had been our way of checking on each other.

"Yeah, Josh, I'm good." I knew that he knew it wasn't the truth, but I appreciated him taking the time to ask.

"See you Thursday?" he asked with genuine concern.

"Of course!" I said, not quite believing it myself.

He nodded, turned to go to the door, hesitated and then left. I wasn't fooling anyone; I was obviously not myself. It was kind of him to check on me, but neither he nor the rest of the students knew what was going on, and it wasn't my place to say anything.

I gathered my things and made the slow walk to the College of Business's main building, which housed the dean and other administrative staff for our group. LaShonda saw me enter and immediately called into Dean Smith's office to mitigate my wait time. Surprisingly, I didn't even have the chance to sit down and was ushered right in. I wasn't sure if that was a good or bad thing but slid into the seat I had sat in only two short weeks ago, set my bags down on the ground next to me and folded my hands.

Dean Smith took one look at me and his demeanor completely altered. I guessed he was preparing to do battle, fully expecting me to come in guns blazing, but when he realized that was not the case, he settled in for a discussion. "How was your Thanksgiving break?" he started.

"Fine," I said. Was he really going to try small talk? I just wanted to get through this.

He must have read my face as he continued. "Let's not belabor this. What are you thinking? Where do we go from here?"

Taking a thoughtful pause, I collected myself. "Well, I know what I'm not going to do, which is alter my teaching methods. Today's classes only solidified that for me even more," I said with much more confidence and resiliency than I expected. Where was this coming from?

Dean Smith looked crestfallen. Had he actually expected me to just back down and change my own, successful, teaching methods because someone had their knickers in a twist? I supposed my higher self was taking over because five minutes ago I felt like a wilting flower, not knowing what I was going to say, and now I was a pit bull standing my ground.

"I can't say I'm surprised, Miss Aitken," he said.

"Dean, it's just not right. Do you know how many students I have positively impacted in my time here? Sure, it's not 100%, but it's damn near close, and I refuse to believe that an institution such as this would be allowing this to happen to one of its best educators if there wasn't more at play here." Now I was on a roll.

This smarted, and he winced. He paused a beat before responding, obviously working something out in his head before he spoke.

"I'm not surprised you are unwilling to change, Miss Aitken, and to be honest, off the record, I would have been quite disappointed if you had."

I was stunned by this.

"However, it stands to reason that we still need to take some action until the dust settles. I am not within my rights to tell you what to do as you are part of the union. However, I am open to suggestions from you on how to move forward."

While he was being supportive, he clearly could only go so far. I threw my hands in the air. "Dean, I honestly don't know. This is new territory for me. I'm from corporate, not academia. The rules that worked there don't work here, because frankly, this conversation would not be happening. Hell, I would be getting a bonus for the work I've contributed, not a slap on the wrist."

That was only half true. Corporate was just as bad with the "very vocal few" having a larger say than they should and impacting the careers of many, but he didn't need to know that. I continued. "Do you have any suggestions you can offer that would better equip me to make a decision? I love this job. It has shown me that it is truly my calling, and I do not want to give it up. The students mean too much to me, and I want to continue to help support the future leaders in the food marketing industry. But I will not compromise my methods, especially when I know they work."

Dean Smith nodded his head in understanding and agreement. "I don't have anything better to offer. However, one thing does come to mind." He hesitated. I waited. "Sabbatical."

I tilted my head. "How would that be possible? I'm not a fully tenured professor yet. I don't qualify."

He seemed to be working it out in his head. "No, no, you are not. However, under the circumstances, I think I could make the argument for it. You are in the midst of getting your doctorate, yes?" I nodded. "Good, then perhaps we can leverage that and say it is a research sabbatical for your dissertation or something," he mused out loud.

Sabbatical. It seemed like the right course of action, given my other options were changing my methodology or quitting, but I needed to think on it.

"What do you think?" he asked in anticipation.

"Well, it seems plausible, but I need to do some soul searching," I said.

"Say no more," he said excitedly. "You go home and think about it and let me know your answer in the morning." I suddenly had a visual of George Bailey being offered a job by Mr. Potter. Was it that "ick"?

I nodded my head and stood. There wasn't much else to say at this point, and I needed to get out of there. I would call Kit on my way home to discuss. I knew she would want to drop everything and come over, but she had already spent way too much time away from her family on my behalf. I would simply get her input and sit with it tonight.

I called as I walked, not wanting to wait until the car, but she didn't answer. Instead of leaving a voicemail, I shot her a quick text.

Meeting with Dean S was interesting. Floated the idea of a sabbatical.

I hit send as I reached Etta. I unlocked the door and threw my bags onto the passenger side. I looked down to the phone in my hand and saw the telltale "…" that indicated she was writing a response. I turned on the car and waited while Etta warmed up.

Sorry, on a conference call. I can come over tonight after Erik gets home to watch the kids.

I knew she would say that.

No need, doll. You stay with your family. I can muscle through this one, just wanted you to know.

That seemed to pacify her, at least for now, as there was no immediate response. I pulled out of the parking lot and once again found myself driving home in a stupor. I reached for one of my Lindt truffles from my latest haul before the holiday – dark chocolate sea salt caramel this time – and popped it into my mouth.

Thankfully traffic was light, and I breezed through almost all green lights. The universe wanted me to get home quickly. I laughed to myself. Sure, now it was speaking up after what had been a tumultuous couple of weeks.

I pulled in the driveway, collected my things and walked inside. Vi greeted me at the door with one of her famous tongue-to-toe stretches and welcomed me home. I grabbed some carrots and hummus out of the fridge and went into the front room. Perhaps some mindless binge-watching of the latest crime series would help me coalesce my thoughts.

Sometime later I woke with a start from the ping on my phone. It had gone dark, and the streaming service had long since paused, asking if I was still watching. I looked at my phone and saw it was a message from Kit.

Crazy thought. Scotland?

Maddy couldn't believe what she had shared with Sophia and Kit, but if she was honest, who else could she have brain dumped on? These last few weeks, with the party, the conversation about spiritual beliefs with Ryan, and now what sounded like a possible shared recurring dream, had completely turned her world upside down. The dream that had kept her traveling – like a gypsy; oh, the irony – all these years was catching up with her now and she didn't know what to do.

She was thankful for Ryan. While they were on opposite ends of the spectrum when it came to their belief systems, that wasn't new for her, as most men were. What was new was the fact they could have an adult conversation about it, and he didn't think she was "too" anything. He had accepted her viewpoint for what it was. Equally as unnatural was the fact that she didn't go running when he explained his. That in itself was unprecedented progress for her and told her everything she needed to know about how much she liked…possibly loved this guy.

The empathy she felt with the evil emanating from her dream counterpart was what startled her the most and made her reconsider her own beliefs.

This had all begun to unravel after the party and the tarot. While the thought scared her half to death, she had a niggling feeling that there were more answers to be found there, if only she knew what the fortune teller had seen in those ten cards she pulled. She had tried to research the Knight of Wands, but none of it made sense to her, and when she did search for a definition, her misgivings were so entrenched it felt like she was betraying some unseen force.

That was it! She needed to see the old Romani woman. Perhaps she could find answers that way. If she was honest, her methods hadn't gotten her anywhere and if she was to honor Ryan's perspective the same way he had hers, she should at least try. How could she get her hands on the woman's real name and contact information without tipping off her employer though? This would require some thought...and strategically worded questions for Mary.

She finished getting ready for the day, threw on her latest shade of magenta lipstick to offset her otherwise natural eye makeup and went downstairs for coffee. If she timed it right, she would catch Mary just as she was finishing and whirling off to her office again, distracted enough to provide information without questioning why it was needed.

She walked down the well-worn carpeted hallway to the winding staircase and descended. She could hear voices from the breakfast room and assumed it was Bill, the porter, and Mary chatting about the lunch needs for the day. Instead, it was Ryan and Mary.

The thought of Ryan made her heart stir, and she smiled. God, was she head over heels for him or what? The conversation floated out to the hallway.

"Are you serious about this one, brother?" Mary asked.

"Sis, you have no idea. She is like a puzzle that I have yet to piece together, and rather than getting frustrated, I'm fascinated!" Ryan said with enthusiasm.

"Well, the fascination part I can clearly see. And why not, she's stunning. But honey, she's 100% homegrown American. Isn't that a tad...beneath us?" Mary said.

Maddy had been smiling up to that point, assuming that they were talking about her and Ryan's relationship, but now she didn't like where Mary was taking this. She thought she liked her?!

"So she is, sis, very observant of you. But isn't it you who in fact hired her to begin with?" Ryan said with amusement, as if he was a cat that had caught a mouse.

"Well, of course, dear, but why wouldn't I? She came with sparkling recommendations, and you can work Americans until they bleed, even over the holidays." She laughed.

This must have made Ryan upset because Maddy heard a chair scrape across the beautiful parquet floor, making her shudder, and Ryan's long stride move toward the door. "Say what you want, sis, but I'm more than smitten, and right now, where she goes, I go!" he said, his voice completely changed. She heard him walking closer to the door. She had to hide. She couldn't be seen eavesdropping on a conversation between her employer and her boyfriend!

"Suit yourself, love. Don't get me wrong, I like the girl. I just don't want to see you go all whompy like you did after the last one...Cecelia?" Mary called after him.

Maddy ducked into the corridor at the bend of the stairs just in time for Ryan to come walking out, past her and toward the back of the house. He was in such a huff that he hadn't noticed her, thank God. That was a close call.

Given what she had just heard, she wasn't sure she wanted to face Mary either. Great, now she had to hide from her employer who only took her on so she could, how did she put it, "work her until she bled"? Ugh. She couldn't possibly ask Mary about the gypsy now.

As she was squatting in the shadows, something under the last step caught her eye. It was sticking out at an odd angle. She waddled over to retrieve the object, only to realize it was a business card. She turned it over in her hands and read, *Gypsy Zabina – mystic, medium, healer,* with her contact information underneath.

Seriously?! She couldn't believe her luck. She looked upward to the sky and said, "OK, universe, I got you." Completely forgetting breakfast, she bounded back up the stairs, taking two at a time, and raced to her room. She needed to email this woman before she lost her nerve.

She sat down at her computer and opened a new message:

Good morning!

I hope you are well. You may not remember me, but you were hired for my employer's party a few weeks back to do readings. I surmised that the reading you had started for me was different than what was typical, and yet I was too scared to say anything. The experience has not left me since and I only now just found your contact information.

I guess what I'm asking is if there is any way we could meet? You noticed I was not a believer at the time, but a lot has shifted in my world since and I need answers. I'm not sure if you are the one that can provide them, but I need to start somewhere...and somewhere different than I have in the past.

Kind regards,

Maddy

She hit send before she could chicken out and took a deep breath. She got up and walked over to the chaise. She suddenly needed to stretch out or she was going to crawl out of her own skin.

She turned her attention to the conversation she had overheard. "Where she goes, I go!" was replaying in her head. What did he mean by that? Was she going somewhere? Was Mary dismissing her? This was all moving so fast her head was spinning.

He was certainly the first, and only, guy she had ever truly fallen for, and it definitely felt like she was heading into uncharted territory, but it seemed it was not so uncharted for him. He had mentioned a Cece a couple times as they walked through their collective histories – the obligatory conversation once you reached a certain point – but was that the same person?

And what about Mary? She thought she was on good terms with her. That conversation made it seem like she saw her as no more than a workhorse, overworked and easily replaced. She had always thought she was naturally passionate about her job, but the tower she had built herself seemed to be crumbling down around her.

Chapter 26 – December 1563 – Lizbeth

It felt good to be out and about and away from the house. Lizbeth could not believe how she had missed the yuletides of the season being locked away in her prison. Richard kept calling it their house, but she knew better. She found it interesting that he never called it home but paid no mind since clearly that was never his intention – to create a home.

After being married to the man for over a month, she was learning his true character even more. She was not surprised, especially based on his behavior leading up to the engagement. She did not blame her father. He was a kind and gentle man and would never have known that someone so vile could exist, let alone marry his daughter. He thought he had done right by her, elevated her station, if only it was that easy.

Still, she must have done something right to have earned herself a day of reprieve. She could not wait to get to the village center and take in all the sights and sounds and post-Christmas celebrations. She had missed Advent and Christmas and hoped against all hope that she could still experience something for this new month. She had started to feel like something had died inside of her and was worried if she did not feel joy again soon, she would lose it forever.

She had been given strict instructions not to seek out Ann or Madge. She did not know what Richard had against them, but surely if she were to innocently bump into them while walking to her father's shop, she could not be blamed for that!

She walked along the path, lost in her own thoughts, until she realized there was a buzz around her. The villagers were murmuring about something, so she started to look around to see what it could be she missed, and then it hit her. They were talking about her.

Had it been so long that she had become an oddity in her own hometown? She supposed it had, which made her remorseful that she had not tried harder to get out of the house. But how could she when Richard had all manner of excuses to keep her locked away?

First, it was to continually consummate the marriage. Though she did not know how much was required, it became apparent he was making excuses and became rougher and rougher each time. She had learned to close her eyes and drift away until he had either finished or fallen asleep from far too much drink.

Then, he was "fearful" for her safety, as there was an outbreak of some illness. Given how he had lost his family to the plague, she was somewhat sympathetic to this and tried to keep from complaining. She could not understand why though, if there truly was something going around, that Ann or Madge had not yet sent provisions. She had asked her husband at one point if she could go visit Mrs. Williams to get some remedies to keep on hand, and he had come undone! He did not let her eat for a day and a half after that, which made no sense in her mind. If he was so afraid of getting sick, why would he not want to be prepared? She could only imagine what she must look like to others since she knew her clothes were now hanging off her once robust frame.

She continued to her father's shop, stopping at other shop windows along the way. She was determined to make the most of her unexpected freedom today and drink everything in. As she approached, she saw two unmistakable figures walking arm in arm ahead of her. Her plan had worked! She would be able to bump into them.

She raised her hand to call after them and get their attention when they turned onto the path to the wood. She paused. Surely, they would not be going there after all this time, and without her?

She slowed her pace, took shelter on the side of the building housing her father's cobbling shop and watched, stared into their backs was more like it, willing them not to be doing what she thought they were doing. With each step they took away from her, she felt what little tether she had left to her old world fraying.

After they completely disappeared from sight, she felt tears prick the corners of her eyes. She did not know what to do. Should she go after them? Wait here? She took a deep breath and exhaled. Perhaps they were just going for a walk. She could go visit her father and brother and stay within sight should they return. She nodded to herself, wiped her eyes and turned to head into the shop she knew so well.

She walked through the door and was hit with a miasma of smells. The worn leather, the smell of the fire, the warm coals set aside to help shape the soles or heat up the tools of the trade to make things more pliable. The few familial lasts that were kept on hand for the gentry on the outskirts of the village hung from the ceiling, with others firmly planted in their holders nailed to the wall.

She caught a glimpse of her father and brother, both buried in their tasks, before they saw her. She witnessed the rhythm they had created since Matthew had started his apprenticeship. Her father must be pleased with his progress. The gentle back and forth while sewing the leather, hammering the nails, setting them aside to move onto the next one. She saw the vat of bear grease in the corner, ready to be applied once the shoe was assembled, to dress the outside of the leather.

The whole scene almost brought her to her knees. She did not realize how long it had been since seeing her family and being in the presence of their warmth. She caught herself sniffling and her father called out, "Be right with you!" without missing a beat or looking up. When he finally did, he jumped out of his seat, toppling his stool over and causing Matthew to prick himself with the needle he was holding.

"Father!" he called out in frustration, not knowing why his father had just startled. When he finally looked up from his work, he saw him in an embrace with a woman. She was unrecognizable at first, the set of her face harder than he had ever seen and her skin glowing, not from health, but from not having seen the sun in a long time.

"Lizbeth?! Is that really you?" her father cried out as he continued hugging her.

She was not sure what to do with this outburst of emotion. When he came at her, she had flinched. After weeks in captivity with Richard, how could she not? But she quickly admonished herself once her father's arms were around her. It was the best feeling. She saw the look of confusion on her brother's face and finally smiled.

"Yes, it is I!" she cried.

Matthew walked over and gave her a quick hug after their father had finished. He looked down at his feet and started shuffling them like a schoolboy who did not know what to do next.

"Well, let me look at you," her father said as he took a step back. "You are definitely a bit paler, but not too worse for wear considering what you have gone through. Poor Mr. Acton has been at his wit's end!"

It occurred to Lizbeth then that she had no idea what her husband had been telling her family as to why she had not been around these last several weeks. It was unlike her to miss any party, let alone the holidays, and yet no one had checked in on her, at least not that she had been made aware of. She had a vague sense there had been visitors at the door from time to time, but with Richard keeping her corralled toward the back of the house, she never knew who it was. She had also never seen her husband "at his wit's end" about anything unless the drink was gone, at which point he became unbearable.

She cocked her head to the side in confusion and said, "Whatever do you mean, Papa?"

It was his turn to look confused. "Mr. Acton. He said you had been fighting an illness, something dreadful, and you have been bedridden for weeks…" His eyes were boring into her now, clearly questioning whether what he had been told was true.

Not wanting to get her father or herself into any trouble, she found her voice quickly. "Oh yes, that. Well, all better now! He, ah, let me out of the house today so I could get some fresh air," she responded.

"Let you?" he questioned.

"Ah, what I meant to say is, we thought it was time that I get some sun and stretch my legs so that I could continue recovering."

He eyed her warily but seemed to acquiesce.

So that was what he had told everyone! No wonder no one ever came to see her. Her father still looked a bit skeptical, so she tried changing the subject. "How were the holidays? I missed you all so."

Matthew chimed in then. "I got a brand-new leather apron for work!" he said, turning this way and that so she could admire it.

"Brilliant!" she said, sure to pay the apron its due.

"We missed you," her father said warmly, "but I suppose we have to get used to that now you are a married woman. Though I hope in the future there will be additional family members with which to share the holidays, running around on little feet requiring little shoes." He winked.

She tried not to wince at the connotation. While she had always wanted children, and dreamed of a large family, the last thing she wanted to do was bear *his*.

Her father read something in her face then. "Matthew, get back to work. You know the Prescotts will be here later today to pick up their order!"

She watched Matthew diligently turn and retreat back to his stool to continue sewing. Her father walked her over to the counter.

"Lizbeth, are you sure you are alright?" He looked at her imploringly.

"Why, Father?" she slowly questioned. Could he see through her? Sense the anguish under which she was living? Could she let him know? What would happen to him if her husband found out? What would happen to her?

"You just don't seem yourself, and it is not like you to take ill for so long..." He was clearly perplexed and starting to unravel everything he had been told.

She had two choices. She could take her chances and reveal everything, taking comfort in the safety of being back in her father's world, or she could lie and keep the fairytale that Richard had spun alive and well. She desperately wanted to tell him, but what would that do to his pride, to know what he had married his daughter off to? She would not be allowed to divorce him – she was not King Henry VIII. The repercussions would be too extreme. Part of her thought...to hell with the consequences. But the pragmatic side was concerned for everyone's safety. Lying it was.

"Yes, Father, of course. Married life is different than I expected. I think the illness is just caused by the structure in which we are temporarily living, which Richard is working to upgrade as quickly as possible, but with this weather, it has halted any build from moving forward. I will be fine," she gushed, as if she could not say the words fast enough.

Her father still looked dubious, but she knew he would not question her. She had never lied to him before, and why would she start now?

"Alright, my dear, if you say so," he finally relented. "Oh, it is good to see you, Lizbeth, but unfortunately you are catching us at a busy time. As I said, the Prescotts are coming later today and with all the lively celebrations, I am afraid Matthew and I have gotten a bit behind," he said as he limped back to his chair. He must be working harder than usual because his cobbler limp was extra noticeable.

"Is there anything I can do to help?" she asked.

"I am afraid not, dove, we just need to keep our heads down and get this done," he said, already back into his work.

"Oh. Alright then." She started to leave, then stopped when she heard him clear his throat.

"Perhaps you would like to come for dinner tonight? I know George would like to see you, even if he may not show it, and then we could have a proper catchup."

This made her smile. Richard had given her strict instructions to return after her walk, but if he truly wanted to keep up the pretense, it would not suit for her to refuse her father's offer.

"Of course! That would be lovely, thank you," she said and truly felt happy.

"Wonderful, we may be a little late here, but help yourself to whatever you can find when you get home later and we can fill in the gaps from there," he said, and then was back to his awl, prepping the soles to be sewed onto the leather uppers.

She turned and walked out of the shop. She momentarily forgot it was winter, having been in the warmth of her family again, and the biting cold surprised her as it brushed across her face. She did not mind. Seeing her father and oldest brother was good for her soul.

As soon as she hit the corner, she remembered what she had seen before, and her heart fell again. She had been inside long enough that if they had simply gone on a walk along the path, they should be returning any moment now. She looked off into the distance, and there was nothing. Could they really be out there, in their sanctuary, without her? She had time before dinner, and she could not return to the house because Richard would never let her out again. She had to find out what they were doing.

She pulled her cloak tight and started down the all-too-familiar path. She mused along the way about what could possibly be found in her father's pantry at home with three men living there. Home. A word and feeling she had not felt since leaving the house in which she grew up. She never appreciated the difference between the words house and home until now.

She kept walking, lost in thought, until she got into the woods and began approaching their space. She tried to blend in with her surroundings, but as the trees were bare, this proved difficult. She walked the perimeter and then she saw them. They had just finished having a conversation on their stumps and were moving about.

She saw the center altar and immediately grew sad. She had held such hope that her incantation, no matter how dark it became, would impress upon Sophia the importance of her request and keep her from marrying Richard. Either she had failed, or Sophia had failed her. Leaning toward the latter, she could not imagine how these two were back here now and doing whatever it was they were doing.

What was it exactly? She crept closer, trying to get a better look, and stepped on a few branches. She stopped in her tracks and froze. She saw Ann look up and around; she must have heard the rustling. Then Ann went back to work, and Lizbeth realized they were clearing out the space.

Were they really going to practice a ritual or conduct a blessing after all this time? Or, she thought with as much anger as sadness, perhaps they had gone on practicing rituals without her this entire time without a care in the world. They had not come to see her since that first day after the wedding. Had her sisters truly moved on and forgotten all about her? And how could they be back here, when Sophia had not provided for her? There was a fire building within her now that felt like it would never be put out.

Her rage started to grow and the tether that had started to fray as she watched them walk away only became more splintered. She had to get away from this place. They started chanting something and she smelled the sage smoke. The smell once held fond memories, but now she suddenly felt compelled to turn around and leave, as if it were forcing her out, only this time she did not care how much noise she made.

Let them find her trudging away from them, as they had done to her. With each step she took from the place that once held solace and safety, Lizbeth grew colder and more distant. She resolved to start her own space with which she could practice her rituals. If they had forsaken her in her darkest hour, just as Sophia had, then she would them. It seemed no one was there for her now and she had to protect herself with her own growing zealotry.

Perhaps this was what her husband felt on the regular, that everyone he had cared for, if he was capable of such feelings, had left him behind and thus he could not dare trust another, nor the rituals and supposed blessings of anything outside of the church. She did not love the man, or even like him, but given this latest revelation, she could understand why he had become the man he was today; which provided a foundation for kinship of sorts.

Forgetting the promise of dinner with her family, she trudged back to her prison and felt the gates of darkness closing in around her with a finality that could be felt by anyone nearby. A wisp of wind that seemed to carry with it a cold unlike any other whirled away from her and back through the village. She did not care who felt it, only that she had completely removed herself from the place that was once her home and the people who had cared for her. The Lizbeth they knew was changed, and it was their fault.

Chapter 27 – January, Present Day – Sophia/Maddy

By the time the new year came, I was chomping at the bit, both from nervousness and excitement. Kit had suggested we basically "get the hell out of dodge" for a bit so I could reconcile what was happening at the university. That last text – *Crazy thought. Scotland?* – lived in my head rent-free for quite a while.

In all of our studying and upgrading of our spiritual knowledge, Scotland had become a nexus of sorts for us. We talked about a "someday" adventure there, clearly thinking it would be far into the future. While I had flexibility, Kit had too much going on to just drop everything and go on a voyage to the great unknown.

It was a crazy thought, but I couldn't get it out of my head, and before I knew it, we were booking flights and deciding it was time. I still didn't understand how Kit had managed to take three weeks off just after the holidays with her thriving business, active husband and even more involved twins, but somehow, she made it all seem like it was going to be a breeze.

Dean Smith had enthusiastically agreed to the sabbatical, and I was staring down the barrel of a work-free spring semester, while still holding my position and being paid. He had pulled the necessary strings since I was, as of yet, not considered tenured, but it was a huge weight off his shoulders, given the ongoing turmoil over my methods. I sensed there was more to it, but also decided I did not need to know right now.

Both Kit and I had tried to get hold of Maddy to let her know we were coming over, but she had been unreachable.

I turned my attention to my suitcases. While I was usually quite an efficient packer, thanks to years of traveling with my parents growing up, this time was different. Kit was going for three weeks and had a ticket booked home; I did not. I had thrown caution to the wind and decided I was only purchasing one way for now.

My biggest concern was Violet. I did not like the thought of leaving my furry companion for an unknown amount of time, but on some level, she seemed to sense what was going on and accepted it. Erik, being the true real-life hero he was, had said he and the kids would be only too happy to take her in and watch her for me while I was gone, so at least she would be with people I trusted.

The weather in Scotland at this time of year was unpredictable at best. It seemed I was going to be trading one cold, windy and snowy climate for another, but at least I had the correct wardrobe! One large suitcase, lovingly named "Big Bertha" many years ago, held all the bulky items I would need: a few different coats, vests, sweaters, boots, alpaca socks, hats, scarves and gloves. The next one had all the varying layers I would need with thermal tops and bottoms, sweat-wicking shirts, flannels and sweaters, though I was looking forward to adding to that stockpile with some Aran sweaters from the Highlands! The last suitcase, a size down, was all the "unmentionables": PJs, toiletries I didn't think I could find over there, and a few other odds and ends. It certainly felt like I was packing up and moving there, though I laughed at the thought.

"Yeah, right. Only in your dreams, Soph," I said to myself.

I walked back into the front room. We still had a week before we left, having decided it would be prudent to get Thora and Tate back into the swing of things at school before Kit left. I thought I'd try Maddy one more time. We were flying through to London and staying overnight so we could catch the morning train to Edinburgh and get the full view of the beautiful landscape with the sunrise. It would be great to try and catch her for drinks or dinner, but with her MIA, I wasn't sure we could make it happen.

I texted her my favorite meme for when checking on people I hadn't heard from in a while, a picture from the 1996 classic *Cool Runnings* asking, "Sanka, ya dead?" after he had crashed into the roadside stand during the boxcar derby. It was a last-ditch effort but usually attracted attention.

I was pacing. I needed to settle down. I went into the kitchen and poured a glass of wine, then went back to take a seat on the couch. My phone pinged and I picked it up, but it was just my parents checking in on their way to Florida.

Mom: *Hi, hon, just checking on you. I know you don't leave for a week, but do you need to run through anything?*
Me: *Hi! No, I'm good. Thankfully not my first rodeo.*
Mom: *Yes, of course, dear. How is Violet holding up? I know she takes your traveling hard.*

Me: *She seems to be good. I think she's taking it in stride since on some level she knows I need this.*
Mom: *That's good. We are so happy you are doing this for yourself. We're sorry we couldn't have taken her with us.*
Me: *It's OK. She will have the time of her life with Erik and the kids. She may not even want to come back to me when I'm home!*
Mom: *I highly doubt that. Well, we are almost at our stopover. Let us know if you need anything.*
Me: *Will do! Good night. Love you.*
Mom: *Good night. Love you.*

I set the phone down, took a sip of my wine and turned on the TV. Perhaps a movie would quiet my nerves and let me relax. I didn't know how I was going to make it through the next week.

Maddy cautiously walked through the door of the small shop with the weird moon phase graphic painted on the window. It wasn't the first time she had been in a shop like this, but it was the first time she had willingly entered of her own accord and not because she was too embarrassed to tell whatever friend she was with that "No, she didn't want to go in because the devil lay inside." She started to cross herself out of habit but stopped. This was no time to invoke that spirit.

Gypsy Zabina had responded to her email a few days later. While it caused her angst to wait, she assumed that the woman, for all her intuition, did not play well with modern technology. She almost had her message back memorized, burned into the recesses of her brain.

Good evening, Miss,

As it happens, I do remember you. Your aura was blocked when you sat down, and hot, almost too hot to touch, as if you had the largest protective barrier around you. The cards I pulled that night were much more aligned with a traditional reading, like I do in my shop, than the simple party favor it was meant to be. I knew you were not ready to hear what old Zabina had to say, so I did not interpret, but I confess I was compelled to keep pulling.

I am happy to hear you have had a shift, I think you called it, and would be honored to help you through this time. I may not have all the answers, but your people do and have been coming through fast and furious since I received your note.

Please come by my shop after the winter holiday. I think it will be profound for you to be here on January 3, around 4:00PM. I am located at 209 Great Weymouth St. You will recognize the shop by its door. You can't miss it.

Yours truly,
Gypsy Zabina

It seemed like forever ago since she received the email, and yet now she was here. What did today have in store, and why had she been so precise with the date and time? Did the numbers hold some special meaning? She presumed she was about to find out.

Zabina called her to the back room where she already had her table laid out with her deck, and a sweet-smelling smoke filled the air. Maddy set her things down on the forest-green velvet wingback chair against the wall and walked over to the table where she was seated.

Feeling incredibly nervous and self-conscious, Maddy started babbling. "Thank you so much for agreeing to see me. I honestly didn't know what to do, and I've never done anything like this before…"

Zabina held up her hand to stop her spewing. "Calm down, my child, you are in no danger here and should not be so nervous. What we are going to do has been done for thousands of years. It predates your chosen god, and even helped inspire him."

Maddy doubted that but did not want to be rude. Instead, she took a deep breath, let it out slowly and sat in silence. At least until she could no longer. "What is that smell? The smoke. I smelled it when you were at the party as well."

The old Romani smiled as she continued to shuffle the deck of cards. "That, my dear girl, is palo santo. A simple type of tree, but when burned and the smoke is allowed to work its magic, it will ward off any evil spirits that wish to take hold in your person while doing lightwork." She continued shuffling.

Maddy considered these words. She only understood about half of what this woman had said, but it seemed to jive. She watched her shuffle the cards and place them down on the table. "I thought we were going to review the cards that were pulled last time?" Maddy queried.

"Cut the deck," Zabina requested. Confused, Maddy did as she was told. "We can't, my dear girl, for unless you are meant to see the same message, the message will shift and change as you do. What came through last time was what you were meant to see or experience then. You yourself have admitted having changed, so the message may very well change too."

Disappointed, Maddy's face fell, but she understood. She wished she could remember the cards that were pulled, but she could get behind the message changing as needed. The gypsy started.

"First, the basics, as I presume you are entirely new to this, and it may help quiet your inner voice to understand what we are doing. When considering a deck of tarot, there are traditionally seventy-eight cards. The first twenty-two are what is referred to as 'Major Arcana' and the remaining are 'Minor Arcana,'" she said, watching Maddy's face for understanding. Maddy was engaged, so she continued. "The Major Arcana are what they claim, representing major life events and themes. The Minor represent small events, themes and issues, more day-to-day type things if you like."

Maddy said, "OK, I'm with you."

Zabina was pulling cards now and moving them around in a different order from which she pulled them. "Typically, you want to read the Major Arcana first, as they represent the larger overarching themes, and then the Minor will provide more detail. It is not uncommon for someone to have all of one type or varying combinations. If I recall from your previous pull, there were several Major Arcana."

She had pulled ten cards so far. Looking at them upside down, it was hard to understand all of them, but Maddy saw enough to pull away. Was that the Devil again, looking back at her from one of those cards? And a burning Tower with people jumping from it? Suddenly, she wasn't so sure this was a great idea.

Zabina sensed her discomfort and looked up. "The first rule of tarot is to understand that the pictures or words are not always a bad thing. For instance, you have the Devil card in your pull, but that does not mean what you think it does." Maddy just stared back at her. "Observe," she said and started the reading.

"As I see these cards and put them in order, a pattern emerges, or a story. Your story, at least for the immediate future, is one filled with major themes and events with more than half of your cards residing within the Major Arcana," she said and waited for Maddy to look at what she was describing. Maddy saw the following, which Zabina had positioned at the top of the table in a single row but differently spaced:

Devil & Moon (side by side)
Hermit
World
Justice
Tower

However, she noticed only the Devil card was facing upright while all the others were turned upside down. She wondered if that carried any significance.

"These Major Arcana cards mean serious business for you, with major change or changes coming," Zabina said with emphasis.

"OK, and what about these?" Maddy asked, pointing at the remaining four cards that had formed a small cascade of sorts underneath the upside-down Tower card:

Ace of Wands
King of Cups
Queen of Cups
Three of Cups

Again, all but the Three of Cups was reversed. Curious. "Does it mean anything specific when the cards are upside down?" Maddy asked.

"You jump ahead, young one, but yes. If the tarot card is reversed, it simply means it is the opposite of the meaning when it is right side up," she explained.

"Oh, so that's bad, then." Maddy looked crestfallen.

Zabina smiled. "Not necessarily." Maddy threw her hands up in the air in frustration. "Patience, I show you," she cooed and started from the top.

"The Devil card shows you are anxious; you have been avoiding something for a long time that is buried deep within you. You consider yourself a victim and have not made peace with inner turmoil," she said and moved onto the next card. "When you have an upside-down moon, especially paired with the Devil card, it means you have cycles at play that have been suppressed for a long time, possibly even related to Karma. The moon is shining its light to help bring awareness, release fear and bring forth truth. If you listen, it will help unblock your intuition."

Maddy didn't like the implications this woman was making. They were uncomfortable, but if she was honest with herself, all too accurate. And something about a moon shining made a part of her brain buzz.

"The Hermit is as it seems. When reversed, one is avoiding themselves instead of others, because they are afraid of what they might discover. The World card usually represents great success through change; however, since this is upside down, it means you are not addressing those cycles and lessons that should be learned. You will be stagnant in all you try to do, until you make the necessary changes." Zabina was growing more emphatic as she went, as if propelled by an unseen energy.

She pointed at the reversed Justice card. "You are still not learning from past experiences. A situation will arise that will throw you off balance and you will be reactive." Then she pointed at the last Major Arcana, the one of a burning tower with people falling from it, and Maddy held her breath. Sensing her angst, Zabina smiled. "This one happens to be my favorite."

Maddy let out the breath she had been holding. "What?! How can that be?! The scene looks awful!"

The wise woman smiled. "The Tower card represents change and letting go. Change is hard. You have to be brave with change. The good news is, when the Tower card is upside down, the change won't be as hard or challenging as it could be, so it will go easy on you. But the effects of the change will bring about personal development far beyond what you can imagine."

This made Maddy feel a touch better. OK, so the Devil card did not mean the devil incarnate was after her, nor did the Tower card mean she was going to spontaneously combust.

"So, what you're saying is that I have been running away from myself for a long time, and I had better come to terms with it quickly and learn from the mistakes I've made and do some self-reflection to understand where it all stems from, or it's going to go south quick?" she summarized.

Zabina looked impressed. "Are you sure you have not worked with tarot before? I think you trick old Zabina."

Maddy smiled and shook her head.

"Ah, OK, well, we move on. Each of the suits of the Minor Arcana represent something. In this case, you have two of the four suits represented in wands and cups. Wands can represent energy, creativity, ambition and new beginnings, while Cups are related to emotions. So here" – she pointed at the cascade below the Tower – "it is saying you are showing a lack of initiative and blocking your own ambitions, and here." She pointed at the last three cards. "Your masculine and feminine energies are out of alignment, making you easily overwhelmed and suspicious. This last one is indicative of a reconnection with the past and a pending celebration."

That wasn't all bad. At least the second half wasn't so revealing. She was feeling seen, and not in a way that she liked. Zabina pulled one more card from the deck she had set aside.

Knight of Wands

Zabina smiled. "What, what does that mean?!" Maddy exclaimed.

"Well, my dear, it's a literal Knight in Shining Armor. Someone who is charming and adventurous who has or will present himself to you to further shake up your world and make you question everything you believe."

Ryan.

She had to admit – this was pretty spot on, eerily so. She sat in silence as she synthesized everything the fortune teller had shared. It was a lot, and she wasn't sure what to do with it.

"So, now what?" Maddy asked.

Zabina shook her head. "I do not know, dove."

Maddy looked confused. "What do you mean you don't know?"

Zabina smiled. "As I said in my email, I don't have the answers, just the inputs. It is up to you what you do with this information moving forward. If you want to reverse any of the cards you don't like, now that you are aware of them, then you must take action, otherwise you will continue to repeat the same cycles you always have and generations have before you."

I woke up with a start. I must have fallen asleep on the couch again. At least I had finished my wine and not spilled the glass. The past few weeks had taken their toll. I looked at my phone; it was 3:11AM. Violet was asleep in her corner of the room, having somehow curled up with a blanket. I had a missed message. While I wanted to drift back to sleep, I thought I better check it.

Maddy: *Sorry, doll, it's been wild. Lots of moving parts here. Yes, I'm alive. Let me know what's up when you're awake!*

I couldn't risk not getting her in her own time zone, so I texted back.

Me: *No worries. Just wanted to check in on you and also share that there's been some developments here too. Will share more details, but any chance you are available to meet near Heathrow on Tuesday? Kit and I are flying in and should be landing around 8AM. I figure with immigration and baggage, we could meet up for a late breakfast? We're staying overnight in Kensington before we leave in the morning for Edinburgh.*

I hit send, completely expecting it to go unseen, then I saw the three dancing ellipses at the bottom of the screen.

Maddy: *First, what are you doing up at this hour, and second, what the hell are you doing coming over here?! So many questions. I will see what I can do but shouldn't be a problem to make my way there. I've been meaning to get to the city to pick up a few things anyway. Send me your flight info and we can just meet at your hotel if easiest. OMG!!!*

I could feel her confusion through the phone and just smiled. Good, for once I wasn't the one throwing her off!

Me: *Got it. Nighty night.*

Before I knew it, it was the Monday of our flight. We swiftly made our way to JFK where we had a four-hour layover until our flight to Heathrow. I thankfully had enough miles saved from my old corporate travel days that I could fly over on Delta One for the full first-class experience, which also got Kit and I into the lounge. Kit said she had to work the entire time and was happy to fly in Comfort+, but little did she know I had a trick up my sleeve with a travel voucher to upgrade her.

After the lounge and free champagne, we were lining up to board. It never ceased to amaze me how assumptions were made when lining up. I often remembered times early in my career when I would be upgraded to first class because of status, but the old guys in blue sport coats with gold buttons would always budge in front of me while waiting for their boarding group to be called, because I, a young female, couldn't possibly have dibs over them. The looks on their faces was priceless when First would be called and I had to say "Excuse me" as I broke through them to pass.

I smiled to myself at the thought and Kit caught me. "What?" she mouthed. I shook my head as our cabin was called and we lined up with the others.

With 2A and 2B all to ourselves, we unpacked what we would need in our little cubbies and happily took the glasses of champagne offered. We both couldn't wait to get to London and meet up with Maddy; there were so many things to catch up on from both sides. In no time, the wheels were up, and we were making our way across the pond.

I thought Kit would probably be relishing the time to herself, so I left her to enjoy a hot meal and a movie. I knew she missed her family already, but it must have been a relief to finally have some alone time. We both eventually fell asleep and enjoyed the smooth, turbulence-free ride, snuggled into the soft blankets and lay-flat seats. Poor Kit wanted to get some work done on the trip over, but clearly that wasn't going to happen now.

The next morning, we enjoyed our hot towels before breakfast, tore open the amenity kit with toothbrush, toothpaste, moisturizer and, my favorite, face spray, and freshened up. We collected ourselves, landed and made our way through the melee that was passport control. Thanks to our superior position on the plane as well as having Global Entry, the wait time was short, and our luggage was out first.

I turned on my phone to text Maddy that we were already through when something caught my attention out of the corner of my eye. Before I knew it, Kit and I were set upon by a mad woman running straight at us. I dropped my bags and braced for impact.

Maddy was always a little ball of fire and would take full advantage of her small stature against my large pouncing on me whenever possible. Kit stood back in both horror and amazement while gathering the bags I had dropped.

"Now. What the bloody hell are the two of you doing here?!" Maddy greeted us in her full British accent.

Chapter 28 – January 1564 – Ann

January hit hard in our village. The biting cold at the end of December only increased with the changing of the month, for the New Year was still three months off in March with the Feast of Annunciation. It had been enough to keep most from joining the frivolity that normally fell upon the village post-Christmas celebrations. It had also kept Madge and I from our sanctuary after we had spent so much time cleaning it up. It was as if someone had placed a cold spell over the town so no one could enjoy the last holiday cheer.

I greeted the day as I had every day these past few months, by checking to see if my siblings had already gone downstairs or were still sound asleep so that I may try my hand at speaking with James. With more and more practice, I was getting better, and the conversations were lasting longer. It was simple at first; we would talk about what he witnessed the day before, and I would talk about any news from my father and brothers. We each seemed to skip around any heavier topics as though neither of us were ready to go deeper.

This morning, however, was different. We had been mid-conversation when Izzy stirred. James seemed like he had been about to share something with me when I had to get up and check on her.

Unfortunately, her head was warm to the touch, and she seemed to be sweating profusely, while I was wrapped up in my thickest blanket and still shivering. I looked back at my bed in the direction James's voice had last come from and sighed. He seemed to understand, and our conversation ended.

I walked back over to my bed, changed into my winter undergarments and gown, and softly padded downstairs. I went over to the cupboard where we stored some of Mrs. Williams' tonics to see what we had.

"Good morning, Mother," I whispered to her. She was cooking breakfast and clearly in her own head because I startled her, and the piece of bread she had just been about to put on the fire to toast went flying.

"Oh my word!"

I stifled a laugh.

"Ann Hughes, you gave me a fright! I did not hear you come downstairs, like a cat you are!" she said as she looked up at the stairs, pondering how I could have come down without her knowing.

"Sorry, Mama. I was only trying to be quiet for the sake of the children still sleeping and you having your morning time."

"'Tis alright, love, I must have just been lost in my own thoughts is all. What do you need?" she said as she picked up the bread, brushed it off and skewered it on the toasting fork to hold it over the fire.

"Izzy stirred a bit. I went to check on her and her head felt rather warm to the touch. I thought I would see if you had any coriander or some of Mrs. Williams' feverfew tonic," I said.

"Oh dear. Well, I do not think I have any coriander after all the holiday celebrations, but I do think I have some tonic. You can give that to the poor dear and then make your way over to Mrs. Williams' later to grab a few more provisions and the like," she said, distracted.

I nodded, searched around in the cupboard and found the little bottle she had indicated. Mother turned around with goblet in hand and some hot fresh small beer, a drink I fondly remembered from childhood.

She threw a few cloves into the cup and said, "Best hide it in something she will drink."

I opened the bottle and poured out what little was left. I carried the steaming-hot cup up to the loft again and jostled Izzy awake. I would have liked to have been gentler, but Izzy was a hard one to wake under normal circumstances.

She lazily lifted her head. "What?" she asked, still half asleep.

"Drink this," I said, wanting to keep it short before she woke all the way and refused.

She took the goblet from my hands. "What is it? What for?" She lifted it to her mouth. I was not about to tell her until she had at least half down her. She sipped and made a face while trying to hand it back to me. Lord, eight-year-olds were so difficult.

"No, you have to drink it all down," I cajoled.

"I do not want it. It tastes awful," she whined.

"Do you feel all wet?" I asked. She woke up more as she started to feel her night shirt. "You have a fever. Now, if you would like to get out of bed at all today and play, you will drink this as quickly as possible. Otherwise, you can stay up here by yourself while I go see Mrs. Williams, Amelia and Rebecca."

This seemed to perk her up. She brought the goblet back to her mouth, took a deep breath for added effect and drank it as quickly as she could. She swallowed, stuck her tongue out for extra emphasis to let me know she did not like it and handed the goblet back to me.

"Good. Now stay in bed a little longer and rest. Hopefully, you will be better in no time." I walked back downstairs to clean the goblet and set it aside.

"How is she?" Mother asked.

"She drank it down with much drama and is calmly resting in her bed," I responded.

"I am sure of that!" my mother said as she laughed. She knew all too well how each of us handled taking medicines and was probably grateful I had sacrificed myself for this one.

Breakfast was smelling so good! I did not realize how hungry I was, but with the toast, meat and what looked like fresh tea, the aromas were making me weak in the knees. I pulled up my chair so I could get to the food before any of my siblings. I was usually patient and let them grab what they wanted, but between this cold and the melancholy hanging over the town, I was in need of some warm food and drink in my stomach to start my day right.

Just then, as if they knew I was getting to the feast before them, Thomas and Susan came bounding into the kitchen on cue. They sat down and immediately started grabbing at the breakfast before I could even get some on my plate.

My mother witnessed this and the expression on my face and laughed. "Now, now, your sister has already been up helping me. She gets to take food first, so keep your grubby hands off!"

They looked crestfallen, but I shot my mother a quick "thank you" look and dug in.

We all sat in calm silence, showcasing how hungry each of us was. It must have been the cold. Just as quickly as they had made their presence known, Susan and Thomas were gone again. I suspected Thomas was going to run over to the Whites so he and George could continue whatever adventure they had concocted yesterday, and Susan would go back to her corner in the front room to finish reading whichever book had taken her fancy this week. She had gotten not one but two new books over the holidays and was enthralled with each.

I set to washing the dishes in the sink. I was anxious to get to the Williams' to see what Mrs. Williams had in stock but equally as hopeful that I might see Madge. While we had a wonderful time together in the wood a couple weeks ago, she had been absent since. I was not sure if it was something I had done or purely because her and Simon were so deeply in love that every waking moment needed to be spent with each other, even if he was farming.

I finished washing the plates and forks, grabbed another cup and filled it with some warm mulled wine from the kettle. My mother looked at me to see what I was planning.

"I did not think a small sip would hurt Izzy while the fever breaks. Perhaps it will let her sleep a little longer."

She continued to eye me but seemed to concede as she knew it would give her some respite, and she could continue prepping Father's midday supper. "Oh alright, but do not take too much, as I'm mulling that for this evening's supper!"

I nodded in agreement, took the cup and gingerly carried it upstairs. Izzy stirred at my presence. I leaned down conspiratorially, whispered, "'Tis a bit of wine!" and put my finger to my lips to indicate she should be quiet.

She giggled. "Really?! What if Mama finds out?!" She was practically squealing now.

"I will not tell her. Will you?"

She shook her head vehemently, and I handed her the cup. She drank every last drop and smiled at me.

"Good girl. Now rest and hopefully by the time I come back from running some errands, you will be well again."

She nodded enthusiastically, shimmied herself back under the covers and laid her head down. I felt her forehead again, and it seemed the fever was already breaking. Damn this cold weather, making everyone worry.

I walked downstairs, washed the cup out one last time and headed to the door to put on my boots, cloak and hat. My mother looked up to check I had concealed myself enough but did not say a word. I declared, "I will be back after I visit Mrs. Williams and get a few more things for our stock cupboard."

My mother nodded. "See if she has any more of the honey and wine mixture as well. If anyone is going to catch anything in this cold, let it not be a cough that rattles the lungs! Oh, and we could do with some more of that balm too."

I nodded, grabbed the basket and walked out the door.

The wind whipped at my face as I walked, but my thoughts had returned to the conversation James and I were having this morning before we had been interrupted. What was it he was saying? It seemed like it was important and that we might be on the brink of him sharing something about his time in Scotland.

Oh, darn you, Izzy, for having to wake.

I quickly berated myself for being unkind. She was only a child and clearly in need of aid.

I was about to return my thoughts to James when I realized I was already at the Williams' doorstep. I put aside the reminiscing and knocked on the door.

This time it was quiet Mary who answered the door. "Yes, Miss?" She looked up at me with her great big brown eyes. She had a few freckles peeking through around her nose, adding a curious quality to her face. My, she was going to be a right beauty, just like Mrs. Williams and all their girls.

"I am here to see your mother, Mary. We need to restock a few provisions in this cold!"

She curtsied at me, and I had to keep myself from laughing at the formality, then she stepped aside to let me in.

Mrs. Williams was in the back and the house was all abuzz, though this wasn't hard to achieve with a family as large as theirs. However, this was an energy of a different nature. I cautiously walked back to the kitchen and found Madge sitting at the table with her mother standing by the fireside. They were talking excitedly about something and had not noticed when I came in.

I walked up to the table expectantly and said hello. They both nearly jumped out of their skin at the sound of my voice. Madge was beaming as she pushed her chair back and ran around the table to come give me a hug. I was startled myself at this but opened my arms all the same.

"Whatever is it, my dear one?!" I asked as she squeezed.

Her mother just looked on, beaming herself.

"Oh, Ann! I am so happy you are here. How incredibly fortuitous! I was just saying to Mother how I simply had to come see you this morning!" She was positively vibrating out of her skin; it was quite infectious after all this cold.

"Well, my sweet one, pray thee tell what is going on that has you so flustered?!" I responded.

She dropped the hug, took my wrists and stepped back to look me square in the face. "Simon proposed!" My mouth dropped. "I am engaged to be married!"

Her mother put her hands together in prayer and I heard her whisper, "Thank you, Lord, it is about time!"

I smiled and gave her a wink. I knew it was not because Madge had no prospects that they were relieved, only that the courtship seemed to be taking so long. With the amount of time the two of them spent together, as well as he with the family, everyone had expected this weeks ago if not over the holidays. I do not know what had caused the delay, but it had the intended effect. I had not seen Madge so happy in so long…or possibly ever!

I must have been staring in stunned silence because Madge dropped my wrists and cocked her head to the side. "Are you not happy for me, friend?" she asked quietly.

"Oh, Madge, of COURSE I am thrilled for you!" I said, coming out of my stupor. "I was saying to my own mother just a few days ago how surprised I was it had not happened yet because I had not seen you for a fortnight! I am elated for you, dear one. It is what you have been hoping for all this time!" I brought her back in for another embrace. Her shoulders relaxed at that.

Mrs. Williams patted the table so we would come over and sit down. "I was making this for dinner tonight, but I think perhaps a wee sip to celebrate these glad tidings is in order," she said as she ladled out three small glasses of mulled wine.

I laughed to myself as I suddenly heard James. "See, show kindness to others and it comes back around." I knew he was referring to my stealing a bit of mulled wine for Izzy and thought it appropriate at this time.

We each raised our glasses, and Mrs. Williams spoke. "To my firstborn, finding her preferred mate. Cheers, my daughter, and may your love prosper forevermore and bring you much luck and happiness in your marriage!"

We clinked and sipped.

The whole scene was very reminiscent of when I had made the announcement that James and I were to be wed. Madge and her mother were talking excitedly again, and I was left to my own thoughts. I smiled, albeit a bit sadly, and heard James.

"Aye, I know, lass. It was us at one time," he said, his voice low and sorrowful. I nodded my head in agreement.

Madge noticed me then and reached her hand out to mine. "I am sorry, Ann, this must be difficult."

I looked up out of my reverie. "Not at all, dear one. What happened, happened, and it has nothing to do with you and your happiness. This will be a wedding to top all weddings, and I cannot wait for you to be married to your sweet Simon. What be the plans?"

That seemed to settle her, and she dove into what she and her mother had already discussed. Given the courtship had been so long, most of the planning was already done, at least in their minds. It would be a quick engagement, and they would be married in a few weeks' time, as long as all the traditions were marked and no complications ensued.

As Madge continued to plan out loud, her mother started gathering what she could from my list of requests and filled my basket. She must have been in a better mood than usual – which was hard to do since she was a pleasant woman to begin with – because she gave me extra of everything.

I wanted to remove myself from the merriment as soon as possible. While I was thrilled for Madge, hearing James's voice in my ear, and his own melancholy at the news, had made me poor company and I did not want to be a damper on my friend's happiest of days. I thanked Mrs. Williams, gave Madge another hug and took my leave so they could continue in their excitement.

As I slowly walked back home, I could sense James on my right side. It was the side he always took to shield me from the streets when we walked along together. It was comforting but also aggravated my already raw emotions.

Instead of heading directly back to the house to share the news with my mother and give her advanced notice of another dress needing to be made, I found myself turning onto the path to the wood. It was cold, but I did not care. I needed some respite. I crunched my way through the snow to the sacred space, laid the basket down atop the center stone tower and brushed off my stump.

I was not usually the one to become transfixed on the past, knowing there was nothing I could do about it now but move forward with grace, but this had hit me hard. Of the three of us, I had originally been the first that was to marry, and now, I was going to be the last, if ever. In a sudden fit of rage, anger and pure despair, I cried out, "Why did you have to leave me?!" and broke down sobbing.

It was the kind of crying that courses through your whole being, outside in to inside out. I felt the waves of emotions writhe through me, as if they were twisting me around and wringing me out to dry. I had cried after James had not returned, but not like this. This was otherworldly. I found myself shaking and screaming. I had to get up and pace to release this energy. I found I could no longer carry the weight of my cloak and loosened it so it could fall to the ground. I felt the walls I had built over years cracking and breaking away.

Since no one was there to witness me, I kept going. I kept going until I dropped to the cold, snowy forest floor and felt the flakes between my fingers. I quieted then and let the cold envelop me. Not to overtake me or my soul, but to cleanse me from whatever it was that just happened. The cool white snow, melting to water in my grasp, washing away the turmoil. My breathing quelled and my tears subsided.

I stood then, not wanting to catch my death on the ground, and stretched my whole body. I felt a lightness that I had not experienced in quite some time.

My throat, sore from the wailing and shouting, was on fire from the cold air I had so heavily breathed in and out. My muscles ached from the pure rush of emotions that had made them tighten and release. My cheeks were cracking from the stream of tears that had frozen to my face. I wrapped my cloak around me and took a seat on my stump. I closed my eyes, brought my breathing back to its normal rhythm and let out a great sigh.

"Ye alright, lass?" I heard to my side. I nodded my head, not ready to test my voice. "Aye, ye needed that. Ye have held onto it for too long." I nodded again, tightening the cloak around my shoulders. He was silent then. But just as I was about to speak, he began.

"I was on my way back to ye, though it took longer than expected. That March. I had finished helping my auntie with training her bairns, my cousins, the basics of tending to the land, and while they did not want me to leave and offered me to stay, I reminded them of ye and my promise."

I sat frozen to the spot, not wanting to interrupt him lest he never start again.

"Ye know the reason my family left Scotland. Too many politics and challenges to regents and rulers. We wanted none of it. Ironic, given the circumstances." I shot an unamused look toward his voice. "I know, love. But all the same." I imagined his handsome face with a sad smile. "At any rate, it was mid-March, and the winds of change were about. I set off south toward Glasgow, hoping to make it as far as Renfrew lands and even Paisley. There had been talk that members of the Protestant Congregation were on their way over to the city to fight the latest grievance against Mary of Guise and her French loyalists. I wanted to get as far away from it as possible. I packed my bags and began the journey home."

Here he paused. I knew this must be difficult for him, but somehow it was giving me peace.

"I will not do ye the dishonor of telling you all the detail, but suffice to say, I was in the wrong place at the wrong time. Mary's French were winning, and unfortunately for my fellow Scots, they were brutalized beyond the bridge. Anyone that was left was taken prisoner and the leaders were...hanged."

I gasped. I knew he had died but hoped it was not in such a manner.

He continued without having heard me. "I was near the area when the battle came to an end and the bodies were being sorted. Unfortunately for me, my tartan resembled that of the clan who had come from Fife to fight among the Congregation, and I was taken for an escapee. I tried to tell them that I was merely a passerby on my way back home to England. However, after so many months back in Scotland, my brogue was as thick as ever and they did not believe that a thoroughbred Scot would be living with the 'dogs of England' so willingly."

At this, I scoffed, but then again, the French had never liked us, given all that had occurred between our previous king, Queen Elizabeth's father, and their king. He must have hung his head at this moment because the pitch of his voice changed.

"I was a resistor among opposition forces. I was placed with some others in the castle to be held for further questioning. A few days later when some of the French returned, they came in to check on us. One of them set their torch down near a keg they did not recognize. I knew immediately what had happened and tried to get over to the torch to remove it, but I was still bound to the others, and they would not let me move. The keg was full of gunpowder and it lit, causing an explosion, and the tower crumbled on us." He fell silent.

I had heard of this incident before. The Battle of Glasgow was a small precursor to the Siege of Leith. What he was not aware of was that only a few months after this, the Treaty of Edinburgh was signed, causing all of this in-fighting among the Scottish lords and France to cease. Four months. It was a matter of four months between his battle and the treaty.

My stomach turned. Somehow, it was even worse that he had not been part of the original battle, for if he had, at least there would have been some sense to it. I could comfort myself knowing that he had died valiantly for a cause which he believed in, but this? His family had left Scotland for this exact reason. For him to have so blindly been caught up in such a small skirmish and then tragically killed because of someone else's ignorance...What were the odds?

"I am sorry, my bonnie lass. I know ye did not want me to leave ye then. Yer intuition ken something at the time, but I dinnae listen. I should have."

I felt like the wind had been knocked out of me. He was right. I had asked him, begged him, not to go. I thought of the foreboding feeling I had that last day, and the great owl that had followed us from the wood, a harbinger. But then I realized something else too that instantly sucked the breath from my lungs.

I cleared my throat to test its vitality. "Yes. However, had you not listened to my wishes for you to come home as soon as you could, then you never would have been passing there at that time. Had I not insisted that we still had a spring wedding, you would have stayed with your family longer and returned later, missing this battle." I hung my head then. What an awful realization.

"Nae, ye must not think that way! I would have come home as soon as I was done whether ye bade me to or not. I could nae wait to marry ye, and I was bound and determined to make it as soon as possible. The path that led me there that day is the same path that originally led me to ye. I have come to accept that what comes with the good is the bad, and I would not trade it for the sun, moon or stars if it meant I would not have had ye in my life, even if only for a brief while."

I started to cry again then, but not with the vigor from before, simply a quiet, steady stream of tears. For him. For us. For the life we were supposed to have. For the life we never would.

"I love you, James Clarke. From the moment I first laid eyes on you, I have loved you. It pains me to know we will never be together in life the way we had hoped, but it does bring me comfort having you by my side now and hearing your voice. I do not regret the path that brought us together, even though it saw fit to keep us apart. I still carry hope that one day, there will be a way. I will never love another in this lifetime, or the next, until our souls shall meet again."

A sudden burst of wind swirled around our sacred space and whirled up to the stone altar. The basket I had set on top spun as if it were a spinning top and fell to the ground. All manner of leaves, twigs and other forest debris whirled around me, as if it were dancing.

"I think ye may have invoked your dear Sophia on that one, love," he said with amusement. I laughed. What a romantic notion. And yet something so familiar twinkled on the edge of my consciousness.

With the spilt basket contents on the ground, I realized Mother would have expected me home and poor Izzy likely needed another dose of tonic. I rallied myself, gathered the gifts from Mrs. Williams and went to leave, but not before I could bestow a blessing on the space. Once again, it had come to my aid. It had helped me release a burden I had been carrying for far too long and allowed James to finally tell his story.

This space today, is sacred to me
Keeping me safe, so mote it be
With grace and love I say unto thee
Gratitude in abundance, so mote it be
I fall, I quicken, you hold and put asunder,
No more shall I fear the fateful thunder
Always sacred unto thee, I bless you now
So mote it be.

I did not know where it came from, other than my heart, but every fiber in my being vibrated as I spoke the words. I sealed it with a kiss in the air and turned to walk home.

Chapter 29 – January, Present Day – Sophia

It took us about two cups of coffee and an English scone each to get to the crux of the conversation at breakfast. The black cab ride from Heathrow to our hotel in Kensington didn't take too long, and our room was surprisingly ready when we arrived, so the three of us trekked up the stairs with all the luggage and settled in before heading back downstairs to the café. Thank goodness Maddy was there, otherwise I'm not sure how Kit and I would have managed all the luggage between us.

"So, you're taking a sabbatical among all this and, what, decided Scotland was the right place to go?" Maddy said as she reached for another scone and the butter dish.

Kit and I exchanged glances. We knew this was going to be the tricky part of the story. How could we tell her a plausible reason without venturing too far into the supernatural?

"Well...you see..." I started.

Maddy placed her scone on the plate in front of her to listen more intently, clearly picking up on the fact I was trying to tell her something important. I didn't know where to go from there, so Kit stepped in.

"You see, it's just related to some topics that we know you are sensitive about, and we don't want to make you uncomfortable." *Well put, Kit.* I high-fived her in my head.

Maddy looked between us. She picked up her coffee cup, took a sip and set it down, regarding it a bit longer than was usual. "Right then. I see it's my turn to chime in." Kit and I once again exchanged glances but stayed silent. "I know I have been MIA as of late, and I apologize."

I opened my mouth in shock. She never apologized for anything, least of all when she dodged calls and texts. She raised her eyebrow in contest, and I shut my mouth before I said anything.

"Anyway, I know I haven't been present, and I should tell you why." She took a breath. "Do you remember that party I went to?" Kit and I nodded in unison. "And the theme, and gypsy woman?" It was Kit's turn for her mouth to fall open. She started to interject, but Maddy held up her hand to stop her. "I know. I did NOT have a positive reaction to it, but as I said, if Ryan hadn't been with me, I would have run for the hills. However, as he was, and we so rarely had the opportunity to get this dressed up and go to a party together, I went along with it."

Kit and I remembered this. How could we forget? We had talked about the recurring dream that night, at least from my perspective, and Maddy had hung up on me. I assumed that was why she had been ignoring me all this time.

"Well, after that night I couldn't shake the feeling that there was some important information I was supposed to know within all those cards."

I remembered then that I had never told her what I found out about that card, and it was because of that catalyst that I had discovered tarot – and my affinity for it. I really did owe her.

Kit and I were riveted now. A tarot card reading? She was intrigued? Maybe there was hope for our friend yet. I laughed to myself.

"So, what did you do?" I asked, assuming she shook it off like normal.

"After a couple of weeks, I couldn't take it anymore. I was going to ask Mary for her information, but then her card appeared on the floor in the hallway in front of me where she had been sitting, so I took it as a sign and emailed her."

"You what?!" Kit said and quickly covered her mouth with her hand. She clearly hadn't meant to say it out loud, or at the volume at which it came out.

Maddy smiled. "I know, I must be losing my mind."

"Well, did she get back to you?!" I queried.

"Will you let me finish my story or not?" Maddy pouted.

Kit and I , on cue and in unison, zipped our lips shut and threw away the key.

"She did. I went for a reading just last week. I was incredibly skeptical, but Ryan and I had a few chats that helped me see things differently and opened my eyes to the possibilities, not just the night of the party, but afterward too. Anyway, the reading hit eerily close to home. I felt seen, and what she had to say resonated with me on a deep level. I am still processing, but all of that is to say...whatever it is that has brought you here and why you are going to Scotland, I will not go running as I would have in the past. It was identifying with the darkness in my dream that gave me pause, and cause, to turn over a new leaf." She finished and took a sip of coffee to punctuate her conclusion. There was a definite twinkle in her eye and I had never seen so many black flecks there before. Curious.

I picked at my oh-so-delicious vanilla scone and Kit tried to sip her coffee but found it was empty, as was the carafe in front of us, having drained it quickly between the three of us. Perhaps it was too early in the morning to declare that I needed a drink, but with the revelation Maddy had just shared, and what we were likely about to divulge, we needed something stronger than coffee.

I motioned for the waiter, who promptly came over. "May we have a round of mimosas, but...light on the orange juice?" I lowered my voice conspiratorially on the last part. He winked at me with understanding and was off. Maddy and Kit just stared in amazement. "What?! Coffee clearly isn't going to cut it after that." I waved my hand in the direction of Maddy, who laughed.

We waited in silence, eating our scones and bacon while the waiter brought three glasses with a bottle of champagne and carafe of freshly squeezed orange juice back to the table. I could tell it was going to be amazing juice at the sight of the color and clearly shouldn't be "wasted" in the champagne. He must have thought as much as well because he set three empty water glasses down too, indicating we could use it for the juice. I thanked him and poured for each of us.

"Right," I began, quickly picking up on the British conversational filler. "To us, and our collective awakening, which seems to be coming fast and furious these days.”

We raised our glasses, clinked and sipped.

“So, circling back…what exactly is it you guys are doing here? Why Scotland?” Maddy asked.

“I still want to put a pin in your reading and revisit that, because that is too juicy for you to simply gloss over, but so as to move things along…” I took a breath and dove in.

I went backward in our journey, explaining how Scotland had become a place of wonder for us as we learned and researched and educated ourselves on the spiritual world. We had a natural connection to it and were both completely drawn by its beauty and wonder. I moved further back into the summer and explained all the goings-on, the synergies, synchronicities and everything else that had presented itself. Kit sensed I was coming to the big finale, the thing that we were not sure we could ever tell her, but now it seemed we could, so she stepped in to give me a break.

“…and this was all started by a conversation Sophia and I had about one of Tate’s dreams.”

Maddy had been engaged and nodding her head along with me as I spoke. She seemed to be rather calm, given all we were divulging, which was good. I was not sure what she was going to do with this next part. The word “dream” seemed to resonate. We hadn’t yet spoken about that last call where we realized that she and I were dreaming about the same story from opposite perspectives. I wasn’t sure how this third piece was going to go…

Kit continued. "Well, you know what Sophia shared about her recurring dream, and how it jived with yours, only from a different viewpoint?" Maddy set her champagne glass down carefully. Kit stalled a bit, watching and evaluating Maddy before she continued. She must have made up her mind because she continued with, "Tate had the same dream as Sophia, from the same side of the chase as her, but as a different person, and he was insistent it was me."

Maddy stayed silent, quietly processing. Kit and I both watched her, waiting for her to bolt, but she didn't.

"So, what you're saying is that the three of us, in some way, are connected to the same recurring dream, only I'm chasing the two of you...and it ends with me shooting a bow and arrow at you?" she surmised.

I was surprised she remembered that bit from the previous conversation given the haste with which she hung up. "Maddy, it's a bit more than that," I started.

Her head swiveled to look at me. I could see in her eyes that she already knew what I was about to say, but she also didn't stop me from speaking. While she looked directly at me, I realized fewer black specks could be seen now. I felt myself pausing for too long.

"Kit and I went to a Shaman after Tate told her about the dream. We didn't know about you yet, obviously, but we could sense there was a deeper connection and needed answers." Maddy just stared, so I cautiously went on. "The Shaman helped us to understand a few things. First, that what I, we, are dreaming, is a memory from a past life." I stopped to make sure she was still with us. "A past life in which Kit and I were killed by a close friend who had turned dark, the second piece to the puzzle."

Maddy nodded. "OK, I'm with you. But if it is the three of us, why did Tate have the dream and not Kit?"

I swallowed. Oh man, would I lose her on this part?

Kit sensed my hesitation and spoke up. "Because Tate is a fractal of my soul and was the one meant to help me see it but not experience it because of the trauma it wreaked in that life." I had to give her credit. Only Kit could make something so wonky sound remotely sane and professional.

Maddy picked up her champagne glass and finished it. I re-poured for all of us, if only to keep her at the table. "So, what you're essentially saying is that we were all together, possibly as friends, in a past life, but something happened to me that was so bad that I ultimately chased you through the woods and killed you both, and because it was so traumatic, at least for one of you, you couldn't experience it directly for yourself and your – what did you call it, fractal? – had to recall it for you?"

Well, she had summed it up pretty well. It still sounded foreign to my ears, especially hearing it out loud from Maddy's lips, but it was the same conclusion Kit and I had come to.

"And what exactly is a fractal?" she asked, sipping.

"Essentially," Kit started, "a soul can have many parts unto itself, and at times these pieces can live in different times and places, but they are still the sum of its parts in the end. It's all very Gestalt," Kit said, waving her hand.

Maddy cocked her head at this. "Huh?"

"Oh, sorry." Kit laughed. "Gestalt psychology. Never mind. Trust me, it jives."

Maddy shrugged her shoulders. As she considered everything, Kit and I relaxed in our seats. We hadn't been sure we'd ever be able to have this conversation with Maddy, let alone have her take it so well. A weight had been lifted, and it seemed the reason for our trek was already coming to fruition.

"I have to be honest," Maddy started, and we both tensed. "I am still new to accepting all of this, but... Damn!" A sudden realization occurred to her. "Well, I'll be damned. Zabina was right again." She laughed to herself.

"Maddy dear, what do you mean?" I asked.

"Oh, sorry. It's just, in my tarot reading, I know I didn't go into the details, but part of what she said was that I would be faced with something from my past. It will throw me off balance and I will be reactive, but I also have an opportunity to learn from it to move forward and break the cycle, or cycles, that I'm currently stuck in." She laughed again. "I guess this fits quite well. I just didn't realize how far back in the past she meant!"

Kit and I couldn't help but laugh at this. All too true. The three of us finished the drinks, paid our bill and decided to explore London together for the day, before we had to get some shut-eye for the early morning train to Edinburgh.

We walked out into the early afternoon sunlight and walked down the street, arm in arm. It felt warm and safe, despite the season, and as we turned the corner, we came upon Kensington Gardens and thought it the perfect place to keep walking. The moment we entered, a warm breeze whirled around us, almost in a circle and upward, creating a reverse funnel. The warmth was impressive for this time in January, and since the walk had otherwise been so brisk. The garden was mostly dormant for the winter, but it still held a "woodsy" character, and we smiled. Kit and I had come to appreciate these odd moments and were thrilled we could have one with Maddy.

All too soon, we were back at the hotel and Maddy was taking her leave of us. We hadn't spoken about the revelations from earlier that day except when Maddy spilled the beans about the card associated with Ryan. There was a calm still between us that had not been there before. Maddy promised she would find time to meet up with us in Scotland before Kit left in a few weeks and then she was off, back to the countryside and her knight.

If we wanted to catch the sunrise over the countryside, the train to Edinburgh left the station at 5:45AM. Thankfully, it was a direct route and would only take about five hours, but having done it before with my parents long ago, I felt it was important that Kit experience it in the best way possible. In my mind, nothing could replace the experience of watching the sun rise over the Scottish hills as you approached such a mythical old town.

We got to our seats, unloaded our luggage, and immediately ordered coffee and scones. I added a side of bacon because I couldn't help myself and nestled into the plush velvety seats. Kit had not traveled by train in Europe before and didn't believe me when I said it was my favorite mode of transport. I think she was starting to see why now. None of the hullabaloo with air travel and security, spacious seating areas with tables, you could get up and walk around as you pleased, and there was a whole car dedicated to food and drink. She was well into a book about "anomalous cognition," something I would likely hear about at a later date, when it was time for her to witness the magic.

"Hey you, book worm," I said to her across the table. She grunted. "It's time," I said casually.

"Time?" she said, confused, still not looking up. "Time for what?"

"For this," I said, but didn't give away any more because I didn't want to ruin it. She finally looked up at me and I pointed out the window. Her mouth dropped.

While it was not as green as Ireland, there was a magnificent beauty to the landscape. Rolling hills, groupings of pine trees speckled over the ground, mountain ranges in the background, spots of white snow here and there to remind us it was still winter. It was breathtaking. The way the sun shone off the train tracks seemed to make it sparkle.

"I get it," she said.

"Get what?" I said playfully.

"Why you said we should take the train and not fly. I would never want to miss this view in a million years."

I smiled. It had been decades since I had seen it myself, but it always gave me a sense of belonging that I couldn't quite comprehend.

Soon, we were coming into Edinburgh station and disembarking. While the plan was to stay mostly in bed and breakfasts while traveling the countryside in the coming weeks, we wanted to start this trip off right and had booked ourselves in The Balmoral for the first few nights. The bonus was that it was adjacent to the train station and thus easier with all our…well, my luggage.

We checked in and were surprised with an upgrade to one of their famed Forte Suites with a note, *Enjoy your stay, ladies! We miss you. Love, Erik.* I gasped, and Kit smiled. She didn't seem surprised.

We were whisked away to our accommodation and were not disappointed. Having just been redone, we were one of the first to experience the Scottish luxury: Original wood floors had been refinished, walls painted with an antique white that both expanded the room and complemented the wainscoting. The ceilings had elegant plaster carvings in every corner, and the bay window had a set of gorgeous green and cream drapes pulled aside so we could see the city below. The furniture was elegant with its rich forest-green and amethyst tones, but neatly understated, something I took to be part of the Scottish charm, and there hung an elk head on the wall near the built-in bookcase.

We peeked in the bedroom, and it was more of the same, only an old-style cloth headboard that extended up to the ceiling and came out to hang slightly over the bed accented the same antique-white wall. The bed was huge, and I resisted the urge to run and jump like a starfish into the center. After a few days of travel, even having stayed overnight in a hotel, I was ready for the rest.

We tipped the bellman and set to work unpacking the basics. Unfortunately, we had only planned on staying here for a few days as we got our bearings before we settled into a B&B just outside the city. However, we were clearly going to make the most of it!

Kit walked into the bathroom to have a look around, and next to the branded skincare and toiletries was another surprise note. Kit walked out and handed it to me. "Look," she said and smiled.

"What, another surprise from your Viking?" I asked.

She laughed. "No, look!"

I read. *Dear girls, we hope you have an amazing stay and are beyond thrilled you are doing this. Enjoy! Love, Mom and Dad.* With it was a certificate to the onsite spa. "Of course," I said and quietly thanked my parents. They were known to do things like this when I would travel for work.

Anxious to get the day going, and to keep ourselves from going headlong into the bed that was beckoning both of us, we quickly changed our clothes, grabbed our crossbody bags and ventured out into the streets. The cold hit our faces as we launched onto Princes Street and made our cheeks flush, but with excitement or chill, I wasn't sure. We were here! We were on our way to one of my most favorite places in one of my most favorite cities in the world.

It was honestly a toss-up for me between Edinburgh Castle and Tower of London, I felt at home in both, but it was absolutely the first place to take Kit as we got used to our surroundings. The trek up to the castle was not for the faint of heart, and it felt good to stretch our legs after the plane ride and this morning's train.

As we climbed the stairs to the entrance, I brushed past someone's shoulder, and they slightly bumped me. It almost sent me teetering, but thankfully their reflexes were faster than mine, and a hand stretched out to steady me.

"Careful there, lass. Ye dinnae want to be falling over the edge."

I smiled. I could only understand about every other word with the thick Scottish brogue. It would be a long trip if I didn't figure this out soon.

"Thank you. I'm so sorry. We've been on a long journey, and I must be more tired than I realized," I said. Kit had gone so far ahead I worried I would lose her, but something about my rescuer's presence made me stay.

"Dinnae fash," the voice said. I finally looked up at him. He was tall and broad-shouldered, but the sun was in my eyes, and I couldn't see his face well. I nodded my head and said my thanks again before I ran off after Kit. He too went on his way in the opposite direction. I looked back once to try and get a glimpse, but he blended into the crowd.

I caught up with Kit after a few minutes of hoofing it and was completely out of breath. "What happened?" she asked, noting my haste.

"Oh, nothing, I bumped into someone and almost fell over, but they caught me and set me straight."

She laughed. "What, bumping into your Prince Charming on the way to the castle? Pretty cliché if you ask me."

I smiled. "I hardly think so, dear friend," I said, brushing it off. "Now, let's get you some authentic Scotch whisky!"

We entered the castle gates for admission to the next tour.

Chapter 30 – February 1564 – Ann/Lizbeth

January came and went, and soon we were entering February, with Madge's wedding drawing near. Neither of us had heard from Lizbeth, even though poor Madge had tried. She desperately wanted her friend to be at her nuptials, and her father had sent word to Mr. Acton, hoping, as he had helped to build the first structure on their property, the invitation would be better received directly from him.

We had not held our breath for the message to have been communicated to Lizbeth, but we still held hope. It seemed as if there had been multiple attempts from family and friends to see her, but ever since the last "sighting" a few weeks ago, there had been nothing.

Madge had visited my house more frequently for a change. I thought it was a double benefit of having my mother work on her wedding gown and also getting some peace and quiet. Her house always moved at a frenetic pace, and ours was calm in comparison.

I had decided, after the happy news was shared and my own personal declaration in the woods, that Madge should have what would have been my wedding dress. My mother was a bit shocked and had strong reservations; however, after some convincing, she had acquiesced.

As it had already been started, this gave her a leg up, which was helpful given the quick turnaround from announcement to the blessed day. I was not going to need it anytime soon myself and did not want all of that work to go to waste. Madge was positively beside herself that I would give it up, but I reassured her it was an honor, and she should consider it her wedding gift. Since then, she had come over practically every day to work out the details of how to make it into her very own dream gown.

It was difficult for me at times to witness the tailoring, and this morning was one of those times. I decided I needed to take a walk and clear my head. I found myself strolling by Mr. White's shop when I was set upon by the man himself.

"Good day, Miss Hughes," he said as he peered out the shop door.

Startled, but happy to see his kind face after all this time, I said, "Good day to you, Mr. White!"

He beamed at hearing his name from my lips after such a long time.

"Do you have a moment?" He beckoned as he opened the door wider, inviting me to come in. I did in fact have more than a moment and said as much as I stepped into the warmth of his shop. I had forgotten how much I loved being around the scents and sights of his work.

He limped back over to his workbench to sit down and pulled up another stool for me. His limp looked worse for the wear, and I wondered how hard he had been working. Michael was nowhere to be found, which was odd for this time of day.

He sat regarding me in silence for a moment before he spoke. "It has been a while, Miss Hughes," he mused.

"Please, Mr. White, you can still call me Ann. It has not been so long that you should not!" I said.

He chuckled and the lines by his eyes crinkled. "Yes, of course, Ann. How are you?" he asked.

"I am well, thank you, sir. And you?" I responded. I felt it strange that he should call me in for small talk, but at the same time I was happy to be out of the cold and somewhat close to my lost friend in a way, this being one of our old haunts. How many times had we three come here to play hide and seek during the winter and occupy ourselves so as to get out of doing chores at home? They were fond memories and made me smile.

He seemed to know what I was thinking, as he said, "Yes, happier times they were. I miss having you girls run underfoot." He stared off behind me, as if he was having visions of his own.

"How is Lizbeth?" I ventured.

His gaze snapped back to mine and the soft smile playing at his mouth fell.

"I had hoped you would be able to tell me. Mr. Acton has not been around for quite some time with an update, and Lizbeth ceased writing to me months ago." His forlorn tone was enough to break your heart.

"I am sorry, Mr. White. I too have not heard from her in quite some time. The last I heard was at the beginning of January when she was spotted in the village. Madge and I had hoped we would run into her, but we did not." I steadied my voice, as I could tell it was about to crack.

That day had been particularly difficult, especially since we had done all the work of clearing our space, only to find out that our dear friend had made an appearance, but we had missed her.

He knew the day of which I spoke. "Yes, that was the last time I saw her too. She came to the shop, and it was almost like old times. However, Michael and I were behind in our work after the holidays, and I am afraid I dismissed her faster than I should have. She was supposed to come for dinner that night, but she never showed." He hung his head.

This was so hard. How could I offer comfort when I knew the one piece of information that would clarify what kind of man Lizbeth had married and that her absence was likely not of her own doing? I had made a promise to my friend that her father would never know, but under these circumstances, I wondered at the necessity of the promise and if it was doing more harm than good. Perhaps if I told him of it now, he would know what to do and be able to rectify what was going on with my dear friend and bring her back. However, it may break him further, and for that, I did not want to be responsible.

He was watching me weigh my options. "Do you know what keeps her from her family, Ann?" He looked at me imploringly.

I looked back at him, then finally shook my head and sighed. "I wish I did, Mr. White. Madge and I feel her absence deeply. Especially as we approach what should be a happy day among friends and family."

He nodded in agreement. We sat quietly again for a moment, and he seemed to decide something for himself.

He slapped his knees and propelled himself up to walk over to his workbench in the back. He turned and carried something delicately in his hands. They were satin slippers.

"I had hoped that we would be able to present these as a family to dear Miss Williams in anticipation of her special day, but it seems the task falls to me," he said as he handed the shoes over to me.

I gasped. They were beautiful. "What an incredibly thoughtful gift, Mr. White!" I exclaimed, turning them over in my hands to inspect the exquisite work. "Are you sure you would not rather give them to Madge in person?" I asked.

He shook his head. "No, my dear girl, I would be honored if you could do it."

I nodded my head in understanding. "They are beautiful. She will love them, and I am sure she will not want to take them off ever!"

He smiled a sad smile at that. This must have been hard for him. He did not have to make such a gift for family, let alone for one of Lizbeth's friends, but I suspected it was a gesture done out of grief for our lost friend.

"I will see that she gets these," I said, clutching them to my person.

"Excellent, then it has been a successful visit all around," he said. He suddenly looked tired, and I decided that was my cue to leave. I stood slowly and trekked to the door.

"Please say hello to Michael and George for me. I hope they are well," I said.

"I will, thank you. And they are. Michael is off running an errand for me to pick up supplies, as I myself can no longer make the journey. George is probably off with your brother somewhere, stirring up mischief. I do hope those boys come down from their clouds soon. They must mature at some point," he said to himself more than me.

I turned to face him once I was at the door. Looking him in the eye, I said, "Thank you again, Mr. White. I will pass along your tidings to Madge and hope to see you at the happy event in a few days."

He looked a bit wistful then. "I appreciate that Ann. However, I do not think I will be able to make it for the celebration. I am an old man, and the excitement is too much." He smiled, even though his tone conveyed a different emotion. I am sure it would have been difficult for him to have come and witness one of Lizbeth's friend's getting married when a marriage ceremony had essentially been the last time he had seen his own daughter.

I leaned in and kissed him gently on the cheek. "I understand," I said and turned to walk out the door.

He watched me as I left, and I had to keep myself from tearing up. Poor Mr. White. I wished there was something I could do for him, but I was in no better position to help, even with the information I had. I thought on it as I walked back to my house.

I entered, not sure if Madge would still be around after the latest fitting. I should not have been surprised when I walked in to find my mother and Madge sitting at the table having some tea and deep in conversation. The dress had been set aside and must have been completed based on the way it lay across the chair in the front room, half bundled to take back to her house, no doubt. I approached the table, and they turned to look at me.

"What is that you have in your arms there?" my mother asked. I had almost forgotten but turned the bundle out of my cloak. Not unexpectedly, they both gasped when I revealed the delicate satin slippers Mr. White had given me.

I turned to Madge. "I ran into Mr. White today. He called me into his shop to chat and then handed these to me to give to you." Madge stared as I continued. "It seems he will not be able to make it to the wedding but wanted you to have something from the White family with you on the day."

At this, Madge's eyes teared up. I handed the shoes over to her so she could inspect their detail for herself. Light-blue satin, with thin soles, a small heel and delicate embroidery around the edges.

My mother regarded me in silence, reading me to see if my mood was much altered. She probably suspected there had been more to the conversation with Mr. White but put this aside, given the present company. I gave her my best reassuring smile, and she turned back to Madge.

"They are beautiful, my dear. Shoes fit for a queen, I dare say!"

Madge bobbed her head in enthusiastic agreement. Suddenly she jumped up. "I must go! I have to show everything to Mama so she can see how it has all come together!" She was up and gone before I could remove my cloak and set it by the kitchen fire to dry.

It was the day of her friend's wedding. She had so desperately wanted to be there and share in the celebration, but she knew her husband would never let that happen. Too many people. Too many witnesses to her changed form. Her once lustrous hair now flat, eyes sunken, and hips no longer plentiful. Who could have an appetite living with him?

He definitely could not risk her reuniting with her friends. But what did it matter? They had clearly forgotten about her already. Ever since she had seen them in the woods that day, her spirit had broken, and she had completely given in to her circumstances.

Her husband had even taken note of her increased silence, reverence and pliability. He seemed pleased as he began rewarding her with solid gold and silver trinkets and religious artifacts. He had even decided it would be appropriate for her to learn archery with him, a sport he thoroughly enjoyed because he could surprise his prey with a silent weapon.

However, as glad as she was for a distraction that got her out of the house, she was not nearly so taken with it as he. The gifts and gestures meant nothing to her, but it made him happy, and as she had learned, if she kept him happy, he would leave her alone to her thoughts, at least during the day.

Because of her recent piety and his appreciation for her silence, he had allowed her to leave the house and go for a walk without having to be escorted. Thankfully, he had not recalled that it was the wedding day, and they were far enough from the village not to hear any merriment or chatter. He had ripped up the message from Mr. Williams as soon as it had been delivered and scattered it into the fire, but not before she had seen the top with the date. She decided that instead of making her way to the wedding, she should go for a walk among the trees.

Her relationship with nature had changed. She knew it had ever since she tried invoking Sophia and nothing had happened. It was as if the blood she had spilt, even though well-intentioned, had been a step too far and she was being shunned by everything and everyone she once loved. However, she still took comfort in being in the outdoors, especially since she had now been secluded for the better part of three months. The cold fresh air made her lungs heave a bit, but she knew it was to help clear out the dust that had started to settle there. There was an unmistakable heaviness overtaking her.

She could hear the frivolity as she made her way to the woods. Her heart ached to be in among it. She was supposed to be by her friend's side on this happy day, not walking alone, but she knew she could not show her face there without Richard finding out, and she had come to understand what kept the peace, tenuous as it was, within her own walls.

She walked silently into the woods and was lost in her thoughts again when she bumped into something. Startled, she let out an "oomphf" and stepped back. She looked up to find Robert standing before her, just as stunned. Her mouth opened and closed a few times before she could find her words.

"Good day, sir," she managed, wiping her hands down the front of her dress in a nervous motion.

At this, Robert's eyes fell to the ground. She knew the overly formal greeting would have crushed him in the past, but after all this time? Surely, he had moved on. It seemed a lifetime ago that they had been making plans for a future that would never come to pass, and yet she realized it had only been about half a year since that last encounter before her world had been taken from her.

If he was not going to speak to her, she thought it best to keep going, so she made a move to pass him when his hand shot out and grabbed her forearm. His touch stung after all this time. Seeing the look on her face, he softened his grip, and she just stared at his hand on her arm. There was a time she would have given anything to have had his hand touch her anywhere; it would have sent sparks flying. It seemed this was no longer true. He was visibly confused by this change. They finally looked at each other.

"Lizbeth?" he seemed to whisper. Well of course it was she. How could he not know?

"Yes," she said, rather more emphatic than she had intended. He winced.

"Oh, Lizbeth, how you have changed. Are you alright?"

She did not know how to answer that. It hurt that the former love of her life should speak to her so, and she felt her new armor start to envelop her. "I am fine, thank you. Whatever do you mean?" she said offensively, this time on purpose.

This seemed to sting him too and he let go of her arm. He stared off into the distance over her left shoulder. Oh no, was he going into one of his fits again? She did not have the energy to deal with this right now, though she had time enough. She did not want to go back to the house yet, but if he was off for one of his round-abouts in the woods, she would not be able to avoid him. She turned to leave, but he stopped her.

"Lizbeth, I must tell you – no, warn you – of something."

At this, she turned. It had been some time since he had spoken one of his visions, and she was not sure how she felt about them anymore. In the past, she would have listened with zest, fervor even, but now with her husband's religious zealotry completely overtaking her, she found herself wanting to cross herself instead as he spoke.

Robert carried on, as if he had not seen her small motions. "Lizbeth, do you remember, last spring or late summer, when we went for a walk in the wood and I stopped, then walked away from you?"

She nodded. She could absolutely remember that time. He looked like he had seen a ghost. She had talked about it with the girls, and they had found it quite odd, which was saying something when it came to Robert.

"The first part of that vision has come to pass. I did not know what it meant at the time, but seeing you here and now confirms that it has," he said. He was staring into her eyes and, she thought, seeing into her soul. She froze to the spot, not knowing what to do.

"What I saw then was a darkness overtaking you. A darkness out of your control. However, you did not fight it. It is because of that darkness that you will be consumed and something tragic will occur by your hand.

To you, and to your friends. If you are not careful going forward, you will carry out an act so wretched that your soul and the souls on which you inflict this tragedy will be propelled into another lifetime to learn this lesson again. You will continue to repeat this cycle until you do," he said with ominous finality.

She? Do something horrible? And to her friends? The implications were preposterous, and yet she knew he spoke truth. Her recently found rage bubbled to the surface with such heat and intensity she surprised even herself.

"You take that back, Robert Evans! I know not the actions you speak, but it is a false prophecy, and one said in malice. Are you so cross with me to be married to another that you now scorn my very existence?!" she cried.

He stepped back from pure shock at her outburst.

"My husband was right to call me away from you, and them. You have all forsaken me and left me to my own demise. I no longer feel anything toward you, or anyone here in this village. If you have done anything in this moment, it is to remind me of how utterly alone I am, and it is you who will propel me to this dark action!"

Robert stared blankly at her. He seemed to no longer recognize the soul to which he spoke, as the darkness he foretold completely consumed any light that had been left behind her once brilliant eyes. Her raven hair, once lustrous with warm red and even gold undertones turned cold with blues and grays. Whatever evil lay in her household was coursing through her veins at this very moment. It almost constricted Robert's breathing.

She spat at him. "I no longer wish to see nor hear from you again. Should you see me out as you have now, you should turn the other way so as to escape whatever wrath I may set upon you. You think I will cause wretched acts? Then avoid me altogether. And tell the same to my former kindreds as well, or I will be forced to question Madge's healing heritage with my husband."

At this, she cocked her chin up in the haughtiest gesture he had ever seen. "He has great connections, my husband, and will see anyone who is considered ungodly hanged, or worse. This village should all be under a watchful eye, and perhaps I am the eye to watch it!" She did not know where this sudden burst of support for Richard came from, but it was having its intended effect and made the roiling in her stomach stronger. She felt more in control than she had in a long while.

Robert could not believe his eyes. The transformation which he kept to himself all those many moons ago was unfolding before his eyes. He was aghast and profoundly sad he had been the one to set the visions in motion. And for her to completely turn on her friends...He would warn them. Hopefully he could still prevent the tragedy which he had seen. He was not sure how or when it would happen, but there was darkness that blurred his vision even now.

Chapter 31 – January, Present Day – Sophia

The time roaming the countryside and Highlands with my friend had gone by in a flash. I couldn't believe it had been almost two and a half weeks!

After staying in Edinburgh for a few days and enjoying a luxurious spa treatment compliment of my parents, we moved onto a bed and breakfast in the Cairngorms. We had selected the site based on recommendations I had found online that it would move us north but also allow for several day trips to keep us from having to constantly pack and repack.

The Rowan Tree Country Hotel and Restaurant – we had come to respect the rowan tree and its folklore in the previous months – was perfect for our needs, aside from the name, which we had come to respect the Rowan tree and its folklore in the previous months, the property itself set among the trees and a small lake.

The accommodations were refreshingly modern in such an old building. Our room was perfectly suited to the two of us with a large, comfy king-sized bed, armoire and my favorite red plaid curtains. As we kept staying in historic places with limited rooms, we gave up on dual queen beds and elected not to get two rooms for cost-saving measures, so bed sharing it was!

The white walls gleamed when the curtains were pulled aside to let in the natural light. Our favorite spot, however, had been the restaurant on site. To say the food was marvelous would be an understatement. From the beautiful breakfasts to the robust dinners, we started and ended our day well, gaining invaluable insights on our next day's adventure and advice from the locals.

"Be sure to meet Murdo the Coo when ye go to the castle!" was one such sliver of knowledge. "Dinnae forget to have lunch in Aviemore. Ye will nae be disappointed" was another. We visited Fort George, Linn o' Dee and, of course, the Cairngorms National Park. Each landscape was more spectacular than the last. We made sure to bring water and snacks with us as we hiked through the terrain.

There were a few points where we each needed to rest, and learned those were perfect times to find a secluded area to meditate. Neither of us was brilliant at it, but we found the more we did it, the easier it became to reach a state of calm and peace. The world would melt away and it was just you, your breath and your thoughts. I felt little pieces of my soul awaken that had long been dormant. I started to understand more about my professional situation at home, though not how to rectify it.

It was during one such meditation that I had gone deep into what I referred to as "the ether," a dark nothingness devoid of any light. As I was allowing myself to be enveloped in the warmth and familiarity of this place, I heard a voice. It was rich, warm and smooth like honey. A man's voice, masculine but soft. I saw a field of heather, a purple flower I had come to appreciate that would bespeckle the fields in the coming spring. Then I heard the voice again, a little louder this time. It was saying something that I couldn't quite make out, but it ended with "bonnie lass." Not surprising given how we had heard people talk to each other here. It was clearly a term of endearment, and the tone in which I was hearing it now definitely exuded warmth.

I must have sat there too long, enjoying the richness of the experience, because I was suddenly being brought back down to earth by another voice, calling my name and shaking my shoulder.

"Sophia, earth to Sophia...we are going to miss our ride out of here if we don't step to it!" Kit said enthusiastically.

I snapped back into my body and opened my eyes. She stopped laughing when she saw the look of confusion on my face. "Where did you go?" she asked.

I paused, composing myself for a moment. "I'm not sure," I admitted. I gathered my things, and we went on our way, though in silence so I could process what I had just experienced.

We then went over to Gairloch, followed by the Isle of Skye. I was definitely excited about Skye, having heard so many mystical stories about the place, and it did not disappoint. I understood quickly why they were known for their whisky; it was the best we'd had thus far along our route.

Poor Kit wasn't as big of a fan of the brown liquor as I was, but she was a champ and didn't refuse a tasting when it was offered. "I will make you a Scotch whisky lover yet!" I laughed as she sampled yet another year.

Kit's favorite part of this adventure had been the Quiraing Walk. Once again, the landscapes were beyond breathtaking. The mountains themselves looked like they were covered in the softest green moss you could ever imagine, and the rocky trails that cut through them led to other small lakes and ponds that gleamed in the sunlight. We elected to pass by some of the local castles but did dip our faces in the fairy pools for good measure. Kit knew the kids would get a kick out of it and it would make for good bedtime stories once she returned.

Fort William, Glencoe and Glasgow were last on our list before we ventured back to Edinburgh to meet up with Maddy. She had planned on aligning her visit with the last part of Kit's trip so we could all be together and not disrupt our plotted-out voyage.

Maddy may have changed in the past few months, but not so much that the city girl wouldn't be caught dead roaming the countryside trails and cliffs as we had been. At least in Fort William we were taking a reprieve from being one with nature and enjoying another historical train ride on the Jacobite Steam Train! A personal request of mine because of my love for a certain series of books.

It was a nice change of pace to take in the sites of the area from a warm, plush seat. I think we had clocked an average of thirty thousand steps a day since we had left Edinburgh. We also took advantage of the local Jacobite collection, housed within the West Highland Museum, to delve deeper still into the history of our now favorite country. There were some interesting exhibits about the Jacobite rising and how it stemmed back to some original spats with the Scottish lords, the French and such.

It wasn't until Glasgow that I had my next odd experience. Everything else had been pretty ordinary, with the pair of us focusing on experiencing everything the local culture had to offer. There was something about the city that almost chilled me to the bone. I couldn't place it. The people were friendly enough, the food warm and inviting, and by now I considered myself a true connoisseur of Scottish whisky, enough to know what I preferred. There was just a feeling of melancholy I couldn't shake.

Today, we had visited the Kelvingrove Art Gallery and Museum. Mary of Guise had been mentioned in the exhibits, and that sent a chill up and down my spine, of which I took note. It had been a while since Kit and I had been able to pause and meditate, so I added this to the growing list of things that I had to ruminate on. I had been listening to my body and its reactions more and more, noticing patterns to my awareness.

Lost in my own thoughts, I was waiting for Kit to come out of the latest shop she had ventured into on Buchanan Street when I was bumped into by someone walking by. I muttered an apology but quickly realized I was not the one that had done the bumping and looked up.

"Aye, it's me who should be apologizing, lass."

I quickly brought myself back to the present. Wait, I knew that voice. I looked up. The sun was in my eyes, but it seemed it was the same set of broad shoulders I had encountered weeks ago while climbing the stairs to the castle. There seemed to be mutual recognition judging by the way the silhouetted head cocked to the side. I pointed at him and had a look on my face that must have invited conversation because he said, "Do I know ye?"

I laughed and found my voice. "Know may be a strong word, but I believe you saved me from certain embarrassment a few weeks ago on my way up to Edinburgh Castle." I shifted my position so I could finally get a look at his face. I realized I had to look up, as he was taller than me. Impressive, since I was tall for a female. I gasped and then caught myself.

He was quite possibly the most handsome man I had ever seen, but in an understated, purely masculine way. For every hard corner of his face and jawline, there was a smoothness to it as well. There was a bit of stubble, and it created a shadow on his otherwise pristine complexion. Soft freckles punctuated the structure of his nose, which then met with his beautiful dark-sapphire eyes, perfectly proportioned to his face, on top of which lay a messy head of dark, wavy hair. If there was a Scottish version of Adonis, then I was staring at him. He watched me regard him and seemed to be amused. I'm sure he had this effect on everyone he met.

"Travel weariness still have ye then?" he asked.

I nodded my head. Electricity jolted through me. "I mean, no, just boredom. I'm waiting for my friend to finish her shopping. It's not really my thing and she has gifts to bring back home."

"Aye, I see. Well, seeing as we keep bumping into each other, I best introduce myself. Bryce McCollum." He stuck out his hand.

As I extended mine, I responded in turn, "Sophia Aitken."

Our hands met and there was a brilliant blue spark that rose and fell. We both watched it in awe, hand in hand,

and then looked at each other. It was as we were staring at each other that Kit finally came out of the shop and nearly toppled over us. She stopped to assess the scene.

"Soph?" she asked gently. I blinked and looked her way, not letting go of Bryce's hand. "Who is this?" she queried with amusement. She looked at our still clasped hands.

I quickly dropped mine while introducing the man. "This is Bryce, Bryce Mc...I'm sorry, I've forgotten your surname."

He broke his equally confused gaze from me and answered, "McCollum. I'm sure ye've each met your fair share of 'Mc's in these parts. Hard to keep us straight, I'm afraid." His voice was smooth as honey.

Kit smiled. "Indeed we have, though none that have captured our Sophia's attention thus, Mr. McCollum." I glared at her. "I'm Kit," she continued. "Charmed." It was his turn to smile.

There was a silence between the three of us, as we each tried to figure out what came next. "Well, I'd love to stay and chat with ye ladies, but I'm afraid ye caught me while running some errands. However, if yer both around this evening, I will be heading to Barrowland Ballroom to catch some live music. Always a grand time there if ye enjoy some authentic bands from the local area." He looked imploringly at me, as if he desperately needed me to go.

Kit must have caught it too because she winked at me and said, "Sounds great! We didn't have anything set in stone tonight, as we head back to Edinburgh in the morning. We might just have to pop by." I was glad Kit could speak because my brain was still stuck on the blue spark. What on earth was that?

"Excellent," he said, looking straight at me. "I hope to see ye there then!" And he strode off. I turned to watch him go. He cut a lean figure with long legs and a strong back and shoulders by the fit of his wool peacoat. Kit watched me watch him and chuckled to herself.

"Well. Who knew you could shop for that?! I say, Scotland does not disappoint, does it, Soph?" She smiled. I continued to stare off after him with wonder written all over my face. "He's a proper mix of Outlander and Superman that one."

"Huh? Oh, yeah," I said.

Kit looped her arm through mine, and we walked off in the direction of our B&B. The Alamo House had been a splendid find for our short stay in Glasgow. With its unassuming exterior, we weren't sure what was in store. Overall, it had a darker interior than the other places we had stayed, but that only added a coziness to the history of the place, and matched the odd heaviness I felt in the air. Our favorite space was actually the entryway. Its deep peach walls, gold framed mirror and accent furniture evoked a welcoming ambiance from a time gone by.

As we walked through the doors and on to our room, Kit continued talking as she had the entire time since we left Buchanan Road. I hadn't heard a word. Bryce's voice had sparked something in the recesses of my brain, but I couldn't quite put my finger on it. And speaking of a spark, what the hell was that blue flare when we shook hands? I had certainly experienced static electricity before, but that was outrageous.

Kit opened the door to our room and shuffled me inside. "Soph, honestly. You haven't heard a word I've said, have you? It's not like you haven't met a man before!" she said, partly in jest and partly in frustration.

"I'm so sorry, Kit. I didn't mean to ignore you. There was just something about him." I paused. "It's illusive, but I swear there is something more to it."

She smiled at me with a knowing glance. "Yeah, I'm sure there is. That's a more manly man than we're used to seeing in the States!" She laughed. "Well, at least for you."

"Yes, yes, I know. Erik the Viking is ALL man!" I exclaimed. She threw one of her many bags she had acquired while shopping at me, and I ducked. "Hey, watch it! You'll break whatever you bought!"

She turned and walked over to the center table where a decanter of whisky sat with two rocks glasses next to it. Without asking, she popped the stopper, poured, and motioned me over to the freshly upholstered chairs and ottoman opposite the bed.

"For not having been a huge fan of Scotch a few weeks ago, you certainly have gotten the knack of it now. What will Erik think?!" I said mockingly.

She just stared at me while she handed me my glass. "Are you complaining?" she retorted.

"Not in the least. Cheer-ahs, Slàinte Mhath!" I said and we clinked glasses and took a sip.

"So, spill," she encouraged. I took another sip and let the warmth of the whisky sit in my mouth as I thought of the best way to start, then swallowed – caramel with a hint of slate, not as mossy as others.

"Do you remember the first day we arrived, and I fell behind you as we climbed our way up to the castle?" I asked. She nodded. "And I said there was a gentleman who had bumped into me, but had then quickly saved me from tripping?" I continued. "Well, that was him." Kit's eyes widened. "I know, right?! I hadn't recognized him at first, but then I saw his shoulders." Kit chuckled. "No, really! The sun had been in my eyes that day, so I only saw his silhouette. But as soon as he apologized for bumping into me this time, I recalled his voice."

Kit saw me swooning again and pulled me out of it. "Great, so why were you basically holding his hand when I came out of the shop?" she inquired.

"That's the weird part," I said.

"That's the weird part? Soph, all of this is a little off if you ask me," she said.

"Well, he introduced himself and we shook hands. When our hands touched, this blue spark appeared out of nowhere!" I said, recalling that exact moment. I looked at my hand and turned it over to check if there were any singe marks.

Kit was about to make a snide comment, but she watched my confusion as I examined the point of impact and decided not to. She settled on, "So...what does that mean?"

I took a sip again, contemplating the options. "I'm not exactly sure."

She got up from the chair and went over to the closet. "What are you doing?" I asked.

"Picking out what you will wear tonight, of course!" she said as she rifled through my side of the cabinet.

"Oh, you can't be serious," I said. She turned around and looked at me with what I assumed was one of her mom looks. I was glad not to be on the receiving end of those on the regular. "Kit, there is no way I'm going to some Scottish club to try and find this guy who may or may not show up. I'm sure he was just being polite."

She continued browsing through my things. "You really didn't bring anything with you that screams 'meeting my future soulmate,' did you…" She turned to her side of the closet.

"Kit!" I called.

"Honestly, Soph, you were coming over here for the entire semester and didn't pack one thing worthy of meeting a guy. What the heck were you going to do after I left, hole up in a B&B in the countryside and hermit away the rest of the time?"

I winced. That had been exactly what I planned. It sounded like perfection to me. "Give me one good reason why I should go tonight," I said.

"Because" was all I got out of her.

"Well, I will give you one good reason why I shouldn't." I paused, and she turned to look at me. "We are leaving first thing tomorrow morning. We have to be back in Edinburgh to meet up with Maddy, and you know she won't be pleased if we are late. We still have to eat and pack up tonight."

"Now you are making silly excuses. Of all the people who would understand, our siren Maddy would be top of the list."

Just then the room phone rang. We looked at each other. Who would be calling us? Erik and the kids would have called our cell phones. Kit strode over and picked up the receiver. "Hello?" she said in her sweetest voice. "Oh really! Why thank you." She hung up and turned to me. "You have a delivery at the front desk, my dear."

I looked at her, confused. "Um…OK." I grabbed the key to the room and went down to the reception area.

Avery, the girl who had checked us in just two days ago, grinned at me and flicked her eyes to the table across the way. I looked in the direction she indicated and saw a small vase full of heather. My heart stopped and my breath hitched. I pointed with amazement on my face with a look saying, "For me?!" and she simply nodded.

I gingerly picked up the green glass vase and walked back to the room. There was going to be no living with Kit now if this was from who I thought it was. I opened the door and carried the embarrassing display inside, setting it down on the side table between the two chairs we had just occupied. Kit's eyes were as wide as saucers.

"I'm sure it's just from my parents or something," I said. Her look said otherwise. I found the card and opened it up.

Miss Aitken,

Please forgive my forwardness. My plans have changed for the evening as I've been called back to work unexpectedly and I did not know how to get hold of you. However, I picked up a card your friend had dropped out of her bags as she came to greet us, and it had the name of a local B&B on it. I took a shot that it was the place you were staying. I did not want you to show up tonight and feel as if I had stood you up after my bumbling invitation. I think your friend mentioned you will be back in Edinburgh soon. I hope to bump into you again. Here is my number should you wish to make it an official bump instead of happenstance.

0131 222 1234

Le taing mor agad,
Bryce McCollum

PS. As I said, I am not usually this forward, but please tell me I am not the only one to have witnessed the fae spark?

I let out the breath I had been holding. Kit was watching me intently. She gave me a minute to gather myself, but only a minute as she was apparently on tenterhooks.

"Well?!" she cried, exasperated.

I handed her the note. She would just have to see it for herself. She gasped, then giggled, then made another odd noise somewhere between a snort and a wheeze.

I got up and went to the window, looking over at my now empty glass. No amount of whisky was going to untangle this one. "Well, I'll be" was all I heard from Kit's direction. "It seems we won't need to find you an outfit for tonight, but we will definitely have to find something once we return to Edinburgh tomorrow! Man, I wish I would have known your wardrobe was so paltry today while we were on Argyle Street. There were SO many options," she mused. "What is a fae spark?" She glanced up at me.

I shook my head. "I'm assuming he is referring to the blue spark I told you about. God, he is Scottish, isn't he." I laughed at his reference to the fae people.

The rest of the evening was spent packing, going downstairs to grab a bite to eat, and then settling into our room so we could catch some sleep before our early rise and return to the city. I slept with the vase of heather by my head, releasing its deliciously light scent all night. I had visions of heather fields in my dreams, romantic tumbles, and at one point I could have sworn I heard the same warm voice whispering, calling me to him. I still couldn't quite make out the first part, but it always ended with, "bonnie lass."

Chapter 32 – March 1564 – Ann/Lizbeth

Ostara. The village was busy with its only revelry this time of year. The Spring Equinox meant the return of the full farming season where everyone would be able to refill the bounty with which our town survived and thrived, and the New Year would soon follow. Winter had been colder than usual, and the harshness brought about an anticipation, or more so an anxiety, for the sun to return and come out from the depths of its slumber.

Madge had happily settled into her life as a married woman at Simon's property and dutifully taken on the role of "milkmaid," as I jokingly referred to her. I could tell she loved having her own home and hearth to tend to, and equally loved being around Simon.

"Perhaps ye should consider what this new spring brings and mend yer ways in finding a husband," my invisible companion said to me as I walked along the streets to escape the latest row between my sister and mother.

"Are you so anxious to be rid of my company in the next life that you would see me wed off to someone I do not love?!" I whispered over my shoulder, not wanting to draw unnecessary attention to myself by appearing to talk to no one.

"Nae, but I will also not have ye growing old with nae one to care for ye because ye are stuck in the past," he said matter-of-factly.

It hurt when he would say these things, and he had begun to say them increasingly since Madge's wedding. I did not know what he wanted me to do. There were not many eligible bachelors in the village, and even they were too much my junior to be a good match. I had resigned myself long ago to becoming a spinster. My time had clearly passed, and I had accepted it.

With Madge now married and otherwise engaged with her own household, I had taken back up with her mother to continue my teachings in the art of healing. Someone would have to take over that role as she continued to grow older, and who better to take up the mantle than I? I whispered quickly a phrase he would understand, "dinnae fash," and kept walking.

James seemed to sense my discomfort with the topic of conversation and thankfully recognized that we were coming to a busier part of the village where I would not be able to respond as readily. Where did he go when he went quiet? I wondered. Did he stay by my side the entire day? Or wander off to walk among the people he used to know? Robert was the only other person he could interact with, and I was sure he did so when he craved being seen. I made a mental note to inquire as to his whereabouts when he was not actively speaking with me.

I was bringing Mr. White an ampule of laudanum that he could use in the evening to manage the increasing pain from his cobbler's leg, and a tea containing turmeric and a few other herbs that I was experimenting with to see if it would help ease the throbbing he experienced during the day. The ointment of camphor, peppermint oil and garlic had long stopped working, and I think he was a bit relieved since the combination was rather malodorous.

As I approached the shop, I could see through the window a most curious sight. Michael had his arm draped over his father's shoulders and both their backs were turned to the door. Suddenly concerned Mr. White's leg had completely given way, I rushed through the door to provide whatever aid I could. Instead, I found them both bent over a letter with tears in their eyes and hurt on their faces. They looked up at me, as I had not made a quiet entrance. Michael's face completely dropped at the sight of me, and Mr. White tried to shield me from seeing his tears, quickly wiping them away with his sleeve.

"Whatever is the matter, Masters White?" I asked.

Michael walked away from his father, wiping at his eyes, and Mr. White stretched out his sinuous hand with the piece of paper lightly held between his fingers, almost as if it was burning him. I took it from his proffered hand and read.

Dear Sirs,

It is with a heavy heart as well as great pride that I write to you. After much thought and dutiful prayer, I renounce my ties to you, my former family, and will only claim the Actons as my kin moving forward. Having been forsaken by you my blood and the rest of the village, I want no association with you or anyone else and ask you respect my wishes. Should you see me out in the streets, please turn the other way so as to avoid any unnecessary hurt on your part.

You are no longer my family. I only recognize Mr. Acton, my pious and generous husband, as my true kin.

Sincerely,

My mouth was agape. What on earth had besieged my friend with such madness and compelled her to write something as awful and offensive as this? Her generous husband? She was forsaken by everyone? Was it not the absolute reverse, as she had never responded to anyone who reached out, likely because Mr. Acton, her "pious and generous husband," had kept her from doing so if he had shared any of the messages at all! And prayer?! When had Lizbeth become so religious that she was praying or taken her full birth name instead of her preferred nickname...

I turned to look at Lizbeth's father and brother. They were destroyed. I could not blame them. While not directed at me specifically, she was renouncing herself of any and all ties to the village, which included myself and Madge. My head was spinning. How could this have happened? I had no words of comfort for these two souls. I slowly handed the note back to Mr. White. He took it and set it aside on the bench in front of him, clearly not wanting to touch it.

"I..." I started, but nothing came. Honesty was best. "I know not what to say."

Her father looked up at me then, the full weight of what Lizbeth wrote, as well as his own decisions that led to this moment, showing on his face. Michael was pacing over in the corner, his shock and grief quickly turning into anger. He was muttering to himself, and I thought it best to leave him be. Mr. White just hung his head.

I had hoped James would be with me to offer some words of comfort, but none such words came, once again causing me to wonder where he went when we were not communicating. Was he acutely aware that any act from him would cause me to reveal myself in front of others? I resigned myself to my next thought.

"I will go speak to her, Mr. White. This is not our Lizbeth. Something must have happened to cause this or perhaps it is Mr. Acton himself who writes these despicable admissions," I seethed.

"Why do you say that, Ann? What cause do you have to blame Mr. Acton in this?" he asked. I could no longer hold back; he clearly already knew or had some inkling of the person he had his daughter marry.

"Because he is a horrible, cruel and vile human being who has abused his influence over Lizbeth," I cried. He regarded me with his soft, light-blue eyes. I had never noticed the clearness in them before, as if you were looking into the lightest shade of blue glass.

"No, my dear girl. You are as upset as we are. We cannot blame Mr. Acton." I started to protest, but he continued. "For even if he is all of those things, my Lizbeth would not be swayed so easily. These words cut like a knife direct to the heart, and only a daughter upset with her father could speak them so fervently. I know now that my decision to agree to Mr. Acton's proposal is what brought this to bear. Was I so wrong in wanting a better life for my daughter? I think not, but I also knew not to whom I betrothed her so willingly, and now there is nothing to be done."

My heart was breaking for him. I had never heard anyone speak with such sad conviction.

Michael stirred from his pacing. "No, Father, you will not blame yourself. It is HER fault. Not yours." He was seething now.

"Hold your tongue, my boy, before you say something which you cannot take back," Mr. White admonished. It was hard, as I could read plainly on his face, but he did as he was told and took a seat opposite his father to quell his rising anger.

This was a difficult scene to witness, and I desperately wanted to relieve myself of it. I had to tell Madge. We had to develop a plan. I would not let Lizbeth think herself so alone that she had lost her sisterhood, Mr. Acton be damned. Little did I know, it was us who were damned.

Mr. White sensed my mood and addressed me. "Go, my dear girl. I know you had not meant to come upon us at such a time, and it is for us to now resolve. Promise me you will not take action. No one can be made to reason when they are in this state of mind."

I could make no such promise but bobbed my head all the same, as I was aching to go. He seemed satisfied and turned back to the center of the room. I quietly left and set in the direction of Madge and Simon. She would likely be out with him and the cows, but this could not wait.

I had originally been bearing in their direction when I started my venture today. Madge and I had wanted to set plans for the Ostara ritual we were planning for that evening. We had only been back to our sanctuary once to be sure it was still clear, and we wanted to celebrate the blessings that had come upon us over the past year, even if not all of the memories were positive. Now, more than ever, I was certain that ritual needed to take place.

I quickened my pace and found myself almost in a run to close the gap between me and Madge. I halted at the front door and knocked thrice. When no response came, I ran out back to the barn. I could hear voices from inside and did not think twice before I burst in. I immediately regretted my action, as I had interrupted a fairly intimate moment for my friend and her husband. I blushed and instantly turned around.

"Ann! Whatever are you…" Madge started as they parted and fixed themselves. She was trying to be forthright, but I heard the giggle escape.

"I am sorry, my friend, Simon, but this news could not wait. Madge, when you are decent and of mind, will you please follow me to the house? We must speak."

I walked out of the barn and back in the direction of the house to give them time to gather themselves. I heard them chattering and then the solid footsteps of my friend approach.

"Whatever is the matter, Ann?!" she cried.

"Not here. Inside," I said in a low voice. I did not know who would be around to hear us, but being outside in the light spring air seemed to carry with it the unknown. We walked inside, removed our respective shawls and sat at the kitchen table.

"Now, what is going on?" Madge said, winded from all the activity and excitement.

"It's Lizbeth," I started. Madge's face brightened, thinking I brought glad tidings, but when she saw my expression, it dropped. "I was making my way into the village when I came upon Mr. White's shop to deliver some remedies. I looked through the window and saw a most unsettling scene and thought something had happened to him. I rushed inside only to find out they had received a letter from Lizbeth," I said and took a breath.

"Lizbeth? Why on earth would she send her father a letter instead of coming to see him?" she asked.

I dropped my gaze, then continued with my story. The contents of the letter, the reactions, the plea to not get involved. Madge sat, completely dumbfounded.

"I know" was all I could muster once I had completed, and she sat frozen to the spot. "I think what we had planned for this evening is even more crucial. We have to see if we can invoke help for our friend, bring her back around and perhaps change her mind." Madge was biting her lip now. "What is it? Do you not agree?" I said, confused.

"No, of course I agree. In fact, I would go so far as to say we should get word to her to join us. It's just..." She paused.

"Yes?" I asked.

She had an odd expression on her face. "I only..." she tried. "I had hoped that we would be adding to our celebrations this evening that I..." She paused again. "I may be with child."

I gasped. She looked up at me from under her lashes. "Why on earth would you be shy of a thing like that?!" I squealed.

"Well, 'tis only that you came with such awful news, and yet I had planned on telling you this evening. I am not saying we should not include Lizbeth in our blessings, but I was not sure how to tell you after your morning!" Now she was squealing with excitement.

I got up and embraced her. "Of course you should tell me. Lizbeth aside, these are glad tidings and should be celebrated. However, you say you may be with child. Are you not entirely sure?"

She shook her head. "I believe I am, as my courses are late. It is too soon to tell if a quickening has happened, but I have been praying we would start our family as soon as we wed and wanted to use our Ostara blessing as an opportunity to bring it forth," she gushed.

What a day. To be taken so low and then so high. She was right; we should find a way to invite Lizbeth this evening. It seemed imperative now. We set to planning everything we would need to bring with us, with a special emphasis on fertility now, and plotted our timing. I wrote the note to Lizbeth in such a way that when, or if, her husband got hold of it, he would think it harmless, but she would know how to interpret it.

I just hoped we were not too late.

She was glad she had done it. The last vestige of her old life finally thrown off, like cutting a cord that had grown too cold and heavy to continue carrying. She had not even let her husband know that she was going to write to her father and brothers to sever any ties, but suspected he would know all the same since he took it upon himself to read her post. She had hoped it would make him happy, if he was capable of the feeling. At the very least, it may afford her a few nights off from their bedchamber, or perhaps he would not be so very rough.

She had gotten used to his careless lovemaking over the past few months, but it did not make it any more pleasurable. She wondered what he had been attracted to since he clearly only loved himself, until one day she realized. He prized exotic-looking things but wanted none of the rebellion that came with it.

While the village had taken in her Romani mother as a child and was accepting of Lizbeth's heritage, she had all but forgotten that she did not look like the typical English woman. She certainly did not act as a gypsy, nor did she practice as one, but with Richard's religious fervor, she was sure it was always at the back of his mind. Distancing herself even further from her heritage would be a good thing, at least she hoped.

While it had been her decision to write, it had still broken her. What her father and brothers would not see were the tears that were rolling down her face while she was writing it. It was as much for them as it was for her; she knew that now. She had become a different person entirely, one they would not understand. She was dark, and cold, and she could feel it in every inch of her body.

She hoped that Richard's God and his Bible would help to fill the void one day. Until then, her anger and despair kept her company. She hoped, somehow, that Ann and Madge would be sent word and they would leave her alone too. Not that they seemed to have checked on her at all as of late, but she could not find the strength to write to them as well. The one letter would have to suffice.

Just then she heard the bang of the front door. Richard must be back from wherever he had gone off to. He hadn't been home in a few days. She always wondered what he got up to, but at the same time, she did not want to question him.

"Where art thou, my pretty little wench?" he slurred. Lizbeth rolled her eyes. Well, at least he would be too drunk to actually do anything to her this time. When she didn't answer, he called out again. "Well?!"

She stood from her chair in the bedroom, smoothed her skirts and walked out into the hallway. The house was not much to speak of at present, given the season and the fact that Richard's money kept disappearing, but she maintained hope for the spring.

"There you are!" he burst out, almost toppling into her as she came around the corner. "I have a surprise for you," he said with what she was sure he meant as a smile but came across more as a grimace.

She had become accustomed to his "surprises" and was not sure she would like this one any better. They seemed to come out of nowhere with no reason behind them, but she plastered on her look of gratitude regardless.

"Where is it?" she asked dryly.

"You must come outside," he said and turned around to lead the way. She could not imagine what would be waiting for her outside but followed all the same, grabbing her now threadbare cloak by the front door on the way out.

She thought she heard the whinny of a horse and wondered what one would be doing all the way out here.

Richard had long since lost his horse in a betting match and had taken to borrowing one of his men's as they passed through.

They turned the corner and there it was. A massive ebony steed fit for a king. The black coat shone in the morning light like obsidian. She wasn't sure she had ever seen a more gorgeous beast.

"Why, Richard, she's splendid!" she exclaimed, and she genuinely meant it.

He nodded his approval but was quick to correct her. "He, woman. Do you think me so daft as to obtain a female horse?! What good would that do?" he pontificated to himself and then turned to her with a sly grin. "Besides, I already have my well-worn mare..."

His colorful jokes were enough to make anyone ill, but she learned she had to at least acknowledge them for her own sake.

"Wherever did you get him?" she went on. "And where have you been these past few days?" she added without thinking.

He seemed perplexed by the questions, given his state, and he genuinely had to think on it. "I...I won him in my latest conquest, and where I have been is none of your concern," he finished in his harsh tone. He watched her look the horse over with amazement.

"He is spectacular, isn't he?" he said, quite proud. She wasn't sure that he would have been able to win this horse fair and square, but she would not question him either. She was just confused as to why it was hers when he was more in need of one than she.

He must have read her mind in that moment. "I will of course take him at my leisure, but I am rewarding you for coming to your senses," he shared. Her perplexed look made him continue. "For disavowing yourself from your family and those heretics, of course!"

So, he had figured out what she was doing. Ah well, it had had its intended effect then. Perhaps she could finally win his favor so she could have the freedom to at least wander as she saw fit. "Oh, that," she said demurely.

"Yes, that. And because of that, I thought it fitting you should be able to 'take the reins,' so to speak, when you have need of it. Our property is vast, and I will need you to work it as the woman is expected to. As I said, I will use the beast as needed as well, but I wanted you to have something for your act all the same," he finished.

She was certain his mind was still befuddled by whatever drink he had imbibed, as most of what he was saying did not fit with how she had been living her life since their marriage, but she stayed quiet. Her ribs were finally healing from the last time she thought he had let his guard down.

Having tired of his grand entrance, he turned on his heel and headed for the house. "Go make me food so that I may rest from my journey," he bellowed.

"As you wish," Lizbeth said and turned toward the door.

Chapter 33 – February, Present Day – Sophia

By the time Kit and I rolled into Edinburgh the next morning, Maddy was already at our planned meet-up spot, the café inside the second grand hotel we were staying at in the city center, 100 Princes Street. Maddy's boss Mary had pulled her celebrity-status strings and gotten three rooms for us at the secluded and private property. Each of us was psyched and could not wait for the experience.

The lack of a doorman was interesting, and instead, we were greeted by a black "100" flag at the main entrance. We sat in the leather-walled lounge of The Wallace, the bar area on the second floor, to enjoy some coffee and morning pastries. Our rooms were not yet ready since it was still before traditional check-in time and we were simply enjoying each other's company, bags stowed away at the front desk.

"So…how goes your adventure thus far?!" Maddy gushed as she took a deep sip of coffee from her pristine porcelain cup.

Kit and I looked at each other, not quite sure where to start. As I was clearly still gathering my wits, not having slept all that well the night before, Kit forged ahead. It was probably best I let her recount all that had transpired since we left Maddy back in London. Her memory was better, and she was a much better storyteller. I sat back munching on a slice of Dundee cake – basically a Scottish version of fruitcake which I had come to love during our time here – while Kit did all the work.

Maddy's eyes kept growing wider and wider as Kit got further into our trip. As I listened, I was really impressed with all we had accomplished and seen. Having been to Edinburgh before, the Highlands were what I had been most excited to experience, and I was not disappointed. I was pondering where I would go back to after my girls left when I realized the conversation had come to an abrupt halt. "Sophia, earth to Sophia."

I zeroed back in on the conversation. "Yes?"

Kit smirked. "Dreaming about your Scotsman, I see."

I froze. Had she already gotten through the travel stories and made it up to yesterday? I looked at Maddy. Judging by the expression on her face, she had.

"Right," I started, "so it seems now it's up to me to fill in the gaps?"

Maddy laughed. "I would say so, starting with who this hunk is."

"I know not of what you speak." I winked.

"Sophia Aitken. You have not had any sort of romantic relationship since that awful band guy who only flirted with your friends when your back was turned. Spill!" Maddy said with far too much enthusiasm.

I knew it had been a while since I had properly dated, but little did she know there had been a few since Greg, the one she practically forced me to break up with because she was so offended by his actions. I couldn't blame her and loved her for it, but ever since that experience, I had kept any romantic entanglements to myself.

"Yeah...why is that, by the way? You've only ever alluded to a purpose behind your self-imposed celibacy," Kit started, and I blushed. "And we never did get to that juicy little detail on this trip."

Maddy leapt back into the conversation. "Yes, yes, Dr. Kit, you can inquire as to her state of mind later. I want to hear about the guy from yesterday, now!"

I dove into the two meetings, the how, when and where, leaving no detail out. Maddy, of course, was less interested in the meet-cute and more in the physical description of my apparent rescuer, even though he was the reason I needed to be rescued.

"SO, have you called him yet?" she asked, hands cradling her face and eyes staring directly at me, way too excited. The fuzziness of the dream from last night hung over me, the visions and smells of heather fields, a warm soothing voice. I wasn't sure why, but I hadn't shared that part of the story with either of them, yet it seemed so significant. "Hello?" she continued.

I caught myself in my reverie. "No. Of course not! We only just returned to the city, and I couldn't wait to see you!" I answered, still thinking about the dream and realizing that was also what was keeping me from reaching out. What did it mean?

"Well, why on earth not?!" she admonished. I looked at Kit, and she seemed equally interested in the answer.

"Because..." I left it at that. They looked at each other then back at me.

"Nope, the court does not accept that plea. Try again," Kit said.

I groaned. I didn't know why, and certainly wasn't ready to explore it further myself, so I changed tactics. "How about, instead of focusing on my love life..." I started.

Kit interjected with, "Or lack thereof." Maddy high-fived Kit and I glared at the two of them acting like we were back in high school.

"...we focus on what we will do today and while I still have you both on this side of the pond. As Kit and I have already realized, time moves fast when you're having fun, and the end of the week will be here before you know it!" I finished. This seemed to create the distraction I was hoping for, and they switched topics.

We agreed that we wanted to find things to do that were more local and not just the tourist hot spots. As much as I loved Edinburgh Castle, Kit and I had no need to revisit the place, nor Maddy the interest. Thankfully, where we were staying was known for its view of the grand castle, so we at least had it in the backdrop for the rest of the trip and could appreciate it from a distance.

We decided that we should walk the Royal Mile up to the Palace of Holyroodhouse and explore where Mary Queen of Scots had stayed as our tourist adventure for the day and find a pub later in which to relax. After that, we would let fate take its course and hopefully solicit some local advice at the pub in the evening.

Our rooms were still not ready, but thankfully we had all we needed to get started. We walked and caught up along the way, Maddy telling us the latest fashion-related tales concerning Mary and her line, as well as updates on Ryan.

"So, he's *not* still walking around the property following you like a little lost pup?" I teased.

Maddy looked upset. "No! He had to take a job in Thailand. He will be back next month, but it has been agony without him. I didn't realize how much time we had been spending together, or how much I relied on him to make me smile throughout the day. Not that Mary isn't lovely, but..." She seemed to hesitate.

Kit picked up on the tone shift. "But what?" she asked, looking over at Maddy as she took a sip of water.

"I don't think she likes that Ryan and I are together," she admitted.

Now it was my turn to gasp. "But why not?!" I asked a little too enthusiastically.

Maddy looked crestfallen. "Well, I overheard their conversation a few weeks back, over a month ago now, and she didn't seem to support the relationship. She had clearly said something to rile Ryan up and his response was 'Where she goes, I go.' I honestly thought I was being fired, but then nothing happened," she finished and shrugged her shoulders.

"Hm. That is odd," Kit said thoughtfully. "Maybe she was just worried her brother had been hanging around too much and wasn't taking the jobs offered to him. They seem to be an ambitious family," she mused.

"Yes, and he had been refusing jobs, which is why I told him he had to take this last one. He was not happy I was sending him away, but I was not about to be the reason he lost out on income or abandoned his passion," Maddy said.

We walked a bit farther in silent contemplation.

Kit spoke up. "And how has it been with Mary since he took the job?"

Maddy seemed to ponder this. "Fine. She didn't know I had overheard them and has always been gracious with me, but now I'm not sure if it is professional courtesy or because she genuinely likes me," she admitted.

"You're overthinking it, doll," said Kit. She was clearly in professional mode. "Think if roles were reversed and you had a brother who all of a sudden was hanging around with your assistant and not doing what you know he loves to do. You would be protective and concerned too, no matter how much you liked that person. I wouldn't take it too personally. It seems like it was more a kick in the butt," she concluded.

Maddy seemed to think on that. We both knew she had a brother, but her family dynamic was certainly different to his.

We arrived at the entrance to the palace and went through the gates. While not a huge structure, it was bigger than I remembered it. We toured its luscious jewel-toned bedrooms, filled with rich woods, wallpapers and furniture, as well as tapestries galore. We listened quietly to our hand-held self-guided tour, electing to use the somewhat outdated tech over our Wi-Fi and the QR codes. We took our time and at certain points broke off from each other so we could linger longer at personal favorites.

By the time we were done, it was three hours later, and we were all ready to go put our feet up. We headed back in the direction of the hotel, as our rooms had to be ready by now. Once we returned, we each secured our room keys and were told our bags had already been taken up. We agreed we would meet up again around six to head to the pub and grab food, giving us about three hours to rest up.

As much as I loved traveling with Kit, and appreciated she was cool with splitting one room for cost-saving measures, I was ready to have some space to myself, as, I was sure, was she. My room was a traditional Scottish affair with walls lined in plaid paper, richly tufted armchairs and a matching bedspread on a thick mattress. Unlike the first time at The Balmoral, I did not restrict myself and dove headlong into the bed to stretch out.

I must have dozed off, because I was once again having visions of heather fields and hearing a voice. This time, the voice was starting to materialize into a figure, walking toward me. The sun was shining, so I couldn't see his face, but he was tall, broad-shouldered and wearing a kilt.

I saw my hand reach out toward him, and then he started to speak, only, instead of a voice, I heard something ring. I rolled over onto my back and bolted upright when I realized it was the room phone beckoning me and not a burly Scottish lover. I wiped my eyes and mouth and picked up the receiver.

"You coming?" I heard Kit ask. What time was it? Surely, I hadn't slept for three hours, but as I looked over at the clock across the way, I realized I had.

"Ugh, give me five," I said into the receiver and hung up. I ran to the bathroom, brushed my hair and slapped some mascara and lip-gloss on. I was only going to the pub with the girls, so I wasn't too concerned with being all dolled up, but as I had just slept for three hours on the side of my face, I thought I had best make an attempt.

I ran over to the wardrobe and discovered that the staff had taken the liberty of unpacking my hanging clothes, bless them. I pulled a cream-colored Aran sweater off the hanger, replacing the long-sleeve shirt and vest I had been wearing, and threw on my boots. I ran down the stairs as quickly as possible without drawing unnecessary attention to myself, noting the beautiful mural that stretched the length of the dark-wood staircase.

"The staff recommended a few places for us to try, but Kit and I have made the executive decision. Let's go," Maddy said and linked her arm through mine as we turned and walked out the door.

"Oh really, where is it?" I asked.

They smiled and we walked a quarter mile up the road. We stopped outside two black barn doors that were swung wide open. The sign above proudly proclaimed, *Devil's Advocate*. I laughed and looked at my two friends. We had come a long way if Maddy was not only willing but had chosen to go into a place with that name. They were also amused with their choice, and we walked in.

It was quite a cozy setup, with dark-wood beams spanning the ceiling, a well-lit showcase of all the liquors and spirits available, with a small loft area lit by candlelight and containing some well-loved wooden tables and chairs. I nodded. "I approve."

We ventured up to the somewhat modern-looking bar and took a seat. It was still early evening, and the work crowd had not yet descended, even though they traditionally finished their day by four o'clock. "Three Glenkinchies on the rocks, please."

"Make mine neat, please," added Kit. Maddy and I both looked at her in amazement. "What? So I've learned to like my whisky, I mean Scotch, while we've been here. Is that a crime?" she said, shrugging in contempt.

I laughed, Maddy nodded her approval, and we clinked our drinks as soon as they were placed in front of us.

We sat at the bar as long as the crowds would allow, but as it got thicker with people, we decided we would be better served retiring to the loft above. Kit and Maddy made their way up there to find a seat while I took care of the next round.

As I walked away from the bar, I stumbled on someone's feet and fell into a body that was headed my way. Strong hands steadied me, and I looked up.

"We must stop meeting like this," he said.

"Bryce!" I cried, a little too loudly.

"'Tis I," he said, uncertain of my reaction. "I hope ye got my note and did not try to meet up at the venue last night. I felt terrible but dinnae know what else to do," he said with anxiety behind his eyes. What a gentleman he was to be so concerned.

"I did, thank you. It was most kind and thoughtful of you," I said, thankful the lights were low and he couldn't see me blushing.

"And yet, ye are grateful but have not called me since making yer way back into Edinburgh," he said with a raised eyebrow.

I looked at my shoes then back at him. "I'm sorry. I had planned on calling you in a few days' time. It's only we were meeting a friend back here and I didn't want to—"

"'Tis OK, Miss Sophia. I only jest. Ye owe no such explanation to me. I'm just glad to have bumped into ye again," he said with a smile. It was perfect. Not overly flashy, but genuine, all his facial features engaged in the smile, including his eyes.

Those gorgeous dark-sapphire eyes. I swear I could lose myself in them and drift away forever. Were there flecks of gold hidden in there too, or was the low lighting playing tricks on me? Again, electricity jolted through me being in his presence.

Sensing the awkward silence, I took a step back. "Sorry, I do seem to be beating your shoulders up a bit with all this bumping."

Really, Soph? That was worse than "I carried a watermelon." Ugh, I had to remove myself from this situation before I made a bigger idiot of myself than I already had. I was not good at this, even though I wasn't quite sure what "this" was.

I looked up toward the loft to seek out my friends. They had halted on the stairs and were witnessing this whole thing take place. Bryce followed my gaze and recognized Kit. He waved, and she waved back. Then she did what I had hoped she would not and motioned for both of us to follow.

I looked back at him with a pained smile. "Please don't feel like you have to," I said.

"It would be an honor. Ye lead. I would hate if ye tripped on the stairs and I wasn't there to catch ye." He winked.

He must think me a bumbling American that couldn't stay on her feet. I wanted to let him know it was he who had that effect on me, but perhaps that wouldn't be welcome information either.

We successfully made it upstairs and Kit and Maddy had secured a table with just enough space for three to sit comfortably, four at a squeeze. Not surprisingly, they had taken the two available chairs opposite the small bench.

I glared at them, and they returned all too innocent smiles. "Subtle, guys," I said before Bryce came up behind me.

"Well, this is cozy," he said, looking around at the seating arrangement and trying to find an additional chair to swing over. "Are ye sure ye want me joining you? I would not want to crowd ye."

Kit spoke up then. "Oh absolutely, you won't be crowding us, will he, Soph?"

I smiled apologetically at him and slid onto the bench toward the wall. I patted the space next to me and said, "Not at all, we can scrunch."

His eyes seemed to playfully grin at me, as if he was accepting an unspoken challenge.

"Alright!" he said, and he sat down.

His strong frame could only just fit between the wall and the table, but he made it work. We proceeded to jump into introductions. The conversation flowed effortlessly and by the end of the night, you would have thought we were all old friends.

Maddy regaled us with stories from the English countryside and Kit took a moment to step away and speak with the kids. She had been wonderful at keeping up with them while we had been gone, and they with her through email, but I could tell they were ready for Mom to come home. When she came back to the table, she looked at me and said, "Everyone says hi and Violet sends a hug." I smiled.

Bryce looked at me. "Yer bairn?" he inquired.

"My what?" I said, confused.

"Yer bairn," he repeated. "Yer child?"

"Oh, goodness no!" I exclaimed.

"Violet is her dog," Kit clarified. "Our Sophia is completely unattached and child-free." She winked and then quickly picked up her drink to hide the smirk spreading on her face.

"Ah, I see," Bryce said and also picked up his drink to hide his expression.

"So, Bryce. We've talked all about ourselves. What do you do?" Maddy asked.

Bryce finished his sip and set his glass down. "I don't talk about it much, but as I can see I am in an interview of sorts…" He cast a knowing look at me. "I am a historian."

I could see where this was going to go quick and tried to stop the freight train that was Maddy. Too late.

"Well, aren't you a modern-day Indiana Jones! If I knew historians were of your ilk, I may have paid more attention in class!" she gushed. I threw my palm to my face.

Thankfully, he laughed. "Well, I don't know about that, Miss, but I thank ye for the compliment."

He looked at me and I mouthed "I'm sorry" as I kicked Maddy under the table. She yelped and I smiled sweetly in her direction.

"What does a historian do these days?" asked Kit.

He smiled at me and said, "Well, mostly we read and try to make sense of the past. But I…" He stopped to acknowledge Maddy. "I like to collect any local artifacts I can get my hands on and go on fact-finding missions for the local museums. I dinnae teach on the regular, though I do hold an office at the University of Edinburgh. Otherwise, I do a fair amount of work for the National Museum of Scotland – helping them secure whatever is needed."

"Oh, how marvelous!" exclaimed Maddy. Seeing where this was going, I tried cutting her short again but failed miserably since Kit beat me to it.

"Our Sophia is a proper university professor, on sabbatical at the moment, but you two have so much in common being in academia!"

I rolled my eyes at her and once again gave him an apologetic look. He took it in stride, though I could see him taking a mental note for future conversation.

I could sense the discussion and evening was coming to an end. Bryce likely had to get up early for work in the morning, and we had yet to figure out our plan for the rest of the week, having expected to get some ideas from the locals.

Almost as if reading my mind, Bryce asked, "What do you ladies have in mind for tomorrow?"

We all shook our heads. "We were planning on asking around for some more local or off-the-beaten-path type things to do or see," I explained.

"Well," he continued, "since I am a historian, and it is my area of expertise, what if I took you all on a tour of some of those haunts instead?"

The girls looked elated, but I held them off. "We couldn't possibly take you away from your work!" I said quickly.

"Nonsense, my work is learning more about the area and helping to record what it is I encounter. I dinnae have much planned myself tomorrow and it would be an honor to show three beautiful Americans around our fair city."

I could see I wasn't going to win this round and acquiesced.

"Wonderful!" he exclaimed. "I can be by yer hotel in the morning after ye have breakfast. Just call that number I gave ye...if ye still have it." He raised his eyebrow in contest.

"Fine," I said. He seemed to be gaining amusement from my discomfort and my friends' obvious game.

We all walked downstairs and said our goodbyes. Bryce seemed to linger behind, as if he wanted to say something to me in private, so Maddy and Kit made for the door.

"Yes?" I looked at him expectantly.

"I..." he started but stopped himself. He seemed to be wrestling with whatever it was he wanted to say, so I filled the gap so I could get back to my group.

"Thank you for this evening. I'm sorry my friends were being so ruthless. If you don't want to hang with us tomorrow and play tour guide, I completely understand."

He glanced up at this. "Not at all, Miss Sophia. It's just..." he stammered.

"I think by now you can simply call me Sophia," I said.

He smiled at this. "OK, Sophia, I look forward to our day tomorrow." He seemed more relaxed now, no longer distracted by something else. I smiled.

He took my hand in his to kiss it and there was the blue spark again! We both looked down at our hands, dumbfounded. I quickly removed mine from his grasp and muttered "goodbye" on my way out the door.

Kit and Maddy had already made it halfway back to the hotel and I had to trot to catch up.

"So, what was THAT all about?" Maddy said with a wicked grin.

I blushed. "Nothing. He seemed to want to say something but couldn't find the words. I made sure you two hadn't bullied him into playing tour guide tomorrow, and that was that," I concluded.

"So, why did you run away then?" Kit asked.

"I didn't!" I said, with more emphasis than I intended.

"Well, whatever it was, there were definitely sparks flying," Maddy said, amused.

I cocked my head at her. "Why would you say that?" I asked.

"Soph, you may not be used to the whole dating thing, but I certainly am, and what we saw up in that loft with the two of you was pure magic!" she gushed. Kit was nodding her head in agreement. Boy, we were in for a long day tomorrow.

Bryce was true to his word and picked us up the next morning with hot coffee in hand. "Madainn mhath!" he said in a bright tone.

Man, he looked good. He was wrapped up in a well-worn leather jacket, plaid wool scarf with a blue, black and white tartan pattern that looked oddly familiar, and fitted jeans that looked like they were custom made for him. His hair was playfully wavy, blowing slightly in the breeze, and his five-o-clock shadow from last night was now clean shaven.

I approached him to take the coffee to distribute and noticed a warm, musky, masculine scent wafting from him. It made me weak in my knees if I was honest, but as I didn't want to have another stumbling incident, I managed to stay upright. The normally talkative girls must have noticed it too because they remained quiet and wordlessly accepted the proffered coffee cups.

"What is on the agenda for today then, Sir Tour Guide?" I asked, trying to lighten the mood.

He turned his sapphire gaze on me, radiant in the morning light. "I have a few ideas." He smirked and walked off in the direction of Blair Street.

The day proceeded much like the evening before. You would have thought our foursome had been the oldest of friends. The day turned into the evening, with another stop at the Devil's Advocate. We talked about all we had seen, having gotten several private tours throughout the city, not least of which included the Underground Vaults, some private rooms within the palace we had not seen the day before, and a few antique stores where we were able to see some amazing historical pieces he himself had found throughout his travels. By dinnertime, we were trying to figure out how we could top the day during the rest of our time there, and before we knew it, Bryce had planned out the week.

The private prep rooms at the National Museum of Scotland, a private tour of the Royal Yacht Britannia and Leith, and even a personal tour of the Real Mary King's Close. The latter was a bit on the fanatical side but hard to pass up given all of its supernatural mystery. I thought we might lose Maddy a time or two, but it turned out to be quite fun!

It was amazing having a historian at our beck and call. His focus was on the city of Edinburgh itself through the ages. He liked following the evolution of the entire area and not just focusing on one era or another. It was refreshing from other guides who, when they chose to focus on Scotland, most often landed on the Jacobite time period and stayed there. His ability to see through the timelines and share his passion of his home country made the week an elevated experience for all. He walked us through the Old Town, explaining how unique Edinburgh was for its lack of skyscrapers within the town walls, in keeping with the old architecture.

By the time Friday night came around, Bryce had to take his leave of our little group and head back to Glasgow for a few days to visit family. He promised to call when he returned and if I was still in Edinburgh, we would go grab coffee. I was sad to see him go. I had truly enjoyed our time together, group or no group, and hoped that he would come back as soon as he had said. In the meantime, the girls and I had concocted our last adventure before they left the next day – tattoos.

We had seen a tattoo parlor on our travels during the week, and the idea had come to me then. This trip was further solidifying our bond in this life, and while none of us directly spoke about it, it seemed to be healing whatever had happened in the last one. Maddy was much freer from her religious fervor, Kit had found a way to be herself again and not just the consummate professional, mother and wife, and I...I wasn't sure what was healing for me, but I had a sneaking suspicion Bryce was a part of it.

"Are we sure, ladies?" I asked as we sat down in three chairs lined up next to each other. Maddy and Kit looked at each other and then me and nodded. "Alright!" I cried.

Thankfully, the parlor had a setup where we could each have the tattoo done at the same time, and the chairs were close enough for us to be able to hold hands during the process, at least partially since it was our wrists that were receiving the mark.

We had chosen a Celtic knot to mark our time here, having seen the symbol around town. In truth, I had seen it elsewhere throughout my life and it always stuck out to me as a beautiful and intriguing mark. It was called the "triquetra," and while it meant many things, we felt it best represented the three of us and our unending soul connection. The placement on the left wrist was as much about the throughlines to the heart as it was practicality, as wearing a watch would cover them as needed. We sat down and each squealed as the tattooing implement came close.

Lathered in Aquaphor, we went to what had become our favorite old haunt for a nightcap. Out of habit, I looked around the place as we entered to see if I could find Bryce's now familiar outline, knowing full well he was not there. Even so, I was a bit disappointed. I had gotten used to seeing him throughout the week and enjoyed his presence. There was a safety and calmness that came when I was with him, unlike any I had felt before.

We grabbed our order of Scotch whisky, neat, and headed up to our table in the loft. It was while we were inspecting our individual works of art that I suddenly blurted out, "It's because I've never felt like anyone was right."

Kit and Maddy looked at me with blank stares. I shook my head, surprised by my own outburst and realizing I couldn't turn back now.

"I've always felt like there is someone specific I am meant to be with, and I don't know why. And while I have no idea who that person is, anyone else I was with not only felt wrong, but it was as if I was being disloyal," I admitted and hung my head sheepishly, knowing full well how crazy that sounded. The two of them just continued to stare at me, but it was Kit who spoke up first.

"Well, honey, of course most people feel like there is a soulmate out there for them, but dating along the way isn't wrong, and if anything, it should help the law of numbers find them sooner," she said.

I shook my head again. "No, it's deeper than that," I said and took a breath.

I had been looking into it a little since Kit and I started down this journey and began learning about fractals. I sensed, more than anything, that what I was feeling was tied to the past life that had been plaguing all three of us. It was at that moment that I realized what all those dreams were, with the voice and the man who had started to take shape. Much like my dark dream had helped me to understand the concept of a past life and death, the man coming to me in the field of heather in the light dream must have been whom I was betrothed to in that life. But why now? And why here?

My facial expression must have showed the wheels turning because Maddy and Kit were watching me intently, waiting for me to say something.

"Sorry. I just..." I began, trying to work it out in my head. "I think I've just realized something about a dream I've been having."

Maddy spoke up this time, finding her voice. "Say more."

I was silent while I gathered my thoughts, not sure I could coalesce them into a coherent sentence. "I'm not sure. Let me ruminate on this a bit and get back to you," I said, deep in thought.

"Oh, Sophia, only you could find a way to divulge a deep thought and then reel it back in while incorporating a word like 'ruminate'!" Maddy said, exasperated.

Kit could sense that I was indeed trying to work something out and it would take more than a whisky-laden toast to get me there. "I think it's time we all turned in!" she declared.

None of us wanted tomorrow to come because it meant their departure, but a part of me was aching to be alone in my thoughts and try to figure some things out for myself. I nodded in agreement, downed my last dram of whisky and proceeded to bundle up. While we weren't far from the hotel, it was a cold night, and it required a certain number of layers to stay warm in between locations.

We all walked slowly, linked arm in arm once again, back to our hotel. 12:34AM. It seemed serendipitous that we should end our trip together at that time. We laughed, hugged and went to our separate rooms. I set my alarm so I could wake up and walk with them to the train station and send them on their respective trips.

Even with the help of whisky, I had trouble falling asleep. My admission at why I had never been successful at dating hung in the air around me. I turned on some music, hoping it would help. While my mind wandered all over the place in the first few songs, I soon realized I was humming along. The dulcet tones of the Righteous Brothers were lulling me to sleep. Something made me hone in on the lyrics of "Unchained Melody," the relevance of the waiting and longing...

As I put my head on the pillow, I dreamed of what these next few months would bring and couldn't help feeling that destiny had crept in as I fell asleep.

Chapter 34 – March 1564 – Ann/Lizbeth

It was an unusually dark night, though the moon shone bright. It seemed we would be blessed not only with the equinox and coming of spring, but also a full moon, surely a night for miracles and blessings.

Or so I told myself as I nervously made my way to the clearing. We had sent word to Lizbeth earlier that afternoon by way of Madge's brother, William. He grudgingly ran the errand as long as Madge promised to talk with their father about something for him. We had hoped his aloofness would seep through when addressing Richard, should he be the one to answer the door. He also would not know him as Madge's brother, but at least Lizbeth would, and perhaps she would take it as a sign of hope. We had not seen William the rest of the day, which only added to my anxiety as the time approached.

Madge and I agreed we would meet at our sacred space when the moon reached its apex in the sky. That time was fast approaching, so I moved with haste. We had to set up all the items we had brought with us for the Ostara blessing and, hopefully, for a reckoning with Lizbeth, who seemed to be slipping away from us at a rapid rate if she was not already completely lost.

I carefully walked through the wood so as not to trip. It would not do to bring about Robert's vision, nor did I want to spill the contents of my basket, which held a few eggs, a fresh loaf of bread and some green ribbon. Madge had agreed to bring whatever dried flowers she could find from her mother's stores.

As I approached the space, I saw a figure moving about and had hoped perhaps it was Lizbeth, but as she turned, I caught sight of Madge's profile and breathed a sigh of relief in equal measure. She was already working out a Celtic knot in the form of a triquetra atop the stone altar for which we were to lay the goods and make the pattern. She'd managed to get some dried clover and tulips to add to what I brought, as well as some biscuits.

The symbol had once represented us three, and we had hoped that by using it now, we might bring forth our friend. She was working with her runes one last time, hoping they would provide some insight on the outcome of the evening. It had been a while since each of us had worked with our gifts in front of each other, but I could see that she had been practicing. Her face held a look of concern or concentration; I could not tell which. She saw me approach and rearranged her expression into one of excitement, though it did not seem genuine as she collected the runes and put them back into their leather satchel.

We set to work quietly to get the rest of the pieces for the offering and blessing ready. I was in charge of channeling the blessing and had to prepare my mind for the activity. Usually when I settled down, James would start to speak to me, but this evening he remained quiet, whether by choice or because he was not with me, I did not know.

Madge lit the three white candles at each of the points of the triquetra and we were ready to start. It was only then that in the recesses of my brain, I recognized a faint flutter of wings overhead.

Lizbeth was furious. How dare her former friends send Madge's brother to her door, and with a note such as this! It was a good thing she had been the one to receive it and not her husband. While she no longer cared about the ramifications for them and their *ways*, she would not want to be labeled guilty by association.

To Mrs. Acton,

*We hope this letter finds you well on such a beautifully **sacred** day. We heard you were unwell and wanted to send good tidings for your **space**. We trust you are to have a splendidly wonderful dinner **tonight** as you continue the work on your new home. We hope your family will be able to **join** you soon, as they miss you so. Here is to fireplaces shining as bright as the **moon** so you can finish the **apex** of your embroidery, a pastime you so enjoy.*

Yours truly,
Your sisters in arms

Did they truly think themselves clever in this ruse?! Anyone with half a brain could have seen through their so-called secret message, though she did have doubts about her husband since he was inebriated most of the time.

Her temper flared once again at the thought that they had been carrying on without her in what was their shared space. It truly was the last straw. The last few months of solitude flooded her all at once. She had been married off to a loathsome man, forsaken by all those she held dear, ripped from her true love, and all the magic she once felt inside herself was lost. She had at least hoped that the others would suffer as she had and their sacred space would be forgotten, like her.

She decided that she would join them tonight, but not for the reasons for which they had planned. She would put a stop to them using what was theirs once and for all, no matter the cost. This offense could not stand.

She walked over to the fireplace, already aglow to keep their paltry dwellings warm. She wanted to destroy all evidence that the letter had ever reached her, and it gave her something to focus on other than her wrath for her husband at not constructing what was supposed to be their grand home. He had at least built her a room in which to keep all the religious tokens he had bought for her, but beyond that, he had neglected anything else that would bring her comfort. Some "lord," as he increasingly referred to himself.

She heard the whinnying then outside the window. She should probably go check on the latest gift. It was cold out and she was sure the makeshift barn was not much warmer than the house. She donned her cloak, hat and gloves, and walked out to the structure. Inside, she found the large stallion. He truly was a sight to behold. Dark as night, fifteen hands high, a remarkable creature that her husband had won in his latest card game, at least that was what she had surmised.

What they were to do with such a beast, she did not know, but she did like the look of him. She glanced around for some more hay to throw on the floor to provide additional warmth.

Her thoughts drifted back to her friends. The wrath was gone and all that was left was hurt. She broke down then, in the stall with her stallion, and let the tears flow free. How could her life have gotten so derailed? She was now friendless, homeless and had declared herself an orphan. Her marriage was a complete sham, and no one cared.

The horse, whom she had yet to name, sensed her emotion and sidled up alongside her so she could bury her head into its side. It was the first display of affection she had received in months, and she relaxed into it. It provided a strength she had not known for quite some time and seemed to rally her.

She decided then that she would ride this horse tonight to surprise her friends during their ritual. What would be more appropriate than that? Her, riding a dark beast of the apocalypse into a once sacred space to put an end to the trio that once had been, destroying the sanctuary as her friends had destroyed their bond in her eyes.

She saw the glint of her bow and arrow hanging on a hook nearby. While she didn't think it was needed, she also wasn't sure what animals would be about in the middle of the night and wanted to protect her new "knight" in black armor should wolves think him a feast. She grabbed it, slug it over her cloaked shoulder and jumped up onto the stallion's back to head out into the night.

The ride was cold but lit well by Diana until she entered the woods. She mustn't think of Diana anymore. She crossed herself thrice.

She had only meant to come upon them and scare them, to get them to stop, save them from this blasphemy. That was it. Maybe if she saved them from themselves, Richard would let her be friends with them again.

Then she stopped. She saw small flames up ahead and heard Ann's voice chanting. She suddenly felt a longing inside of her core that she wanted to be with them, encircled in the magic of what was once a sisterhood of divine souls, guided and supported by Sophia.

Something inside of her broke then. She found herself tensing and then digging her heels into her ride to get him to gallop forward. She knew not what she was doing, only the blindness of rage coming to the surface.

We had waited as long as we could. We removed our shoes so that we could more readily ground ourselves with the earth and wore only our white shifts. With the candle lit, I stood, and we began. Walking around in a sunwise direction to bring in the blessings, I led:

Ostara blessings come to we
Renewal, rebirth and fertility
We welcome new beginnings and offer our thanks
Hoping to add more to our own ranks
Blessed Sophia, we offer to thee
Said times three, so mote it be!

As we circled the stone altar the second time, the candles began to flicker. I started to say the blessing a third time when I heard a familiar voice in my head shout, "RUN!"

I stopped short, causing Madge to bounce into my back. There was no time to explain. I heard the desperation in

James's voice, so grabbed Madge's hand and yelled the same warning to her.

Before I knew it, we were running.

Bare feet running through the forest. It was pitch black and becoming ever darker. Only the light of the full moon on this vernal equinox could be seen through the trees, and only then because the branches were still bare and the moon so bright tonight.

And her. Gaining on us with full force on an ebony thoroughbred, her jet-black hair falling around her shoulders in long tendrils, coupled with the dark-violet, velvety cloak flowing behind her, creating the illusion that she was flying through the dense night air right at us.

Suddenly, I tripped. The root had come out of nowhere on the soft emerald floor of the forest so familiar to me. I knew these woods like the back of my hand. Where had that come from? But I could not focus on that right now.

"Get up!" I heard James yell. It was as if he had reached Madge too, because she stopped in her tracks and reeled around.

No! I thought as I tried to yell, but my throat was raw from breathing in the cold night air. My blood was rushing through my ears, and I could feel my heart about to pop out of my chest. I wanted my beautiful soul sister to keep running, but instead, she circled back to try and help me up. It was but a moment but allowed our pursuer to get within reach. We huddled together, each trying to shield the other.

Madge was curled into a ball under me as I wrapped my body over hers. "Lizbeth! Stop! What are you doing?!" I cried, trying to break her from her stupor, the look in her eyes so unlike any I had ever seen on a human, let alone my friend. I swore I could see black flames alight in them. It was as if she and the horse on which she rode were both possessed and could not hear anything but their own fervor.

Just then, the duo stopped their advance. I looked up to emit a sigh of relief when instead, all I saw was Lizbeth, sitting atop this great beast that was now standing beside us, her silhouette outlined in the moonlight. I saw her raise something in her arms. What was that?

James knew before I did, and before I could do anything, I caught a flash of him trying to shield me from whatever was coming. Lizbeth continued to raise her arms, and the next thing I knew, I heard the "whoosh" of a bow releasing its arrow. I curled myself around Madge even tighter and heard James whisper in my ear, "I love you, my bonnie lass."

And it all went dark.

Chapter 35 – March, Present Day – Sophia

The rest of February was a whirlwind. Since my girls left, I moved just outside of the main city center and set up "shop," as it were, in a small B&B that was more conducive to my singular needs...and wallet. I had anticipated moving around the country a bit and seeing the sights, but something had me tagged here. That something was a 6'3" Scotsman who knew his way around the surrounding area, and all the history that came with it.

In our time together, which was increasing by the day, I had learned more about this man. Not only was he a historian, but he had been in the Scots Guards, which was impressive considering they had a reputation for being one of the British Army's toughest fighting units. It didn't seem to jive with his overall demeanor, but I gathered it was a sense of duty to family and country that had driven him to be a part of it.

We had fallen into a nice rhythm over the past few weeks. I would wake up and enjoy the breakfast from my host, Annie, a lovely woman in her late sixties who loved cooking as much as she loved having company in her home. It was a quaint house, built in the early 1900s, a young'n by comparison to most buildings in the area, and everything you could want from a B&B in the Scottish countryside. It had all manner of plaid décor throughout, handmade lace curtains, and a fair number of wild game heads mounted in each room.

Her husband had been a hunter and died a few years ago in a tragic work accident. Annie started the B&B then so she could keep busy and never be alone. The reason for the business was sad, but she truly was brilliant at it.

After we would have our coffee conversation over a hearty breakfast of toast, eggs and bacon, I would wander out. The wanderings varied by the day and the weather, but I was venturing farther and farther, both with Bryce's help and the waning winter weather.

If I wasn't joining Bryce on his latest historical endeavor, we would meet up for dinner somewhere. He wanted me to experience all the local fare, which was admittedly limited, but I enjoyed his enthusiasm. We would stay up to the wee hours of the night talking about anything and everything, and then he would take me back to Ms. Annie's and we would go our separate ways.

It was getting increasingly hard to say good night to him at the end of the evening. I had come to know him on a completely different level than I had ever known anyone and didn't want to be out of his presence even for a moment.

My dreams were also becoming more frequent. The same heather field, the same figure in a kilt coming toward me, or at least from my first-person point of view, because the hand that outstretched from my body was not my own, and yet it was at the same time. However, every time the figure bent to come into view, the whole thing would descend into mist and I would lose it.

Before I knew it, we were well on our way into March. Ignoring the fact that I would have been halfway through the spring semester and all the work that entailed, I was thoroughly embracing my sabbatical life and enjoying the break I had been given.

Instead of eating out tonight, I had suggested that we take over Annie's kitchen and eat in. She had kindly agreed it was a wonderful idea. She had no other lodgers right now and she had a date night planned with some of her girlfriends in town, so said we would have the house to ourselves. I tried my best not to blush at the insinuation but failed miserably and Annie just laughed at me.

It had been a while since I had cooked for anyone, let alone a man. I wasn't quite sure how to refer to Bryce. We had made no formal declaration to each other and yet found that neither of us were seeing anyone else and could barely stand to be apart. Perhaps I would get an answer this evening.

I was preparing my famous, and only, dish – freshly made pasta with a vodka sauce, crispy brussels sprouts and cheesy sausage bread. Bryce had insisted on bringing the wine, even though I had said tonight was my treat after all the other meals he had paid for. I still had a bottle of Barolo at the ready just in case. I had only ever seen him drink whisky and was unsure of his taste in wine.

The hour of his arrival approached, and I found myself bustling about, so much so I almost didn't recognize myself. It was then that my phone chose to ring. Thinking it might be him saying he was going to be late, I answered it absentmindedly, not realizing it was a video call.

"Girl, what on earth are you doing?!" I heard from the speaker. It snapped me to attention, and I whipped my head around to see Kit's smiling face staring at me.

"Oh! Hi, doll. I'm just—"

"And is that makeup on your face?!" Now she was toying with me.

"Ha, ha. Yes. Bryce is coming over for dinner and I'm just trying to get everything ready."

There was no avoiding what came next. "Oh, is he now?! Well, that must be why, after traveling the countryside with you for three weeks and getting you away from reality, I haven't heard hide nor hair from you in over a month!" She smiled. Had it really been over a month since we had spoken?

"I'm sorry. I have been busy enjoying my time here and completely unwinding," I responded.

She nodded her head knowingly. "Oh, I'm sure you have, though I doubt it has been in solitude. Wait...are you making your vodka sauce?! Oh, this is serious!" she squealed.

"OK now, Nancy Drew, I have got to go! He will be here any minute and I'm not nearly ready," I hurried. I could swear I heard a car pull up the driveway and a door close.

I started to hang up the call and heard her yell, "Don't forget to shave!" I rolled my eyes even though she couldn't see it and laughed. Forget to shave...wait, had I?

There was a knock at the door. I straightened my hair and made sure my shirt was lying as it should be. It was a sheer cashmere turtleneck with a matching cami underneath, paired with my best pair of jeans. I didn't want to be too overdressed but thought dolling up a bit wouldn't hurt.

I hustled to the door and opened it to find Bryce standing there with a bottle of my favorite red, Cline – Cashmere blend – and a bouquet of heather. I gasped. Where on earth had he found heather at this time of year? And how did he know that was my favorite wine? Thankfully, he hadn't noticed my gasp as he was looking me up and down, clearly approving of my outfit choice. I had mostly been wearing large heavy sweaters or flannels and vests, so it must have been the first time he was seeing my actual figure.

"Come in! Winter may be going away, but I don't want to let all the warm air out!"

He stepped over the threshold. For as much time as we had spent together, I couldn't fathom why this was so awkward. Perhaps because I was entertaining a man in someone else's house? He broke the silence first. "Smells good."

I smiled. "Thank you."

"These are for you, and here is the wine I promised," he said as he offered the goods to me. "It's a personal favorite," he said with a little smirk.

"Oh, is it now?" I said, raising one eyebrow.

"Ok, I may have had some help. I wanted to be sure I brought the right thing. You make me a bit nervous, Miss

Sophia Aitken," he admitted, and I blushed. Would I ever not blush in this man's presence?

"You are too kind, gentle sir, and have absolutely nothing to be nervous about with me! I am pretty easy." I caught myself with the double entendre. "I mean..." I stuttered, and he just laughed.

"Oh, are you now? Well, that's new information."

I turned and walked to the kitchen to put physical space between myself and the direction of this conversation.

"Why don't you pour the wine into the decanter, and I will find a vase for the heather," I suggested. He found the decanter and opener easily enough, and I found what I hoped was an unimportant vase of Annie's for the flowers. We moved around the kitchen in sync, as if we had been doing so for years. After letting the wine sit for a minute, he poured two glasses and approached me at the stove.

"What shall we toast to?" I asked.

He thought for a moment and then said with a devilish grin, "To unexpected truths...and being easy."

I had already started to sip and almost had to spit out my wine. "Whatever am I going to do with you, Bryce McCollum?" I said and turned back to the stove.

I could feel his presence at my back as I stirred the vodka sauce. The energy was practically vibrating between us, and I could imagine the electrons bouncing off each surface and back at each other in pure chaos. I sensed there was tension in his body, as if he was trying to decide what to do.

I started to swivel around, and he turned away to go sit at the small table in the corner of the kitchen. Disappointed, but also relieved, I announced that dinner was almost ready, and he could take his seat at the table out in the dining room.

Annie had let me use some of her fun Scottish china, decorated with plaid borders and rimmed with gold. She had found some crystal candle holders and set out a simple tablecloth so that the dishware did all the talking.

Bryce carried his wine and the decanter to the next room, giving me a moment to breathe since it felt like the air had been sucked out of the room when he had left me at the stove. I plated the fresh pasta and sauce and grabbed the bowl of crispy brussels sprouts, adding a quick drizzle of balsamic glaze. The cheesy sausage bread was already on the table, and we each sat down. We cheers-ed again and got to eating.

We were both silent for a bit, again an odd occurrence given our typically lively conversation over the past few weeks. Had we run out of things to say? He had been through almost his entire childhood and adult life leading up to the present. I had already shared mine and why I was over in Scotland in the first place. We had conferred on the pros and cons of teaching, me much more for and him much more in favor of research and being in the field, though he empathized with my current plight. Perhaps that was that.

"Do ye ever feel like there is just one person for everyone, and until ye find that person, the rest is just...wrong?" he said out of nowhere.

My fork stopped in midair. I set it down. He looked at me from under those long dark lashes, contemplating my now awed expression. Not knowing how to gauge my reaction, he said, "Never mind, I speak too plainly" and raised a bite of brussels sprout to his lips.

"Yes!" I interrupted. He stopped and looked at me. "Yes, I do. In fact, I was just having this conversation with Kit and Maddy before they left. They looked at me like I had two heads when I explained that whenever I tried dating, I felt like I was cheating on that unknown or as yet unmet soul."

It was his turn for his mouth to drop. "Exactly," he said in a satisfied whisper. We continued to eat, cautiously regarding the other and not knowing where to take the conversation from there.

I thought I'd better be the one to break the silence, otherwise the evening would be lost. "So, since you bring it up, how many almost Mrs. McCollums have there been?" I joked, trying to ease the tension building between us. It had the intended effect since he laughed his warm guttural laugh and set his fork down to wipe his mouth. It brought unexpected attention to his lips, which I suddenly wanted to kiss.

I stopped my daydreaming in time to hear his retort. "None, I'm afraid, lass."

I laughed. "None?! How is that even possible?" I mused.

"Well, for one, being in the Scots Guard is not for the faint of heart, nor did I want to entangle anyone in that life," he admitted.

"You haven't been a part of that for some time. Surely there has been someone since then," I said.

"There have been a few, but none of them lasted. They've never felt right, and rather than leading the poor lasses along, I cut and run as soon as I knew." He took another forkful and then reached for some of the bread to dip in the sauce.

"Poor lasses indeed. Having a hunk like you in their clutches and then losing you?! I would be heartbroken for sure," I joked and took a sip of wine. In all honesty, I *would* be heartbroken if it were me, then had the realization that it could very well be. My face dropped at the thought.

"Would ye now?" he queried with a knowing look on that chiseled face of his. My maternal grandmother would have referred to him as a "handsome divil," and now I truly understood the meaning of the phrase. Being that she was where I got my Scottish heritage, I thought it immensely appropriate and grinned to myself.

"What are ye smiling at now, lass?" Bryce asked as he finished his plate.

"Just a thought from my grandma."

He smiled. "Ah, grandmothers have wisdom for sure!"

Indeed, I thought to myself.

We each collected our plates and other dishes from the table and brought them to the kitchen. I had planned on retiring to the parlor with the fire and a bottle of our shared favorite whisky, a Macallan I had secured for the occasion, but wanted to get the dishes washed up and kitchen set to rights. I couldn't possibly leave Annie with the mess! I suggested that he take the bottle and Glencairn glasses into the other room, and he insisted on helping.

There we stood side by side at the sink, shoulder to shoulder in a tight configuration given the size of the kitchen, washing and drying like an old married couple. The "dinner party" playlist I had started earlier kept playing, then just as we wrapped up the cleaning, my all-time favorite song came on, "Moonlight Serenade" by Glenn Miller.

I started unconsciously humming and the next thing I knew Bryce had whisked me into his arms and we were dancing around the kitchen. No words exchanged, I laid my head on his strong chest and enjoyed the sensation of being in his arms. I could almost picture us in USO attire from the 1940s at a dance club, listening to Glenn Miller live.

Once again, as if my playlist knew what I needed, "La Vie En Rose" began to play, another personal favorite. I expected him to release his hold and stop moving, but thankfully he just held on tighter and kept swaying me around the tiny room.

Completely lost in the moment, I hadn't felt him stop but became acutely aware of an energy shift as his hand gently tipped my chin upward. I opened my eyes just before he leaned in and gave me the strongest, most enveloping kiss I had experienced in my life. If our hands created blue sparks by touching, I could only imagine what was happening now.

We both stopped and leaned away from each other, trying to catch our breath. "Wow" was all I could muster.

He smiled at that and chuckled. "I concur," he said. We dropped from each other's arms, and I turned.

"Come on, let's get the fire in the other room going and relax," I said as I walked out of the kitchen.

"I think we already got the fire going, wouldn't ye say?" he joked at my back.

We sat on the couch together, sipping our whisky and enjoying watching the flames dance. I don't know what time Annie returned, but before I knew it, it was morning. I woke up with my head on Bryce's chest, both of us stretched out on the little couch and covered in a blanket that had seemingly come out of nowhere.

It was the best night of sleep in my life, no dreams, no darkness, just peace. I got up, trying not to wake him, and made my way into the kitchen, stretching my arms as I went. Annie was up and moving about, clearly making a breakfast fit for a king. She took one look at me, smiled an all too knowing smile and handed me a fresh steaming cup of coffee with a pinch of cinnamon. We wordlessly exchanged a conversation, and I sat down at the table next to the stove with a satisfied smile.

Bryce soon followed suit, blocking the small doorway with his large frame. Annie did not let anything slide. "Well, Miss Sophia. Are you going to introduce me to your man, or do I have to do it myself?" She looked between the two of us.

"He's not my—"

"Bryce McCollum, Mrs. McGinty. A pleasure to make yer acquaintance. Thank ye for the use of yer home last night. It was most generous." I thought I saw him bow a little as he said this. Whatever he had done won Annie over in a second, and she blushed. It was nice to know I wasn't the only one that he had that effect on.

"Yer most welcome. Miss Sophia has been one of my most favorite lodgers I've ere had, and I was only too happy to oblige her request since I myself had plans. It's nice to know that young love can still spring from these walls after all these years."

I blanched. She was making some grand assumptions. I shot Bryce a wary look to see if he was going to run for the hills, but he seemed to be taking it all in stride.

Annie shooed us to the dining table so she could finish the breakfast she had started and bring it to us. She brought Bryce a cup of coffee with some milk on the side, as if he had specifically asked for it. He looked up at her in amazement.

"It is my job to ken how my guests take their coffee," she said and walked away.

I sipped my coffee and said, "She's good."

Bryce nodded in agreement as he poured a splash of milk into the black coffee and stirred. He picked up his mug and before he put it to his lips, I was momentarily distracted again, thinking of that kiss from the night before...and several others that followed by the fire.

He said, "So what shall we do today, young lass?"

I blushed, having been caught daydreaming. "I could use some fresh air," I decided out loud.

"Great!" he said. "I had wanted a drive myself. We will take off after breakfast," he declared.

"Don't you have work today?" I asked.

"No, I left the day open, not knowing how late I would be out. Besides, I finished up my latest assignment early and could use a few days to myself."

Annie came in then, plates heaping with food in hand. She set them down in front of us and we got to work, as if we hadn't eaten in days. Her cooking was so good, and I had even come to appreciate the haggis she made for the morning protein.

Once finished, Bryce insisted he help clean up, to which Annie winked her approval to me when his back was turned. When he was done, we both grabbed our coats and walked out to his car. Since I didn't care where we went, and he seemed to have a certain destination in mind, I let him drive. We talked about all the small towns we drove past and whether they had been part of the Jacobite Rebellion.

He had put his playlist on random in the background. I hadn't been paying much attention to it, but as there was a lull in conversation while he checked the map, I started to smile. There Billy Joel was with a perfect song for the situation, crooning about "The Longest Time." I giggled to myself; the music Gods had done it again.

My giggle caught Bryce's attention. "What are ye laughing about?"

I smirked. "Oh, just a private joke with myself. I do love this song though!"

Not missing a beat, he formed a rakish grin, showcasing his dimples. "It does seem appropriate, does it not?"

An hour later we were driving through Glasgow city center and my interest was piqued. I hadn't been back since our last run-in here when Kit was still with me. He didn't seem to be stopping but instead headed toward the water. The same melancholy had hit as we drove through city center but then dissipated as we got farther away.

When I said I wanted some fresh air, he had taken me seriously and was driving me to the other coast! There were a few places along the water we could walk and that was where he parked.

We got out and he reached out for my hand. The blue sparks had lessened each time we touched, but they weren't gone completely. We had just grown accustomed to them and the warmth we felt in each other's touch.

We walked along the River Clyde in comfortable silence. After a short while he cleared his throat. "Do ye believe that a soul can live more than one life?" he asked, continuing to look forward.

I pondered this for a moment. I mean, of course I did, given all I had experienced and learned that had brought me here, but would that sound crazy to him? I had nothing to lose. "Yes," I said resolutely.

He looked at me then. "Good."

"Why do you ask?" I questioned him.

He stopped walking and turned to face me. "The more I learn about history, the greater sense of connection I feel to it, but not all time periods, just certain ones. And certain places. For instance, I may live and work in Edinburgh, but for some unexplained reason, all my life I have been drawn to this area of the island, just outside of Glasgow. I know it sounds crazy, but I almost feel as if I had a past life here and something significant happened to me in this place," he said, looking into the ether around us.

I shivered. There was truth to what he was saying, especially since I had felt a draw to Scotland myself. He seemed to be gauging my response and I didn't want to keep him in suspense. "I know what you mean. I've always had a recurring dream that felt otherworldly, or at least other-timely, where I knew it was me on some level, but it wasn't me. Over the past few months, Kit and I have discovered...well, a lot," I said, not sharing too much so I could wait for his reaction.

He nodded his head and turned to keep walking hand in hand. "Recurring dreams can be gateways into the past for sure," he said contemplatively.

I was somewhat surprised at his understanding. Perhaps he wouldn't think me crazy.

"I'm glad you think so," I said and launched into the last part of my story that I had been holding back. At this point, I had nothing to hide and everything to gain. I somehow knew he would be able to understand. At the conclusion, he merely stayed silent and stopped to look out over the water.

We stood there, for how long I wasn't sure, quietly enjoying each other's company and drinking in what felt like an incredibly important moment. I sensed I was on the cusp of a discovery I had been waiting for my entire existence. He turned and took both of my hands into his.

"This may come as a shock after so little time, Sophia Aitken, but I believe you are the one I've been waiting for."

I smiled, and without hesitation, I said, "I believe you are the one I've been waiting for too, Bryce McCollum."

He grinned, making those dark-sapphire eyes dance, and then pulled me into his embrace for another kiss.

It was an earth-shattering, time-altering, souls uniting kiss. I felt us melt into one being and the space-time continuum shift. I lived a thousand lifetimes in that kiss and knew I had found my home. Not in Scotland, but in him. His soul was the one I had been waiting for all my life and had known on some level existed. The reason those few others had felt so wrong. The reason I was OK on my own, until now.

We stayed on the shore of the river for a bit before heading back to the car. There was no returning to the B&B tonight, and instead, we drove back toward Glasgow. With his reputation preceding him in the history world – man, he really was like Indiana Jones – he secured us a room at the gorgeous 17th century property, Crossbasket Castle.

We opted for the Peter Large Double Room, picked because he recalled my favorite color being purple and the décor included beautiful amethyst accents and plush purple plaid chairs in the lounge. We could have stayed in the stables for all I cared. Now that I had found my person, I was never letting go.

We stayed in that evening, ordering room service and taking full advantage of the restored castle room and en suite. The food was purely for sustenance's sake so we could continue to explore each other in every sense of the word. I gave myself to this man, mind, body and soul, and he in return.

It was a connection unlike any I had ever experienced, and I doubted many ever did. What had I done to deserve this type of love? If that was even the appropriate word for it. It had only been a short time, but I could feel his love for me on every level.

The next morning, we decided we should extend our stay and hide away at this amazing place to further explore the grounds and our budding relationship, feeling as if it had already withstood the test of time.

We drove back to the B&B and gathered my things so I could clear out the room for Annie to rent. It was coming up on the Spring Equinox and a popular time for out-of-towners to visit for unique festivals and events.

Annie gave me a long hug and flashed me a motherly smile. "I ken it. I ken it the moment I walked in and found the two of you snuggled on the couch. There is an energy about ye two that is unmistakable. Good for ye, love."

I thanked her for everything and was out the door, back to the car with Bryce and back to our hideaway.

Unfortunately, the same room was unavailable, also because of the pending holiday. However, they were able to accommodate us in one of the lodges on site. A tad large for our needs, but we would at least be able to squirrel away and enjoy our time together in a completely separate space with ample access to the grounds.

It was as we were unpacking that I received a text.

Maddy: *Earth to Sophia? Come in, Sophia.*
Kit: *Seriously. A girl ventures over to Scotland and then forgets about her life back home.*
Me: *Hi, guys.*
Maddy: *There she is!*
Kit: *How now, brown cow?*
Maddy: *LOL – moo!* <Highland cow gif>
Me: *Seriously, guys? I'm alive. I'm fine.*
Kit: *I bet you are. How'd it go at dinner the other night?! Did you remember to shave* 😊
Maddy: *Dinner?! Shave?! What did I miss??? Spill. Immediately.*

I looked up to see where Bryce was. It was going to be too much to type, so I wanted to send a voice message but also needed to be sure he was not within earshot. He must have still been in the front room, as I was in the back bedroom unpacking my things.

I held down the microphone icon and began speaking, recounting the last forty-eight hours. It was divine to be replaying it in my head and sharing it with my friends. I hit send and put the phone down on the nightstand. It wasn't long before the pings started coming through. They were going crazy with all sorts of memes and gifs. I laughed.

Bryce walked in then and asked what was so funny. Before I had a chance to answer, he toppled me onto the bed, and I lost track of what I had been doing.

A few hours later, we got up and dressed to go to the main castle for dinner. We had decided we would go into town tomorrow to grab provisions for the small kitchen in our space, but tonight we would have a proper meal.

The next week passed in a blur, and we were suddenly upon the equinox. Bryce and I had been in our own little world, essentially playing house in this lodge built for six. It was amazing how we quickly fell in step with each other, as if we had been together for decades, or centuries. It was a quiet appreciation for having found each other.

We spent the day walking the grounds, as we had come to do on the regular. There were plenty of parks for us to explore. Today's energy was different, as the entire place was throwing an "Ostara" celebration to welcome spring. Also known as "Lady Day" I found out, a time when before 1752, they actually celebrated the New Year in March rather than the beginning of January. There was going to be an amazing feast in the main dining area and a bonfire planned at the hunting lodge on site at Chatelherault Park. Bryce and I had decided we would take part in the dinner but had our own fire to conjure back in our rooms that night.

I had messaged the girls earlier saying I wanted to check in with them the day after, as we had each planned a small celebration with our own chosen families. It was an incredibly momentous time for us given all we had experienced. While we had been able to celebrate with each other in a way, this felt like it marked a new beginning for all of us. New Year indeed. I chuckled to myself.

I was curious to see how all our personal celebrations went. Kit had been prepping the kids with a child-appropriate version, Ryan had brought back some special gifts from Thailand for Maddy to incorporate into their ritual, and I had plans of my own.

The dinner was grand, and quite filling. I was happy for the walk back to the lodge afterward to settle all of the baked goods and heavy dishes we had consumed. We saw the bonfire light in the distance and smiled. Walking hand in hand back to our "home" was the most at peace I had ever felt.

As we fell asleep, entangled in each other's embrace, Bryce placed his chin atop my head and was stroking my hair. I had my hand on his chest and felt his soft breathing. I was just drifting off when I heard him say, "I love you, my bonnie lass."

That night, instead of heather fields, kilts and faceless men, I dreamed of going back in time. I ventured far back through a mist that covered a wood outside of a 16th century English village. From above, I saw three girls, working around a stone altar, laughing and talking with each other, as if they were sisters. I saw the seasons change and their relationship evolve before my keen eyes, and as I felt the energy shift, I swooped in closer to try and warn them of what was to come.

I realized from my vantage point that I was flying. When I looked over at how I was accomplishing such a feat, I saw dark-brown feathers. I was a harbinger, sent back to help bring forth the souls that were meant to heal from the past, to the present, to the past once again.

I felt someone move in the bed beside me and realized I had been dreaming. In all the goings-on and happenings leading up to the equinox, I had all but forgotten my usual angst around the recurring nightmare. But this time, on this night, after having reconciled all possibilities and built a new bridge between myself and my friends and finding this man to call my own, I saw beyond the nightmare and into the sublime. My soul had been on an adventure, had gone through a dark night with death and loss, only to come out on the other side, completely redeemed and whole once again.

Epilogue

I was running, my face being whipped by the cold bitter wind in the night. I tripped. Madge must have heard me fall and she stopped to turn around and help. I tried to tell her to keep running but could not find my voice. Then, Lizbeth was on us.

Before I knew it, she was raising a bow and arrow in our direction. I covered Madge and the unborn baby she carried in her womb and tried to call out to Lizbeth to stop, but she was too crazed. Whatever had possessed her was not taking its leave. I heard James cry out, "I love you, my bonnie lass" and it went dark.

When I woke, it was no longer dark, and I was not alone. I watched as my hands changed before my eyes. They were my hands, but also not. I looked ahead of me and saw Madge, alive and well, but then her form shifted too. It was as if our souls had catapulted out of our bodies and into another. I was myself, but not, and she the same. She seemed to have a small piece of herself standing beside her as well. Had her child been born?

There we waited, for what seemed like forever, until another form approached. This time of Lizbeth. She was shrouded in all black, a sense of foreboding all around her. The fire in her eyes had gone out and dark ash had been left behind.

Madge and I were tentative but still tried to approach her. It was not until she lifted the veil herself that we were able to do so. She shifted form then too, and there we were, the three of us, whole again.

Or at least, almost whole. I was still missing a piece, but what was it?

I closed my eyes and when I opened them once again, I was lying in a field of heather. A figure approached. It was a man of strong build, in a kilt. He had a voice warm and inviting as honey.

When he knelt down to take my hand and help me up, I could not see his face for the sun was in my eyes. When he lifted me to my feet, I saw my beloved James. He smiled at me and said, "I told ye I would come for ye and we would be together for always."

As he spoke, his form shifted into a man of great character and the darkest sapphire-blue eyes I had ever seen. I fell into his embrace and let him take my mouth to his. I had finally found him, after all this time. He let my chin drop from his hand, but I kept looking at him anyway. I heard myself speak. "I will never love another in this lifetime, or the next, until our souls shall meet again."

About the Author

A once burgeoning author redirects her passion for creative writing into "more practical" means as the whimsy of childhood stalwartly turned into adult tenacity. Parlaying the creative processes into strategic marketing has had its advantages certainly, but as that dreamer is rediscovering herself after experiencing life, she realizes that there is a book...or several, still inside of her.

From a very young age, Sarah was fascinated with story-telling. Whether it was listening, reading or creating, she had a natural affinity for strong narratives. Fast forward and she is harkening back to her original passion, leveraging all she has learned in her professional career to create something wholly new and aligned with her original calling.

Now? She's tuning into that passion and sharing her love of writing, historical fiction and mystical intrigue with you! So thank you, for holding space for one person to pursue their dreams and bring to the page what was once lost for so many years.

 sarahheximer.com

Photo credit: Water&Moon Photo Co.

Also by Sarah:

- Stay tuned for the next in the series, coming early 2026!
- Finding Your True Colors & Manifesting Your Dreams: One Journey to Self-Actualization

Thank you for reading.

If this story moved you, inspired you, or kept you up late turning pages, ***please consider leaving a review on Amazon or Goodreads***. Your feedback helps other readers discover the book – and means the world to independent authors such as myself. Just a few words can make a big different in helping others find it!

www.ingramcontent.com/pod-product-compliance
Lightning Source LLC
Chambersburg PA
CBHW030328120726
47901CB00007B/1716